The Untied Kingdom

The Untied Kingdom

Kate Johnson

First published 2011 by Choc Lit Limited
Penrose House, Crawley Drive, Camberley, Surrey GU15 2AB, UK
www.choclitpublishing.com

A CIP catalogue record for this book is available from the British Library

ISBN-978-1-906931-68-1

Printed in the UK by CPI Cox & Wyman, Reading, RG1 8EX

To the men and women who have fought down the centuries for less tangible goals and in worse conditions than Major Harker. I salute you.

Acknowledgements

With grateful thanks to Amy Edwards for sharing her medical knowledge. If there are any mistakes or inaccuracies in the book, they're purely down to my desire to make the reality fit the fantasy – in other words, that's me taking dramatic licence. A similar disclaimer can be applied to my brother Richard and any musical misinformation that made it into the story.

There are so many other people to thank, simply for their encouragement, advice and friendship. I've made so many wonderful friends through the Romantic Novelists' Association that I simply can't thank them all individually! A big shout goes out to my Twitter friends: you kept me going through the dark spots. And of course to my family and those rare creatures, my real-life friends, who still hardly ever tell me to get a real job.

And to the Choc Lit Tasting Panel: without your recommendations this book quite literally wouldn't be here!

With thanks also to three men who don't know I exist, but without whom this book would never have been written at all: Bernard Cornwell, Joss Whedon and Terry Pratchett. Your brilliant, imaginative and intelligent writing, attention to detail, world-building, and especially your vivid characters have inspired me for years. Without Richard Sharpe, Mal Reynolds, and Sam Vimes there might never have been a Will Harker.

Prologue

Eve Carpenter was having a bad enough day, even before she fell through the hole in the world. Since she'd suffered eleven hundred bad days in the past three years, however, she failed to notice the significance.

It started with a phone call from Louisa Butcher, smugly enquiring if Eve might like to come over for 'kitchen sups' at her farmhouse in the Cotswolds next week. Eve knew that Louisa knew that her farmhouse was exquisite, that her tennis pro husband was both rich and handsome, that their toddler was adorable and their nanny a treasure. Eve also knew that Louisa knew that Eve was living in a council flat in Mitcham with a damp patch on the wall and that even if she could afford to travel to the Cotswolds, she would be too busy filming a TV show whose working title had been Let's Humiliate Has-Beens.

She told Louisa to go and put her head in a bucket, and it set the tone for the rest of the day.

The rest of the show's participants were almost more pathetic than Eve. At least she'd actually once been famous, and recently, too. Well, infamous at any rate. Now she was recording reality TV with ex-wives and stepmothers of minor celebs, a glamour model and a children's TV presenter who hadn't worked since the 1980s, probably because he was the most appalling old letch she'd ever met.

She was so disgusted it didn't occur to her to protest about being sent paragliding on her own with only about half-an-hour's tuition, until she was being strapped into the damn thing. By which time it really was too late, and anyway, she was distracted by the glamour model, who was having enormous difficulty fastening her flight suit over her obscenely large breasts. Thankfully, the TV crew were pretty distracted too, so there was virtually no one to see her make a pig's ear of her first several attempts at getting airborne.

And then ...

And then City Airport was miles behind her, and she was soaring over Victoria Dock and the Isle of Dogs, and she could see the Tower, and the sheer exhilaration of flying made her forget that she'd spent more of the afternoon fending off the revolting attentions of the children's TV presenter than listening to the instructor telling her what to do.

And then her wing collapsed.

And then the high, spiky gothic parapets of Tower Bridge were looming and Eve saw her death right in front of her.

And then the bridge *wasn't there any more*, and cold hard rain was splattering her face, and a sudden wind was buffeting her, and it was dark, and the river was getting closer very, very fast.

The water hit with a slap that left her breathless, which was just as well because Eve wasn't great at breathing underwater. As the wing which had been pulling her upwards five minutes before started dragging her down, she heard a scream and realised it was her own.

Oh God. She had a radio, but her arms were tangled in the ropes, and besides now she was wet all over, icy water soaking through her flight suit; it was a miracle the radio wasn't electrocuting her. Vaguely she recalled mention of a knife, but did she have one? Had they given her one?

The water was black, and sucking at her. Something was tugging at the wing, and she hoped like hell it was an undercurrent because otherwise there were much bigger fish in the river than she'd ever realised. Submerged to her chest now, she fought desperately against the ropes but nothing was working. She was trussed up like a turkey and the current pulling at the wing was getting stronger.

Something yanked at her ankle, and the wrenching pain that shot through it jolted her and tugged her deeper.

I don't want to die like this, she thought. *I don't want to drown, I don't want to freeze, and I sure as hell don't want it in my obituary that I died filming Let's Humiliate bloody Has-Beens.*

But the throbbing pain in her ankle and the ropes lashing themselves ever more securely around her were making it harder and harder to fight off the black water. The cold was seeping through to her bones now, weighing her down almost as much as the sinking wing. Only her head above the surface now, Eve caught glints of gold on the surface and raised her eyes to see what her last sight would be of.

Horrified, she realised it was going to be the giant buttresses of a bridge with arches so narrow the water was churning through them. It should be London Bridge and yet it ...

... wasn't. Mad frothy waves thrashed the wooden pier at the base of each arch with a force that would reduce a boat to splinters. Eve didn't want to think about what they'd do to her. Above them, huge buildings loomed, six and seven storeys high, the glowing windows of a chapel in the middle of them. A chapel in the middle of London bloody Bridge.

Oh crap, Eve thought, *I must already be dead. I'm bloody hallucinating.*

She hallucinated a bell tolling in the chapel, and fires gleaming from the Tower of London. Then, as her head sank under the icy water, she hallucinated something hauling her back up. But it didn't matter, because Eve was already dead. She knew that because the heaviness of the wing and the ropes fell away from her and the water cleared from her mouth and nose.

Dreamily, she lapsed into blackness.

Chapter One

The day the alien landed in the river wasn't the best of Major Harker's life. But then considering that life, it wasn't the worst, either.

It was all fairly routine until Charlie handed him a list of all the new blood conscripted to fill the gaps in C Company, signed with the name of his ex-wife and current commanding officer. That in itself wasn't so bad, until he noticed the same surname repeated in the Private Soldier column.

Colonel Saskia Watling-Coburg's much adored, intensely sheltered and hugely cosseted little sister had been conscripted into the army as a foot soldier. A foot soldier in Harker's company.

He wondered if he should blindfold and shoot himself now, to save the army the trouble of doing it later.

Saskia's office smelt like paper and coffee, an olfactory combination that took him right back to the schoolroom. Of course, back then teachers had been able to drink coffee. It hadn't all been reserved for high-ranking army officers.

'Why?' he asked, for about the hundredth time since he'd been given the news.

'Why not, Harker?'

'Do you hate me?' he asked. 'I mean, do you really, really hate me?'

'No, of course not.' Saskia shuffled some papers, her eyes on the desk.

'Then why in the name of all that is holy have you assigned your eighteen-year-old sister to my company? I saw your signature on the chit. It was your idea.'

'Well, of course it was.'

'But why? Now I'm going to spend the rest of bloody forever making sure she doesn't get shot at, or blown up.'

'Yes,' Saskia said calmly, 'you are.'

Harker threw himself at a chair. She hadn't offered him one, but he figured it was his right as an ex-husband to flout a protocol or two. It was bad enough he had to take orders from her; the least he could do was make it clear when he was unhappy with them.

'Sask, we're at war,' he pointed out.

'Yes, I had noticed.'

'We're an active company!'

She gave him a level blue stare. Apparently she'd noticed that too.

'Do you hate Tallulah?' Harker asked uncertainly, and immediately regretted it as the air in the already frigid office got a little colder.

'You know I don't.'

'Then why not put her in – in, I dunno, some admin corps, or ... QM stores or something ...'

'Because she's not stupid, Harker, and she doesn't like being patronised. Besides, she's perfectly able-bodied and there's always the possibility that someone else will spot that fact and have her on the front line before I can do anything.'

Harker groaned. He'd met Saskia's younger sister, of course he had, but it was back when they were newlyweds, before the war had blown up, and the kid had been – well, just that, a kid. And of course, now she was of age she'd been conscripted. They were at war, after all.

'I'm going to play the "active company" card again,' Harker said. 'She could still end up on the front line.'

'Yes, she could.' Saskia's expression tightened just a little.

'With me as her CO.'

'Yes.' She gave him a significant look.

'Come on, Sask, give me a break. I ain't baby-sitting her–'

'I'm not asking you to.'

This time Harker gave her a look.

'All right, I am asking you to. But no more than you do with your other men.'

'Actually, most of them are women–'

'Military term, Harker, military term.'

'I've got a war to fight. I can't give her special treatment,' he tried.

'I don't expect you to.' At his incredulous look, she insisted, 'I really don't.' Saskia put down her papers and took off her reading spectacles. She pinched the bridge of her nose. 'Do you really not know why I've assigned her to you?'

He raised his palms. 'You were lying to the divorce lawyer and you really do want to hurt me?'

Saskia, quite sensibly, ignored that. 'Because your men come back, Harker.'

Harker opened his mouth. He shut it again.

'Look, the matter's closed. If you think about it, it's actually a compliment.'

'Oh, sure.' Harker slouched lower in his chair. 'When you order me a court-martial because she's got trench foot I'm sure I'll feel really complimented.'

Saskia put her glasses back on. Harker resisted the urge to punch the desk.

'Have I said how bad I think this idea is?'

'Goodbye, Harker.'

She turned her attention back to her paperwork. When Harker didn't move, she said, without looking up, 'I said–'

'Yeah, yeah.' He stood up, scowling, and flicked the little brass sign reading Col. S.E. Watling-Coburg. 'I want it put on record that I'm not happy with this.'

'Work your way up to a higher rank and challenge me,

then,' Saskia said, still not looking up.

Harker gnashed his teeth at her and opened the door.

'And, Harker?' she said.

He glanced back. She still hadn't looked up.

'If she does get trench foot, I'll have your head on a pike.'

Harker slammed the door. Dust fell from the rafters as he stomped away.

Bloody Saskia! Higher rank, indeed. She knew he was perfectly happy as a major. Had been perfectly happy with being a captain, truth be told. The higher up he was promoted, the more responsibility they laid upon him, the more paperwork he was stuck with, and the more toffs he had to hobnob with. And each time he moved up a rank, he was put in command of more men, most of whom he didn't even know, and none of whom he wanted to see die.

Your men come back. Well, of course they did. He looked after his lads, it had never occurred to him not to. Soldiers looked after each other. It was what they *did*. It never failed to amaze Harker how many officers just couldn't grasp this concept.

He mooched back to the mess, snapped at Charlie and immediately felt bad about it.

'It's okay, sir,' she said when he apologised.

'Maybe I'm no different from the rest of 'em,' he said moodily, kicking his boots up on his desk and narrowly avoiding a paper landslide.

'Of course you are, sir,' Charlie said, handing him a cup of tea. 'The rest of them would never say sorry.'

Harker slurped his tea, which garnered a look of annoyance from the captain at the next desk, so he did it again. The air inside the office was chilly, and stale with smoke and cold coffee. Outside, the world beyond the small windows was dark and damp.

He swung abruptly to his feet. 'I need some air,' he said,

and Charlie raised her eyebrows, eyeing the packet of cigarettes in his pocket.

'It looks like rain, sir,' she said.

'I like rain,' Harker said stubbornly. Charlie gave him a look he seemed to get a lot from women, which was interesting since he rarely, if ever, thought of her as a woman. Saskia had done it; his mother, God rest her, had done it; and even General Wheeler did it. It said he was being difficult, just for the sake of it.

Harker liked being difficult. It made life more interesting.

'Rain is good,' he insisted. 'Makes things grow.'

'So does sun.'

'Aye, but imagine if all we had was sun? Country'd be a desert. Might as well go and live in Spain.'

Charlie muttered something that sounded like, 'You've had worse ideas.'

'I hope you're not being unpatriotic, Lieutenant,' Harker said.

'Disliking rain is unpatriotic?'

'It is in England.' He shrugged into his greatcoat. 'We ain't made of sugar.'

'You certainly aren't,' Charlie opined, which made several of the younger officers snigger.

Harker ignored them. 'Where've they put Tallulah?'

He collected his former sister-in-law from her chilly, draughty barracks, and mooched down to the river. Not far away, the crowded little world of London Bridge was lit up against the darkness. The water rushed, deep and black in the shadow of the Tower's mighty walls, churning towards the narrow arches of the bridge, fast and deadly.

Torchlight flickered on Tallulah's pale, fine features. She had her sister's dark hair and straight bearing, but she was so young, younger than Saskia had been when Harker first met her. Like a past version of his wife he'd never known.

No. She might share her blue-diamond eyes and porcelain skin with Saskia, but she wasn't the same person. Saskia would never have slogged through the ranks when she could cut to the chase and buy her commission as Ensign. An officer to the core. Her head, her very voice ringing with duty. Ambition blazing from her fine pale skin.

Tallulah watched him expectantly, her face perfect in its prettiness, its freshness, its eagerness to please. Barely eighteen, mucking in with the rest of the conscripts. Calling him 'sir'.

Saskia had never been like that.

'You've grown,' he said, trying not to notice the precise areas in which she had.

'You haven't seen me in years,' Tallulah said. 'I was a child then. Sir.'

You're a child now, he wanted to say, but he didn't expect she'd like to hear it. Sodding war, conscripting kids like her.

'Don't call me sir, Lu,' he said moodily, kicking at pebbles. He got out his cigarettes and lit one up, inhaling deeply. Much better. 'You never used to.'

There was a pause, then Tallulah said, 'I'm not sure I ever called you anything.'

No. Well, she'd been a kid, and he and Saskia had been young officers. Why would he have spent any time with her?

'Smoke?' he offered, and thought he saw Tallulah's lip curl slightly.

'No. Thank you. Sir.'

Back with the 'sir' again, he thought, tucking the packet away as rain started to fall. 'Well, you wait until you've been on campaign a few months, soldier,' he blew out some smoke and watched it spiral upwards, 'and we'll see if–'

Light from the Tower's torches glinted off something up high.

'What the hell is that?' he said, staring up. 'A bird?'

Tallulah followed his gaze. 'A pretty big bird,' she said.

The creature gave a cry.

'A pretty big bird that swears,' Tallulah said doubtfully.

They watched it a second or two longer. It seemed to be gliding downwards.

'Lu, you know of any birds with a thirty-foot wingspan?'

'Uh, no,' she said, starting to back away.

'It's spiralling, looks like it's in trouble.'

'Yes, sir ...'

'What the hell is it?'

'I don't know, sir, but it's ...'

Harker instinctively stepped back a little.

'... it's spiralling this way,' Tallulah said, and they both rushed back against the castle walls.

But the ... *thing*, whatever it was, rapidly whipped back towards the centre of the river, and as the light reflected off the giant wings, Harker realised that it was just one wing, one huge curve, and beneath it was suspended ... something ...

'That's a person,' he said, squinting.

'Sir?'

The giant wing was crumpling now, losing whatever force had been keeping it airborne, and the figure suspended by a network of ropes was thrashing about, getting more and more tangled.

And Harker realised the thing was being blown downriver, towards the Bridge, and he didn't even need to look to know the current was smashing water against the piers, churning itself into a mad frenzy against the wood and stone.

His hand went to the gun at his hip, which was a stupid thing to do, because what good would shooting do?

The person tangled in the ropes shrieked, and Harker knew the sound was pure terror.

The Thames would be bloody freezing this time of year. It

was dark, it was deep, this close to the Tower it'd be mostly sewage – and he was going to jump into it.

'Crap,' he muttered, and handed his coat to Tallulah.

'Sir?'

'And these,' he toed off his boots. 'And these.' He handed over his sword and pistols.

'Sir, you're not going to jump in? The river – it's too dangerous!'

'Well, I don't see no bugger else doing it,' Harker said, and started running before he changed his mind.

Chapter Two

'Sir! Sir, are you all right?'

That was Tallulah. Grimly, Harker dropped to the stony shore under the Tower's walls and let the body over his shoulder flop on the pebbles.

'I'm all right,' he said. 'Get a doctor, would you?'

She peered closer at the limp body. 'Is it – is it a person? Is it alive?'

Harker, busy performing mouth-to-mouth and trying not to think about what the drowned woman would be coughing up if she was still alive, didn't bother to answer. In the background, people were shouting. The guards on the walls had seen him dive into the river and come out with some sort of bedraggled alien.

Well, it wasn't an alien, Harker was pretty sure. It was a human woman, and she – yes, there she went, coughing up river water through blue lips.

He rolled on to his back and fought the urge to throw up. Who knew what he'd ingested in the Thames' foetid depths?

People were streaming out of the South Gate now, and a guy with a stethoscope flung over his pyjamas was kneeling by the unconscious woman.

'She all right?' Harker said, and the doctor nodded.

'I think so. We need to get her inside. Can I get a stretcher?'

'Dunno,' Harker said, mostly to himself. 'Can you?' Patting his pockets, he found his cigarettes – a soggy, unsmokable mess. Dammit. Well, if he couldn't have a quiet smoke, he'd have a quiet nap instead.

He lay back, closed his eyes, and tried to block out all the noise and the light. It was a trick he'd perfected after years on campaign. These days he could sleep anywhere, any time.

Then a foot prodded his ribs, and he opened one eye, grumpily.

'Well, then, hero,' Saskia said, her face demonic in the torchlight. 'I suppose you'll be needing medical attention, too?'

Harker waved a hand. Truth be told, he was so wet and cold he was beginning to worry about his extremities. 'Get me a packet of smokes and I'll survive,' he said.

'I think we can run to that.' Saskia extended a hand. 'Come on. Wheeler wants to see you.'

Harker groaned. 'Why? What'd I do?'

Saskia just glared at him.

'Oh, right.' Ignoring her hand, he hauled himself upright. 'Let's go and face the fun, then.'

Dripping wet, he squelched through the gate after Saskia and gave the guard there a damp salute.

'Sir, is it true you pulled an alien from the river?'

Harker rolled his eyes at Saskia. 'Yep. Blue skin, it had, and one giant wing.'

The young man's eyes were enormous. 'Gosh!'

'Yep.'

'That wasn't necessary,' Saskia said, as they made their way to the General's quarters next to the mess.

'Yeah, but it was fun,' Harker said, looking back at the trail of puddles behind him. A slight commotion at the gates heralded the stretcher, complete with blue-skinned alien, but sadly minus any wings.

'You never take anything seriously, Harker,' Saskia said, stepping out of the way of a guard patrol on their way past the White Tower.

'Nope,' he said, knowing it infuriated her when he didn't rise to the bait.

'That's probably why you're still only a major,' she said,

which was an unusually low blow. Harker wondered what he'd done, specifically, today, to make her so angry.

'Probably,' he said, and grinned in the gloom as her scowl intensified.

General Wheeler's office was attached to her quarters in Martin Tower. When the army had moved in, rooms were offered in the Lieutenant's Lodgings and the White Tower, but General Wheeler had been keen to make the point that the army was not here to stay, and so had taken up temporary lodgings in one of the more luxurious towers.

Harker privately considered that five years was a pretty rubbish sort of temporary, but hadn't seen any point in saying so.

He dripped up the worn stone stairs to her office, and stood at attention.

'Ah, Major,' the General said. 'At ease. Do take a seat.'

Harker, contrary to his bones, remained standing. Saskia, looking thunderous, sat down. General Wheeler finished writing whatever terribly important document she'd been working on, and set it aside. Her pale blue eyes fixed on Harker like a searchlight.

'And how is our alien?'

How does she know? Harker wondered. *It happened five minutes ago*. 'Still breathing, sir, although not knowing much about aliens I'm not sure if that's healthy or not.'

'I really don't think–' Saskia began.

'One eyewitness reports that it was, in fact, a dragon,' Wheeler said, glancing at a document.

'No, sir. Not enough wings,' Harker said, beginning to enjoy himself. 'Or scales.'

'Really?' Saskia snapped. 'And how many dragons do you know?'

Oh, come on, she's giving you that one. Harker paused for a delicious second, avoiding Wheeler's gaze, then said,

'Oh, a few, Colonel. A few.'

Saskia made a growling noise in the back of her throat.

'Of course, several watchers thought it was merely a large bird,' Wheeler said, ignoring this.

'Still not enough wings, sir, and too many appendages of the arm variety.'

'But you have no argument with the hypothesis that it may be an alien?'

'No sir. Happy with that, sir.'

'And this is because ...?'

'Blue skin, sir,' Harker said promptly, while Saskia made a noise of impatience. 'Not a natural colour among humans, sir.'

'Of course not,' Wheeler said. She scanned another document – Harker was under the belief she kept a few lying around to make you think she had notes on everything – and added, 'Unless said human has been in a freezing river.'

'Werrl,' Harker said expansively, 'if we're going to look at it that way ...'

'Oh, don't be ridiculous,' Saskia exploded. 'It was clearly a human being in one of those flying machines.'

'An aeroplane?' Wheeler said.

'No sir,' Harker said. 'I think it was a glider, sir.'

'You think, Major? And what do you know on the subject of aeronautics?'

Absolutely nothing, but he'd been listening idly in the mess the other day while a couple of engineers discussed the topic eagerly. If only for want of money, they'd moaned, we could be flying in the air, and that'd show the Coalitionists who was boss! Harker had smiled and declined to comment, because personally he figured that flying in the air would just give the Coalitionists something else to aim at.

'Unfortunately, sir, it's impossible to be certain,' he said. 'Reason being, that flying apparatus is now at the bottom of the river.'

'And why is that?'

'Had to cut it off her, sir. Current had hold of it.'

'So it's a female alien then, is it?' Saskia said sourly.

'Indeed it is,' Harker said, smiling at her.

'Harker, please stop being so silly. You saw her closer than anyone else, you know she's a human being–'

'Who fell out of the sky in a country where the only thing coming from the clouds is rain,' Harker said. 'Makes her a pretty foreign body in my book. Sir.'

She scowled at the 'sir'.

'An illegal alien, Harker?' Wheeler said.

'Well, I dunno if flying is exactly illegal in this country, sir,' Harker said. 'So far as I know, we ain't never arrested a bird for it, but I don't expect we allow people to go around doing it, either.'

'We do have pilots, Harker,' Saskia said reprovingly.

'Either of 'em missing, sir?'

General Wheeler gave a faint smile. 'Not to my knowledge,' she said, and Harker knew that if Wheeler didn't know something, then it wasn't knowable. 'Well, then, Major Harker. It seems clear to me that what we have is no more than an aeronaut blown off course. Naturally,' she went on, before Saskia had even opened her mouth to object, 'since we have very little in the way of an aviation industry, I expect you to investigate where she came from and why. It is entirely possible that she is a spy.'

'Yes, sir,' Saskia said eagerly. 'I can conduct the investigation–'

'Colonel, you have much more important things to do,' said Wheeler. 'This is clearly a matter for the good people at St James.' She let her searchbeam gaze settle on Harker, who shifted damply and sighed. St James. Hell.

'I'll see to it in the morning, sir,' he said.

'Do,' Wheeler said, turning her attention back to her desk in that way Saskia had begin emulating. 'Do.'

Outside, someone was doing construction work. Or maybe firing a gun. Eve thought that was unlikely, but then she did live in Mitcham.

Her head throbbed. Her throat was on fire. She hurt in places she didn't know she had.

'Ow,' she croaked.

'Oh, you're awake.'

An unfamiliar voice. Eve cranked open an eyeball and was presented with an equally unfamiliar face, topping a white coat.

'Apparently,' she rasped.

'How do you feel?'

She considered. 'Like I just got slapped by a really, really big hand,' she said, and the doctor grinned, handing her a small glass of water.

'Well, I wouldn't call the river a hand, but "slapped" is probably about right.'

Eve closed her eyes. Hell, yes. The paraglider. The river. The–

'What the hell happened?' she said. 'It was clear blue sky when I set off. Did a storm fly in or something? It just seemed to switch, bang, like day into night.'

The doctor shrugged. He was scribbling things on a chart by her bed. 'Don't ask me about weather,' he said. 'You were lucky the Major saw you fall.'

'Major?'

'Major Harker, miss. He swam in and pulled you out.'

'Oh,' Eve said. 'Well, I ... I guess I ought to thank him.' She made to push the covers back and get out of the high-sided bed, but as she moved her right foot her ankle gave a throb. 'Ow!'

'Yes. It's a bad sprain. Try not to move it too much.'

Eve's head felt like someone had filled it with lukewarm water, but a pertinent thought managed to swim to the surface. There was a curtain pulled partway around her bed, blocking off a lot of the room from her view, but what she could see of it looked rather ... old-fashioned. The walls and cupboards were painted a sort of jaundiced yellow. It looked like the biology lab at her old school.

Her gaze flickered back to the doctor, who looked terribly young. His lab coat was too small for his gangly frame and an inch of wrist was exposed by each sleeve. Under the coat, he appeared to be wearing khaki.

Industrial paint. Major. Khaki.

'Uh,' she said, as the doctor turned to go. 'This might sound a little trite, but where am I?'

The young doctor hesitated a moment or two. He had a wide mouth, like a child's drawing of a smile, and with his hair sticking up in a dozen different directions he looked like a cartoon character. 'Tower hospital, miss.'

'Is it ... I mean ... you said there was a major ...'

'Military hospital,' he clarified for her.

'Oh.' Something unpleasant was occurring to Eve, who wasn't entirely sure why being in a military hospital might be a bad thing exactly ... but she was also fairly sure it wasn't a good thing, either. 'Um, am I in trouble?'

He hesitated again, which Eve glumly figured probably meant yes.

'You'll have to ask the Major,' he said eventually.

'Major ... what was his name?'

'Harker.'

'Right. Major Harker. Is he in charge here?'

'Well, um ...'

Eve rolled her eyes. 'Can I go see him?'

'No. Sorry, miss. You need to rest here.'

'But, look, I can hop or something. Do you have any crutches I could use?'

The young doctor was already backing off. 'Sorry, miss.'

'Stop saying that! And don't go!'

But the door had already fallen shut behind him.

'Great,' Eve said, slumping back against the pillows, which were lumpy. 'Fantastic. That was a load of help.'

'It's the military,' came a voice from behind the curtain, making her jump. 'They're not supposed to be helpful.'

Eve froze for a long second, then reached out, balancing precariously, and tugged back the curtain. On the other side of it was a man lounging on a hospital bed, his hands behind his head, his ankles crossed. He, too, was wearing khaki, t-shirt and combats the same faded shade of sludge green. His right arm was bruised, and he looked like he hadn't shaved in about a week, or had his hair cut in about a year.

He gave Eve a nod, reached into a pocket and pulled out a packet of cigarettes and then, to Eve's horror, lit one up.

Mistaking her expression, he offered her one.

'Er, no,' she said. 'Um. Should you be smoking in here?'

He shrugged and took a deep drag. 'Don't see no laws about it.'

'Uh,' Eve said. 'I'm pretty sure there is one. This is a hospital, right?'

'Apparently.'

'Then–'

'Ah, military, see?'

She blinked away smoke. 'You can smoke in a military hospital?'

'No one's ever stopped me.'

Privately, Eve didn't consider this to be the same thing at all. 'Been in many?' she said.

'Yeah, a few.'

She ran her eyes over him. There was a long scar running

from his wrist to his elbow, and his nose looked like it had been broken a few times, but there were no obviously new injuries visible.

At first glance, he didn't look like he had a soldier's discipline. But muscles flexed in his forearms and under his t-shirt, and he had a lean look about him, as if he was made of muscle and bone and nothing else. She wondered if he'd ever carried an ounce of fat in his life.

Her eyes went back to the ugly bruise on his arm. Befitting his calling it, too, was khaki.

'What happened to you?' she asked.

'Someone kicked me.'

'In the arm?'

'There, too.' He puffed contentedly. 'You?'

'I, er, I had a sort of accident.'

His eyes travelled slowly over her, and Eve became aware that the make-up she'd painstakingly applied that morning would at best have dispersed in the river, and at worst, still be sliding down her face. Her hair felt heavy, limp, dirty; her head pounded; she felt ... *grey*.

'I was paragliding,' she explained, limply. 'Something went wrong, and I ended up in the river.'

'Paragliding?'

'You know. With the parachute and the sort of sling ... I bloody told them I shouldn't be out alone, I'm really sure you're supposed to have training and stuff – well, more than they gave me.' She made a face. 'But they said it'd make better TV that way.'

'Why were you paragliding?'

Eve winced. 'I just said. TV.'

She waited for him to make the connection. Okay, she was looking really rough right now, and generally speaking she looked pretty different from how she used to in the Grrl Power days, but that didn't seem to stop the people who waved and pointed and, most of the time, sniggered at her in public.

He shrugged, and she realised he really didn't seem to know who she was. Well, under the circumstances that was a good thing, but ...

... it was also really sad.

'Do you know a Major Harker?' she asked, trying to spot if he was wearing any insignia that might clue her in to his rank.

'I think I can bring him to mind. Why?'

'Apparently he rescued me. From the river. Which was pretty nice of him.'

'Aye, it was.'

She frowned. 'Although what the hell he was doing there in the first place I've no idea. Was there, like, a parade or something?'

He shrugged. 'Not that I know.'

'Oh. So what was he doing jumping in the river?'

'Rescuing you. Clearly.'

'... oh.'

Chapter Three

He gave his name as Will.

She seemed satisfied with that, didn't ask for his surname or his rank. In fact, the only thing she did ask for was a telephone. A telephone! As if that was a privilege offered to anyone.

Happily, easily, she gave her name and address, even her date of birth. Eve Carpenter, from Mitcham.

'Mitcham?' he echoed. A smoking pile of rubble, like everything else south of the river.

'Yes, I know.' She made a face. 'Not exactly my choice. Look, is there a phone I can use? I really ought to call the TV company or something.'

'A phone,' Harker said, and she looked annoyed.

'Yes, a phone. A telephone. You know?' She mimed it with her hands.

'We, uh, there isn't one,' he said, and she stared at him incredulously.

'What do you mean, there isn't one?'

'Well, there is, but not for civilians.'

Eve looked astonished. 'Is that, like, some sort of military rule or something?'

Harker nodded. 'Yep. Military.' A telephone. For a *civilian*. 'What did you say you do?' he asked.

'Temp.' She shrugged. 'Office work, mostly. Filling in. Other people's lives.'

'Right. You ever, er, filled in for a switchboard operator?'

'No. Mostly it's filing, typing, that sort of thing. I can do audio typing now though,' she added, as though it was a minor achievement she wasn't particularly proud of.

'Audio–?'

'You know, typing at dictation speed?' She made movements with her fingers, like playing a piano. 'I can pretty much type what someone's saying, as they say it.'

He was impressed. He'd seen the typewriters the clerks used, and they were big, heavy behemoths. 'Don't the keys get stuck?'

She gave him an odd look. 'Er, no.' Then comprehension dawned. 'Wait, you mean like on a typewriter? Hah, I used to have one when I was little, actually it was my mum's, from like the 1960s or something. Nightmare. Used to have to stab at the keys, they got jammed together ... man, I was glad when we got a computer.'

A *computer*.

It was possible, just about, that she really was innocent, that she'd been brought up in Flanders or something, where – Harker was a little hazy on the details – ordinary households had telephones and even computers.

However, she had a damn good English accent for someone born in Flanders.

'You had your own computer?'

'Yeah. Little eighties thing, only used it for playing games and writing essays. One of those nasty dot-matrix printers, used to drive my teachers batty.' She smiled, her face softening.

'Where was this?'

'Just outside Reading.'

Barely forty miles from where they were now.

'Where are you from?' she asked. 'You sound northern.'

'Leicester,' he said absently. She really had her own computer? Nah, she was messing with him.

Maybe all this was a joke. She'd just read about these things in books, or maybe she'd visited abroad or something. Yes: she came from a rich family who took her on holidays to the Continent; maybe rich enough to have their own telephone?

No. Who had their own telephone? In a *house*? Even Saskia's parents hadn't had that.

'You ever go to the Continent?' he asked.

Her brows rose. 'Er, yeah,' she said. 'Not like it's a long way away, huh?'

Not geographically.

'Where? I've never been.'

She looked amazed. 'What, never? Anywhere in Europe? Not even on ... like a day trip or something? Family holiday? Camping in France?'

Was she mad? Camping – the army would never set up camp in France. A tiny little army like this, against all the electronics and bombs of the French Empire? Hah!

'No,' he managed.

'Wow. That's ... seriously, Will, that's weird. You have left the country, haven't you? I mean, you've been outside these shores?'

'Went to Ireland on manoeuvres once,' he said. They'd struck some deal for training with the Irish army a few years ago. Of course, now the Irish wouldn't touch them with a bargepole.

She was looking at him like he'd just said something very strange. 'I can't believe you've never been abroad.'

'I told you, I went to Ireland once.'

'Yes, but that's hardly abroad. You don't even need a passport.' Eve shook her head.

'Well, why would I? Got everything you'd want right here.'

She didn't miss his sarcasm. 'Sure. Land of milk and honey, this is.'

Harker lit up a new cigarette. 'So where have you been then, Miss World Traveller?'

She shrugged. 'Well, Europe for starters. We did a capital cities tour before I–' She broke off, then finished resignedly, 'before I left the band.'

'Band?'

Eve's eyes shifted, as if she was embarrassed. 'I used to be a musician. A singer.'

Since when did singers get to tour the Continent? 'Where did you go?' asked Harker, fascinated.

'Paris, Madrid, Rome, Vienna, Berlin, Copenhagen, Stockholm.' She ticked them off on her fingers. 'Someone tried to talk us into doing Reykjavik but seven cities in seven days is damn well enough when you're seventeen.'

Harker frowned. 'Copenhagen?'

'Yeah. Denmark.'

He shook his head. 'Odense is the capital of Denmark.'

Now Eve frowned. 'No, it's not.'

'Yes, it is. And Berlin – how did you get into East Germany?'

She just laughed. 'Dodged the machine-guns and climbed over the wall.'

Harker stared.

'We flew. Like normal people. It's not 1987 any more.'

Harker opened his mouth. Then he closed it again.

Maybe she wasn't a spy. Maybe she'd just hit her head.

Telephones, computers, and Continental travel.

Yeah. Hit her head *really* hard.

Reveille sounded, apparently five minutes after Harker had closed his eyes, forcing him out of bed. His quarters faced away from the courtyard, and yet the bugle still sounded as if it were being played right outside his window.

Thank goodness that infant doc had put Eve to sleep last night so Harker could go back to his own bed. He'd spent many a night in military hospitals, and every one of them had been hideous. Even worse when the person in the next bed kept talking rubbish.

He sent a yawning Tallulah off to the tax office. Probably he could have found someone else to do it, but Tallulah, like her sister, had that upper-class knack of getting what she wanted very, very quickly, and Harker needed to know whether Eve existed.

A body could hide from the law, from the army and maybe even from God, but Harker knew no one could hide from the taxman.

He wasn't remotely concerned about waking up the good people of His Majesty's Revenue and Customs. Firstly, because he doubted they were good people, and secondly, because he doubted they slept.

Tallulah had only just returned when Harker was summoned from his breakfast to Wheeler's office. *Promotion?* he wondered, climbing the stairs. *Special, exciting mission? Pay rise? Or another bollocking over Crazy Eve?*

'How's our alien?' Wheeler greeted Harker as he saluted.

Crazy Eve it was, then. 'Haven't seen her yet this morning, sir,' Harker said, giving the clock a pointed glance which was ignored by Wheeler. 'Although I think her worst injury was a sprained ankle, so I can't imagine she's dropped dead overnight.'

The General gave a crisp nod. 'What have you found out from her?'

Harker sighed. 'Either she's a very bad spy, or a very, very good one. Or she's mad. I'm not sure.'

Wheeler raised her eyebrows, and Harker told her what Tallulah had discovered. 'There's no record of anyone with her name, date and place of birth at HMRC. She says she was born and raised here, but we can't find her. The other thing is that she says she lives in Mitcham.'

'No Man's Land,' Wheeler said. 'Perhaps she's been away.'

'Well, she does seem to have travelled a lot, sir. All over Europe. I wondered if she was from a very wealthy family.'

'Then I'm sure you would have socialised with her,' Wheeler said. 'You were, after all, married to the daughter of one of our wealthiest families.'

Harker scowled. 'You want me to ask Saskia if she knows her?'

'I want you to find out what she was doing flying over the Tower last night,' Wheeler said. 'Try as I might, Harker, I am having trouble finding an innocent explanation for that.'

'Me too, sir,' Harker said, which was a shame, because he rather liked Eve. Even if she was mad. Or a spy.

'You have until the end of today to find one, Major,' Wheeler said, picking up a sheaf of paper and directing her attention to it. 'Otherwise, she may reside in St James's.'

'Sir,' Harker protested. 'A day?'

'We do not have time to waste on proving innocence, Major,' Wheeler said. 'We are at war, in case you hadn't noticed.'

Harker ground his teeth. 'Yes, sir.'

'The Coalitionists–' Wheeler took off her spectacles and rubbed the bridge of her nose. 'I'm sending out troops this afternoon to clear No Man's Land again,' she said. 'Closing the theatres, too. Doubling the patrols on the Bridge. We've suffered too many losses recently, and the Coalitionists are getting closer.'

'How much closer?' Harker said, alarmed.

'Peterborough, Oxford, and most worryingly, Southend. We're still counting the casualties. They know where we are, Harker. These were organised attacks.'

Stunned by how close the enemy had come, Harker only nodded.

'Find out who this girl is. Unless you can prove to me, conclusively, that she is innocent, I want her in St James's by tonight.' Wheeler put her spectacles back on. 'That is all, Major.'

Harker saluted, Wheeler ignored him, and he left.

Southend! That was close, and more frighteningly, it was coastal. If they took the coast – if they let the French in – the whole army might as well disarm now.

If the French got involved, as they were constantly threatening to, it would be the end of independence in Britain. And Harker would rather burn England than see it annexed to France.

Frowning, worried, he made his way back to the mess, where he started towards Charlie, only to be waylaid by Saskia. She looked tense as hell.

'Sask, that alien from last night. Do you know her?'

She frowned, annoyed. 'For heaven's sake, Harker, why would I know her?'

'She's not someone you've socialised with? Eve Carpenter. She mentioned some stuff that made me think she might come from a rich family, and I thought ...' He trailed off as Saskia shook her head, looking impatient. 'You don't socialise with aliens. Okay. Never mind.'

'Wheeler thinks she's a spy.'

'I know. Wants her in St James's by tonight if I can't prove she's innocent.'

'Well, at least she's letting you investigate.' Saskia looked peeved. 'Do you think she is innocent?'

Harker raised his palms. 'How the hell should I know?'

'Well, find out. These attacks have got Wheeler worried. Very worried. She's scheduled a telephone call with the King.'

Harker whistled. Wheeler must think the situation was pretty terrible if she was going to trouble the King with it. Not that Harker expected he could do anything about it. According to all sources, the royal family was being entertained by the King of California, and were likely to stay there until the fighting was over.

Privately, Harker wondered why the King wasn't soliciting any military aid from the Californians, but whenever he'd voiced this thought out loud he'd been told it was due to 'politics', from which he deduced that the Americans, like everyone else, were scared of the French.

'Well, if I get anything, I'll let you know,' he said, and Saskia nodded. But just as he turned away, she said, 'Will, there's something else.'

He sighed, and turned back. It must be serious if she was calling him Will. 'What? France sending warships? America kicking the King out? Wheeler resigning?'

'No. Nothing *that* terrible.' She said it carefully, as if it was only slightly less terrible than all those things, perhaps if they all happened together.

'What, then? 'Cos I've got to tell you, Sask, I'm having a pretty shitty day and it's not even nine a.m. yet.'

'I saw Sholt outside. He's back.'

Harker went still.

'And unless a bird did something on his shoulder, he's wearing an extra pip.'

Harker closed his eyes. Sholt's pinched, sly face came into his memory.

'And,' Saskia began, then stopped, clearly uncomfortable. Harker opened his eyes.

She was wincing.

'What?' he said heavily.

'I spoke to Lieutenant-Colonel Green. Sholt's been transferred to the 75th. It's already gone ahead, Wheeler approved it.'

Cold hate and revulsion churned in Harker's gut. 'Wheeler? What the hell was she thinking?'

'I don't know, Will.' She looked genuinely upset. 'I'll try

and get him shunted back out again–'

'Preferably into the river,' Harker said viciously.

'–but I don't know if I'll have any luck.'

'And this time, I ain't diving in to the rescue. Sask, what the *hell*? It's your damn regiment!'

More to the point, it was his damn regiment.

'Yes, I know,' she said. 'She went over my head, she can do that, she's the General. And I'll do what I can, but I've got more important things to worry about than checking every single officer coming in when I'm losing dozens every day.'

'I know,' Harker said through gritted teeth, 'but this is Sholt we're talking about. You put him in my company, you can have my resignation tomorrow.' The horrifying thought occurred to him that she just might. '*Sask*,' he said. 'Do *not* put him in my company.'

'I won't,' she assured him. 'He hasn't been assigned to a company yet, that's what he's here for. But you do need a captain.'

'Promote Charlie.'

Saskia sighed heavily. 'I can't just–'

'She's up for it anyway. Been doing Smith's job for ages.'

'Don't tell me what to do,' Saskia said, steel in her eyes.

'Do *something*, Sask,' he said, and he didn't care that by now the whole mess was listening to him fight with his CO. 'Because I swear, if that man comes near me or any of my men, I'll bloody kill him.'

Saskia raised her hands. 'Calm down, Harker. I'll do what I can. Go and see this Carpenter woman, will you, and stop thinking about Sholt.'

She left, and Harker glared at the rest of the mess, daring any of them to make a comment.

Every single officer looked away. Harker looked up at the clock and watched the minute hand thud into place. Nine o'clock, and his day had already gone to hell.

Chapter Four

Also unhappy with the way the world was turning, Eve woke up to find herself still in the sickly yellow hospital ward, her ankle throbbing and her stomach growling. A nurse wearing a starched hat and an apron with a red cross on it appeared with a lap tray bearing a steaming bowl of slop that might have been porridge.

She refused to answer any questions Eve directed at her, including why she was dressed like an extra from *Oh! What A Lovely War*.

Finally, yesterday's doctor with the cartoon mouth appeared, clipboard in hand.

'How are you feeling?'

'Pissed off,' Eve said.

He continued to consult his chart. 'Any pain in your ankle?'

'Yes, but it's not as annoying as the pain in the arse standing in front of me.'

'Any nausea?'

Eve glared at him, irritated that he wasn't responding. 'No.'

'Do you think you can walk?'

'I don't know. But without any clothes, I'm not about to –' she broke off as the doctor held up a bundle she recognised as yesterday's clothes. 'Oh God, I love you.'

He grinned, the first reaction he'd given her. 'Sure, that's what they all say. There's a shower,' he pointed to a door on the far side of the room, 'or if you don't think you can stand, I'll get one of the nurses to give you a sponge bath.'

'I think I can manage,' Eve said in horror. 'Is there any

shampoo?' she asked hopefully, tugging at the strawlike mop that had once been her hair.

'Of a sort,' he said, and Eve nearly swooned.

The shower was rudimentary, and gave her flashbacks to school changing-rooms, and the shampoo was little more than a large bottle of liquid soap, but she felt immeasurably better for having scrubbed the river dirt away. Drying her hair with a threadbare towel, she got dressed in her own clothes, which mercifully had been cleaned, if not ironed, and hobbled out to have her ankle rebound in bandages.

'I'm sorry,' she said as she went back into the ward, where the doctor was talking to someone whose back was to Eve, 'I don't think I know your name, Doctor ...?'

'Haran,' the doctor said, smiling that cartoon smile.

'And it's Captain Haran, actually,' said the other guy, turning, and it was Will.

'Captain,' Eve said, nodding, smiling at Will, feeling better for just seeing him. A friend. Someone who was nice to her. He smiled back, but he looked tense. 'I see you were allowed out,' she said.

'I don't have a dodgy ankle,' he said. 'How is it, by the way?'

'Oh, it's fine. Well, not fine, but you know.'

Any minute now, you're going to start blushing, Eve thought. He wasn't even that good-looking. Clearly, things had got even worse than she'd realised.

How long had it been since she'd even flirted with someone?

'Major Harker wants to see you,' Captain Haran said, as Eve perched on the edge of the bed to have her ankle re-strapped.

'Does he, now?'

'Yes. But his office is on the other side of the courtyard, and up some steps. Do you think you can manage it?'

Eve flexed her ankle, and winced. Wordlessly, Will fetched a pair of wooden crutches.

'You guys really need to modernise,' Eve said, but she took the crutches and made a few experimental hops. 'So, what's this Harker guy like? Do you know what he wants?'

Will and the doctor looked at each other. 'He wants to talk to you,' the doctor repeated.

'Wants to know why you were flying over the Thames with that parachute thingy,' Will supplied.

'I told you, it was a TV thing.'

'Why,' Will sounded uninterested, 'were you on TV?'

Eve chewed her lip, thumping the wooden crutches on the lino floor. 'Uh,' she said. 'I ... Okay, remember I said I was in a band? Well, they used to be kind of famous. I ... used to be kind of famous.'

This elicited no reaction. Eve wasn't sure if that was a good thing or not.

'Thought you said you were a temp,' Will said. 'Other people's lives.'

'Yes,' Eve said shortly. 'I had a disagreement with the taxman.'

'What kind of disagreement?' Will asked.

'You're not very curious, are you?' she snapped. 'The kind where he said I hadn't paid any taxes and I said I had, and then we both discovered my accountant had been scamming me.'

'Not your fault, surely?' Captain Haran said.

'Nope,' Eve agreed, testing her weight on the crutches, 'but the thing about the taxman is, if your money isn't paid, it's you they come after. Even if it's someone else's fault. So now I live in a tiny bed sit with damp on the walls in a building that looks like Cell Block H, and pay pretty much everything I earn straight to those lovely people at the Inland Revenue.'

There was a short silence.

'Anyway. Maybe I'll sue the TV company,' Eve said with a lightness she didn't feel. She was good at pretending it didn't bother her any more.

'If you're paying all your money to the taxman, how will you afford a lawyer?' Will said.

'Well, I'll ...' Eve shrugged, taking an experimental step. 'I'll complain really loudly.'

Will smiled at that, not a proper grin but something more genuine than she'd seen from him so far, and some of the dark cloud that had settled over her when she'd brought up the taxman lifted. She followed him out of the ward and down a broad corridor, where a couple of nurses in their ludicrous starched caps were talking over a clipboard. They broke off, watching Eve hop after Will.

'Don't see many civilians in here,' he explained, and she nodded. He led her out into the cool sunshine, down a set of steps that had a ramp laid over them. At the bottom of the ramp, a soldier in a wheelchair was smoking a cigarette and flirting with a couple of girls in khaki. He had, Eve was horrified to note, no right arm.

'Marley.' Will slowed down to greet him. 'How's it going?'

Marley grinned. He had a vicious scar on his face that skimmed one eye, making the lid droop. 'Can't complain, sir.'

'Can't salute, either,' Will noted. 'Suppose that means you're off?'

'Nah, I'm gonna teach.' Marley grinned at the two girls. 'Off to Basic Training. I can still run drills with one arm, can't I?'

'Don't see why not,' Will said. He clapped Marley on the back. 'Take care.'

'Yessir,' Marley said, and went back to flirting with the two young recruits.

'Will,' Eve said as she hopped after him, 'what rank are you?' The epaulettes where she might have looked for insignia on his greatcoat were torn, but even if they hadn't been, Eve would have been none the wiser. All she could remember were stripes for sergeant, and he didn't have any of those. But did that mean he was of a higher rank, or lower?

He raised his eyebrows. 'Why's that important?'

'It isn't. It's just, he called you sir.'

'Well, he doesn't know me well enough to call me Will.' He grinned at her, and Eve smiled back. He did have a nice grin. 'Smoke?'

He held a battered packet of cigarettes out to her. Eve shook her head. 'No? Well, your loss.'

He lit up and loped across the courtyard, which was busy with troops marching about. Holding open a door for her, he said, 'Now. We have to go up two flights. Reckon you can manage it?'

'Is there any alternative?'

'I could carry you.'

His eyes sparkled a bit as he said it, and Eve couldn't help letting her gaze run over his broad shoulders, remembering the muscular frame she'd seen last night in the hospital bay.

'I think I'll manage,' she said, her voice coming out a little higher than she'd intended.

Will winked and stood by to let her pass, and Eve was sure she was blushing.

'Right,' he said, as she hopped up the steps ahead of him. 'Harker's going to want to know why you were flying over the river last night.'

'I told you,' Eve said. 'TV.'

'Are you sure? You can tell me.'

She looked back at him over her shoulder. He lifted his eyes from her backside in its tight denim, and grinned at her.

'Pervert,' she said, without malice.

'You were clocking me outside.'

'I was trying to assess if you were strong enough to carry me,' Eve said, as loftily as she could manage, and started hopping again.

'I have to warn you,' he said from behind her, 'the office'll be full of men who only get to see women in baggy khaki. Hope you don't mind being stared at.'

Eve looked down at her t-shirt, which was tight and pink, and said, 'I've appeared on stage in hot pants and feathers in front of ten thousand people. I can deal with a couple of soldiers.'

'Hot pants?'

'Yeah. They were lime green.' She shuddered. 'Goodness knows who thought that one up.' And she didn't know how she'd had the nerve to wear things like that. The last time Eve had seen her thighs they'd been in no condition to mince around at the end of a pair of hot pants.

Of course, as she recalled it the hot pants had been Louisa Butcher's idea. Louisa, who'd always had photogenically perfect legs. Eve had always suspected she did it on purpose.

'What stage was this?' Will asked, as she reached the top of the flight, and he pointed round the corner to the next one.

'Uh. I can't actually remember. I think it was the European tour.'

'Recent?'

'No, Grrl Power broke up five years ago. You really don't listen to pop music, do you?'

'Nope,' Will said. 'Was this the tour that took in the not-capital-of-Denmark?'

'Copenhagen *is* the capital,' Eve said, rolling her eyes and smiling to herself.

'It is not!'

'Look, have you been there?'

'No, but–'

'Well, I have.' She turned and stuck her tongue out at him. 'So ner.'

'That's mature,' Will said, but he was smiling.

Eve reached the top of the stairs and he stepped around her to open the door there, into a large, busy room full of people poring over large maps or reading thick sheaves of paper. It reminded Eve of a lot of the offices she'd temped in, only in this one, everyone was in khaki, and there were no computers. Maybe that wasn't 'military'.

Several people, men and women, nodded to Will as he entered the room and made for a desk piled excruciatingly high with paperwork, and plenty of the men did, indeed, give Eve a thorough up-and-down that made Will grin.

Then something caught his eye, and his grin faded.

A man was making his way over to them, and Eve hoped like hell this wasn't Major Harker, because he had a smile that made her feel vaguely queasy. His eyes had an odd flat look to them, and they darted around like those of a lizard.

'Sir,' he said, and his voice had the cakey, whining quality of someone who has spent too long trying to ingratiate themselves. He smiled a sickly smile, a lizard smile, and Will's face grew grimmer.

Thank goodness he was subordinate to Will. If this guy had turned out to be Harker, Eve would have jumped out of the window.

'Sholt,' Will said shortly. 'Heard you were back.'

'Indeed, sir,' Sholt said, and Eve half-expected him to start twisting his hands and declaring that he was 'ever so 'umble', like Dickens' two-faced character, Uriah Heep. 'Transferred to the 75th this week, sir.'

'Heard that, too,' Will said.

'Put a special request in, sir. Wheeler saw to it, sir. Heard

C Company is in need of a captain, sir, now old Captain Smith has gone to Basic Training.'

Will's gaze travelled slowly to the pips on Sholt's shoulder. There were three. Deliberately, he took off his greatcoat, and Eve could see the rank insignia on his jacket. One crown. She didn't know what that meant, but it was still a higher rank than Sholt, it had to be, or else why was Sholt calling Will 'sir'?

'I will take a captain from Lieutenant-Colonel Green's command, or Major Dennison's,' Will said in a low voice that was so full of anger and menace that Eve had a sudden yen to hide behind something heavy. The man who'd looked strong and capable five minutes ago looked big and downright frightening now. 'I will promote from within the ranks. I will take a rat off the street, Lieutenant, before I allow you in my company.'

Sholt's obsequious smile only widened and became more hideous. 'Begging pardon, sir, but I've already put in for the transfer, sir. None of the other companies need a captain, sir. Only C company, sir. And it's Captain now, sir,' he pointed to his pips. 'Promoted in the field, sir.'

Will's face turned to granite, and he leaned in close. Eve couldn't help but notice that all the other officers had gone quite silent.

'Oh no, *Lieutenant*,' Will said deliberately, 'you won't beg my pardon on this. You've a list a mile long of things to beg my pardon on, and they all come higher than this. And one day, Lieutenant Sholt, you will beg indeed.'

Sholt's horrible smile grew a fraction more horrible before he said, 'It's up to the good Colonel now, isn't it, sir? Newly promoted too, sir. Colonel Harker – oh no, sir,' his smile turned, if possible, a little more sly, 'that's not her name any more, is it, sir? Changed back to her maiden name, I couldn't help but notice. No longer using your name, is she, sir?'

Will looked like he was going to punch Sholt, and Eve couldn't blame him. Then what the horrible little man had said penetrated her brain.

She stared at the crown on Will's shoulder.

'Don't you have something else to do, Sholt?' he said, making the man's name sound like a bad word.

'Yes sir, Major Harker, sir,' said Sholt, saluting greasily and oiling away, and Will turned back to her with a face like thunder.

Conversation suddenly resumed around them.

'Well, he was a horrible little man,' Eve said brightly to Will. 'Not one of your friends?'

'If there was a way to blast him off the face of the planet I'd do it,' he said, and the look on his face frightened Eve.

'Can't you just order him to take a long walk off a short bridge?' she said. 'I mean, you are a higher rank than him, aren't you? Major Harker.'

He scowled and threw himself into the chair by the overburdened desk, lighting up a new cigarette and pulling on it furiously.

'Why did you lie to me?' Eve said, lowering herself into the chair opposite him.

Harker ran his hands through his already dishevelled hair. 'I didn't lie,' he said.

'You said your name was Will–' Eve began.

'It is.' He gave her an unconvincing smile and poked gingerly at the debris on the desk. 'There's a sign around here somewhere.'

Wordlessly, the man at the next desk reached to the floor and picked up a desk sign. Into the slot at the front a piece of card had been inserted with a typed name on it. He handed it to Eve, who read *Maj. Wm. Harker*. It had a slightly temporary look about it.

'You let me think you were a rank-and-file soldier,' she

said, edging the sign on to the desk, from which it promptly fell off again.

'Would you have made friends with a major? Would you have told him what you were really doing with that glider...' he waved his hand, 'thingy?'

Eve scowled. 'Yes,' she said, and honesty forced her to add, 'maybe.'

There was silence between them. Eve waved away some of Harker's smoke. 'Thank you for saving my life,' she said, unable to inject much gratitude into it.

Harker dragged on his cigarette. 'Weren't going to let you drown, was I?'

'Well, I don't know.' He didn't talk like a major, Eve thought. Matter of fact, he didn't look like one, either. Majors ought to be stout, hearty fellows with greying handlebar moustaches, who said things like, 'What ho!' and called everyone Old Stick.

A major shouldn't be a man in his thirties who looked like a vagrant, talked like a steelworker and smoked as if it was the only thing keeping him alive.

Harker looked up as a woman approached, her frizzy hair battled into a plait, her face bare of make-up. Eve itched to tell her to get some decent conditioner, but judging by the stuff she'd found in the hospital showers, that sort of thing wasn't military at all.

'Sir,' said the woman, 'I've just been speaking to Major Dennison. They're already clearing people from No Man's Land. They're sending in the fire throwers before it gets dark.'

Harker nodded, rocked his feet off the desk and stood up. 'Right. I'm going to need a driver, Charlie, and some handcuffs.'

Charlie didn't blink, but she did glance at the bandaged ankle Eve had managed to fit her unlaced trainer over.

'How far do you think she's going to get, sir?'

'She could be faking it.'

'I am not!' Eve said. 'The doctor – Captain – whoever he is, he said my ankle is sprained. It bloody hurts!'

They both ignored her. Harker glanced at something on the far wall. Charlie continued to watch him, like a dog awaiting instruction.

'Fine,' Harker sighed. 'Get me a driver though. I'm not letting her out of my custody. Wheeler'll have my head. Get Lu. I'm sure she can drive. Do her good to see No Man's Land.'

'Hold on,' Eve said. 'Custody? Handcuffs?'

Again, she was ignored.

'Byward Tower, ten minutes,' Harker said.

'Sir.' Charlie nodded and left, but she didn't salute, and Harker wheeled round to face Eve.

'So!' he said, voice like a gunshot and a glint in his eye Eve didn't like one bit. 'Mitcham. Mitcham, Mitcham. I don't know much about it, I wasn't born in London.'

'Neither was I,' Eve said, warily.

'No, of course not. Still, you'll have to point it out to me.'

He gestured to a large map covering the far wall, and Eve got clumsily to her feet. 'Am I in some sort of trouble?' she said.

'What makes you think that?'

'The handcuffs conversation? Just because you ignored me doesn't mean I couldn't hear you.'

'Military rules,' Harker said vaguely, and led her to the map. A few people watched her go by – maybe they recognised her. Well, that was humiliating.

But when Eve got up close to the map, she rolled her eyes. 'Very funny.'

'What is?'

'The map. What is this, Elizabethan?'

Harker stared at her a minute, then said without turning

around, 'Ensign Bowhurst, how old is this map?'

A fairly young male voice replied, 'Er, about a month, sir.'

'All right, smart arse,' Eve said. 'What map is it based on? 'Cos I'm expecting to see the Globe on here. The old one.'

'The theatre?' Harker pointed to a blob south of the river. 'That one?'

She peered at it. Yes, it was labelled Globe Theatre, but she didn't see any of the stuff that ought to be near it. Where was the Tate Modern? The Millennium Bridge? Where was freaking Waterloo Station?

Why was there a long, uninterrupted ribbon of river, running all the way from the Tower, whose lopsided pentagon she could make out, off past Westminster and into the countryside? Where were all the bridges? Where were all the landmarks?

Where, in point of fact, was London?

'Found it yet?' Harker said. 'Your house?'

'It's not on here,' Eve said, because south of the river there was virtually nothing. A couple of circular theatres by the river and that was it.

'Hmm,' said Harker, in a voice that was starting to annoy her. 'Well, maybe we'd better get in a car and you can show me.'

Eve scowled. 'And if we drive to Mitcham and I show you where I live, will you let me go?'

'If we get there and you can show me your house, then yes. You can go.'

Eve gave him a distrustful look, and Harker raised his palms. 'Oath of an officer,' he said.

'Considering you allowed me to believe you were no such thing until ten minutes ago, that does not count for much,' Eve said, but she followed him anyway.

Chapter Five

The Wolf rattled down toward the Byward Tower, clanking and jarring. Harker shaded his eyes to see if the poor unfortunate driver was Tallulah, and smiled. It was Tallulah perched behind the wheel, her back ramrod straight, clearly horribly uncomfortable and never likely to admit it.

'Lu,' he said when she eased the rickety vehicle to a halt, 'this is Eve Carpenter. We're going to be taking her home.'

Surprise showed on Tallulah's pretty face.

'To Mitcham,' Harker added, and Tallulah's mouth opened, then closed again.

'Yes sir,' she said, and got out to open the door for Eve.

Harker held out his arm to assist Eve into the car, but she batted him away sharply.

'I don't need any help,' she snapped, and Harker raised his eyebrows at Tallulah, who hid her smile and waited. Harker waited too, arms folded across his chest as if he had all the time in the world. It was perverse fun to watch her struggle, her cheeks going red as she realised she couldn't do it by herself.

She was pretty, his alien, a little softer than most of the women he knew. Good bone structure under that scowl, a tangle of damp blonde hair to her collar, green-blue eyes that she turned, annoyed, on him.

Harker smiled amicably. 'All right?'

Nostrils flaring, she shoved her crutches at him and grabbed the side of the open vehicle, swinging herself in and tumbling on the seat with a total lack of grace. Harker, winking at Tallulah, followed, pushing Eve gently over to one side of the seat and propping her crutches in the corner.

'Isn't there a seatbelt?' she asked, and Harker, who had no idea what she was talking about, just shook his head.

'Well, that's safe. Thank you for helping me,' Eve said, her voice thick with sarcasm, as the Wolf rattled across the cobbles under the Middle Tower. Her fingers clutched the seat, her knuckles white.

'You said you didn't want any help,' Harker replied mildly as they drove out on to the road.

'Well, clearly I needed some! I have a sprained ankle!'

A sprained ankle. Harker had seen men drag themselves uncomplainingly for miles with half one leg blown away.

'Ah. So when you said you didn't want help, what you actually meant was the exact opposite? You'll have to forgive me, Miss Carpenter, sixteen years in the army does dreadful things to a man's capacity to disobey orders.'

Eve scowled.

'Don't take the Bridge, Lu,' he added, picturing the noisy, smelly snarl of people, horses, wagons and donkeys which clogged it at all times of the day and night.

'But you want to cross the river, sir?'

'Yeah. Drive down to Blackfriars, there's a pontoon.'

Eve snorted, but a minute later when London Bridge came into view, she sat up straight and said, 'What's *that*?'

'That,' said Harker, lighting up a cigarette, 'is the bridge you nearly drowned under last night. You're welcome, by the way.'

'What the–?' Eve twisted around to look behind them. 'Where's Tower Bridge?'

'Tower what? The bridge across the moat? You can't see it from here.'

'No, I mean the bridge across the river.'

There was a short silence. Harker gazed at the unmissable bulk of the only permanent river crossing in London.

'That is the bridge across the river,' he said eventually.

'London Bridge. The bridge that crosses the river in London. That's why they call it London Bridge,' he added helpfully.

'But ...'

He looked over at the Bridge, in all its decrepit glory, and tried to imagine it as someone who'd never seen it before. The stone columns, crumbling in places, slimy and lashed by the water frothing over the wooden piers. Even when the river was calm, the water churning through the narrow gaps in the low stone of the Bridge made a dozen or more fierce whirlpools. If Eve had been caught in any one of them, she'd have been smashed to pieces on the rotten wood of the battered piers. There wouldn't have been enough left for him to drag out.

Above the creaking stone, the buildings clustered together, outgrowing the Bridge by horrifying proportions. Some had been extended outwards so far they required supports to stop them toppling into the river. Each building tottered under the weight of six or seven storeys, leaning sideways or even forwards to rest on the structure opposite. Crossing the bridge meant dodging through a dark, narrow tunnel, the overhanging storeys allowing grudgingly little daylight to pass through.

People lived on the Bridge, shopped and worked and even prayed there in St Thomas's Chapel. It had always seemed to Harker as if it could exist entirely separately from the city, and that it might be possible for a person to live their entire life there, without ever stepping on to solid ground.

'... that's not London Bridge,' Eve said forlornly. 'And where *is* Tower Bridge? It should be just ... there, right next to the Tower!'

'Why would we put a bridge next to the Tower?' Harker said, glancing back along the docklands, which looked as crowded and unfathomable as ever. 'It'd be an open invitation to attack the fortress, and nothing could get past to the docks.'

'No, that's why it opens,' Eve said. 'To let ships through. Holds up the traffic something chronic. Where *is* it?'

Silence again. Even Tallulah glanced back upriver where there was, unmistakeably, no bridge.

Eventually Harker exhaled. 'No idea,' he said. 'You tell me.'

Tallulah drove on towards Blackfriars, while Eve bounced around in her seat, exclaiming and protesting. 'Where's HMS Belfast? Where's the Tate Modern? Why is everything so *low*? There's nothing on the south bank!'

'Couple of theatres,' Harker said, trying not to notice how attractively she bounced. 'See, that's the Globe. And that's the Curtain.'

'But ... but ...' Eve said.

'Dunno if the Rose is still there. You go to the theatre much, Lu?'

'Not really, sir.'

'Yeah. It all went to hell after the taverns moved out. No audience.'

'There's ... like ... a shanty town there,' Eve said, disbelief heavy in her voice.

'There is now,' Harker said. Come tomorrow there wouldn't be.

'But ... what is it? Who lives there?'

'Oh, refugees, vagrants, spies, whores. Big brothel industry over there. They get shut down every few months, lie low in the city for about a week, then go back and start rebuilding their huts. They're resilient, you've got to give them that.'

'But ...' Eve said, and Harker attempted to close his ears to her prattling. Soon enough, they'd reach the pontoon, and it'd be nice if Eve shut up long enough for Tallulah to concentrate on driving over it. After all, it was little more than a collection of planks laid over some boats. He could see it now, swaying gently in the tide. One slip of the wheel, and they'd all be in that filthy old river. Again.

Tallulah glanced back, her eyes worried, as they approached it. 'Sir? Are you sure this can take the weight of a car?'

'It can take a fully loaded infantry truck, Lu, it can take us.'

Carefully, experimentally, Tallulah drove on to the bridge, and Harker fancied that she didn't take another full breath until they'd reached solid land again.

Beside him, Eve prattled on about things that she expected to see but couldn't, and then she said, '*Where the hell is Westminster*?'

Harker sighed. He was getting pretty tired of this.

He put one hand on the top of her head and turned it towards the huge, complex bulk of the palace. 'There. Look. That really big building? With the gardens? And them flying ... er, what're they, Lu? Flying buttocks or whatever.'

'Buttresses,' Tallulah murmured.

'Yeah. Them. That's Westminster Palace.'

'It is not!'

'It is.'

'It isn't!'

'It is.'

'It isn't!'

Harker sighed. Again.

'That's not Westminster!' Eve shouted eventually. 'It's not the Houses of Parliament!'

'Yes, it is,' he said patiently. 'Why would there be that many soldiers guarding it, if it wasn't important? See that big long roof there? That's Westminster Hall where the Chancery court is. And that bit sticking out there, that's the House of Commons where all our good elected Members of Parliament sit and try to save the country.' The ones that haven't buggered off to form their own army, he added inside his head.

'It isn't! Where's Big Ben? And ... how come I can see it from here anyway?'

'Wait,' Harker said. 'Are you asking me why something you don't think you should be able to see isn't there?'

'Get lost,' Eve snarled. Harker, unconcerned, lit another cigarette.

'Where are we going, sir?' Tallulah asked, surveying the squalid huts and temporary shelters on the south bank.

Up until recently, this had been the town of Southwark, with proper houses and shops and a rather lovely cathedral. Three years ago, the Coalitionists had made their biggest attempt at taking London, and Southwark had become the battleground. The suburbs and villages south of the river had been overcome by the rebels, burning buildings and shooting civilians, and the army had met them full on.

Harker's fingers flexed, the back of his hand aching. The Battle of Southwark had taken the whole country by shock. Suddenly the war wasn't just a few skirmishes happening miles away, it was a battle raging in the capital. It was the destruction of homes and the slaughter of innocents.

It was a watershed moment for the British Army, and for Harker. He'd taken command of C Company after Major Chesterton had lost half his head to a grenade supplied to the rebels by the French. He'd been awarded a promotion to Major. He'd listened to General Wheeler announcing that after the army's narrow victory, losses were so great that Britain's women were not just to volunteer for the front line, but be conscripted for it.

And he'd turned to Saskia, knowing what this meant for her family. All her brothers and sisters, bar one, had been taken by the war. Only Saskia, the oldest, and Tallulah, the youngest, remained. Sheltered by her parents, he had rarely seen her due to his military duties, although Saskia, of course, had kept in contact.

'It won't come to that,' Harker said, trying to take Saskia in his arms. To comfort his wife. 'The war'll be over before Lu's eighteen. She'll be fine.'

He tried to smile, but Saskia just spat tearfully, 'Don't be a bloody fool, Harker. And how many times have I told you, stop manhandling me in public!'

She tore herself from him, and as he watched her stalk away across the wasteland south of the river, Harker realised he wouldn't be married for much longer.

Now Southwark was a shanty town of buildings so flimsy a good storm would wash them away. No one bothered to build properly, since the army came around every few months to clear the place. The town was a barren sweep of fire-blackened trees and transient shelters. Here and there low walls surrounded large piles of earth. The graves of soldiers.

'Well,' Harker said, clearing his throat as the engine idled and Eve surveyed the desolation in shocked silence, 'I do have one thing to confess.'

'What?' Eve said distantly.

He extracted from his jacket a very grubby, tattered bit of paper. 'I have a map that's about five years old. It has Mitcham on it. Couldn't find your street, but I found the village.'

'Mitcham's not a village,' Eve said, but she took the map, shaking her head as if it was all wrong. Eventually she said, 'Well, okay then. Drive … um … this way.'

She handed the map to Tallulah, who took it gingerly as Eve asked, 'Do I want to know what those stains are?'

'Most likely blood,' Harker said, and Tallulah hurriedly put the map on the dashboard as she set off again. 'I was carrying that at the Battle of Southwark.'

'The Battle of Southwark,' Eve said, sarcasm heavy in her voice.

'Yep.' Harker stared at a tree stump. He remembered sheltering under its huge, high branches. 'Lost a lot of good men then.'

'But no good women?' Eve asked archly.

'Lost a lot of them, too.' He kept his voice even.

'I thought women didn't serve in combat situations?'

'*They do*,' Harker said, and even Eve didn't argue with that.

'Stick to the marked paths, Lu,' he said. 'There are still some mines in the fields.'

'Excellent,' Tallulah muttered, her voice nearly lost under the rattle of the ancient Wolf's engine.

They drove in relative silence. South of Southwark, and the swarm of army wagons clearing people out, there was nothing but rubble and the skeletal remains of buildings. Some of them were black with fire. The fields surrounding them were pockmarked with shell holes, and in one meadow there was a big crater, with mud spattered for miles around, and bits of the unlucky animal who'd set off the mine decorating the rubble and the stark trees.

A sheep mine, the lads called them.

Occasionally, something in one of the ruined houses gleamed white, and Harker looked away, because he'd seen enough naked human bones in this lifetime.

After about half-an-hour of weaving around the remains of Brixton, Clapham, and Streatham, Harker leaned over Tallulah's shoulder, peered at the map, and said, 'Reckon this is about it.'

'This is about what?' asked Eve.

'Well, this is Mitcham.'

Tallulah stopped the car. There was grass growing on

what once had been a street, between some lumps in the ground where buildings had stood. Off to the right was half a stone wall. A hundred or so yards ahead was part of a wooden house frame. It stood like a dead tree, listing to one side and creaking in the wind.

Harker vaguely remembered Mitcham before the battle, and what he remembered was the air, thick with the scent of lavender from the bushes growing for miles around in all the fields. Now, the fields were stark and empty but for the flock of crows feasting on some dead animal.

'This is not Mitcham,' Eve said.

Harker ignored her. He couldn't even be bothered to sigh at her any more.

'Look. My Mitcham has tower blocks, and shopping precincts, and, and, and people, and buses, and cars! This looks like something out of a war film!'

'It *is* something out of a war,' said Harker, politely ignoring the last word, which he didn't understand.

'This is ridiculous! This is – wait.' Eve's voice changed. The hysteria vanished, and in its place came a sort of relief. 'I'm still being filmed, aren't I?'

'Um,' Harker said. All right, she was crazy. Pity. That soft little body next to his in the car had been a pleasant thing to be thrown against.

'This is – oh my God, this is like, what do you call it? That thing on MTV. Where they do something to celebs – well, not that I'm much of a celeb any more, but this is all Let's Humiliate stupid Has-Beens, isn't it? You've been filming me the whole time!'

Tallulah turned in her seat to exchange a look with Harker. Her expression said she didn't know what the hell Eve was talking about, either.

'All right,' Eve called cheerfully, 'you can come out now. Where's the camera? There's probably one here, isn't there?

In the car?'

'A camera,' Harker said. Who the hell was she talking to? What the buggery bollocks was MTV? A Multi Terrain Vehicle, maybe that was what the Coalitionists called them. 'The army doesn't have any cameras.'

'Yes, but this is not the army, is it?'

A pause, then Harker said, 'I'm pretty sure it is.'

'I bet it's in one of those building things. Where are we? 'Cos you just *told* me we were in the Tower of London and I believed it, but I bet it's a set, isn't it? A film set? It's pretty elaborate, but wow, I'm impressed.'

She sounded pretty cheerful, Harker thought. Of course, that was because she was completely insane.

'Where is it?'

Eve made to open the car door, but Harker leaned across. 'Where do you think you're going?'

'To look for the camera.'

'What camera?'

'Come on, guys, the game's up. Unless – oh, *you are kidding*; you don't know, either?'

Harker gave her a measured look. 'No, I really don't,' he said. He started to get out of the car. 'You can get out and look around if you want, but I'm coming with you.'

'Fine.'

Eve waited for him to come around and help her out of the car, smiling conspiratorially at Tallulah, who smiled nervously back. Hand on gun, Harker watched Eve hop confidently over to a fragment of stone wall and peek around behind it. She seemed disappointed not to find anything there.

Poking at the rubble and weeds around the base of the wall also produced nothing. Eve hopped over to the wooden frame, her smile fading, and peered around it. She squinted off into the distance, where there were barren fields, several of which were undulated with shell holes.

Starting to hop over to one of them, Harker halted her, his hand firm on her shoulder.

'I wouldn't,' he said. 'Not unless you want to further the cause of the British Army by detecting landmines for us.'

She paused, and looked up at him uncertainly. He stared back steadily.

'Well, maybe the camera's on the car,' she said, and started back towards it. She poked at the doors, at the spare tyre on the back, at the camo netting strung along the sides. She was about to go for the gun on the bonnet when Harker once more stopped her.

'Please don't touch that.'

'But what if it's–'

Harker flicked the safety catch, aimed at the empty field, and a spray of bullets kicked up mud.

'But–' she began, and Harker lost his patience. He leapt into the car, grabbed the submachine-gun from the seat and, raising it over Eve and Tallulah's heads, sprayed bullets into a circle twenty feet wide around the car.

Eve went white.

'There's got to be a camera somewhere,' she whispered.

'There isn't,' Harker said. 'And if there was, there isn't any more. Now get back in the car.'

Eve, looking shocked, did so, this time without complaining.

'Lu,' Harker said, tucking the gun down beside him, on the opposite side to Eve, 'back to the bridge.'

Tallulah did as she was told, and rather faster than necessary. In the back of the car, Eve sat still and quiet, her face pale and her eyes big with confusion.

'But it doesn't make any sense,' she whispered at one, apparently random, point, and Harker replied, 'War rarely does,' and put his arm around her.

Chapter Six

'Wheeler wants to see you,' Charlie said as Harker tugged off his jacket and looked for somewhere to put it. But unless he started colonising Captain Turner's desk, next to his, there wasn't anywhere.

'Of course she does.'

Charlie grinned and made a T with her hands. Harker nodded, in desperate need of something to take away the bad taste in his mouth that St James's always left him with.

'Did she say what it was about?'

'No. But I'm guessing it's our alien. What have you done with her, anyway?'

'St James's,' Harker said. He threw his jacket on the floor and sat down, swinging his boots on to the few inches of desk that Charlie kept clear for such a purpose.

'Shame,' Charlie said. 'She seemed to have spirit.'

'Yeah.' Harker frowned as he thought about the silent ghost curled up next to him in the car on the way back to the city. She'd had spirit, until he'd fired that gun and she'd … deflated, like someone had sucked all the fight out of her.

He'd handed her over to the halfway house at St James's, explaining that she'd be fine there, and well-treated. It wasn't a prison as such, more a place to put people they weren't sure about. People they suspected of nefarious deeds, but didn't have any proof of.

The army was big on proof.

But Eve hadn't really seemed to listen. Stumbling, shivering, like a person in shock, she'd huddled into his greatcoat and avoided eye contact. In the end, Harker had given up trying to talk to her, and just left.

Coop had been there, though. Good old Cooper, one of his best sergeants. On light duties after getting shot. Again. He smiled. Cooper's fiancée, Rosie, said that if he collected any more lead they could use it to fix the guttering.

Your men come back. Well, yes; if Coop hadn't, Rosie would be wearing Harker's entrails as lingerie.

Charlie handed him a cup of tea and leaned back against his desk. She didn't have one of her own, although she ought to. But then, Harker ought to have his own office and didn't.

'Any word on our new captain yet, Charlie?'

She shook her head.

'I put you forward for it, by the way.'

He didn't need to tell her. Half her promotions had come through him. Wheeler herself had seen to the rest. Wherever Harker went, there was always Charlie Riggs. Some of them called her his spaniel, behind both their backs of course.

Harker considered that a folly. For one thing, they ought to know he heard everything said behind his back; and for another, if they thought Charlie was a spaniel, they clearly didn't know much about dogs. Or about Charlie, for that matter.

'Thank you, sir.' She looked at her watch. 'Drink up. Time and Wheeler wait for no man.'

Harker did so, grimacing. When he'd joined the army as an enlisted man, a nice cup of hot, sweet tea was almost his constitutional right. But now he was an officer, he never had the time any more.

'I dunno,' he said. 'Three months back pay I'm owed, and I still can't finish a cup of tea. Never had to put up with this shit when I was a sergeant.'

'Sir?'

'Never mind.' Harker grabbed his jacket, now dusty and creased, which was just the way he liked it.

Wheeler was donning her own immaculate coat and

gloves as he entered her office. 'You wanted to see me, sir?'

'Yes, Harker. Walk with me.'

He did, following her back down the way he'd just come.

'Lieutenant-Colonel Green's men are clearing No Man's Land,' Wheeler said. 'In about an hour I will be sending in the Grenadiers.'

Harker waited to see where this was going.

'Did you drive your alien into the area?'

'Yes, sir. Found an old map and took her to Mitcham. Nothing there, of course, sir. She went a bit ...'

'Yes, Major?'

'Well, a bit mental, tell the truth, sir. Still don't know if she's mad or a spy, but I've sent her to St James's anyway.'

'Good. That's one less thing. See if they can get anything out of her.'

Harker bristled at the implication that he hadn't been able to, and almost forgot to open the door into the courtyard for Wheeler.

'Now, Major. Colonel Watling-Coburg passed on to me a recommendation from you for the position of captain in C Company.'

'Did she?' Harker shivered; it was damn cold out here.

'You know she did, Harker. And you know it was for Lieutenant Riggs.'

'Yes, sir. I really think–'

'I agree with you, Major. She would make a fine captain. And as I understand it, she's been the *de facto* second-in-command of C Company for as long as you've had it.'

'She's been the *de facto* second-in-command wherever I've been. No disrespect to Captain Smith, sir, he was a fine officer, but Charlie's the best second I've ever had.'

'Yes, I know. I've often considered the two of you as brothers.'

'Er, d'you mean she's like my sister, sir?'

There was a pause as both of them brought to mind one Charlotte Riggs, the most ruthlessly unfeminine person on the planet.

'All right, brother,' Harker conceded.

'And a very good officer. It's shameful it took us so long to get her out of the ranks. But nonetheless, I am going to have to turn her down for the position.'

Harker blinked. 'Might I ask why, sir?'

'No, Harker. Not today, you may not.'

Anger boiled up within Harker, but years of experience had taught him to squash it, quickly.

'I see, sir,' he said, which was a direct lie.

'No,' Wheeler gave him a faint smile, 'you don't. I don't expect you to. I would explain it to you, Harker, but I'm afraid it's on a need-to-know basis right now, and you don't need to know. Colonel Watling-Coburg has made her recommendation, with which I agree.'

'Do I get any choice in this?' Harker asked gloomily.

'No,' Wheeler said cheerfully. They'd reached the car, and its crisply saluting driver. Harker glanced at the kid; you didn't get boots as shiny as that unless all you did was drive around in them all day. They were not, Harker considered, boots that had seen many muddy battlefields.

'Do I get to find out who it is?'

'A Captain Wilmington. I don't think you know him. Exemplary service record.'

'Then surely I would have heard of him?' Harker muttered, but Wheeler caught it.

'Not every officer is promoted for heroism,' she said sharply. 'I have been known to look kindly on soldiers who have simply done nothing wrong.'

Harker refrained, but only just, from rolling his eyes.

'And then there are officers like you,' Wheeler said, looking him over in much the same way Harker imagined his mother might have done, had she still been around. Despairing, but with, he hoped, a touch of affection. 'Harker, where is your overcoat?'

'Oh.' He thought about it. 'Damn. I left it with Eve.'

Wheeler let out a theatrical sigh. 'How have I promoted this far from the ranks a man who can't even keep track of his overcoat?'

'Don't know, sir. Must have done something else right, sir.'

Wheeler gave him another faint smile. 'Yes, Harker. You must.'

'So. For what did they catch you?'

The speaker was a black girl with a French accent. She was dressed in jeans and heeled boots and looked, to Eve, like the first normal person she'd seen since her glider collapsed.

Eve closed her book but kept her finger on the page. They were in the small, pleasant library of the Palace of St James; smaller than Eve might have expected, but a quick inspection of the titles on offer gave one explanation: there just weren't enough books printed in English for a large library.

'Paragliding over the Thames.'

'Para ... ah, *oui*.' The girl nodded. 'You were doing the spying?'

'No! But they seemed to think I was.' Eve glared angrily at the book in front of her. 'And how do I prove I wasn't?'

'You can't,' said the girl. 'It is why they put us here, yes? My name is Lucille.'

'Eve,' Eve said distractedly.

'You are English? From where do you come?'

At that, Eve let out a laugh. It was the sort of laugh she'd become familiar with in the months following the news that her accountant hadn't paid her tax bill, and her mother had taken all her money and run off to the Bahamas. It was the kind of laugh that came from hearing something so mercilessly unfunny that it had gone round the other way into hilarity.

'London,' she said. 'But not this London.'

Lucille frowned. 'Not this London? But how many are there?' she said. 'Perhaps I am not understanding. I do not have the good English.'

'No, your English is really good. Where are you from?'

'Mozambique. I come to England to help with the children, and the hospitals, you understand?'

'An aid worker,' Eve said heavily.

'Yes, just so. But when there was the Battle of Southwark it was decided I was doing the espionage, and I was put here.'

An aid worker from Africa. It made total sense, in a way that didn't.

'When was this?'

'It is since three years.' Lucille shrugged. 'But it is not so bad. The food, it is good, I have my own bedroom and there is much to do.' She waved a hand at the book on Eve's lap. 'What is it you read?'

Eve looked at the mistyped title page of the book, which had a sad, cheap, hand-printed look about it. '*A History of the Untied Kingdom*,' she read bitterly.

'Ah, yes? Me, I don't know a lot about the history of your country,' Lucille said, totally missing the malapropism. 'Perhaps to the last fifty, or sixty years.'

'Yes,' said Eve, flipping towards the end of the book, 'sixty years including the Third Civil War, the secession of Scotland and Wales from the United Kingdom – to which no part of Ireland ever belonged, apparently – oh yes, and the World War, the *only* World War, no numbers, which we *lost*.'

Lucille was nodding politely. 'Yes. The French Empire, it

was too strong. And with the Americans also ... I think no one expected for Germany to win.'

'Germany *didn't* win,' Eve said. '*We* did, but Germany *didn't*. We were fighting *against* Germany. We didn't ally ourselves with the ... the ...' she glanced at the book, 'the Austro-Hungarian Empire!'

'*Oui*?' said Lucille nervously.

'And look at this.' Eve stabbed the page. 'In 1914, absolutely nothing happened.'

'Uh,' Lucille said.

'No! No, something did, but not here. You want to know what?' Eve dragged over another book, this one larger, proclaiming itself to be a history of the Austro-Hungarian Empire in the twentieth century. 'Because look. Here. In 1914, Archduke Ferdinand was assassinated ...'

Lucille was nodding as if this all made perfect sense to her.

'... *and his capable wife Sophie stepped into his place*, ruling the Empire and bringing about a period of peace and prosperity that lasted until the rise of Hitler, who we *supported*–'

She broke off, because fear had come into Lucille's eyes. And she couldn't blame her. She was ranting like a crazy person.

In the last three days she'd started to believe she might *be* a crazy person.

'None of this makes sense,' she said, calming her voice. 'I'm living in a blasted typo. There's all this stuff ... there was never an empire. Not a British Empire. No ... no Colonial India, or America, or Australia – it's all French! It all belongs to the damn French!'

'Yes, this is so,' Lucille said, starting to back away.

'Apart from America, which they – wait, I've got it here–' she grabbed a shiny book about the New World, 'which the French investigated in the eighteenth century, because of the tales about seafarers going there and not returning, but they decided it was just marsh because they'd sailed up the Mississippi Delta, and ignored it. And no one knew there were people in America until an experimental Japanese flight sailed over buildings in Hawaii! I mean – how did anyone learn to fly? Have you ever heard of the Wright Brothers?'

Lucille looked at her with a worried expression. 'I do not think so. Are they English?'

'No, they're American.' She felt like sobbing.

'Wright,' Lucille said thoughtfully. 'It does not sound American to me. Perhaps they are *émigré*?'

Eve's fingers clutched the book tightly. 'Who invented flying, Lucille? Modern aviation? The biplane, powered flight?'

If she says the Wright Brothers I'll know I'm sane. It's just a practical joke. A really, really big practical joke.

'Ah, it was the Frenchman Robert Esnault-Pelterie,' Lucille said. 'He founded the Fédération Aéronautique Internationale, yes? My father, he is an engineer for the–'

'But how did no one know America existed?' Eve yelled. 'I've heard of Isolationism but this is ridiculous!'

'Yes,' Lucille said, smiling. 'It is the thing unimaginable! A nation complete with the aeroplanes and the television ... can you imagine how it is not to know what television is?'

'*What, you mean like every single person in this country?*' Eve snapped.

'Uh, perhaps I should be fetching someone,' Lucille said, taking another step backwards.

'Well, unless it's Doctor Who then I can't see them being any use.' Eve closed the books all on top of each other, and looked up at Lucille. 'It's just all wrong. These books have us as basically a third-world country. We used to be just another part of Europe but then they all advanced and we were left behind and we made bad choices, one after another. We lost every war we've ever had, even the ones against ourselves! We're on our fourth civil war, Lucille, our *fourth*, and that's counting all those in the seventeenth century as one. I mean, look at this place. Clearly there was money here once, but it looks as if nothing has changed for hundreds of years. The rest of the world continues to evolve and this place goes *backwards*.'

Lucille nodded, but continued to back away.

'When I was at school they told us no battles had been fought on British soil for two hundred and fifty years. And now we're at war with ourselves, again.'

Lucille was almost to the door now.

'No wonder Harker thought I was mad,' Eve said. 'I'm the only person in the world who's heard of the British Empire.'

Lucille gave her an encouraging smile that in no way reached her eyes.

'Which must mean that Harker was right,' Eve concluded, her head drooping to her hands. 'I am mad.'

Several annoying days passed, during which Harker met his new second-in-command and hourly invented ways to kill him and General Wheeler.

It wasn't that Captain Wilmington was a bad man. He wasn't even a bad officer. It was just that he was a terrible soldier.

'I checked into his history, sir,' Charlie whispered as they watched Wilmington blundering about in No Man's Land. 'He's never actually seen active service. He can train and drill the men at home, but he's never been out in the field.'

'If he took my men out in the field, I'd have to shoot him,' Harker said grimly. He took a cigarette out of his top pocket and lit it, cupping his hand against the wind. 'I swear, Charlie, she must have something against me.'

'Wheeler, sir?'

'No. I bet this was Saskia. What did I do to her?'

'You did divorce her,' Charlie pointed out mildly.

'No, she divorced me. I just allowed myself to be divorced. It's entirely different.'

Charlie, showing some restraint, stayed silent.

'He can't even read a map!' Harker exploded, watching Wilmington turn the paper around and around, and point off vaguely in the wrong direction. 'Jesus wept.'

'Seventh Platoon!' Wilmington's voice carried across the empty ground, cleared of all the shacks and tents clustering it a few days ago. Guarded every few hundred yards by soldiers with very large guns, it was nonetheless an ideal space to test manoeuvres. 'To me!'

Seventh Platoon milled about hopelessly until the very capable Sergeant Milson got them into order. She caught Harker's eye and gave him a despairing eye-roll.

'He's going to kill them,' Harker said, closing his eyes. 'We go out into the field, he's going to get them all killed.'

'Technically, sir, he won't be the one giving commands,' Charlie said.

'Yeah, but unless I tie him up somewhere and gag him, he'll still manage to do something wrong.' He thought about it for a second, then opened his mouth.

'No,' Charlie said.

'I didn't say anything!'

'You didn't have to. You can't tie him up anywhere.' Harker opened his mouth again and she added quickly, 'Or gag him.'

'Excuse me, who is the Commanding Officer here?' Harker complained. Brotherly relationship, yeah right. Sometimes he wondered if Charlie forgot he was her CO and not just her mate. He sucked on his cigarette, inhaling deeply, and regarded it with suspicion. 'I read the other day these things are bad for you.'

'You gonna stop smoking them, sir?'

Harker put the cigarette back in his mouth. 'Nope.'

Charlie snorted.

'In fact, after this, I may take up drinking as a hobby.' He blew out a cloud of smoke. 'This is a bloody joke, Charlie.'

'I don't see anyone laughing, sir.'

Back at the barracks, he made good on his promise to take up drinking, leaving the company in Wilmington's hands and heading straight for the mess, where the barman, seeing his face, got out a whisky tumbler.

'No,' Harker said, 'I hate that stuff.' And it was expensive, as it had to be imported from Scotland. Or smuggled over the border. 'Give me a beer.'

'The whisky will get you drunk quicker,' said a voice behind him, Saskia's voice, and he turned with a scowl.

'Don't you start,' he said. 'Don't you bloody start.'

Several other officers went very quiet.

'He even asked for a batman,' Harker said, disgusted.

'Did you assign him one?'

'I told him he could have one while we were at base, but he was on his own in the field. My men have better things to do than wash and dress their superior officers.'

Saskia, who had always employed the custom of taking a batman to act as her personal servant, said nothing.

'And you know what he said, *Colonel*?'

'I can't possibly imagine. Major.'

'He said he'd never been in the field before, and was it frightening?'

'And what did you tell him?' Saskia asked pleasantly.

'I told him that with his command skills, it wouldn't be frightening for long.'

Saskia made the mistake of smiling at that, and Harker had to resist the urge to throw his drink at her.

Right then a creak of the door heralded Captain

Wilmington himself, and Harker forced a smile.

'Ah, Captain,' said Saskia. 'We were just talking about you.'

'Yes, sir?' Wilmington looked at them with a hope that rapidly faded when he saw Harker's expression.

'Major Harker was telling me of your bravery in the field,' Saskia said, and Harker turned away before he thumped one or the other of them.

'On second thoughts,' he said to the barman, 'whisky would be great.'

In the morning, head pounding and mouth dry, Harker woke up cursing Saskia, Wilmington, Wheeler, the barman in the mess, and all whisky distilleries. His mood wasn't improved when, over breakfast, he was summoned to General Wheeler's office.

'Major Harker,' she greeted him as he saluted. 'At ease. Take a seat.'

Harker did, with bad grace.

'How are you getting on with Captain Wilmington?' Wheeler asked, without looking up. Which was just as well as Harker was pressing his hands to his forehead, trying to stop his brain from expanding out of his skull.

'Harker?'

He sighed and dropped his hands from his throbbing head. 'Permission to speak frankly, sir?'

'I don't believe you have ever required anyone's permission for that,' Wheeler said mildly.

'Why the hell did you send him to me, sir?'

She laid down her pen and looked up at him, eyes sharp in a face only slightly softened by age.

'You don't like him, Major?'

'Oh, I like him fine, sir, but if he takes any of my men out into the field he's going to get them all killed. He has no experience, sir. Where did he come from, QM stores?'

'No, but I suspect that's where he'd prefer to be,' Wheeler said. 'He is very good at drilling the men, I hear?'

'Yes, sir, but he can't fire a weapon. And if he ever took command of the company ...'

'Why would he do that, Major?'

He gave her a heavy look. 'Because sooner or later some bugger's going to hit me somewhere they can't patch up,' he said. 'And in that case –'

'In that case, Lieutenant Riggs will surely step into the breach, Harker, because by the time I send C Company out on campaign, she will be its captain.'

Harker opened and closed his mouth several times before he said, 'What, sir?'

Wheeler smiled. 'You didn't think I really wanted to hold either of you back, did you, Harker? No. I have something I need you to do, a special mission, and I'm quite sure you'll be wanting to take the good lieutenant with you. Were she your second, you could not in all good conscience do that without leaving C Company commanderless.'

'I'm not sure I could in all good conscience do that now, sir,' Harker muttered.

'I give you my word, Harker that, barring unforeseen circumstances, I will not send your company out on active service until you return.'

Harker, who couldn't believe anything had ever happened to General Wheeler that she hadn't already foreseen, nodded warily.

'What mission, sir?' he asked.

Wheeler smiled.

'She wants us to *what*?' Charlie said, as Harker went around the mess kitchen searching out eggs, bacon, and strong coffee to soothe his hangover.

'Go up north, break into a rebel stronghold, steal a computer, find out how to work it, and use it to track the Coalitionists' movements,' Harker said, breaking an egg into a skillet and watching in dismay as the yolk broke.

'Apparently, her intel says that's how they've been tracking ours.'

Charlie closed her eyes momentarily. 'That's how they knew there was only a skeleton force in Oxford.'

'Yep. And in Peterborough. And in Southend.' Harker took a breath and let it out slowly. Wheeler had given him the estimated casualties for those cities, and they hadn't been pretty. The people had gone down fighting; but they'd really gone down.

He laid a couple of strips of bacon down in the pan and watched them sizzle. 'She's set us up to stay with someone in the Lincolnshire Wolds.'

Charlie frowned. 'We're not going to another base up there? We still have Hull, don't we?'

'Aye, but it's too far from the front. And she doesn't want us obvious. I'm to take a small party, stay with civilians–'

'Wear civilian clothes?' Charlie asked, with a gasp of mock-horror. At least, he thought it was mock. Briefly, he wondered if she'd been born with dogtags round her neck.

'Mock not, Charlie. Wheeler wants us to start looking in Leeds.' A city which had been under Coalitionist control for a while. 'Shame Smiggy's not with us, that were his old ground. Wonder if we might bump into him.'

'And who is "we", sir?'

'Well.' Harker flipped the bacon. 'She's letting me choose–'

'She is?'

'–but she has recommendations.'

Charlie smiled. 'Of course she does.'

The door opened, and a man in a grubby chef's coat came in. Harker and Charlie stared at him until he went away, then Charlie asked, 'Who's she recommending?'

Harker added a generous helping of salt to the pan. 'You, obviously, and Tallulah.'

'Tallulah Watling-Coburg? People are going to start thinking you have a favourite.'

'How many other poor kids in this army have been named Tallulah? Apparently she speaks fluent French and German, so if we run into translation difficulties–'

'In Lincolnshire, sir?'

He gave her a look. 'Clearly, that's why she's sending me. No, she thinks the computer may be in French.'

'Do they have languages, sir?'

Harker raised his palms. 'How the hell should I know?' He didn't even know what a computer looked like, never mind how one worked. The whole mission was a disaster waiting to happen, but then weren't all army missions? He continued, 'Which brings me to her next recommendation. A Captain Darren Haran.'

'Darren Haran?' Charlie said, her eyes wide, her mouth twitching.

''Fraid so. Joined us recently from the Medical Corps. Wanted to be an engineer, but couldn't get the training, so joined as a doctor, and learnt medicine at the army's expense.' At Charlie's look, he added, 'Well, it's all a sort of engineering when you think about it. Just ... squishier.'

Charlie made a face. 'Remind me not to get injured when he's around.'

Harker, unconcerned, turned off the heat and flipped his splattered egg and bacon on to a plate. 'Pass us that bread, will you?'

She did, and Harker cut two thick, uneven slices, slathered them with butter, and squelched egg and bacon into a sandwich.

'Hangover?' Charlie asked, watching him eat it.

'If you tell anyone,' Harker began, and had to chew and swallow before he could continue, 'I'll have to kill you.'

'That whisky gives you a headache?'

'Whisky does not give me a headache. Whisky makes me feel wonderful, and then in the morning I feel like a piece of old carpet. And I do not want my men knowing I feel like old carpet.' He glanced around the kitchen, nodded at the larder. 'Any juice in there?'

Charlie raised her eyebrows and went to look. Finding a jug, she sniffed experimentally. 'Reckon that's apple,' she said, and at Harker's gesture, poured him a glass. He drained it, and gestured for more as he finished the doorstopper sandwich.

'I think that's the healthiest thing I've ever seen you consume,' she said, fascinated, as he picked up the glass.

'Charlie, I get shot at on a reasonably regular basis,' he said. He considered that, and added, 'Probably daily if I have to work with Wilmington. What's the point of eating healthily?'

Charlie just shook her head and put his plate in the sink.

'But if it makes you feel any better, I'll take the men on a march around the city. Blow away some cobwebs.'

'Good idea, sir,' Charlie said approvingly.

'Right. Now, where are my fags?'

Chapter Seven

Cobwebs duly dispersed, Harker dispatched Charlie to find Captain Haran while he decided on who else to take with him. On returning from the march with his men, he found her on the green where the cars were parked, talking to a Wolf with a pair of legs sticking out from under it.

'Bleedin' freezing out here, Charlie,' he said. 'Did you find our sawbones?'

The legs flailed for a second, then the body attached to them revealed itself. Under the greasy smudges, Harker discerned the cartoon-faced doctor who'd treated him last week after his dip in the Thames.

Charlie said, as politely as she could, 'Sir, this is Captain Haran.'

Harker winced. 'Right. Sorry.' He nodded at the man's hasty salute, and added, 'Wheeler said you were something of a mechanic.'

'Yes, sir. In my spare time.'

'Really? And when do you get that?'

Haran's ears turned pink. Charlie hid a smile, but Harker didn't bother. 'We'll leave tomorrow, Captain. Get all your stuff, I want a full and comprehensive medical kit, no telling what sort of trouble we'll get into, and we won't be attached to a base. Do you know anything about computers?'

'Not very much, sir, but I'm good at working things out.'

'Fantastic,' said Harker, and judging by Captain Haran's smile, he hadn't caught Harker's sarcasm.

Harker walked away wondering who else he could possibly add to this band of misfits to make it any worse. Charlie clearly didn't have a high opinion of the doctor, but he'd seemed reasonably competent when he was treating Eve, and if he knew his way around a complex piece of machinery like a car, or a human being for that matter, then he could probably figure out a computer. After all, how hard could they be?

He pinched the bridge of his nose as he walked out under the Middle Tower, nodding to the guards there.

Wheeler had told him to take between six and ten men, and so far he only had four, including himself. He'd spent the afternoon march observing his men, mentally taking notes as to who would be due for promotion soon, and who would never rise higher than private. He'd taken them to the targets in Southwark and shouted them, personally, into line, then watched to see who the best shots were.

They'd marched out over the Bridge, which was hell this time of day, but he needed to sort the wheat from the chaff and hell was a damn good place to do that. Southwark, a desolate wasteland, had given him thinking space. Leaving Captain Wilmington to take the company back to the barracks, he'd kept a few of the best shots back. And then they'd taken the old horse ferry across to Westminster and marched up Whitehall on his way to the targets at St Giles-in-the-Fields, to remind the men who they were fighting for. Shooting at them as they tried to take aim, to test their ability in battle conditions, all but one managed to dodge his fire; and according to the medic, his ear would be just fine with a small nick in it.

Harker blamed himself; he'd been distracted. For the march, unfortunately, brought him perilously close to the only other person he'd ever heard talk about computers. And, damn it, it had dawned on him as he took his men home that he was going to end up taking Eve Carpenter with him.

The guards on the gate at St James's weren't familiar

to Harker, but they saw his rank insignia and let him in anyway, and he trudged up to the handsome brick building. It had once been a royal residence, but the King had signed it over to the army for their own use after it became apparent that he didn't need quite so many palaces when he wasn't even in the country.

Lucky sod, Harker thought. *I'd sure as hell like to be in America right now*. So much electricity they used it for street lights. Televisions in every home. *I've never even seen a damn television.*

And no war. No sodding, ugly, bloody war.

'Eve Carpenter,' he said to the officer at the desk, after showing her both his rank insignia and a copy of Wheeler's orders that he could take any soldier, officer or civilian he deemed necessary to the mission.

And then he cursed himself. She'd actually written that word, civilian. She knew he was going to get Eve. Hell, the guards on the gate had waved him straight in. And the officer at the desk had seemed to be *expecting* him.

'She's probably in the ...' The woman listened, then smiled. 'Yes, the Garden Room.'

'And where's that?' Harker said, wondering what she was listening to. He could hear faint music, was that it?

'Straight down the hall, through those double doors, and keep going until you see the piano,' the officer said, and Harker turned away, slightly confused.

It was one of those grand buildings where each room opens on to another by means of double doors. Saskia's parents had lived in a place like this, and back then they'd been able to employ men to open each door, at least when they had company. Now there was no one to open the doors for him, although there were plenty of people standing around, reading books or sewing or playing endless games of chess.

Most of them, on seeing his uniform, glared.

The sounds of music, piano-playing and singing got louder the further he went, until there was only one set of doors between him and a woman singing. The melody was sad, haunting, but the words weren't clear, so he opened the door on her singing something about yesterday coming suddenly, which made no sense to Harker.

Then he realised that the singer was Eve, and that she was sitting at the piano with her back to him.

She didn't seem to have heard him, but continued playing and singing the sad, beautiful song. Quite taken with it, Harker found himself moving closer, and then a floorboard squeaked and Eve glanced back over her shoulder.

When she saw him, the music stopped abruptly.

'Hi,' he said, and she turned back to the piano, still for a second.

Then she hammered the keys and yelled at someone named Jack to hit the road.

'Who's Jack?' Harker asked, but she ignored him. The only other occupant of the room was a young African woman, who was giggling a little.

He wasn't getting any reaction from either of them, so he brought out the big guns. Reaching inside his jacket, he placed a small gold box on the top of the piano, and stood back.

Eve faltered a little when he moved close to her, but stopped altogether when she saw the little box. It was tied with a green ribbon.

The music dying away, she reached for the box, then pulled her hands back.

'Lucille?' she said to the African woman. 'Do you see a box of chocolates on the piano?'

'Yes, I see it. And the cocoa is very rare in England, is it not? It has to be imported. I think they must be very expensive.'

Damn right they'd been expensive. Harker had a feeling Eve wasn't the sort to be won over easily. He could use force if he wanted to, but he'd prefer to use Ogilvy & Kent, who had at one time supplied chocolates to the King.

'And do you see a lying, sneaky, scum-sucking weasel standing behind me?'

'A weasel?' Lucille peered at the floor. Harker stifled a laugh.

'A *man*,' Eve spat, 'in an army uniform.'

'Ah. I am all comprehension.' Lucille squinted. 'I think he is a major,' she offered.

'Dammit,' Eve muttered, and turned to face him, her face sullen. 'I was doing well ignoring you, but it's impossible to ignore chocolate.'

Harker grinned at her. She didn't return it.

'Of course, it's entirely possible that it's a hallucination. I'm hallucinating chocolate. If I can hallucinate an entire city, I can hallucinate chocolate.'

'Smell it,' Harker said. Eve ignored him.

'What are you doing here?' she asked, as if she owned the place.

'I came to see you.'

'Bearing chocolates. Which, as Lucille has kindly explained to me, are very hard to come by in this country, and it's all jolly expensive.'

'It is,' Harker said.

'So you must want something. Unless, possibly, my insanity is catching and it's infected poor Lucille, too.'

'Well, I'm sure I'm here, if that's any help.'

'No,' Eve said. 'It's not.' She stood up abruptly, grabbing the chocolates and shoving the piano stool back into his leg.

'You sing really well,' he said, limping slightly as he followed her out of the room.

She ignored him.

'And play. You play well. The piano.'

'Well, there's no guitar here,' Eve said shortly.

'What was that song? I don't know it.'

Eve gave a mirthless laugh. 'There are little old men in Outer Mongolia who have never even seen a radio, let alone heard one, who know what that song is,' she said.

'Are there? Well, I ain't a little old man in Outer Mongolia,' Harker said cheerfully.

'No. And yet you don't recognise one of the most famous songs of the most famous band the world has ever seen.'

Harker darted round her to open the first set of doors before she could. She didn't appear to appreciate the courtesy. Stalking through, she snapped, 'That was *Yesterday*, by the Beatles. And the fact that you don't know it, that no one knows it, only confirms what I've become totally sure of in the last few days.'

'What's that?' Harker asked, following her up a staircase. She still favoured one leg slightly.

'That I've had a complete mental breakdown and I'm imagining everything around me.' She paused, looked again at the hideously expensive box of chocolates, and handed them back to him. 'Including these.'

Harker was stunned. So stunned that she was almost at the top of the stairs before he caught up to her.

'Eve,' he said, 'are you serious?'

'No,' she said, 'I'm mad.'

'Mad as in angry?'

'That too.' She started off down a wide corridor that had once been decorated with rich wallpaper and many large portraits. Now, the paper was peeling, and had many large, dark squares where the portraits had once been.

'Because I brought you here?'

'Score one for the Major.'

Harker tried to figure out what she meant, and gave up. 'Look, it's not a bad place,' he said. 'They feed you okay, don't they? And you can use the grounds.'

'Sure, the food's great. Only it involves no tea, coffee, chocolate, rice, pasta, or anything else that's not indigenous to this country. I mean, haven't you people heard of citrus fruits?'

'Yeah, coffee's at a premium,' Harker said. 'The army's restricted it to officers only.'

'So you get all you want?'

'Well, not all *I* want,' he said, smiling at her. She didn't smile back. 'And, hey. You have a piano to play.'

'Whoopee,' Eve said, and shoved a door open. Her bedroom was small, part of a large room that had been cheaply subdivided. It had half a window, and that half was crisscrossed with bars. She stomped to the foot of the narrow bed, opened the locker there, and pulled out a familiar bundle of khaki fabric. His greatcoat.

She held it out to him, but Harker didn't take it.

'Yours,' she said, as if he might have forgotten.

'You can keep it if you like,' Harker said generously, wondering if he was going to be able to cadge another one before the winter set in. Probably not.

'No,' Eve said shortly, holding it out further. 'Thank you.'

'I didn't come for my coat,' Harker said, gently.

She faltered a little, then pushed the coat further towards him. 'Then what did you come for?'

'You.'

She stared at him a moment, then burst out laughing. Throwing the coat down on the bed, she shook her head and said, 'Okay, I'm mad. What's your excuse?'

'You're not mad,' Harker said, despite the evidence.

'Yes, I am,' Eve said, as if he was being silly. 'I think London has skyscrapers and an ethnically diverse population. I think

Britain is one of the richest countries in the world, thanks to the empire – the *British* Empire – and the Industrial Revolution. I think the last battle to take place on British soil was against the Scots in the eighteenth century, and that we won both world wars, and that every home in Britain has electricity, and TV sets, and computers and DVDs and–' Her voice, having wound itself faster and higher, suddenly broke off. Shook her head. 'And clearly, none of that is actually real, so, you know, I must be mad. It's okay, I've come to terms with it. Last few days weren't pretty, but I'm okay now. Happy in my insanity.'

She sat down on the bed, and stared determinedly at the wall.

Harker sighed, and pulled the locker around to sit on in the absence of a chair. Eve avoided his gaze.

'I can get you out of here,' he said, and saw her fingers twitch. 'Look, the only reason you're in here is because the army thinks you're a spy.'

'Because *you* think I'm a spy,' Eve said sulkily.

'No, I don't.' He wasn't sure what he thought she was – mad probably was about right – but he really didn't think she was a spy. 'Look, Eve, I need you.'

She snorted.

'You said where you come from, every house has a computer.'

'Well, not every house, but ... yeah. Most. Lots.'

'Right. So you're familiar with them? Know how to work them?'

'Of course I do,' Eve said.

'Right. Well, that makes you pretty unique around here.'

She snorted again. 'Having a *passport* makes me unique around here,' she said.

'Ye-es,' Harker said doubtfully. 'Look, I need someone who knows how to use a computer. It'll get you out of here.

It might even get you a pardon.'

At that, she gave him a sharp look. 'Why? What do I need to be pardoned from?'

Harker wasn't sure, but he knew the army would think of something. Besides, Wheeler had hinted strongly that honours and promotions would be given to anyone who aided the war effort in such a gigantic way, and he figured that ought to include Eve, too.

'Eve, I can set you free,' Harker said, going out on a limb somewhat, but it didn't get the response he expected.

Eve just shrugged tightly, her eyes once more avoiding his, and said, 'What's the point? I don't have anywhere to go.'

Eve leaned back against the wall, her eyes stinging a little at the prospect of her life going on like this, day after day. If anything, it might actually be worse than the stinking, graffitti'd concrete block she'd been living in before. No TV. Not even any electricity. The lamp by her bed ran on oil, for goodness sake.

The last few days hadn't been pretty. Well, that was by way of being a colossal understatement. She'd been shown to her room, where she'd alternately sat and stared at the wall, sobbed until her eyeballs ached, and screamed that she'd had enough and *could this just be over now please.* No one listened. No one came.

The staff had offered her food. They'd told her to read whatever she wanted in the library, to walk in the grounds. They'd told her, basically, to come to terms with it, and Eve had wondered briefly if everyone else here felt the same as her.

Maybe everyone in St James's was a victim of the same practical joke. Maybe they'd all drunk from the same water and were having the same hallucination. Maybe they were all mad and she was just the latest to come down with the delusion. Some sort of imagined grandeur. But no one else seemed to understand a word she spoke. The ones who'd heard of computers and TVs and trains were the ones who belonged in other countries. Nobody at all had heard of the British Empire or the Industrial Revolution.

Nobody had heard of Eve Carpenter, of Grrl Power, of a pop star's fall from grace.

She'd spent three years being a cautionary tale. Three years of jeering and snapped photos that ended up in Where Are They Now? features in magazines. Three years of ignoring the world around her.

It had occurred to Eve in the last slow, sleepless hours before morning that the world she knew and everything in it could have turned into this in the last three years, and she wouldn't have noticed.

'Do I have any choice in this?' she said after a while, during which Harker had been admirably silent.

'Sure. You can stay here until the war is over.'

'I'm not sure I'll live that long,' Eve said, because at this rate she was going to die of frustration in about a week.

'Or you can come with me. It'll be fun,' Harker said, and actually seemed to mean it.

'What will?' she said, turning to look at him. 'You haven't actually even said what you want of me yet.'

Harker grinned in a way she was sure she'd have been more susceptible to if he wasn't a bastard and she wasn't mad, and said, 'I want you to help me capture a computer and use it.'

'Capture? What, do they breed in the wild here?'

'I don't know,' Harker said innocently. 'Do they?'

'Oh, for–' Eve looked down at her hands, which were in the same ugly state they'd been in since she stopped getting regular, expensive manicures.

Do you really want to spend the rest of your life just

existing? she asked herself. *A life which, if Harker's side loses the war, and it doesn't look incredibly likely that they'll win, probably won't be all that long?*

What war? she replied to herself. *None of this is real! It can't possibly be!*

In that case, what have you got to lose?

'What the hell,' she said. 'I'm in.'

Harker gave her a more genuine smile, the sort of smile he'd given her when she thought he was just another soldier, and stood up. 'Right then,' he said. 'Get your coat–'

'*Your* coat,' she corrected him.

'–we're leaving.'

She didn't actually have many possessions, just the clothes she stood up in, the changes of underwear she'd been issued with and the box of chocolates, so once she'd said goodbye to Lucille, it didn't take long to leave.

Outside the building, Harker looked her up and down and said, 'How's your ankle?'

'Better,' Eve said. She could walk okay, so long as she didn't put too much stress on it.

'Glad to hear it,' Harker said. 'Unfortunately, it means I have to use these.' And before she could react, he'd locked a handcuff around her right wrist, and his left.

'Bastard,' Eve said, with feeling.

'You say that like it's a bad thing,' Harker replied, without rancour.

Expecting a car, she was surprised when Harker just walked out of the compound, past the guards who raised the barrier for him.

'No Sergeant Cooper today?' Harker said to one of them.

'No, sir. Getting married, sir.'

An expression of horror came over Harker's face. '*Hell*,' he said. He looked at his watch. 'Double hell. Corporal, I need a ... a car, a horse, whatever you have. I need to be in

Cheapside, *now*.'

Whatever authority Harker had clearly put the fear of God into the guards, because a fully saddled horse was produced from apparently nowhere at lightning speed, while Eve looked on in amazement. 'Why do you need to be there?' she said. 'Are you related?'

'Coop's one of my men,' Harker said. 'We fought together. That's closer than "related".'

He lifted her sideways into the saddle, swung up behind her, and had the horse moving before Eve could protest that she didn't know how to ride.

'It's easy,' he said, grabbing her leg and lifting it over the horse's neck so that she sat astride the saddle. Eve was so shocked at the intimacy of it that it didn't occur to her to protest.

In order to hold the reins, he had his left arm wrapped around her waist, for which Eve was mildly grateful, given the horse's eager gallop.

'You go to all your soldiers' weddings?' she shouted over the noise of the streets, which looked to her like something out of *Deadwood*.

''Course I do.'

'Are you always this punctual?'

'On days when I don't have to go and get prisoners out of jail, yes.'

So she had been a prisoner. It was the first time anyone had actually admitted it.

The horse thundered through the streets, people scattering before it. Eve couldn't even begin to figure out where they were; nothing looked familiar. The streets were full of timber-framed buildings listing drunkenly towards each other, the roads either broken or unpaved, and full of people and animals. Horses and donkeys seemed to be the preferred way of getting about, and any motor vehicles she saw were painted khaki and resembled leftovers from WWII.

Cutting through backstreets and reeking alleys where the buildings overhung so low they had to duck, Harker came out by the river and the pontoon he'd taken her over those few days before. Across the river, the skeleton of a timber theatre stood, stark in the afternoon light, the whole south bank behind it bare of anything but rubble.

Last week it had been bleak, but not that bleak.

'What *happened*?' she gasped, as Harker turned the horse sharply left.

'What?'

'To the south bank!'

'The Royal Grenadiers did,' Harker said. 'Duck.'

The horse clattered through an alley so narrow, low and stinking Eve thought for a moment Harker was going to use it to hide her dismembered corpse, but then they emerged into sunlight, raced along another unfamiliar street, and skidded to a halt outside a pretty church.

Over the road, a crowd of people were clustered around a piece of paper nailed to the wall. Many of them were sobbing. Harker, seeing Eve's interest, muttered, 'Casualty lists. Never pretty.'

He leapt down, yanking Eve with him, and she fell into his arms just as a pony-led carriage came to a halt behind them.

'Mister Harker!' someone gasped, and Harker righted Eve and turned to smile at the passenger of the open carriage.

'Rosie. You look wonderful.'

The young woman, dressed in white with a short veil, beamed at him as she climbed out. 'Mister Harker, I knew you'd come. And you sent those coupons for the reception. I just can't tell you how grateful we are. We've enough for a cake!'

'Well, I'm glad,' Harker said, his tone warm, his smile

genuine. As Rosie's gaze darted between him and Eve, he added, 'This is my … friend, Eve.'

Eve plastered on an instant smile, the sort she'd learned how to do in the Grrl Power days, and said, 'Congratulations.'

Rosie beamed at her, and Harker tugged her away, taking her hand and pulling the long sleeve of the great coat down over her wrist to hide the cuffs.

'So I'm your date now?' Eve muttered as they went inside the church. Harker, to her surprise, crossed himself with his free hand.

'Until we leave this wedding, yes. Create a fuss and I will have you shot,' he muttered back, and there was menace in his eyes. Eve raised her palms in surrender, noting with a giggle that his hand came up, too.

To her continued surprise, the service was in Latin. It occurred to Eve that, with everything else about this place that was different, England might well be a Catholic country. She mumbled along with Harker's responses, relieved to be at the back so no one could see she hadn't a clue what was going on. He, along with everyone else, seemed to know exactly what to do.

When the glowing bride and groom walked back down the aisle, Harker and several other men in uniform saluted them, and she noticed for the first time what a state his right hand was in.

The palm wasn't too bad, but the back of his hand and fingers bore several puckered scars. A particularly vicious one ran across the back of his first three fingers. The last finger ended in a stub.

Eve stared for a long moment at that stub. His little finger had been cut off at the first knuckle. There just wasn't anything past it.

If she was mad, why had her brain come up with that detail?

Outside the church people were throwing petals at the newlyweds, who stood beaming and absorbing congratulations. The groom was in a uniform with shiny buttons, bearing medals on his breast. The bride wore a dress which, while white and undoubtedly bridal, lacked the volume of fabric usually associated with such outfits, and her shoes were quite ordinary.

'Say nothing,' Harker ordered her, and yanked her forward to greet Sergeant and Rosie Cooper, who both thanked him again, profusely, for the ration coupons he'd sent them.

Eve glanced up at the sky, half-expecting to see barrage balloons floating there.

'And you must come and have some of our cake!' Rosie insisted. 'It's for family only, but you can have a piece, Mister Harker.'

She called him Mister as if it was a privilege, Eve thought. And he didn't seem to mind.

'That's so kind of you, Rosie, but I couldn't deprive you of it. You enjoy it.'

Rosie looked at him as if he were mad, but Cooper said, 'Now Rosie, Mister Harker's made time to come and see us wed, and he's a busy man, don't ask for more of him.'

Rosie nodded, and Eve wondered what kind of hero she was handcuffed to. For a second, she entertained the idea of telling them that he'd tricked, imprisoned and handcuffed her, but she wasn't cruel enough to destroy anyone's idols. Even if she didn't understand them.

Instead she reached inside the greatcoat and brought out the box of chocolates. 'Here,' she said, holding them out to Rosie. 'A wedding present.'

To Eve's horror, tears welled up in Rosie's eyes. 'Thank you!' she cried, hugging Eve to her and nearly crushing her bouquet. 'Oh, look everyone! *Chocolates*!'

People turned to stare at them, and Eve felt herself go

pink. Even Harker was looking at her in amazement.

'Well, congratulations,' she mumbled.

'Oh, Mister Harker.' Rosie flung her arms around him, and Eve hoped she was the only one to see his expression, 'I do hope we'll see you down this aisle one day!'

At that, Harker's eyes slammed wide open, but when Rosie looked up at him, he was smiling normally.

'Don't expect that'll be any day soon,' he said.

'Not even when you've found a lady what gives people chocolates?' Rosie said, looking at the box in her hand as if it contained diamonds.

'Not until I find a chaplain who'll marry a divorced man,' he said gently, and Rosie went pink.

Eve felt an immediate bond of sympathy with Harker's ex-wife.

Harker kissed Rosie's cheek, shook Cooper's hand, saluted them both, then tugged Eve away into the street.

'Well, that was interesting,' Eve said, to no one in particular, as Harker untied his horse and hefted her into the saddle. He swung up behind her, took the reins in his mangled right hand – Eve couldn't stop looking at it – and they set off, this time at a more leisurely pace.

Passing yet another ramshackle church, Eve asked over her shoulder, 'Was that a Roman Catholic service at the church?'

'Course it was.'

'Are you Catholic?'

'Course I am.'

'Oh.'

After a minute or so, Harker said, 'Aren't you?'

'Er, no. Church of England.' In truth, Eve had been baptised, and then hadn't set foot in a church until her father's funeral.

'Church of what?'

'Never mind. Is the whole country Catholic?'

'Of course.' Harker paused, then said, 'Eve, are you sure you're not from abroad?'

Eve sighed. 'Yes, I'm sure.'

They rode in silence a while longer. Which was to say neither Eve nor Harker spoke, but the crowds ebbing around them were in constant chatter, people shouting above the general noise, dogs barking, bells ringing. Eve looked around at the people, at what they were wearing, and couldn't quite put her finger on what was wrong.

There were men and women in trousers. She saw t-shirts and jeans. Very few men in suits, or women in heels. In fact, a large portion of the people she saw, male and female, were in uniform.

There were few children. Even fewer old people.

'What about Henry VIII?' she asked after a while.

'Sorry, what?'

'Henry VIII. The King. Fifteen hundreds.'

'What about him?'

'Well, how many wives did he have?'

'Oh, was he the one with loads? Divorced a couple.'

'Yes!' Eve said, massively relieved. 'He broke with the Catholic Church because the Pope wouldn't give him a divorce from his first wife.'

'Um, no he didn't,' Harker said. He shifted behind her. 'I don't know a lot about history, but I do know we never broke with the Catholic Church.'

'Yes, we did!'

'No,' Harker said wearily, 'we didn't.'

Eve floundered a moment, then asked 'What abut the Protestant Reformation?'

'The what?'

Well, that answered that question. A thought occurred to her and she asked, 'Then how come *you* got divorced?'

'Because ordinary people like me don't have to petition the Pope,' Harker said. 'We just get a lawyer.'

'I thought the Catholic Church disapproved of divorce.'

'I don't think they really care any more. Not about some damp little island on the edge of the world.'

'England is not on the edge of the world,' Eve said.

'Yeah, but it might as well be.'

Another silence. Eve ducked as the horse went under a low, dirty brick bridge. Behind her, so did Harker, his hard body pressing against hers in a way that might have been pleasant if he wasn't holding her prisoner.

'So, if they don't care, how come you can't get married again?'

Harker sighed. 'Is this important?'

'Or was that just to shut Rosie up?'

'It was to stop her asking when I'm going to marry someone I only just met, who is suspected of being a spy,' Harker said.

Eve made a face, glad he couldn't see her. The Tower was up ahead, its high walls rising over the lower buildings surrounding it.

'So are you not actually divorced, then?'

Harker made a sound of annoyance, and jerked on the handcuffs so she looked at his left hand. 'See a ring there?'

'Well, I don't know if soldiers wear them!'

'Yes, I'm divorced,' Harker said, his voice terse. 'I was married, it didn't work out, she wanted a divorce, I gave it to her. Happy?'

'Any children?'

'No.'

'Then yes, I'm happy.'

'Why does me not having children make you happy?'

'Because divorce is hell on kids,' Eve said bluntly.

She felt Harker draw breath, but it was a moment or two

before he said, 'Your parents?'

'Yes.'

'Sorry,' Harker said.

'Yeah, me too.'

Neither of them said anything else as they approached the castle over a moat Eve wasn't entirely sure had always been there. The guards at the gate saluted Harker and waved him straight in, and Eve had to admit it was sort of cool riding a horse into the Tower of London while armed guards saluted her. Even if they were missing the shiny uniforms and the big hats.

'Hey, what happened to the Beefeaters?' she asked.

'The what?' Harker said, and Eve sighed.

He handed the horse over to a female sergeant, and it occurred to Eve that there were an awful lot of women around. They all wore the same uniform as the men, and they looked, as Harker had said on that rather distant and frightening day south of the river, as if they were prepared to face 'combat situations'.

'Is your whole army female?' she asked.

Harker gave her a pissy look. 'I look female to you?'

No, and half-an-hour on horseback with him had made it abundantly clear that he wasn't.

'It's just, there are a lot of women around.'

'Aye, well. Time was, we only conscripted men over eighteen. But then a load of them went and got shot, and we ran out of men to conscript.'

'So you actually put women on the front line?'

'If we didn't, we'd have no front line.' He held a door open for her. 'After you.'

The false courtesy didn't impress Eve the way it had when he'd done it a few days ago. She stomped inside, then wished she hadn't, because her ankle was still a little sore. Limping slightly, she followed him down a corridor lit only by the light coming in through small windows. It was enough to illuminate the peeling paint on the uneven walls. The stone stairs they reached echoed madly.

'Um,' she said. Harker sighed for about the dozenth time. 'Well, it's just that I'm a prisoner, right?'

'Technically.'

'Technically, meaning yes.'

'All right, yes.'

'So ... well, are we leaving on this mission today?'

'No. First thing tomorrow.'

'Right. So where am I staying tonight?' Eve asked, full of trepidation as they reached another dark corridor lined with incomprehensibly labelled doors. She was a prisoner in the Tower. Surely that sort of thing led to damp dungeons and rats?

'With my lieutenant,' Harker said. Hammering on a door and yelling, 'Charlie,' he leaned back against the wall, head back, looking tired.

'Who's Charlie?' Eve ventured.

'Lieutenant Riggs. My right hand,' Harker said, again with that ghost of a smile. Eve's gaze shot down to the stub of his little finger, but before she could ask what had happened to it, the door opened and the woman with the frizzy hair looked out. 'Sir?'

A woman. Thank goodness.

'Charlie. This is Eve Carpenter. She's coming with us tomorrow. Knows something about computers.'

Charlie looked Eve up and down and didn't seem too impressed with what she saw.

Well, at least I'm on speaking terms with conditioner, honey, Eve thought, flashing a smile at the other woman.

'Wheeler'll have my head if I put her in the brig. Has Bly's bed been reassigned?'

Charlie shook her head, and Eve glanced at the crossed-out name on the door. Dead woman's bed. Nice.

'In that case, Eve's your new roommate for tonight.'

'Yessir,' Charlie said, not looking particularly happy about it.

'Leaving at oh-seven-hundred,' Harker said, unlocking the handcuff bracelet from his wrist and locking it to Charlie's. Eve rolled her eyes, and was ignored.

'See you in the morning, sir,' Charlie said, and then Harker was gone, and Eve was left chained to another total stranger.

'If you snore,' Charlie said, 'I'll have you shot.'

'It's nice to meet you, too,' said Eve.

Chapter Eight

Over the river, a faint mist danced, but Harker wasn't in the mood to appreciate its beauty. He'd been up since the early hours, making sure everything was packed in the wagon – not a truck but a sodding wagon – and that C Company would run properly in his absence. Since Captain Haran was attached to the Medical Corps, it wasn't necessary to find a replacement for him. He had, however, glanced through the Captain's file, and found that he was usually known by all and sundry as 'Daz', which was certainly an improvement on Darren Haran.

He'd spent a large part of the evening briefing Wilmington on what not to do in his absence. Namely, interact with the men or take them anywhere, at all. The remainder of the evening he'd spent with the junior officers and sergeants of C Company, telling them to keep up what they'd been doing and maintain the high level of competence they'd become used to. He'd pretty much said everything but, 'Don't listen to that idiot Wilmington,' and he was pretty sure they'd understood the subtext.

And then this morning, as he was leaving the mess with his own pack, ready to join his squad, Captain Wilmington had caught him and said, 'I say, good luck, sir.'

Harker winced at the 'I say', but nodded and smiled. 'Thank you, Wilmington. Take care of my men, and don't do anything ... stupid.'

'Oh, of course not, sir. They'll be in tip-top shape when you return, sir!'

'Jolly good,' Harker muttered.

'And besides, sir, only this morning a fellow officer

approached me and offered his advice, any time I needed it.'

'Kind of him,' Harker said, trying to get away.

'Oh indeed, sir. And he's a lot of experience in the field, sir! Came up from the ranks like yourself, sir.'

Harker turned, slowly, and looked at Wilmington's eager pink face.

Very few officers were promoted from the ranks. Harker could count the ones that weren't him or Charlie on one hand. And the ones currently at the Tower on one finger.

But Sholt hadn't deserved his promotion. He'd earned it not through grit and hard work, but through blackmail and bribery. There was no proof, of course, and the officer in charge was now dead. Harker didn't see that as much of a coincidence.

'Did he, indeed,' he said evenly. 'And what's his name, this friendly, helpful officer?'

'Captain Sholt, sir. Said you and he go way back.'

Harker knew his rage showed on his face, because of the way Wilmington stepped back, alarmed. He closed his eyes, but that didn't help because all he saw was Corporal White, and Mary. Poor bloody Mary.

'Oh, we go back,' he said softly. 'Sholt and I go back a very long way. And shall I tell you something about Lieutenant Sholt, Captain?'

Wilmington was up against the wall now, quaking with trepidation as he said, 'Um, technically he's a captain, now, sir.'

'Yes,' Harker said, through gritted teeth, '*technically*, he is.'

'And, um, what is it you wanted to tell me about him?' asked Wilmington, who was evidently either braver or stupider than Harker had given him credit for.

'That if you listen to a damn word he says he'll get you and the company all killed.'

With that, Harker turned to go.

'Oh, I protest, sir!' Wilmington cried, running after him. Harker didn't break stride.

'Do you, Wilmington? Do you protest at my feelings about Lieutenant Sholt, or that I voiced them out loud?'

'It's disloyalty to a fellow officer, sir!'

Harker spun around so fast that the smaller man ran into him. 'That man is *not* my fellow,' he said. 'In no way is he my fellow. My loyalty is to my army and my country, and not to venomous parasites like Sholt. Now, you follow my orders as regards my company, Captain, and don't listen to a word that poisonous shite tells you, and maybe there'll be a company for me to come back to. Is that clear?'

Wilmington quivered with indignation.

'I said, is that clear, Captain?'

Wilmington saluted. 'Yes, sir. Perfectly clear, sir.'

'Good.' Harker started off towards the wagon again. 'As you were, Captain.'

Now he sat beside Charlie on the wagon's front bench, steaming with fury. Damn Sholt's bloody hide! At least Saskia was there to keep an eye on things – and it was a rare day that Harker appreciated his ex-wife's seniority so much.

'Sir?' Charlie said. 'Are you going to brief the men?'

Harker stared out at the dilapidated suburbs of Moorfields. 'When we're outside the city,' he said, 'we'll stop.'

Charlie just nodded and kept her eyes on the road. Good old Charlie. She knew when to push and when to keep her mouth shut. It occurred to Harker, and not for the first time, that he'd never have come so far without her.

When the wagon had rattled out beyond the last straggle of buildings and there was little ahead but fields and woods, Harker told Charlie to stop, and the squad piled out.

He regarded them critically. Was it a good squad? Had he chosen well? Aside from Charlie and Daz Haran, the rest were junior ranks. And Eve.

She looked sullen, standing there between Private Banks and Lance-Corporal Martindale. Well, the hell with her. At least she was chained to someone sensible. Sarah Martindale was a Lance-Corporal solely because Harker had no room to promote her further. A small, dark-haired girl, she kept herself quiet but always got the job done. She reminded him a lot of Charlie when they'd first met.

Of course, then there was Private Banks, who was a joker to his core and was really only on the squad because he was a damn good shot. Well, and he could drive. Harker had made his choices before Wheeler had informed him that a truck was too conspicuous, and they'd be using a bloody wagon instead.

Tallulah stood at attention. Harker studied her for a second, relieved that Saskia hadn't cottoned on to the fact that Harker was taking her little sister on a potentially dangerous mission. She couldn't have, or she'd surely have bawled him out for it. But Harker figured Tallulah was safer here than she would be with Wilmington.

'Right then,' he said, getting out a cigarette and lighting it. 'Some of you have a better idea than others of why you're here. But the main reason you're here is this: I picked you. I looked over the whole company, and even beyond it, and you were the best of the bunch. That's a good thing. I'm proud of you. Because we've got a very important job ahead of us.'

He paused, surveying them, then went on, 'You might be aware of the recent fighting in Oxford, Peterborough, and Southend. If you're not, you're a bloody disgrace to this man's army. The Coalitionists have captured those three towns. The casualties are still being counted. Most of the deaths were civilian. And do you know why?'

He waited to see if one of them was going to be a smart

alec. To his minor annoyance, they all kept silent. He'd kind of wanted an excuse to shout at somebody.

'Because those three towns were short on troops. Underdefended. Now, what's got General Wheeler and yours truly worried is that the enemy *knew* they were underdefended. They picked on our weak spots. We're stretched tight for troops, men, which is something you all know. But how did the enemy know it? How did they know that the garrison at Oxford was flooded out? How did they know that the Buffs had left Southend to patrol further up the coast? How did they know that the 9th of Foot were busy further north than their base?'

It was Eve who spoke up, in a dull, belligerent tone that said she'd lost her patience with Harker's behaviour, and wasn't going to play along any more.

'It's a computer,' she said. 'You said they've got a computer. They're probably watching everything on Google Earth or something.'

'On what?' Harker said.

'On the Internet.'

Harker narrowed his eyes at her, and she sighed. 'Oh God, the Internet. Um ... it's like a sort of .... worldwide network where anyone can connect with anyone else.'

'And it can be used for information?' Charlie said.

'They call it the Information Super Highway,' Eve said, 'or they did, before that got lame.'

'This Internet,' Harker said, 'who can access it?'

Eve shrugged. 'Anyone with a computer and a modem.'

'What's a modem?'

'It's ... the thing that connects you to the Internet. You need a phone line,' she added.

'A phone line,' Harker said. 'Eve, how do you know all this?'

Eve sighed again. 'Because I'm crazy,' she said.

'Remember? I think I come from a world where everyone has computers. But clearly, that's not the case, so I must just be mad. And don't yell at me, all right, I'm not one of your soldiers, I didn't ask to be here, and I have no idea what crawled up your butt and died this morning but get over it and stop snarking at us, okay?'

Harker stared at her. He was aware of Charlie's hand settling on the hilt of her pistol.

And all of a sudden he wanted to laugh.

'Okay,' he said, and Charlie exhaled. 'Right. Thank you for that, Eve. Form up, lads, we're on foot for a while. Give the horses a rest. Captain Haran, you may drive the wagon. Charlie, you're with me. Rearguard.'

The squad, the smallest he'd ever commanded as an officer, formed up, with Eve still looking very sulky. Harker toyed with the idea of telling them to put their packs on, but decided against it.

'Scouts pace,' he said. 'March!'

Tallulah, Banks and Martindale immediately set off at a jog. Eve stumbled.

'You're being cruel, sir,' Charlie said, as they waited for Daz to set off after the men.

'What, by making the infantry go on foot?'

'By making our prisoner go with them.'

'Hah,' Harker said. He stubbed out his cigarette with his boot. 'She ought to learn to march. Toughen her up.'

Charlie just rolled her eyes.

He pulled out a map from inside his jacket and showed it to Charlie. 'Latest intel Wheeler could give me said the Coalitionists had control of the area twenty miles to the north of Peterborough, and about ten to the east. To the west, they've joined up with their own territory.'

Charlie winced. 'They can only be about ten miles from the coast.'

'Yep,' said Harker. 'We've a blockade about halfway along the Fen Causeway, twelve miles from the coast. And it's that twelve miles we have to manoeuvre in. They take that last stretch, and not only do they have sea access but they've effectively cut off the north from the south.'

'Are we still blockading the Wash?'

'Far as I know, yes. Thing is, Charlie, we've got too many bleeding miles of coastline. Can't blockade it all.'

Charlie took the map and peered at the strip of land between the sea and the red blotch that signified Coalitionist-controlled territory.

'So we follow Ermine Street to Godmanchester–' she began, and Harker shook his head.

'No, I don't want to run into any trouble. We'll take the Icknield Way from Royston,' he pointed to the old Roman road on the map, 'and go north from Newmarket. I want to go right by the coast, as far away as possible from being spotted.'

Charlie nodded. 'Where do you want to stop tonight?'

Harker tried to calculate it in his head. He wasn't going to make the men march all the way, that would take days. If they alternated with short, fast trips in the wagon ... he looked up at the sky. Sulky grey clouds hung low. If it started to rain, they'd have to find somewhere to shelter the wagon, or it'd get stuck in the mud.

'I don't know yet,' he said. 'Wait until it starts getting dark. I want to at least get past Royston tonight.' He peered at the map again. 'It's about sixty miles to Newmarket, but we could set up camp there in the Devil's Dyke. Nice defences, and it's sheltered.'

'I remember,' Charlie said, and of course she did, because when the Coalitionists had gone after Newmarket they'd used the earthworks to shelter themselves before attacking the town. They'd been unsuccessful, although they'd taken plenty of casualties on the way. One of them had been Lieutenant Marston, into whose place Charlie had stepped, still only a sergeant, to lead her platoon.

'It is ... empty, isn't it, sir?' she said, and Harker had a nightmarish memory of the piles of bodies heaped around when daylight came.

'They buried them at the north end,' he said. 'We'll camp at the south. It's miles away.'

Charlie nodded, but she didn't look happy about it.

Eve's feet were entombed in the cheap trainers she'd bought for a fiver from one of those gigantic sports shops always on the verge of shutting down. Aside from the low-heeled courts she wore to work, they were the only shoes she had, which was heartbreaking when she remembered the mountains of shoeboxes on offer in her Grrl Power days.

Unfortunately, because her shoes were cheap they were also rubbish, and after an hour on the move her feet were killing her. They rubbed at the back of her heels, the sides of her toes and where the tongue was stitched in. After she was dragged through a puddle by the humourless girl she was handcuffed to, one foot was also soaking wet.

'I protest,' she said, as the squad slowed from jogging to walking for the millionth time. 'I have a sprained ankle!'

'Which the doc examined this morning and pronounced fine,' said the male Private, behind her.

'Well, I'm sure you're not supposed to run on it, not straight away.'

'You sprained it last week,' said the other Private, a very young girl with a long and stupid name Eve couldn't currently remember. She looked vaguely familiar –maybe the girl who'd driven them around Southwark. Eve wasn't sure. She'd been trying not to think about that day.

'How do you know?'

'I was there.' After a second or two's silence, she went on, 'I was with Major Harker when you fell out of the sky.'

'Right – look, what's your name?'

'Watling-Coburg,' said the girl, a touch defensively. Eve couldn't blame her.

'Right, Private ... Watling-Coburg, so can you tell him I wasn't spying?'

'I couldn't say what you were doing,' said the girl, infuriatingly.

'Hey, can you fly?' the other Private asked.

'With the right wings.'

'No, seriously?'

'Anyone can fly with the right wings, Banks,' said the girl to whom Eve was cuffed. She started jogging again.

'Oh, come on, I'm in real honest pain here!' Eve protested.

'Shoulda seen my feet, first week in training,' Banks said. 'Blimey, what a state. Thought I'd never walk again.'

'Me, too,' said Watling-Coburg. 'Hours and hours of marching in full gear. I thought they were trying to kill us.'

'Well, that's what the army's about, ain't it, Lance-Corporal?' Banks said. 'Train you up and send you off to be shot?'

'Banks,' she said sharply.

'Well, it is, isn't it? We're the infantry. Cannon fodder.'

'Well, that's not why we're here now,' the Lance-Corporal said.

'Yeah, but why are we here? I mean, us three?'

Us three. Clearly, Eve wasn't included.

'You tell me, Banks,' the Lance-Corporal said.

'Werrl, I reckon you're here 'cos he needs someone to keep me and Tallulah in line,' Banks said.

Tallulah Watling-Coburg? *Jesus Christ, her parents must have hated her*.

'That's probably right,' she replied. She gestured to the

white band on her arm. 'See this, Private?'

'Yes sir, I see, sir.'

'This means that in the absence of a sergeant, I'm your NCO.'

'Absolutely, sir, yes, sir.'

'And stop making fun of me, Banks.'

'Yes – uh – sir. Anyway, I reckon that's why you're here. And I'm here 'cos I'm a crack shot–'

'And also because you're so modest,' Tallulah murmured, as they slowed to a walk again.

'Yeah, and that too. And, because the Major said we was gonna steal something, right, and that's what I'm good at.'

'Stealing?' Tallulah said.

'Yep. 'Course, I'm reformed now, on account of being caught and hauled up by the magistrate.'

'Let me guess,' Eve said. 'It was death or the army, and you're wishing you'd chosen death?'

Banks laughed. 'Nah, miss, it was jail or the army. Course, I'd forgotten we was at war ...'

'How could you forget?' Tallulah said.

'I have a very sunny personality and am always looking upon the bright side of life,' Banks announced self-importantly, making Tallulah giggle.

Private Joker, Eve thought. Well, at least he might cheer things up. Harker seemed to have lost all traces of Will, the nice guy she'd chatted to in the hospital, and turned into a surly bastard. Although this might have more to do with the presence of the humourless Charlie, who had ignored Eve for half the night and left her alone, chained to her bunk, for the rest of it, while she went for a drink.

'And we all know why you're here,' Banks said to Tallulah, and there was a chilly silence. Eve felt the Lance-Corporal tense beside her.

'Do you?' Tallulah said, ice in her voice.

'Yeah. It's 'cos you can drive and speak French.'

The Lance-Corporal relaxed.

'And also 'cos your sister is in charge of the regiment,' Banks went on, and the Lance-Corporal snapped, 'That's enough, Banks.'

But Eve, who wasn't a soldier and was rather beyond caring at this point anyway, turned her head and said, 'Really?'

'*Yes*,' Tallulah Watling-Coburg said, and Eve turned back, realising that anyone who'd grown up with that sort of name would have nerves of steel as a matter of course.

Right then, Harker came trotting up, turned and actually jogged backwards, facing them. He was smiling.

'Having fun?' he said to Eve, who stuck her tongue out at him. He grinned. 'Right then, squad. Back in the wagon. We're not making good enough time.'

'Thank God for that,' Eve said loudly, as they finally stopped running and the wagon came to a halt behind them.

'Not enjoying it?' Harker asked. He looked like he was having a whale of a time. Great, so he was one of those hideous people who actually got cheered up by exercise. Either that, or he was enjoying her misery. Probably, she thought darkly, it was both.

She gave him a poisonous look. 'My ankle hurts.'

'Shame.'

And that was all she got. She was hauled back into the wagon, which if Eve had been feeling polite she'd have described as cosy. But she didn't feel like being polite, not remotely, so the words that came immediately to mind were more like cramped, dark, and uncomfortable.

Charlie, Harker's very own right hand, took the reins again, with Harker and the doctor seating themselves inside. Eve caught the doctor's eye and tried for sympathy. 'I'm not sure my ankle is fully healed yet,' she said.

'Um,' he said. His eyes darted towards Harker, which infuriated Eve. 'Well, when I examined it this morning, it seemed fine.'

'Yes, but that was before Captain Sadistic here made me go running for an hour.'

'Hey, I object to that,' Harker said, lighting up another of his damn cigarettes. 'I'm a major, not a captain.'

'But you'll admit to the sadistic part?'

He gave her a smile that didn't reach his eyes. 'This is the army,' he reminded her.

'And you are a vicious fiend from hell,' Eve said, which seemed to amuse him. She turned her head away, staring pointedly out of the back of the wagon at the rutted, unmade road which jarred and jolted her spine. None of the others seemed to mind, or even notice, but Eve supposed that was something else the army instilled. Endurance.

Some time around midday, long after the paltry dawn breakfast Eve had been given had worn off, Harker called a halt and ordered Tallulah to distribute lunch. This consisted of bread that was already a little stale, slimy slices of ham, and water.

Tallulah caught her looking at it and said, 'Be thankful we're not further into the journey. Then all we'll have is dried meat, and it's twice as bad.'

'Marvellous. And how long is this journey expected to take?' Eve asked.

Tallulah shook her head. 'I honestly don't know,' she said.

After lunch, which was eaten by the side of the muddy road, Harker announced that they'd be marching again.

'Okay, now that's just bad for digestion,' Eve said.

'Tough,' Harker said. 'Form up!'

Eve refused to move.

The Lance-Corporal tugged on the handcuffs, which hurt, especially as she was clearly much stronger than Eve, but she still refused to move.

'Sir,' the Lance-Corporal said, 'problem.'

Eve, who would have folded her arms if one of them hadn't been attached to the furiously tugging Lance-Corporal, stood her ground and glared at Harker. He heaved a heavy sigh and said, 'All right, come here.'

They did, and when Harker took the handcuff key from his pocket Eve nearly sang in relief. He unfastened the cuff from the Lance-Corporal, who shook her wrist and gave him a grateful look ... and then fastened it on his own wrist.

'What?' Eve shrieked. 'I have to be chained to *you* now?'

'Shut up,' Harker said, 'or I'll chain you to the back of the wagon and gallop the horses. And don't think I won't do it, 'cos I will.'

He probably would, Eve thought, resigning herself to trying to jog at his pace. It wasn't fair, he was a lot taller than her and he'd have a longer natural stride, and – wait, he was climbing into the driver's seat of the wagon.

'Oh, frabjous day,' she moaned, taking the weight off her aching and, she suspected, bleeding feet.

'Squad,' Harker yelled to the men, who were now being led by Captain Haran. Charlie had taken up position at the back of the wagon. 'Quick *march*!'

They set off at a fast walking pace, and Harker flapped the reins in such a manner that the horses followed suit.

Eve fumed for a while, staring straight ahead at the small group of marching soldiers, watching as Tallulah, who was quite short, kept up with Banks, who was quite tall, while they followed Daz, who seemed to want to go at his own pace, and the Lance-Corporal, who stopped him from doing so.

'She's a good soldier, Martindale,' Harker remarked. 'Make a great sergeant.'

So that was her name. Eve hmphed.

'She'll probably get it when we get back, too. Only trouble is, I've nowhere to put her, and I don't want to lose her. Suppose I could transfer someone else out.'

Eve ignored him, and started unlacing her trainers to get some air to her feet. Yep: at least one blister had burst, and the blood was soaking through her sock.

Unconcerned, Harker lit yet another cigarette.

'Where do you even get them all from?' Eve said, waving away a puff of smoke.

'I buy 'em. What d'you think?'

Eve glared. 'No, I mean ... you can't grow tobacco in this country, can you? You need a hotter environment for it.' Certainly hotter than this weather. Charlie had procured for Eve a rather old and suspiciously patched redcoat, which made her feel like a gigantic target, but at least it was warmer than her t-shirt.

'Yeah. They come from the Americas.'

'Can you afford that?' Eve had no idea what the country's economy was like, but between the rationing and the lack of telecommunications, it didn't look particularly strong.

'Got bugger all else to spend my pay on,' Harker said.

'No, I mean – oh, never mind.'

They drove on a while longer. Eve couldn't quite manage to guess where they might be; she didn't even know where they were going. North of London was all she knew. Nothing at all looked familiar, and there were no road signs.

After a while, Harker said, 'Have you ever killed anyone, Eve?'

Eve, who'd been leaning against the side of the wagon, massaging her feet and idly watching the fields roll by, sat up in surprise. 'What kind of question is that?'

'A valid one. Have you?'

'No!'

Harker shrugged. 'I have. Charlie has.' He pointed to the soldiers marching ahead of them. 'Martindale has. Banks I ain't sure about, but being a poacher I wouldn't be surprised if he had before he joined us. And Daz, poor sod, probably has, even if he didn't mean to. Only one I can say for certain hasn't ever killed anyone is Tallulah, and that's 'cos she's only been out of Basic Training a week.' He considered her for a moment. 'Although if she's anything like her sister, she was probably born lethal.'

'I feel so comforted,' said Eve, who honestly hadn't given much thought before that to the idea that she was travelling with a bunch of paid killers.

Why should I care? It's not real. None of this can possibly be real. I hit my head and I'm in a coma.

Only, the presence of the large man to whom she was handcuffed was so utterly real that she couldn't bring herself to believe she was just dreaming. She could smell the damp wool of his jacket, the pungent smoke of his cigarette, the earthy scent of horses and leather and the faint, acrid scent of something she thought might be gunpowder. She felt the heat of his rough skin whenever his hand brushed against hers. When she breathed in, smoke crackled inside her lungs.

If I'm not dreaming then what is this? Have I gone mad? I must have gone mad.

I'm sitting next to a self-confessed killer. Either the world's gone mad or I have. Somehow neither thought made her feel better. Fear, a cold nasty fog that crept around inside her, rose up inside her chest.

'Yeah, well, you should. Reason being this. Do you know how many people, civilians, are killed by strangers? Not many. People only commit murder when they've a damn good reason to.'

'Or if they're insane,' Eve said, wondering if that qualified her. She shoved down the fear. It was no good to her now.

'Yes, all right, but my point is this. People, ordinary sane people, don't go around killing strangers, do they?'

'Not unless they're in the army.'

'Ah,' Harker said. 'Yeah. That's it. Not unless they're in the army. Where it's our job to go around killing complete strangers, often en masse. And that's not something a normal person is any good at. Now, in peacetime, we can happily hire all those psychos who like killing people, although it tends to make a bloke a bit uneasy, sharing a barracks with some bugger who wants to know what your insides look like. In wartime, though, we've a bit of a shortage. Not enough volunteers. Got to start recruiting from the populace.'

'Conscription,' Eve said.

'Yep. And that means we've got a load of men–'

'And women,' said Eve, who was still faintly amazed that women were on the front line now. Part of her, the feminist part, cheered, but a big chunk of her cowered.

'Military term, military term,' Harker said, waving his hand. 'We've got a load of men who don't really want to run around murdering complete strangers. It's not a normal human thing to do. The Bible even tells you not to.' He blew out a cloud of smoke, most of which went Eve's way. 'Which is something the padre at the barracks could never quite reconcile to my satisfaction. Anyway. The point is, we've got to take these men, who've been brought up nice, and turn them into people who will kill without a second's hesitation. And do you know how we do that?'

'I don't know,' Eve said, still feeling belligerent. 'Brainwashing?'

'We drill 'em. Day in, day out. From the first minute they put their boots on. Basic Training involves day after day of being shouted at until you obey orders without even thinking. Squaddies don't need to think. They need to obey. They need to have it hammered into them that when their sergeant tells 'em to march, they march. When he tells 'em to run, they run. And when he tells 'em to fire, they get their guns, they aim, and they kill the bloke standing in front of 'em. That's why we drill. Every day.'

'So you can beat the compassion out of ordinary people?'

'Absolutely. Don't you look at me like that. If we didn't then we'd have an army of men who felt sorry for the enemy. And then the enemy'd kill 'em.'

Eve said nothing. She couldn't think of anything to say.

'Now, the reason I have my men marching on a full stomach is this. It's a damn sight better than marching on an empty one.'

'An army marches on its stomach,' Eve said, trying to remember who'd said that.

Harker looked at her like she was mad. 'No, they march on their feet. But they've got to be ready to march at any time. Whether they're tired, or hungry, or hurt – even if they have sprained ankles,' he said, looking sideways at her, which Eve didn't really appreciate. 'Whether they've just eaten, or they haven't eaten in three days. When I was defending Newmarket, they had us under siege for weeks and one of their shells hit the food stores. We were on such tight rations I was giving serious consideration to eating my own horse. But I still had to get up and fight, didn't I?'

'Aren't you the hero,' Eve muttered.

'No,' Harker said, 'I ain't a hero. I'm a soldier. Big difference. But the next time you tell me it's bad for my men to march on a full stomach, or with blisters on their feet, or whatever, you consider that there are far worse conditions they're going to have to march in, and fight in, and if I don't toughen 'em up, and keep 'em tough, then I might as well wave a white flag at the Coalitionists right now.'

Eve knew that was intended to keep her quiet, and for a little while she *was* quiet, remembering every war film she'd ever watched, remembering history classes at school and pictures of soldiers in trenches at Ypres and the Somme. She supposed he had a point. Soldiers had to be tough.

But then, she wasn't a soldier.

'Who are the Coalitionists?' she asked after a while.

Harker made an exasperated sound. 'You ain't very curious, are you?'

'I'm just asking,' she said. 'If they're who you're fighting, and I'm stuck with you, then I think it'd be nice of you to tell me.'

Harker was silent a moment. Then he said, 'Fair enough. The Coalitionists are, in brief, a group of people who think we should take the French up on their offer of a "coalition".'

Eve saw Harker's sneer. She nearly heard his inverted commas.

'A coalition,' she said. 'Like an alliance?'

'Yeah. Well, that's the way they phrased it. But can you see France, the biggest power in the world, forming an equal alliance with a country that gets aid workers – what's so funny?'

'*France* is the biggest power in the world?' Eve said.

'Yeah.' Harker gave Eve a look that she was getting used to. It said, 'You really must be mad if you don't know that.'

'Okay,' she relented, 'I am crazy. But France?'

'The French Empire,' Harker clarified. 'They own a third of the world.'

Eve, whose grandmother had related the story of colouring in the world map and running out of pink when she did the British bits, could only shake her head.

'Anyway. They couched the offer in very pretty terms, but what it basically means is they want to annex us to the Empire. And we don't want that. Well, the majority of us don't. But there were some ministers who thought it'd be a good idea. They developed a bit of a following. It was all just political until they stormed out of Parliament and attempted to get the army behind 'em.'

'And the army said no?'

'The army did. More to the point, General Wheeler did. But two of the MPs who walked out represented Manchester and Leeds, and they raised militia and took over those two towns. Since then, it's been us against them. Parliamentarians against Coalitionists.'

Eve digested this. It all sounded vaguely reminiscent of – well, every civil war she'd ever heard of.

'The King declared military rule, and–'

'I'm sorry,' Eve said. 'The *King*?'

'Yes,' Harker said patiently. 'You know, posh bloke, sits on a throne, wears a crown.'

'A king,' Eve repeated. Not a queen. The *History of the Untied Kingdom* that she'd read hadn't got that far. 'What, uh, what's his name?'

'Charles,' Harker said, and Eve nearly choked on her own breath.

'Charles? Charles – son of Elizabeth II?'

'Yep. See, you have heard of him. You know, I'm wondering if you just hit your head or something, I've heard of cases where amnesia's set in–'

'Yeah, maybe,' Eve interrupted with a wave of her hand. 'Look. What happened to the Queen? The old Queen?'

'Elizabeth? It was pretty nasty, actually. There was a fire at Windsor Castle and she was killed. Thankfully, Charles and Diana and the princes weren't there, or the whole line might have been wiped out.' Harker chucked his spent cigarette on to the ground, where the wagon wheel rolled over it. 'Plenty of people, of course, reckon that was the idea, but no one's been able to prove it.'

'I remember that,' Eve said, frowning. 'The fire at Windsor.' She'd been a kid, maybe eight or nine, but she remembered news footage of ordinary people helping to rescue priceless works of art. Remembered that the damage had been so expensive the Queen had opened a couple of her houses to the public to pay for it.

Remembered, too, that the Queen hadn't been anywhere near the place at the time, and that arson hadn't even been suggested.

Then something else occurred to her. 'You said Charles and Diana,' she said. 'His wife?' Harker nodded. 'Is she ... still his wife?'

Harker shook his head. 'No. The divorce came through in 1996. I remember that; it was the year I met Saskia.' He laughed, but it didn't indicate that he found anything particularly funny.

'Saskia ... your ex?' Again he nodded. 'What ... happened after that?'

'Well, my CO had recommended me for promotion and Saskia's father bought it – well, she denies it, but–'

'No, I mean with the – the King,' Eve said, although her inner gossip hound shelved that bit of information away for later.

'Oh. Well, not much, really. He has a lady friend, but I think there's a lot of opposition to her becoming queen, what with her being divorced and all. Seems a little hypocritical, seeing as he is, too, but then that's the monarchy for you.'

'His lady friend,' Eve said. 'Would her name be Camilla?'

'It would,' said Harker, looking pleased. 'See, it's coming back to you. And Diana's walking out with an Egyptian guy; it's because of him we get imports of things like–'

'Wait,' Eve said, with such urgency that Harker hauled on the reins and stopped the wagon. 'Diana's alive?'

Harker gave her a strange look. 'Of course she is.' His eyes narrowed. 'Why, shouldn't she be?'

Realising she probably sounded like a terrorist, Eve said

quickly, 'Oh, no – I mean, yes, I just thought … never mind.'

Diana was alive. Wow. Did the tabloids still put her on their front pages?

They reached the Devil's Dyke a few hours after nightfall, and Harker started handing out duties before the wagon even stopped rolling.

'Private Banks,' he said, 'take one of the horses – you can ride? Good. Follow this ditch to the north and keep on for three miles northwest and you will find a river. Fill this,' he chucked a large water can at him, 'and bring it back here. Spot anything we can eat on the way, you shoot it and bring it back. Tallulah, you take care of these three nags and the other one when Banks returns, and Private Banks,' he added suddenly, as the younger man made to ride off, 'when I say shoot something for our supper I do not mean animals that belong to anyone else, do you hear me? You poach another man's livestock, that's a flogging offence. Clear?'

Banks nodded. 'Yes, sir. Clear, sir.' He rode off.

'Lance-Corporal Martindale, the tents, please, and get Eve to help you.' He unshackled himself from Eve and fastened her wrist to a longish chain that was attached to the wagon.

Technically, he knew it ought to be Charlie giving the orders, because whatever her rank, she'd always performed as his sergeant, but a big chunk of Harker remembered being a sergeant himself, and he recalled being happier then than he ever had been since his promotion to the officer classes.

'Charlie, you take first watch. Someone'll relieve you in a couple of hours. Up on top of the ridge, if you please.'

The dyke had been built, however many years ago, by the simple method of digging a big ditch and piling the earth up to one side. It made a pretty decent defence, as Harker had discovered when the Coalitionists had made their advance on Newmarket.

Then, the ridge's height had been supplemented by bodies, and the ditch had been a foot deep in water. Harker rubbed his right hand absently. He'd been made captain after Newmarket, four years after Wheeler had first offered it to him. Four years after he'd married Saskia.

He'd turned it down back then, having come to the unsettling conclusion that his promotions to ensign when he met Saskia, and then to lieutenant when he proposed to her, hadn't been mere coincidences. Saskia, who'd just accepted a wedding gift of promotion to the rank of major, hadn't been thrilled.

Looking back, he probably ought to have learnt something from that.

Since he'd run out of men to collect firewood, excepting Daz who, he surmised, would bring back green twigs and be unable to light them, Harker went off himself to do that, taking the small axe included in the wagon's kit. *Mental note*, he told himself, *make sure Eve has both hands and feet bound at night and chain her out of reach of the wagon.*

It was perhaps over the top, but Harker hadn't got where he was by taking silly chances. Well, he had, but not that kind of silly chance.

With a fire burning and the tents up, the camp looked much more appealing. Banks returned with a couple of rabbits, at which Eve looked horrified – especially when he proceeded to skin them and set them in a skillet over the fire.

'Fried rabbit?' she asked, going a little pale.

'Nah,' he said. 'Just sautéing it before I chuck it inna stew. Got some vegetables, too, make a nice meal out of that.'

'And where did you get those vegetables, Private Banks?' Harker asked, making the kid jump.

'Found 'em, sir,' he said, his face open and innocent.

'And where did you find 'em?'

'Just lyin' around, sir.'

'Speaking of lying, Private, you'd better not be telling me falsehoods.'

'Would I lie to an officer, sir?'

'I don't know, Banks, would you?'

Banks grinned. 'Honest as the day is long, me, sir,' he said.

'Yes. Unfortunately, it's October, so the days ain't that long, are they, Private?'

Banks continued to grin, but said nothing more.

Banks turned out to be a decent cook, and over bowls of comfortingly hot stew, he entertained them with stories of his thieving days. He didn't seem remotely ashamed of them at all.

While they were eating, Daz turned to Eve and said, 'Tell me about this Internet. What is it?'

Eve blew out a long sigh. 'God,' she said. 'I don't even know where to start.'

'At the beginning,' said Harker, one ear on their conversation and one on Banks's exploits.

'Like with ABC?' Eve asked. 'Right, anyway,' she said quickly. 'The Internet. It's like a ... a worldwide network.'

'You said that bit,' Harker said, and she glared at him. He was beginning to enjoy provoking her.

'What kind of network?' Daz said, and Eve put down her spoon.

'Well,' she said thoughtfully. 'Okay. You asked me if I'd ever temped on a switchboard,' she said to Harker, 'so you know what they are?'

'I know *of* them,' said Harker, to whom the wonders of technology were a closed book. But Daz was nodding, so she addressed herself to him.

'Right. What you're sending down a phoneline is your voice, yes? You're sending sounds. Do you ... know how they do that?'

'Yes,' said Daz. 'The voice produces acoustic pressure waves, which affect the electrical current being picked up by the transmitter contained in the telephone. The varying electric current is transmitted along a copper wire to the other telephone, making the coil in the receiver move back and forth to reproduce the sounds from the first person through a microphone.'

For a long moment, there was no sound above that of the fire. Even Eve looked stunned.

'Yes,' she said eventually, her voice a little weak, 'that's ... right. Although I think you meant 'speaker' there, at the end, not 'microphone'. A microphone is what you speak *into*. The speaker is where the sound comes out.'

Daz frowned. 'Is it?'

'Yes. Trust me on that.' She cleared her throat. 'All right. So a telephone can transmit sounds ... in the way you said. What about if the signal could be modified to send pictures, too?'

'How?' Daz said, and Eve looked as if she was trying to work that out ahead of him.

'Well, a similar ... sort of ... way,' she said. 'With ... variations in the current.' She looked at Daz hopefully. He looked back with a similar expression. It was almost comical.

Eve slumped. 'All right,' she said, 'I don't know exactly how it's done. But the basic principle of the Internet is that it sends information through a phone line. I don't know how exactly, but it is to do with those current variations. I think.'

Daz looked a bit disappointed. Harker asked, 'What kind of information?'

'Well,' Eve said, reviving a bit, 'images, for one thing. Static images, but also moving ones. And there's also a method of communication called email. Electronic mail. It's basically a way to send private message online ... er, on the

Internet. You have to have a password, and then you can read it.'

'And anyone with the password can read it?' Harker asked.

'Well, theoretically, yes. You have your own email address – like a phone number, it's individual and specific. Say, if I wanted to send you a message, an email,' she said to Daz, 'I'd type in your email address–'

'Type?' Harker asked. 'Do they use typewriters?'

'Something very similar,' Eve said. 'I'd type in your address and send you the message. And when you wanted to read it, you'd log on – er, you'd type in your email address and your password, and then you could read it. So long as you keep that password private, no one else can read it.'

Harker looked at Charlie. She was nodding. 'Yes,' she said, 'I know. This could be what they're doing.'

'What who's doing?' Eve asked brightly.

'Never you mind,' Harker said.

'Oh, cheers, I just sit here giving you the hotsheet on the Internet, which, by the way, is a very complicated thing and not easy to explain to people who've never even seen a television, and you won't even tell me why you want to know.'

'It's a need-to-know thing,' Harker said.

'Well, I need to know!'

'No, you don't.' He stood up. 'Well, troops, I don't know about you, but I'm bloody knackered. Time to turn in. Up at sunrise. See you in the morning.'

'Wait,' Eve said. 'I haven't even told you about Internet porn!'

'You can use it to sell stuff?' Daz said, and everyone else went po-faced.

'Uh, no, not pawn as in shop,' Eve said. Her cheeks were pink. 'Porn as in …'

She looked around as if for help, and the rest of the squad suddenly found the canopy of trees fascinating.

All except Harker, who grinned at her. 'I think I like the sound of this Internet,' he said. Eve scowled at him, and he winked. 'All right. 'Night, everyone. Sweet dreams.'

Charlie snorted, and Harker went to bed to fight against images of telephones and naked girls, who all seemed to look rather like Eve.

Chapter Nine

Morning came, and with it heavy mist and a hideously early start. *You've got up earlier than this,* Eve reminded herself. *Remember those days full of planes and rehearsals and interviews and performances? You'd be on the go from six in the morning until after midnight. You had the feet of a ballet dancer and skin like tracing paper.*

She shuddered, and thought wistful things about coffee.

An hour after Charlie had barked her awake, the camp was dismantled, the only evidence of it a couple of rectangles of flattened grass and a burnt circle where the fire had been. Charlie and Harker spent some time conferring on their route, pointing and talking about roads on which she half-expected to encounter Bilbo Baggins.

'If we follow this road until we get to the Peddar's Way, that's ... thirty miles just to Downham Market, and if we want to change horses we'll have to stop at the blockade on the Fen Causeway, which is another twenty-odd miles. Charlie, that's another day's travel. Whereas if we go cross country, we can get to the barricade by lunchtime, get fresh horses and be at Boston by nightfall.'

'In this fog? Sir, we've been in that country before,' Charlie said. 'We'll get stuck in the mud.'

'Then we lighten the wagon, carry our packs, and hope we've all lost weight.' Harker glanced up, saw Eve watching them. 'Any bright ideas?' he said.

'Try the A10,' Eve said, which he didn't seem to find funny.

'We go cross country, Charlie,' Harker said, folding up the map with a sort of finality. 'There are markers and things along the way.' He gave Eve a humourless smile. 'And how about this. We send Eve on ahead. That way, if the fen turns marshy, she can warn us.'

'Oh, *thanks*,' Eve said.

The ground squelched underfoot, but held. Fog crept in patches, sometimes obscuring her view to only a few feet ahead. Even when it cleared there wasn't much to see. Around her the trees were sad, windswept affairs, huddling together in small woodlands here and there. For mile after damp, foggy mile, Eve trudged on, still chained, but ahead of the others, searching out the path, muttering about bloody Harker and the bloody marshes, until he called a halt for lunch and she muttered about bloody cold rabbit meat. On her back was a pack that apparently contained cooking equipment, but into which she was certain Harker had just piled a load of rocks. She fully expected to sink with every step.

At least she wasn't handcuffed to anyone, although she was still attached to the long chain that Harker had put her on last night, like a dog. She'd even slept with it clinking coldly beside her.

Bastard.

Their progress was cautiously slow, so it was mid-afternoon by the time they approached what Harker called the Fen Causeway and which, Eve discerned, was a road running east from Peterborough. As they got closer, Charlie and Harker discussed earnestly how close they should go to the barricades, and whether the whole party should go, or just a couple of them, with the wagon, to change the horses.

As it happened, they didn't get to do either.

The path they were following, itself not much more than a solid bit of ground between the marshes of the fens, had been empty for their entire journey. But within five miles of the Causeway, people started coming the other way.

Lots of people.

Carrying things.

After the third family hurried past, all burdened with suitcases and leading a pig on a piece of string, Harker stopped and said, 'Okay, something's up.'

'You don't say,' Eve muttered.

In the distance, through the fog which had never entirely lifted, more figures were heading their way. Even when she squinted into the distance, Eve found it hard to tell if she was looking at a crowd of people or a huddle of trees. She eventually worked out that the static group was a wood. Harker took off his coat and replaced it with a blanket from the wagon. He handed his sword to Charlie, who hustled the rest of the squad, including Eve, out of sight behind the wagon.

As he walked, Harker's feet trailed in the mud, and Eve thought he might be limping a little. His shoulders visibly slumped and he clutched the shabby, patched-up blanket as if it was his only friend in the world. Eve, who hadn't really paid much attention to his military bearing, aside from noticing how broad his shoulders were, was amazed at the transformation.

He looks even more like a vagrant than usual.

He approached a young couple. The woman was pregnant and the man, carrying a heavy pack, walked with an awkward gait that Eve later realised was because he had a wooden leg. Clearly, if the army was conscripting all able-bodied men, there weren't going to be too many of them hanging around outside of the military.

'Hold a minute, friend,' Harker said, approaching them with an open smile. 'What's the hurry?'

The young man glanced backwards over his shoulder. 'Fighting,' he said. 'The army's fighting the rebels in March.'

'March?' Alarm showed on Harker's face. 'They broke

through the barricades?'

The woman nodded. 'Word got to us this morning. They broke right through, and they've been pushing back towards Downham Market. They're taking the whole Causeway.'

Eve saw the line of Harker's shoulders tighten, straighten a little. Beside her, Charlie's movements mirrored Harker's. Eve wondered if the Lieutenant's ears were pricking up under her bushy hair.

'Do you know how far they've got?'

'We came from Tipps End,' said the woman. 'They hadn't got there yet, but a runner came ...' She trailed off, tight-lipped and shaking.

Her husband put his arm around her. 'A runner came from Christchurch,' he said. 'He said only a couple of them got out in time.'

The woman gave a sob.

Eve glanced at Tallulah and mouthed, 'Is this bad?'

Tallulah nodded and whispered right in her ear, 'The barricade was further west. If they've got as far as March, that means they're pushing along the Fen Causeway towards the sea.'

She leaned back, and saw the incomprehension on Eve's face. 'If they close the gap between Peterborough and the sea they could cut us off from the north.'

'They've got the whole of the Midlands?'

'No, they've got hardly anywhere.' Tallulah looked troubled. 'At least that's what they tell us.'

Charlie tapped Eve on the shoulder and frowned, putting her finger to her lips. Eve nodded and continued to watch Harker talking to the couple on the path, her mind racing.

The Coalitionists only had a little bit of territory. *That's what they tell us*. But how well informed was Tallulah? Her sister was high-ranking – higher than Harker? – but how much had she passed on? How much did the average soldier know?

Propaganda. Tallulah and her fellow squaddies probably thought they were winning the war, that there were only a few rebel strongholds to overcome. But if the enemy already controlled Manchester and Leeds – her mind composed a quick map – then they'd already got a strong foothold in the north. Pushing east from Peterborough was probably only a localised part of the plan. Hell, they could hold the entire Midlands and the average soldier on the street wouldn't know about it.

With any luck there was no such thing in this world as the M62, so crossing the Pennines would be–

Eve shook herself. This world. It was the same goddamned world as always. All of this was just a ... a dream or a nightmare or a hallucination. Not real. Even if the smell of the horses and the wetness of the mud and the fear creeping through her veins *felt* pretty damn real.

Beside Eve, Charlie silently took off her pack, quietly placing it into the wagon. She gestured for the others to do the same, drawing from a box several belts of ammunition. Charlie the gundog. She handed the belts silently to Martindale, Banks, and Tallulah, draped one over her own shoulder, and then handed Daz an armband with a prominent red cross on it.

He shook his head and pointed to her ammunition.

Charlie shook her head. Daz mouthed, 'Lieutenant!' angrily. Charlie shook her head again, then tilted it at Harker.

'We've seen no trouble further south,' Harker said. 'Are there many more coming from your village?'

The woman shook her head. Her eyes were huge and frightened. 'No,' she said, 'we were the last. They've all gone on ahead. They–'

A muffled boom from behind made her jump. All heads turned in that direction.

'You,' Harker said to the man, shaking out his blanket and straightening his shoulders, 'you've seen service?'

The ex-soldier glanced once at the insignia on Harker's newly revealed jacket and nodded. 'Battle of Southwark, sir. 109th.'

'Right. So you'll keep your lady well out of it.'

He nodded determinedly. 'We were heading for Ely,' he said.

'Good man. Good man. You have any arms?'

After a second's hesitation, the man produced a pistol. Harker grinned.

'Excellent. On your way.'

They hurried off, seemingly unsurprised by the squad hiding behind the wagon, and disappeared into the fog as another boom sounded, louder than the first but still muffled.

'If we can hear that,' Harker said, striding back towards them, 'in this fog ...'

'Then it's much closer than we think,' Charlie said. She took Harker's blanket from him, tossed it into the wagon, and handed him a belt of ammo. Harker took it and gestured for more, which Charlie, rolling her eyes, gave him.

'And for me, Lieutenant,' Daz said, holding out his hand.

'How close?' Eve asked, and was ignored.

'With respect, sir, you're a surgeon, and there's no telling–'

'What I might have to defend myself against,' said Daz. 'There aren't many shots in my pistol.'

'Neither should there be,' Harker said, buckling on his sword. 'Non-combat officers are not to draw arms except to defend themselves, General's orders. Is that clear, Captain?'

Daz's cartoon mouth closed tightly. 'Yes, sir,' he muttered.

'Good.' Harker handed him the ammo anyway. 'Best line of defence is attack,' he said with a faint smile.

'Defence?' Eve said. 'We're not going *towards* them, are we?'

Towards was bad. Very bad. Eve had seen *Saving Private Ryan*. She'd seen *Gladiator.* And she'd seen that man with the wooden leg.

'What are we, Eve?' Harker said.

'Well, I'm a prisoner,' she muttered.

'We're the army. We don't run away from a fight.'

Daz climbed into the wagon to retrieve medical supplies, while all around Eve the rest of the squad checked and clicked and loaded things with an efficiency that frightened her. *They're killers. All of them. Even sweet pretty Tallulah.*

'So you're just going to join in?' Eve said incredulously to Harker, as he slung a machine-gun over his shoulder by its strap, then turned to unharness the front two horses.

'No, I thought we'd take a picnic and sit and watch,' he said, not looking up at her.

'You don't even know what you'll find,' Eve said, fear mounting in her.

'Course I do. Smoke, mayhem, death, blood, the usual.' He didn't look too bothered by it.

'And it's really foggy! How can you even see anything?'

At that, Harker did look up. He grinned. 'Do you know what fog is, Charlie?' he said.

'Ambusher's best friend, sir,' she said.

'See, if we can't see, then they can't see,' he said. 'They don't know how many buggers are sneaking up on 'em.' He patted the top of her head, which Eve found immensely patronising, and said, 'We'll be fine. Done this before.'

Eve, not so terrified that she still couldn't be bolshie, folded her arms.

'Right,' she said. 'Fine. While I do what? I'm chained to this damn wagon. Are you going to leave me here? In case they come this way? Bait? Or have I outlived my usefulness now?'

Fear was making her babble. Dammit, what if she had

outlived her usefulness? They were using her as a pathfinder, weren't they? She'd told them about the Internet – not enough, but did they know that?

'I can tell you lots more about–' she began, but Harker shut her up with a wave of his hand and a noise of disgust.

'I ain't gonna leave you here to get shot and raped,' he said, which made Eve slightly nauseous. 'You're sticking with Daz.'

Daz brandished his pistol with a total lack of skill, and as Eve's chain was fastened to him she thought she might be sick. He could as easily kill her with his ineptitude as the enemy.

I don't think I can convince myself this is a dream any more.

There was another boom, and the spatter of automatic fire. It sounded hideously close. Tallulah's lips got thinner.

Harker handed Eve an armband like Daz's.

'Um,' Eve said, 'I don't know anything about, uh, field medicine or anything ...'

'Don't need to.'

'But ... isn't this a bit dishonest?'

Harker stared at her. 'Right, so when the enemy comes at you, sees Daz and his armband and spares him, and you tell them you were going to wear one but decided not to because you're not a medic and it'd all be a bit *dishonest*, exactly how long do you think they'll spend listening before they shoot you in the bloody head?'

Wordlessly, Eve took the armband.

Harker checked his map again. 'Right,' he said. 'If we don't find you, meet us in Downham Market.'

He nodded at Daz, which seemed to be his version of an everyday salute, and slung a blanket on the back of one of the horses as a makeshift saddle. Eve watched him mount up to ride into the wood full of smoke, mayhem, death and blood, and blurted, 'Wait!'

He glanced down at her, impatient, and the cold realisation occurred to Eve that she had no idea what she was going to say.

'Come back, all right?' she said. 'Just ... come back.'

He gave her an unexpected wink. 'Count on it. Squad, to me!' he shouted, and cantered off into the woods. The squad followed on foot, like a line of little ducklings.

'They're going to die, aren't they,' Eve said, her stomach churning.

'We're all going to die,' said Daz, then caught her expression and added hurriedly, 'eventually.'

'Advance!' Harker yelled, spraying bullets into the fog. He switched on the toff accent he'd learned while married to Saskia. 'Leave no man standing! Hussars, advance!'

His horse screamed and reared. Poor sod, wasn't used to being ridden, wasn't used to all this noise and terror. In the fog, the woods were an impenetrable nightmare. He and the horse were muffled in their own terrifying little world, possibly miles from everyone else, possibly only a heartbeat. Neither of them knew which until a shape loomed out of the mist, screaming and wielding bloody death.

Harker galloped the horse towards the nearest shapes, yelling and swinging out with his sword. It wasn't a cavalry sword, which meant it was far too short to make any real impact when swung from high up, but it made the soldiers on the ground recoil. Ducking loose bullets – *any bullet, the next one could be it* – Harker swung his left arm around a narrow tree trunk, gripped the horse with his thighs and forced it to veer around the tree, back towards the enemy, returning fire as he went. Evidently he hadn't come away with nothing from his marriage to Saskia. Thank goodness for her daredevil brother, who had taught him how to control a horse with no saddle and no reins.

The horse bucked and Harker nearly lost his seat, but sheer bloody-mindedness kept him on, and he shoved the beast back down to the ground, thundering into the man he'd forced back with his sword.

The body squelched as it hit the mud, and a horrible scream bubbled from the man's throat as he died.

Harker wheeled the horse around again, every muscle he had protesting, and galloped off down the line, zigzagging under a hail of bullets, until he'd driven the Coalitionists opposite him back further, and further still. From the mist and the dark woods came the shouts of surprise and dismay as the rest of the squad made themselves known further along the line. Sound bounced around, the direction impossible to distinguish.

Someone screamed, a woman, terrified and desperate. Hoof beats thundered, making the ground shake, and Tallulah, real plums in her voice, commanded an imaginary cavalry brigade forward. Somewhere a tree, having taken too many bullets, groaned and screeched and crashed to the ground. He heard Charlie bellowing in a raw voice, 'Seven Platoon! To me!' and a lot of gunfire from what appeared to be random directions.

In the fog, five men can be fifty. And fifty men can be followed by a lot more.

Good job half the enemy were cowards.

As the first cries of, 'Retreat! Retreat!' drifted through the fog, Harker smiled, and cantered off in the direction of Charlie's rifle. She swung towards him, finger on the trigger, and in the space between heartbeats recognised him and lowered her gun.

Harker grinned. 'Which bugger was it who said God was on the side of the biggest battalions, Charlie?'

'Napoleon, sir.'

'Well, he was wrong. God is on the side of the biggest bastards.'

A shot through the fog wiped the smile from his face. Harker swung down off his horse, slapped its rump, and watched it run away. He didn't blame it.

'Cavalry?' came a voice. 'Identify yourselves!'

Harker winked at Charlie. '75th Infantry,' he said. 'You?'

The darkish shape came closer, clearer. 'Infantry? But I heard ...' he looked at the horse disappearing into the fog, '... horses.'

The speaker was a lieutenant. Quite young, by the looks of him, dirty and wet with marsh gunk and splatters of blood.

Harker clapped him on the shoulder. 'Old trick, Lieutenant.' The kid was even still wearing his cap, with a badge that identified him as 9th of Foot. 'Reckon they're retreating now, but you might want to give the order for a farewell salvo.'

The Lieutenant nodded, but he was looking around without much confidence. 'Yes, sir, but the thing is, we're all a bit broken up by this fog. They don't fight in neat lines, sir, they just ran at us like a mob!'

Harker closed his eyes for a second. Unbelievable.

He opened his eyes. 'Well, that's the enemy for you, Lieutenant ...?'

'Simson, sir.'

'Simson. Enemy ain't got no manners. Right. Well then, I suppose we'd better form your men back up, hadn't we? Who's in charge of the 9th now? Danbury?'

Simson shook his head. 'No, sir. Wounded at Newark. Major Collington had us, sir, but she was one of the first to fall when the barricades came down.' He swallowed. 'They took all of the first line out, sir. Shelled us at the back. We've only a quarter of the men left, sir; at least, we did when the barricades came down.'

'When was this?'

Simson looked at his watch. Smudged some blood out of the way. 'An hour, sir? Maybe more. Can't quite see the minute hand, sir.'

Harker resisted the urge to swear, loudly, because the poor kid looked as if he'd had enough already.

'All right, Lieutenant,' he said. 'You go off, round up as many men as you can, form a line and advance towards the Causeway, firing and reloading the whole time. There's to be no one else enters this bog, you understand? Unless they're civilians, and you send 'em south. When you reach the Causeway, start curving round west, force them back towards the barricades. Got it?'

Simson quavered for a minute, then nodded. 'Yes, sir. I understand.'

'Well, go then!'

Simson ran off, and Harker turned to Charlie. 'You go that way,' he pointed west. 'Do the same. Force 'em east, back on to the barricades.'

'What about the ones who've already gone further east, sir? Past Simson's men?

Harker glanced at the blood already drying on his sword. *Never stays clean.*

'Those,' he said, 'are mine.'

Mist closed in on Eve and Daz, the rumble of the wagon and the thud of the horses' hooves muffled like the bass beat outside a nightclub. Every now and then something boomed distantly, someone screamed, and fear pounded through Eve until she thought she might shatter.

The woods closed in on them, dark and murderous, full of fear and madness.

Manoeuvring the wagon up the path towards the

Causeway, which seemed to Eve to be the wrong direction entirely, Daz halted suddenly when he heard a burst of fire and the muffled command, '9th of Foot! Advance! Slow and easy, men!'

'They're still fighting,' Eve said, her eyes darting around, desperately trying to see through the fog. 'Should we, er, should we be here?'

Daz gave her a look. 'We're not going near them,' he said. 'We're going west.'

'West?' Eve hitched up the loose coils of chain looped over her shoulder.

'Towards the barricades.'

Again with the *towards*. Towards was *bad*. She grabbed his arm. 'Are you mad?'

'No. I'm a doctor.' At her look, which Eve suspected resembled a startled goldfish, he explained, 'Heaviest casualties will be where the barricade was breached. And probably least fighting, too. Come on.'

She hurried after him, encouraged by the part about 'least fighting'. 'Er, did I tell you I've no medical experience?'

'You'll learn. Amazing how fast it comes on a battlefield.'

'Have you, er, been on many?'

Daz shook his head. 'Not while they were actually fighting. Been in plenty of field hospitals, though.'

Eve had a sudden recollection of the *Gone With The Wind* scene where all the wounded were laid out along the railroad tracks, and nearly threw up.

Large shapes, taller and broader than the windswept trees, appeared in the fog. Buildings.

The remains of buildings.

The stench hit her, even through the fog, as they approached the smoking skeleton of a timber-framed cottage.

A collection of wounded soldiers had already amassed in what Eve assumed had once been the village of Christchurch.

Now it reminded her strongly of the No Man's Land south of the Thames, except that this one came complete with bodies, and fresh blood. Several buildings were still on fire.

'Oh God, it's like the devil's barbecue,' she said, stuffing her sleeve over her nose. Daz gave her a look, but tore off a strip of bandage and told her to cover her mouth and nose. It made breathing more bearable, but now the problem was that the fire was burning away the mist, and she could see.

She could see the rubble, the overturned cart, the dead dog in the middle of the road. Somehow, that was the most upsetting thing.

Until she saw what was waiting for her inside the church.

As the only stone building in the village, it hadn't been burned or knocked down by whatever monstrous weapons the enemy had been using, and so it was being used as a shelter by the soldiers too badly hurt to move any further.

Daz immediately ran to the closest and started checking him over, but Eve stood, horrified, as the stench of the dead and the dying overwhelmed her. It smelled like a sewer, and Eve wasn't sure if she'd prefer that to have been because someone had been using it as a toilet, or because someone's innards had been cut out. The sharp, hot tang of blood was everywhere, creeping inside her nostrils and taking up residence. Over it all hung the smell of burning flesh, like a lamb chop that had caught fire on an open grill. Eve didn't want to know where exactly that was coming from. She had an awful premonition that Daz was going to ask her to find out.

'Eve,' he said, tugging on the chain for her attention. 'Eve! Help me. Set up a triage.'

'What?' Eve said, dazed. *I can't do this. I don't want to be here. I can't* do *this.*

'A triage!' He was already moving on to the next soldier. 'Sort out who's most in need of help. Get the ones who can walk on one side of the church. Anyone who's unconscious, check for breathing and heartbeat. You can do that, can't you?'

Eve looked around helplessly, a muddle of excuses tripping from her lips.

'*Eve*, these people *need* your *help*.'

A woman not much younger than Eve met her eyes. There was blood all over her jacket, which was stuck to her body. A long rip ran across the middle of it.

Eve swallowed. 'Yes,' she said, 'I can do that.'

Chapter Ten

Eve straightened up, her back screaming in agony. She ignored it. Right now, it seemed ridiculous to complain about back pain when she'd just assisted Daz in chopping off a man's arm.

She'd vomited the first time he'd done it. But that was because she'd kept her eyes open while he cut through the bone with a curved knife.

'Eve, compression,' he said, and she nodded and pressed both hands over the cloth that was doing little to stem the blood pumping from the soldier's elbow. Daz, who'd already done something to the veins and arteries that involved thread and very bloody hands, rethreaded his needle and grabbed the flap of skin he'd left hanging from the man's forearm. As Eve removed the cloth, Daz began to sew the flap over the stump, like some obscene sort of dressmaking.

The soldier, thank God, was unconscious. Partly due to the morphine Eve had given him, and partly, she suspected, due to shock.

Relief had come a while ago – maybe minutes, maybe hours – all Eve knew was that it had turned dark at some point and someone had brought oil lamps. The church had become a field hospital, and the pews were full of men and women waiting to be treated. Trestle tables and beds had been set up. Medical staff bustled. Outside was a tent where more soldiers were being carved and stitched.

Daz was performing amputations on the altar, a fact which Eve was sure was going to make her burst into hysterical laughter at some point. Maybe when she was less busy.

When the medical staff of whatever unit had arrived, Daz

had said to Eve, 'You can go now, if you want.'

And Eve, who'd spent the whole time she was assisting Daz praying violently for something to take her away from this, found herself shaking her head.

'No,' she said. 'There's still not enough staff. I'll help. Besides,' she said with what might, in other circumstances, have been a smile, 'I'm still chained to you.'

He unshackled her, but Eve volunteered to stay. She didn't think she could just go and sit outside and allow her conscience to beat her over the head while Daz was still working.

Now the sky outside the church windows was dark, and her back ached, and her clothes were saturated with blood, and even the stench of entrails and burned flesh wasn't overpowering any more. Outside someone had lit a brazier, out of sight of the troops, where the amputated limbs were being burned, although thoughtfully, it had been placed downwind.

She was wrapping a tight bandage around the arm stump when Daz said, 'Hey, that's it. No more amputations.'

'Yet,' Eve said, not looking up. 'They still haven't brought everyone in. I heard someone say they were just five miles north of the Causeway before the reinforcements got there. That's a lot of ground to cover.'

'Yes,' said a voice behind her, 'but we were in line formation, so we found them as we came back.'

Harker. Eve glanced up briefly at him before returning her gaze to the bandage. He looked like hell. 'I was wondering when you'd turn up.'

'I said I'd come back.'

'Expected to see you on this table.'

'Oh, cheers. You think I'd survive sixteen years as a soldier just to get my arm cut off?'

'You got your finger cut off,' Eve said, getting to the end

of one bandage and reaching for another to knot on to it.

'Aye, and that was enough.'

She was aware of Daz and Harker looking at each other over her head. They were communicating something, but she was too tired to care what.

Then Daz took the bandage from her hands and said, 'All right, Eve, I'll take it from here. Time you got some rest.'

'I'm okay,' Eve said, which wasn't even remotely true. A small part of her knew she was in shock, that she was operating automatically. It was exactly how she'd functioned in the days and weeks following that brown envelope from the tax man. All throughout the phone calls and the horrifying figures and the hearings and the paparazzi, she'd retained a kind of numbness.

In three years, it hadn't entirely worn off. Until the blood and fear and stench had slammed through the lack of sensation and woken her up.

On balance, Eve preferred the numbness.

'No, you need to rest,' Daz said. 'Doctor's orders.'

Eve closed her eyes for a second and wondered if she'd ever be able to open them again.

'Banks has another stew on the go,' Harker said. 'Got real beef in it, too.'

'Really?'

'Yeah. Shame to let a dead cow go to waste.'

For some reason, that tipped Eve over the edge, and she turned away, bile rising in her throat, and only just made it outside before she threw up again.

Gulping in fresh air, realising just how fetid it had become in the church, she sat back against her heels and wiped her mouth.

'Eve? Oh my goodness, are you all right?'

It was Tallulah, hurrying over, looking horrified. Eve nodded, but Tallulah was staring at her and she realised she was so soaked in blood she looked like an entrant in the world's most macabre wet t-shirt competition.

'Oh, it's not mine. I was helping Daz.'

Harker came out of the chapel, glanced down at Eve, then said to Tallulah, 'Go and call off Martindale. And see if you can find some clean clothes for Eve and the doc. And some soap and water.'

Tallulah nodded, and ran off. Harker hauled Eve to her feet. 'Better?'

She nodded. 'What's Martindale doing?'

'Looking through the bodies for you and Daz.' Harker took off his greatcoat and propped it around her shoulders.

'No, I'll get blood on it ...'

'It's seen worse,' Harker said, and closed the coat in front of her. Eve, shivering, let him, and when he strode away, she followed him. A camp had appeared, tents stretching away in the darkness, fires flickering against the ruins of the village, snatches of laughter and music penetrating her hearing.

'So, the squad,' she said, and faltered. 'Are they – I mean, did you–?'

'They're all fine,' Harker said. 'And we won, by the way.'

'Yes, I heard.' Realising something else was needed, she added, 'Er, well done.'

Harker flashed her a look that had half a smile in it. They detoured around a clutch of tents, open to the night air, steam escaping from the large tubs of water within. Men and women scrubbed at sheets bearing pinkening stains. Eve turned her head away, towards the vastness of the camp.

'How many people are there here?' she asked.

'Dunno. Probably a thousand, all told. Maybe more. Mostly this is the 33rd, who finally deigned to grace us with their presence. There were only a few hundred of the 9th left, poor buggers, no wonder the barricades fell.'

He walked her past a rather hastily constructed corral, heavily guarded by men with large guns. Peering past them, Eve saw men in uniforms that were khaki, but different from the ones she'd seen so far. They had a more modern look to them, whereas Harker and the rest seemed to be wearing something from a WWII costume drama.

'Are they prisoners?' she asked, looking at the sullen men within. Funny, but they all seemed to be men. Or maybe the women of the Coalitionist army had been put somewhere else.

'Yep.'

'What's going to happen to them?'

'Probably round 'em up and shoot 'em in the morning.'

Eve flinched. So did the prisoners within hearing range. To her surprise though, Harker didn't stop and admit her to their ranks, but walked on past. He murmured softly as they left earshot, 'Actually they'll just be sent to POW camps to make munitions and roll bandages. But I can't resist winding 'em up.'

Eve nodded, her head bobbing back and forth, back and forth, like the bobble-head dolls Grrl Power had promoted somewhere in a universe far, far away. As Harker took out a cigarette and lit it, she found herself watching longingly.

He saw her, and said, 'That's a very hungry look for someone who doesn't smoke.'

'Well, maybe I should.' Maybe it'd soothe her shaking nerves.

'Nah. Filthy habit.' Harker blew out a stream of smoke. He was holding the cigarette in his left hand, she noticed; he always held it in his left hand, pinched between thumb and forefinger, his palm cupped around it.

'What happened to your finger?' she asked.

Harker glanced at his right hand. 'French sabre,' he said.

'You fought the French?'

'No,' he gave her another of those half-smiles. 'But they were supplying weapons to the rebels.' He lifted his hand, looked at the scars crisscrossing it. Eve, with the experience of the past few hours behind her, could tell it hadn't been a wound that had received a lot of attention.

'Bastard tried to cut the sword out of my hand,' he said. 'Kept hacking at it. Had to learn to do everything left-handed while it healed.'

'Can you use it properly now?' Eve asked, because in all honesty she'd never noticed him holding a pen or doing anything that involved fine motor skills. Except for smoking, of course.

'Oh aye, it's fine now. Aches a bit sometimes, but it works all right. Got off lightly. I know plenty of old soldiers who get pain in limbs they don't even have any more. Phantom limb, they call it. Bloody unfair, if you ask – Eve?'

She felt herself wavering, as if her bones weren't strong enough to keep her solid, as if she wasn't quite sure which way was vertical. The tents ahead of her tilted.

Daz had been using the *altar* for *amputations*.

She started to laugh.

'Eve?' said Harker again, from a great distance.

'Like a pagan sacrifice or something,' she giggled. 'Look out, here comes King Kong! What sort of god wants a limb, anyway? That's a bit crappy, isn't it? Like – I know! Like one of those eight-armed pagan gods, maybe that's how they got them–'

'Eve.' He had hold of her by the shoulders, which was odd because he was such a long way away, and impossibly tall, too, or was he standing on something?

She couldn't stop laughing.

It was forcing all the air out of her lungs; she couldn't breathe; she was sucking in huge chunks of air but it wasn't working, and now it *hurt;* she was panicking, laughter turning to sobs, *she was covered in blood*, and he'd been *chopping arms and legs* off, they fell on the *ground* and he *kicked them away* like *debris*, and there was *blood*, there was *so much damn blood, everywhere–*

'We'll wash the blood off,' said Harker, and Eve realised she'd been babbling that out loud. They were on the ground, in the mud, and he was holding her as she sobbed and shook and hiccupped with laughter, even though nothing was funny any more.

'Eve, it's all right. It's just shock. You'll be fine.' He was sitting beside her in the mud, his arm around her, just letting her shudder and bawl all over him. The coat had slipped off her shoulders and she was still wet with blood and it was smearing his jacket, but he didn't seem to mind. He was covered in blood.

Her eyes focused on the spatters of dark red flecking his skin.

'Were you hurt?' she quavered, hearing the weakness in her own voice and hating it.

'No. Nothing serious.'

'But there's blood …' She touched his face, his neck, rough with a week's beard and grimy with sweat and blood. In the hot flickering light of the small fires around them, his dirty skin gleamed.

'Not mine.'

Harker's hand covered her own, and shock travelled through Eve from her palm, right down her arm into her body.

He had grey eyes, the colour of gunmetal. There were smudges of blood and what might have been gunpowder on his face, his hair was tangled and damp with sweat and blood, and she could feel the pulse beating in his neck.

His lips were parted, and she moved towards them without even meaning to.

Towards is bad …

'Ah, Major Harker! Did you find your civilian?'

The moment broke almost audibly. Harker looked up at a moustachioed man in a suspiciously impeccable uniform and said, 'Yes, sir. This is her, sir – Eve Carpenter, Colonel Wilson.' He looked back down at Eve, in whom mortification was rising fast, and added, 'Touch of shock, sir. She was helping in the hospital.'

'Ah, yes. Not surprised.' Wilson loomed over Eve and said in a loud voice, 'Always a shock first time, my dear! Don't worry, it's all sterling work!'

Eve looked back up at him and said, 'I'm in shock, I'm not deaf.'

Besides her, she felt Harker's shoulders shake in what felt suspiciously like a chuckle, but she was too embarrassed to look at him. He still had his arm around her. She'd tried to kiss him!

'Ah. Yes. Capital,' said the Colonel, looking a bit wrong-footed. He recovered quickly, however, and said, 'Young Harker here saved the day, dontcha know! Handful of men against hundreds of filthy rebels. Absolutely capital. There'll be a medal in this for you, Harker, mark my word.'

'Thank you, sir,' Harker said. He picked up the squashed half of his cigarette from the mud and shook his head. 'Sir, if I could beg a favour?'

Wilson beamed. 'Of course, Harker! Anything you need.'

Harker, somewhat apologetically, left Eve sitting on the ground, where she started to feel a little bit foolish, while he spoke in hushed tones to the other officer, who had lots of shiny braid on his uniform, and no blood at all.

Harker lit up another cigarette as he spoke, moving so fast his hands blurred. He smoked when he was upset, Eve thought distantly, or when he was thinking.

He was upset now. A mad woman had tried to kiss him,

of course he was upset!

'Of course, my lad. You come with me and we'll see what we can find.'

Harker turned to Eve and held his hand out to her. She took it, but only because she'd have looked damn stupid ignoring it. What she did try to ignore, however, was the shock that ran through her again when his fingers touched hers.

And anyway, it wasn't his fault. She'd just been overwhelmed, and a man fresh from battle, dirty and heroic, was always going to be sexy. Right?

It didn't *mean* anything. He'd probably barely noticed.

Harker watched Tallulah usher Eve into the women's tent the squad had set up. At least, he tried to watch Tallulah, and not Eve, with her clinging t-shirt and her big eyes and her soft, lush, trembling mouth.

Her t-shirt is clinging because it's soaked with gore and blood, and her eyes are wide because she's in shock, he reminded himself sharply, but even that didn't help, because now he had fantasies of helping the shocked, stumbling Eve remove her dirty clothes and tenderly wash away the blood.

'Sir?' Tallulah said, and Harker's eyes remained on the tent for just a fraction of a second too long to pretend he hadn't been thinking about her. 'There's some fresh water in your tent, if you want to wash.'

Wash. Eve. Warm and trembling and soft and –

Dammit, he'd been doing fine until she'd gone into her tent, and then he'd blinked and in that second had imagined her naked and soapy, and it had all gone to hell. 'Yeah. Sure. Thanks.'

He stumbled into his own tent, hearing Banks's voice through the thin canvas. 'What are you smiling about?'

Tallulah, laughter in her voice, replied, 'Major Harker. I

think he's sweet on our captive.'

If she's not a spy, then she's mad. Either of these things ought to be enough to cancel out big blue-green eyes and clinging t-shirts.

Harker wished he could convince himself on that point.

'What, Eve?' Banks said. 'Well, I wouldn't say no.'

'You'd have to fight the Major off first.'

He threw his clothes on the floor and tested the water, which was annoyingly hot. Cold would have been more useful.

'That's enough,' said Charlie. She was cleaning her sword. 'He's not sweet on anyone.'

There was a pause. Harker nodded to himself. Damn right he wasn't. Being sweet on a suspected spy would be a ridiculous thing to do. *If you feel sorry for the enemy, the enemy will kill you.*

'Jealous, Lieutenant?' Daz asked, and Harker wondered when he'd found his way to their little camp. He must have spent more time comforting Eve than he'd realised.

'I know popular opinion says that I'm Major Harker's lover,' Charlie said, 'but I'm too ugly for him and he's too bitter for me. Besides, I saw him through dysentery when we were campaigning near the Scottish border and unless you're mad about someone it's hard to be attracted to them after that.'

There was an embarrassed silence. Harker frowned at the tent wall, slightly hurt. Bitter? Did she really think he was bitter?

'And I think I'm done with my stew,' Daz said. 'Did you have to bring up dysentery?'

'Sorry.'

'I think if you really loved someone then it wouldn't matter if they had dysentery or something really disgusting,' Tallulah said.

'Really?' said Daz. 'You ever seen any of the really disgusting diseases, Private?'

'Well, no, sir, but I mean ... if you already loved someone, then surely it wouldn't matter?'

Harker threw himself down on his narrow, uncomfortable bunk, while he waited for the water to cool. Great. Now the squad was discussing his love life. Even Charlie! Harker knew half the army thought he and Charlie were lovers – and he'd always been both amused and depressed by the idea. Amused because they had such a lack of imagination, and depressed, because if they couldn't see that what existed between him and Charlie was loyalty, pure and simple, then maybe they were missing one of the basic tenets of the army.

You followed your commander, and you protected your brothers – even if they were sisters. It was what Harker did. It was what he'd always done.

'You're quite right,' Charlie said eventually. 'Love's a fine thing, and so's loyalty, but I'd ask if you could all remember that they're different things.'

'You're very loyal to the Major,' Tallulah mumbled.

'Yes, I am, Private. That's my point.'

It was just because he was restless. That was all. After all, the last time he'd had a woman had been ... well, it had been Saskia. And that had been well before the divorce had come through. Before Southwark. Maybe before Newmarket. He couldn't remember.

That in itself was kind of sad.

Harker realised he was counting not just months, but years, and groaned. Truth was, for a long time the only woman he'd actually wanted was Saskia. The problem was that she hadn't wanted him back. Lack of ambition, she'd thrown at him, and Harker had been baffled.

'I have ambition,' he said. 'My ambition is to protect my men and win the war.'

'Very noble,' Saskia fired back, 'but you could do it better with a promotion.'

Romance had been the first casualty of their private war. Sex had been the second.

He stuck his head in the bucket of cooling water and tried to drown out those images of Eve stripping naked in the next tent.

Chapter Eleven

When they left camp the next day, Harker offered Eve a ride in the wagon, but she chose to walk, needing to pound out feelings she didn't quite understand. She'd always found a physical distraction helped when she needed to think, either walking or playing the guitar or doing housework.

Now she was walking, marching in fact, and with her body occupied her mind could think.

She hadn't dreamed much last night, but she suspected Daz had slipped something into her drink to make her sleep. Probably just as well. She could see the sticky puddles of blood whenever she closed her eyes, see the saw marks in severed bones, the skin flapping loose, the steady pump, pump of veins emptying themselves of blood. She could see all the muscles and sinews, and when she let her guard down she could see the pink squibbly bits deep inside a person that ought never to see the light of day.

She was developing a Lady Macbeth-style obsession with washing her hands, which couldn't be good.

The rest of the squad had been kind to her, in varying degrees. Harker had avoided her somewhat, but she couldn't really blame him. The others had made an effort to talk to her, make her comfortable, as if she was an invalid.

I must have been in shock, she told herself. *I thought I was acting quite normal most of the time.*

When they broke for lunch she talked and smiled and felt quite proud of herself for participating, but was vaguely aware that she shouldn't *have* to be proud of herself for participating. She should just ... participate.

Harker hadn't chained her up, but she got the feeling he

was watching her all the time. Probably wondering if she was going to try to kiss him again. Well, fat chance. She wasn't crazy any more today – well, no more than she had been since she woke up in this mad world – and she didn't tend to want to kiss people who weren't talking to her.

Hah!

When they set off again, Daz was driving and Harker was marching with the squad. He walked alongside Eve for a while, then said, 'You okay today?'

'Fine,' she said.

'How're your feet?'

'They're fine.' *Damn sight better than some of the feet I saw yesterday. They're attached, for one thing.*

'Sleep all right last night?'

'Fine.'

'Three fines. You'll notice I haven't cuffed you today?'

'Yep.' She realised he was looking for something else, and added, 'Thank you.'

Harker gave up, and went to walk with Charlie.

Eve didn't know if they'd run out of Roman roads to travel on, or if Harker was taking back routes on purpose, but they were walking along narrow, badly made tracks between small, squalid villages, trails that were deeply rutted with the tracks of cartwheels. Every now and then, someone had filled in the worst of the holes with rocks and straw, but they frequently had to stop and haul the wagon out of the mud. They were walking with heavy packs in order to lighten the wagon, but it didn't seem to be helping much.

On either side of them stretched endless fenland, the featureless marshes eventually fading off into chilly mist.

When it got dark, Harker ordered a rest, then told them they'd be walking another couple of hours. Banks groaned, Tallulah made a face, but no one complained, least of all Eve, who barely heard anyway.

The scent of the sea came rolling over the dark land as they crossed yet another marshy fen, this time in the dark. Harker himself was scouting ahead, although they were using a track raised above the fens and well-indented with cart tracks, so no one seemed particularly worried.

Isn't the Wash famously unpredictable? Eve thought. *Shifting sandbanks and moveable coastline, full of shipwrecks. Maybe we'll find an unstable bit of coastline and just fall into the sea.*

Would anyone miss me?

She'd probably have carried on in this nihilistic vein had not Harker called a halt for the night. Eve hadn't really noticed, but they'd finally come to the end of the fens and had been walking through an increasingly dark and rather forbidding wood. Or it might be a forest. She wasn't sure. They were in another deep ditch, a riverbed or something, sunk from sight between the trees.

Charlie handed out duties, camp was made, and food served out. Daz ordered everyone to change their socks before their feet went mouldy.

'Court-martial for anyone with trench foot,' Harker added, with that half-smile of his.

Eve took off her trainers automatically, and then realised she'd once again been given a pack of cooking supplies to carry, and didn't have any spare clothes. That morning she'd been given khakis to dress in, with the explanation that her own clothes were still in rather a state. She didn't know if her jeans, t-shirt and spare underwear had been left behind or not. She was finding it difficult to care.

'Here.' Someone was holding out something soft and woollen … yes, a pair of socks. She started to look up to see who it was, but then registered the missing little finger, and said, 'Thank you, Major.'

'Welcome. Sorry, ain't got any spare boots for you.'

'That's okay. I'm fine.'

'Yeah, you must be, it's all you've said all day.'

She looked up to see what he meant by that, but he was gone, vanishing into the darkness outside the firelight. Eve put the clean socks on, and when she looked up he was back again, this time holding out a guitar as if it was a bunch of flowers.

Eve stared for a second.

'I can't put that on my feet,' she said.

Harker grinned at her. 'Can you play it?'

'I ... I'm a bit out of practice.'

'Found it in the 33rd's stores,' he said. 'Probably get used for firewood if no one can find a use for it.'

A stab of feeling caught Eve at the thought of destroying a musical instrument, even one as shabby as this. 'Needs tuning,' she said distantly.

'You can tell by looking at it?'

'Yeah. One of the strings is loose. Might not be any good.'

'Well, maybe we can replace it. Be a shame to let it burn. What're guitar strings made of?'

'Nylon and steel,' Eve said.

'Oh. Well, it's yours if you want it.'

He held it out, and Eve took it. Rested it across her thigh. Ran her hand over its waist, where the wood was smooth, almost silky. The guitar was small, slim, built like a Spanish guitar but with a wider fretboard.

She used to have a Martin like this, and a bigger Gibson with steel strings. Had borrowed the session musicians' instruments, getting a feel for them, learning how to play a guitar with six or twelve strings, memorising chords until she could play them blindfolded, sitting in her hotel room playing softly into the night, calming herself, while the others were out at parties and nightclubs.

Unconsciously, she ran her fingers over the strings–

–and winced.

Blimey, it was out of tune. She turned the pegs, bit by bit pulling the sound into shape, until she could strum her fingers over the strings and get a chord that didn't make her flinch.

'Could use a new top E,' she muttered, 'but you'll do. Yes, you will.'

Her fingers formed a D minor, a D minor 7th, a B flat, an F … familiar chords, chords she'd played dozens, hundreds of times before, sitting alone in her damp poky flat playing on the guitar she'd bought for a fiver in a pawn shop.

'That song,' Harker said softly from beside her. She hadn't even noticed he was there. 'You played that before. On the piano. What did you say it was called?'

'*Yesterday*.'

'It's beautiful.'

'Yes, it is.' She reached the chorus, those quick chords in succession, a work of genius. 'Apparently it came fully formed into his mind, he woke up humming it. Kept asking the others if they knew the song, and he eventually realised he'd written it in his sleep.'

'Very impressive.'

'Well, he's Paul McCartney. He's a genius.'

'He is if he wrote that song.'

Eve played the song out, not singing, just listening to the chords. *That strain again, it had a dying fall*. She used to wish she could write a song that was as good as just one of those chord changes. But the songs never came. She had nothing to sing about.

She played a few more chords absently, a few more McCartney strokes of brilliance. Then some Harrison, her fingers moving into *While My Guitar Gently Weeps* before her brain had entirely caught up.

She didn't sing, just played. Old songs, new songs,

favourites and some too obscure for anyone to know. Although none of her current audience seemed to recognise any of them at all. Some of them chatted quietly as she played, some of them listened. After a little while Martindale came off guard and was replaced by Charlie. Eventually Tallulah, yawning, stumbled off to bed. Before long the rest followed, and Eve realised she'd been playing for an hour, and her breath was clouding in front of her face. Her fingers were frozen, but she hadn't really noticed.

Harker stayed beside her, leaning back against the ditch wall, saying nothing.

'I should stop,' she said, mid-chord. 'I – I'll keep them awake.'

'Haven't you ever heard of a lullaby?' Harker said.

Eve made to put the guitar down, but Harker's hand covered hers, and she went still.

'You can keep on playing if you want,' he said. 'I'll stay up with you.'

And she realised. Her eyes met his and she realised. He hadn't just brought the guitar along on a whim. The wagon was small and guitars were large, not to mention rubbish material for firewood.

How did he know how much music brought her out, soothed her, calmed her? For the first time today, she didn't feel disconnected.

'Wow, you're good,' she murmured.

'What?'

She stood up. 'I think it's time I got some sleep,' she said. 'I'll see you in the morning.'

He nodded, standing also, and watched her carefully fit the guitar back into the wagon and cover it over while he banked the fire.

As he brushed past her, she reached out and grabbed his arm. He glanced at her, surprised. 'You won't,' she began, licking her lips nervously.

'Won't what?'

'Please don't, um, tell anyone about ...' *About me trying to kiss you. About me clinging to you like a life raft. About the way you looked at me.* 'About ... what happened after the ... at the Fen Causeway.'

His eyes narrowed thoughtfully.

'About me having a bit of a breakdown and ...' *Oh God,* please *don't make me say it.*

His hand rested briefly on her shoulder. 'About me fetching you from the hospital and bringing you back to the camp without incident?' he said softly.

Eve nodded gratefully.

He gave her a tired, faded, and above all kind smile. 'Not a word,' he said, and turned away.

Just before he went into his tent, she said, 'Will?' and he turned, barely visible in the darkness under the trees.

'Thank you,' she said, and his silhouette nodded, then disappeared.

Harker let them sleep in the next morning, and travel a while in the wagon. They'd walked a long way yesterday, but he'd wanted to get off the fens before they made camp, and he was damned if he would let them sit in the wagon and sink the bloody thing.

He could have detoured west and taken Ermine Street, which was much steadier for a wagon, but was also currently lousy with army patrols and barricades every few miles. According to Colonel Wilson, the 17th was marching down to help the 33rd retake Peterborough, and Harker preferred to stay well away from that. He didn't need any more delays, wasted days and traumatised men.

Not that Eve was one of his men. But she was no good to him in the zombified state she'd been wandering around in yesterday.

He watched her carefully as they broke camp. She seemed brighter, more like herself again.

Harker had been given some communiqué from Colonel Wilson to take to the 17th's temporary camp at Coningsby. He wasn't intending to stay there, but he figured if they drove the wagon at a fair pace, he could save some time and swap horses when they got there. North of Coningsby, it was another fifty or so miles to Hatfield Chase, the house on the edge of the Wolds where Wheeler had arranged for them to stay. If they'd been able to go closer to Lincoln, it would have been a much shorter journey, but the Coalitionists were apparently making a move on that city, and he didn't really want to risk it.

As it was, they'd have to cross Ermine Street, and part of the reason for going to Coningsby was to find out where the barricades were so they could cross there and minimise their chances of getting shot by their own side.

He drove the length of the disused canal where they'd spent the night, and when it veered off course, set the squad to marching the last ten miles. Once more Eve marched uncomplainingly and he gave the reins to Daz and marched behind her, just in case she had a relapse.

Not to watch her move. Not at all. They'd been going an hour or so when he became aware of someone humming.

'Eve?'

Her steps faltered. 'Sorry.'

'What's that tune?' He didn't recognise it, but he was happy she was humming. Yesterday's silence had been far too loud for his liking.

'Oh ... an old show tune.'

'Show? What show?'

'It's called *Les Misérables*. It's about–' She broke off and sighed. 'About something that probably never happened.'

'Why do you say that?'

'Well, since according to your history books France has won every war she's ever been involved in and been a powerhouse of finance and industry for as long as anyone can remember, I doubt there was much call for a student revolt in 1832.'

And just when he thought she was becoming more normal, she went and said something crazy again.

'What do you mean, "*your* history books"? What other kind are there?'

'The ones ... the ones I remember. It doesn't matter. I'm crazy, take no notice of me.'

Beside him, Charlie shot him a warning look, but Harker pressed on. *Do you really believe she's mad?* 'Tell me about this revolt?'

'I don't really know a lot about it. The script doesn't go into detail. But basically the students in Paris stage a revolt against the government because of the way the poor are treated. It fails terribly and nearly all of them die.'

'That sounds like a fun show,' Charlie said dryly.

'Er, yes,' Harker said. 'What was the song you were humming? Does it have words?'

After a few silent paces, Eve started to sing. Her words had a definite rhythm, as if they were intended to be marched to, and were about the songs of angry men.

Charlie shot him a look, and he knew what she meant. It sounded like a marching song, but not one the army might use. She was even singing about barricades.

Harker winced. She must be mad, because no spy would sing like that.

'All right, that's enough,' he said, when Eve had exhorted them all to join in the fight that would give them the right to be free.

Eve stopped, and Harker felt like hell. Her voice had been

gaining in confidence, singing made her happy, and she'd been so–

Bang.

'What the hell was that?'

Tallulah flinched. Charlie went for her gun.

'Sounded like a shell, sir.'

'Halt!' Harker yelled, and the squad did so, the wagon rattling to a stop slightly belatedly behind them.

They all listened. Another shell exploded.

'Hell,' Harker swore, 'bloody blast and damn.' He fumbled inside his coat for his map. Coningsby was supposed to be a small camp, little in the way of defence. Were they under attack?

Or were they, as Harker suspected, the ones attacking? Sitting in trenches, taking pot shots at the Coalitionists, who were no doubt sitting in trenches taking pot shots back, as they waited for an opportunity to move on Lincoln.

As the aural smash of another shell boomed in their ears, the squad turned to look north.

'Another battle?' Eve said, her voice a little ragged. Beside her, Banks flicked off the safety catch on his gun.

'I don't bloody need this,' Harker said. 'Right. Eve, you're back in the wagon. Rest of you, dump your packs, get your guns out, I'm going to try and avoid this but it might not be possible. Quick march!'

The camp at Coningsby had begun as little more than a base for the newly formed 17th. Now, what had once been a small village had turned into a huge, sprawling camp for what looked like half the army. Harker, bullying his way into the stone keep overlooking the camp, ascertained that it was now a base for several battalions, who had indeed dug trenches. But they weren't shelling an opposing line of dugouts. They were shelling Lincoln.

The Coalitionists had taken the city, and now the army

was having to attack to get it back.

The enemy was advancing all over the north. West of the Pennines there were entirely separate battles being fought to keep them away from Liverpool and the other ports, but over in the east, they were spreading fast.

The problem wasn't just that they were marching from city to city. They didn't always have a damn army on the move. They just sort of formed one right under everyone's noses, and the next thing you knew, they'd popped up like a mole from underground and taken a city.

Harker gathered intelligence and supplies from the camp at Coningsby, and tried not to let his men see how rattled he was. Every time he looked at a map, there were more red splotches on it. Like the sort of rash that came with the plague. Death usually followed.

Time was running out.

Chapter Twelve

Taking a wide route to avoid the trenches, and any shells that fell wide of the mark, Harker led the squad east before going north, riding partway and marching the rest, annoyed because this new attack meant he was having to take a far wider route around Lincoln than he'd planned.

At least they were out of the damn fens and they could walk without fear of falling into a bog, which, since the mist was coming in low and thick, Harker was grateful for. Once the noises of the Battle of Lincoln had faded behind them, muffled by the creeping mist, some of his tension faded.

Things weren't as bad as they seemed. Hell, they couldn't be.

'Hey, Eve,' he said, walking up alongside her. 'How about a little marching music?'

'You didn't like the last song I sang,' she retorted.

'Well, no, because it sounded to my ears like a rebel song.'

'It was a rebel song,' she said. 'Weren't you listening? About the student revolution?'

'Aye, but in case you hadn't noticed, we're currently fighting *against* a bunch of rebels.'

'So? Don't you want to hear their point of view?'

Harker stared at her, but she didn't seem to be joking. 'No,' he said clearly and slowly, just in case she was secretly an imbecile.

'That's very close-minded of you.'

'Eve, they are the *enemy*. I ain't paid to think about points of view.'

'Why? Because you might start questioning why you're fighting in the first place?'

'Careful,' said Charlie, ahead of her.

'Oh, come on, I'm your damn prisoner anyway. If I can't say it, who can?'

'No one,' Harker said. 'So shut up.'

'No, I won't. Why won't you even consider their point of view? They want – what, to join the French Empire? Okay, I know it's abhorrent to you, and I'm British, too, I understand the whole Francophobe thing. But listen. They've got to have a reason. So far as I can tell, this whole country is on its knees. You're rationing everything, from clothes to food, you can't import anything much, because you can't afford to, because what do you export?'

Harker opened and shut his mouth.

'No, really, what do you export? What's your contribution to the world economy? Because listen, if you actually joined the French Empire, then maybe they'd be obliged to protect you, and share trade with you.'

'The hell they would,' Charlie said evenly.

'Why do the French even want to annex England? They must see something about this place that's worthwhile. Because from where I'm standing, we're broke and backwards, and it's just not even worth their bother.'

'They probably want to use us as a jumping off point to invade Wales and Scotland,' Charlie said.

'Why? What have they got? They're no better off than we are,' said Harker.

'From here they could probably invade Norway,' Tallulah opined. 'And they're a much more advanced country.'

'How come? I mean, what do they have in Norway? Snow and pines.'

'They have oil,' Harker said. 'Comes up out of the sea. Don't ask me how, sea must be black over there, but–'

'Wait,' Eve said. 'Oil? Gas and oil?'

'How're they going to get gas out of the sea?' Harker

said. 'Don't be daft.'

'It can exist in bubbles under the seabed,' Daz said. 'I'd imagine they use some sort of siphon arrangement.'

'Yes,' Eve said triumphantly. 'Look, don't you see? It's all in the North Sea. Gallons of the stuff. Right off the coast of England! And Scotland. You must have some rights – er, the whole International Waters thing? I mean, what are your fishing rights?'

Harker blinked at her.

'Equal distance from both coasts,' Banks said, unexpectedly. 'Not much in the Channel or the Irish Sea, but probably a couple of hundred miles in the North Sea.'

This time Harker stared at Banks, and he wasn't the only one.

'Poacher,' he reminded them. 'Lot of money in fish, but all that boat stuff,' he shuddered, 'too bleedin' cold and wet for me.'

'Look,' Eve said, 'if you don't even know it's there, they could be taking it and you'd have no idea. That stuff is worth a fortune. I mean – where do you get your oil from? What do you power your cars with? I know you don't have many, but what do you use?'

'There's oil under the ground,' Daz said. 'In some of the coalfields. Not far from here, actually.'

'Sir,' Charlie shot him a look, 'doesn't that come under the heading "classified information"?'

'What, that we run our cars on oil?'

'No, where we get it from.'

'Oh, leave it off, they probably know that already,' Eve said.

There was a short silence. 'How?' Harker asked.

'I don't know! Probably Google.' She scowled at his look of incomprehension. 'Look, oil refineries are big places, right? Fairly visible from an aerial view?'

'Are you saying they're flying over us and spying?' Charlie said.

'Well, yes, maybe. Or–'

'Is that what you were doing?'

Eve stopped walking and put her hands on her hips. 'For the last time,' she said, 'I am not a bloody spy. I don't know how I ended up here or why it's so different from what I know, but I am not a goddamned spy.'

'But how do you know all this?'

She threw up her hands. 'It's common knowledge! Jesus Christ.' She started walking again – stomping, to Harker's eyes. He noticed Tallulah frowning, and realised that to a nicely brought-up young lady, Eve's language might be considered a bit unnecessary. He grinned to himself. Personally, he loved a bit of unnecessary language, but it was always fun to annoy Eve. 'I hope you are not taking the Lord's name in vain,' he said severely. And the look Eve gave him could have cut glass.

He lit up a cigarette, which went somewhat soggy in the heavy mist, and thought about what she'd said. There had to be a reason the French wanted England. They wouldn't annex a poor, useless country, it'd cost them more than it was worth.

Harker belonged to England body and soul, but even he had to admit the place was hardly a land of milk and honey.

What did they have that France wanted?

If Eve was right, then there were reserves of oil and gas under the sea. He couldn't quite understand that, but then he didn't understand motorcars, and they existed sure enough.

What else? Well, it was a fertile land. Sunshine and rain, great growing for wheat and barley, vegetables, even fruits, although they had plenty of that in France, too. You couldn't grow anything exciting, like oranges or grapes, or even tobacco, dammit. The Americans had become very rich on tobacco, and on cotton, too – although England imported her cotton from Egypt, thanks to some deal ex-Queen Diana had struck with her new boyfriend.

England had lots of coal. It ran most of the things that needed to be run, powered ships and mills, generated electricity for those who could afford their own generators and, ironically, ran the oil drills in Nottinghamshire. But was it enough, and good enough, to export? There wasn't, as far as Harker knew, anything like silver or gold in the ground, although there was some iron and tin. Hard to imagine anyone invading for the sake of iron, tin and coal.

Hard to imagine anyone invading England for, well, anything. And yet people did. The Romans, the Vikings had settled here; even the French, a thousand years ago.

And that'd be the last time, if Harker had anything to do with it.

Late in the afternoon Charlie brought his attention to a ruined priory, in the shelter of which they made camp and burned a couple of large fires to fight the mist off. Banks made another of his stews, which were very hearty but Harker was getting a little sick of them, and Daz handed Eve her guitar.

'I'm not sure that's a good idea,' she said. 'I might play something seditious.'

'Attempt not to,' Harker said, still irritated over the *broke and backwards* comment.

'Well, I don't know,' she said, sticking her chin out. 'I didn't think singing about something that didn't happen more than a hundred years ago was seditious, but you decided it was.'

'Eve–'

'All right,' she said, a mutinous gleam in her eye, 'how about this? This isn't inciting anyone to anything. It's about silence. You should like it.'

And she started playing, just a couple of notes, up and down, up and down, and started singing about the sound of silence, which was a stupid thing if you asked Harker, because silence had no sound.

And then he listened to her words, and realised what she was singing about.

'All right, you've made your point,' he said, and she gave him a smug smile.

'I don't get it,' said Banks. Tallulah patted his arm.

'It'll come to you,' she said.

'I'm going to bed,' Harker said, chucking the butt of his cigarette into the fire. 'Play what you want.'

Damn her, how did she do it? The words were meaningless, they didn't make any sense.

And yet–

'But silence doesn't have a sound,' Banks was still saying as Harker shut his eyes.

And yet, there was something pervasive about that song. Something that made him feel guilty, and he didn't know why.

'All right, all right, I'll sing something normal,' Eve said, and started singing some ditty about love. Harker listened for anything dangerous, found only vacuous sentiments, and settled down to sleep. He woke briefly when Daz came in, squinted at his watch and said, 'Did Banks go on guard?'

Daz nodded in the darkness. 'He's watching Eve. The others have turned in, too.'

Harker nodded and tried to go back to sleep, but Eve was still singing. To herself, he realised, not for an audience.

And it was beautiful.

She was singing about wishes, about leaving clouds behind her, about troubles melting away. A fine sentiment, Harker thought as he closed his eyes. Wishing never got anybody anywhere. If you wanted something, in Harker's experience you had to fight for it. Although lately, fighting didn't seem to be doing much good, either.

Maybe that was what she'd done. Wished upon a star and woken up somewhere … how did she put it? Over the rainbow. Well, that was what you got for gliding over the river.

The longing in her voice was almost tangible, and being flippant wasn't working. *I must be tired,* Harker thought, *because I'm beginning to believe her. She's singing about a better world, and I'm beginning to believe it's true.*

Maybe because she sang it with such conviction. Such purity and strength. Probably the rest of the squad were feeling it, too. Probably it wasn't just him who wanted to go out there and make her feel better.

He wondered if she'd feel better if he went out there and kissed her silly.

No, probably not.

Dammit.

The morning brought more mist, which burned off around midday. By which time the squad had been moving for four or five hours, and Eve's throat was somewhat raw from singing.

Most of the things she sang were inconsequential, but every now and then she threw in something to annoy Harker. He didn't seem to like the one about where all the flowers had gone, or the one about the bells of hell, although she noticed he didn't stop her from singing them. He just complained.

'Can't you sing something uncontroversial?' he said.

'But all the best songs are controversial.' Eve gave a mirthless laugh. 'You want something bland, I'll sing a Grrl Power hit, although they're all so awful you'll be begging me to sing about the glories of revolution.'

'Go on, then,' Harker said, 'sing us one of those songs from your famous band.'

Eve sighed, and did, and about five bars in she could tell they all hated it. She didn't mind. She hated it, too.

Into the following silence, she said, 'See, I told you they were rubbish songs.'

'Then why'd you join the band?' Harker asked.

She sighed. 'Because I was seventeen and stupid.'

'Those two so often go together,' Harker agreed, and Tallulah, who had until recently been seventeen, wrinkled her nose.

Eve said, 'Okay. Here's one that's much more tuneful, I promise, and it's by Sheryl Crow, and she's an absolute poet.'

'Is it one of your "protest songs"?' Harker asked suspiciously.

'No.'

'What's it called?'

Eve hesitated. '*Letter to God*.'

'No.'

'But it's not–'

'I ain't bringing religion into this, Eve. No.'

'It's not about religion.'

'Oh, aye? A song with the word "God" in the title? What's it about, then?'

Another brief pause. 'Well, it's sort of protesting against–'

'No.'

'But–'

'No,' Harker said, more emphatically.

'Oh, get lost,' Eve snarled, and refused to sing any more.

When they broke for lunch, Eve pointedly avoided Harker, and found herself highly irritated when he didn't seem to notice.

They crossed the barricades at Ermine Street without incident, other than one of the sergeants recalling how

Mister Harker had saved his life back in Nottingham in '04, and approached their destination as it turned dark. The mist returned, and a huge gothic tower of a building loomed out of the mist, the setting sun swathing it in an eerie red halo.

'Is anyone else expecting to see a big black dog?' Eve whispered, and then very nearly screamed when a dog barked from inside the house.

Harker, she noticed, kept his face immobile, but his shoulders were shaking.

'This,' he announced as they crunched up the drive, 'is Hatfield Chase, the home of Sir Dennis and Lady Winterton.'

'Not Dracula?' Eve asked.

'Tallulah, you know these people. Are they acquainted with a person known as Dracula?' Harker asked, straight-faced.

All eyes turned to Tallulah, who winced. 'I don't know,' she said.

'Hmm,' said Eve, leaning against one of the pillars supporting the grand entryway. 'Mr Harker and Dracula's Castle. Just call me Mina.'

'Eve–' Harker began, then shook his head and turned away from her. 'Sir Dennis and Lady Winterton,' he repeated determinedly. 'They are friends of General Wheeler and staunch supporters of Parliament. They are also filthy rich, have donated not only large amounts of money but a car to the war effort, plus,' he looked as if he could hardly believe it, 'they have in addition *another* car. They have a private oil supply for said vehicle which also powers the electricity to most of the house.'

'Ooh, *electricity*. Do they have *ceiling lights*?' Eve asked waspishly.

'That's none of your business. You will be polite to them. You will be respectful. You will not leave muddy footprints around and you will watch your language; Private Banks, I am looking at you.'

'Yessir.'

'We will be using this house as a base. As it has electricity, we will be setting up the computer here as and when we find appropriate parts.'

'Gonna build it from the keyboard up, are you?' Eve said, and was ignored.

'Captain Haran, you will stay here the majority of the time and when we are away, Eve Carpenter is in your sole custody. She disappears, you are responsible, is that clear?'

'Yes, sir.'

'Right.' Harker stepped up and lifted the big brass door knocker on the big oak door. It echoed, even through the fog, and when the door opened, it was with a creak which made Eve giggle.

Harker saluted. 'Major Harker of the 75th of Foot, at your service,' he said.

The elderly man standing there looked him over and didn't seem impressed, but he said, 'I will fetch her ladyship,' and disappeared into the gloom of the house.

The squad fidgeted awkwardly on the steps. Behind them, the horses whickered. Eve tried to remember whether Jonathan Harker had married Mina or Lucy – and which of them survived Dracula.

Harker's wife, seduced in a remote gothic castle. She shivered, and not because of the cold.

The clatter of heels heralded the arrival of the lady of the house who, like the pearls and evening dress she wore, had clearly seen better days but wasn't about to admit it. 'Ah, yes,' she said. 'Now, do come in, it's glacial out there. That's it, into the hall; there aren't many of you, are there? Do you have any horses? Benson will show you where to put them.'

Harker motioned to Banks to follow the butler, who looked at him as if he smelt bad.

'Now, my husband and I were just partaking of some sherry,' said Lady Winterton, as she led them across the tiled floor of the cavernous lobby, her heels clicking. As she pushed open a thick door, a cloud of cigar smoke greeted them.

'This is my husband, Sir Dennis. Dennis, do wake up.'

Sir Dennis, who had been snoozing by the fire, snorted and smacked his lips. He had grey hair, a thick moustache, and a purple nose. Eve could *feel* Harker trying not to laugh.

'What? What? Oh,' Sir Dennis said, peering at the squad, who were looking rather the worse for wear. 'Oh yes. Hmm.' His gaze lingered on Tallulah. 'D'you know, that young filly's the absolute spit of Brig Watling-Coburg's oldest?'

Eve struggled to keep a straight face. *I didn't know people actually talked like that.*

'Remember, Margaret, she married that dreadful common little oik from the ranks?'

The squad froze. Inside Eve's head, a memory popped like a burst vein. And in an accent as crisp as a February morning, Harker said, 'Indeed, sir. I think I can bring him to mind.'

Charlie was laughing so hard she could barely stay on her chair, 'I thought I was going to *die*.'

'When you said,' Daz put on his poshest accent, '"Can't trust the rank-and-file at all, sir," I thought that was it. I thought, I can't keep a straight face any more.'

I could, Eve thought, her shoulders tight, not sharing in the fun. Irritation, hot and prickly, spread through her veins.

'But how could he not know?' Banks said, incredulous. They were in the kitchen, having beaten a hasty retreat before the squad all exploded into laughter. 'If he was there at your wedding, sir?'

Tallulah giggled into her mug, which contained something

rather stronger than tea. 'He looks a little different now,' she said.

Eve glanced at Harker, who was cradling a mug in scarred hands. His jacket was unbuttoned and stained with mud and blood. He didn't seem to have shaved once during the entire journey, and had the hairstyle of a man who thinks a comb is for nancies.

Eve wanted to thump him, and the really annoying part was that she didn't really know why.

'Oi, less of it, Private,' he said. 'Just 'cos I ain't wearing my shiny dress uniform.'

Tallulah giggled again. Eve figured the gin was going to her head.

'*You* wore a shiny dress uniform?' Daz said.

'Well, when I got married. So did Charlie, didn't you, Charlie?'

Daz goggled. 'When did you get married?'

The rest of the squad burst into laughter, except for Eve, who still wasn't finding it as hilarious as the rest of them.

Was it the sudden revelation that Harker's ex-wife ran the regiment? It hadn't bothered her when she knew it was Tallulah's sister in charge, and it hadn't bothered her to know Harker was divorced.

But then, she'd sort of imagined that his relationship with his ex-wife was as distant and painful as her parents' had been. She hadn't imagined that he'd still be literally taking orders from her.

Still, when it came down to it, close to her.

It shouldn't be bothering Eve at all. But that very fact made it all the more irritating.

'I didn't,' Charlie said. 'I was best man at Mister Harker's.'

'Best woman?' Banks said.

'We're all men in the military, Private,' Martindale said.

'Yeah? Then why don't we all share showers?'

'Speaking of,' Harker said, getting to his feet, 'housekeeper's made up rooms for us. Seems the West Wing is afflicted with damp, so there weren't quite enough to go around.'

The rest of them groaned, apart from Banks, who perked up.

'We're all sharing?' he said, waggling his eyebrows at Tallulah, who giggled some more and kicked him under the table.

Eve entertained dark thoughts about Harker sharing with his ex-wife.

'The housekeeper apologises but she's only got one room for the male enlisted men and one for the female enlisted men. Which means, Banks, as the only male enlisted man – stop laughing, Lu – you get your own room.'

'I what?' Banks said, astonished.

'Where do I go?' said Eve.

Harker glanced at her and frowned. 'You can sleep with the bleeding servants if you don't stop scowling.'

'... never had me own room ...'

Eve stood up, her expression no less cheerful. 'Fine. Room in the attic, is it? Or shall I curl up in the fireplace?'

'Sleep where you like, then, I don't care,' said Harker, no longer smiling. He nodded at the rest of the squad, and stomped out.

'Well done,' said Charlie, and trotted after him, which only made Eve scowl harder.

'If she was one of my men I'd set her to digging latrines,' Harker said to Charlie as they climbed the servants' stairs.

'Do it anyway,' Charlie said. 'She's not exactly a civilian.'

'Yeah, but she might be. What if she just hit her head or something? Then we're abusing a prisoner.'

Charlie rolled her eyes. 'And what if she's a spy? Then

you're being far too lax with her.'

'Yeah, but what if–' Harker broke off and raised his hands. 'No. I ain't doing this, it's going to drive me crazy. I'm going to take Sir Dennis's car tomorrow, recce around Leeds, see what the security's like there.'

'Can't imagine them just letting people walk in,' Charlie said.

'Yeah. Reckon we'll be looking at guards, maybe identification papers. If that's the case, I'll have Banks nick some.'

'What, and pretend to be people who live there?' Charlie frowned. 'No. What if someone on the gate knows the person whose papers you've stolen?'

Harker rolled his eyes. 'Then we'll use them to make our own copies. I don't know, Charlie, I'm winging this.' He paused, and added, 'But don't tell anyone I said that.'

She grinned, pushing open the door that led to the corridor of the East Wing where they'd been billeted.

'There's a bathroom at the end,' he pointed. 'Yours is the third on the left. Night, Charlie.'

'Night, sir.'

Harker, as the superior officer, had been given not just a room but a suite, which had a bedroom, sitting room, and its own bathroom. Harker had never had his own bathroom before. Hell, until he got divorced, he'd never had his own bedroom.

He wandered around for a bit, turning on the hot and cold running water, flushing the toilet just for the hell of it, flicking the electric lights on and off. Sir Dennis might be an ass, but he kept his guests in fine style.

The bed was divinely soft, a little disturbing for someone used to a blanket on the ground. Not remotely tired, he pulled on his clothes again to go down to the kitchen for a glass of something. Milk, maybe with the last of the gin in it. Or maybe just the gin on its own.

He was only two paces down the corridor when the bathroom door opened and Eve came out, looking freshly scrubbed. She hesitated when she saw him, then scowled and turned away.

'Eve,' he said, and she stopped. He saw, rather than heard, her sigh. Then she turned around, one eyebrow raised, her expression telling him she wasn't nearly done being angry with him.

'Look,' he said, 'I don't know what's got you in this mood, but–'

'Then try and figure it out,' she snapped, and Harker lost his temper.

'Why?' he said. 'Eve, you are not one of my men, I have no obligation to you, and I sure as hell don't care what makes you happy. I have bigger things to worry about than if you're offended or not. But I do need you on my team, so–'

'Oh, do you? Then you might try treating me like I am a member of your team,' Eve said, 'and not a prisoner or a servant, which is what I've been so far.'

'I do not treat you like a servant,' Harker said, surprised. He didn't think he'd ever treated anyone like a servant. He was proud of it.

'Oh, yes? "Sing a song for us, Eve. No, not that kind of song, this kind of song. No, not like that, it might upset *my men*. It might make them *think*." And heaven knows you don't want anyone to think.'

'Oh, *that's* it, is it? Because I told you not to sing that song?'

'Not just that one song, all the songs. Nothing about war. Nothing about religion. Nothing about anyone thinking for themselves. Because if they think for themselves, maybe, ooh, maybe they'll start to think those rebels have a point.

Maybe they'll think they don't want to fight them. Maybe they'll start to question the whole war.'

'Eve,' Harker said warningly, but her face was tight with fury and she didn't look like she was about to stop. He took a step forward.

'Because you know what? Maybe they do have a point. This country is dying, Harker, it is broke and it is starving. You have nothing to sell that anyone would want to buy, not to mention that you've blockaded all your ports – yes, I was listening – so not much could get in or out anyway! You have no industry to speak of, you're surviving on the barest rations of what you can manage to grow and refine yourselves and that's not much. And you're fighting a war that you're *losing*.'

Harker leaned closer and spoke in a low voice because he wanted this conversation leaking through the walls to his squad like he wanted a fresh bullet wound.

'We are *not* losing,' he hissed. 'We have all our main cities defended–'

'What, like you were defending Lincoln? And Peterborough? I know a little bit about trench warfare, Harker, like how bloody slow and futile and horrific it is. All it does is get people killed in large quantities. That's your main industry here, killing people. And don't you deny it, because your army is so desperate it's conscripting, and it's not just conscripting men, but women–'

'Who, as you're demonstrating, are quite able and indeed eager to fight,' Harker said.

'But you're running out of men! They're all dying. I saw the aftermath of even that little skirmish in the fens, and it scared the life out of me, because there were so many men – and women – there, who just won't be coming back to fight. You're losing men every day.'

'Not *my* men,' Harker said fiercely.

'No,' she said, 'so that's okay, is it? Major Harker the Hero is bringing his little band of brothers home, so the war must be going well! Harker, you're fighting an enemy who is better equipped and better informed than you. They're allied with the most powerful nation on Earth, who, may I remind you, is just twenty-two miles away by sea. And they're gaining support.'

'Who says–?'

'They took three cities without even having to attack from the outside! Do you think they could do that if people were happy with the way the army is running the country? Do you think people like being starved and killed? You conscript everyone over the age of eighteen, that leaves no one to grow food and look after children; not that there can be all that many children born with your entire population of child-bearing age going off to be shot at–'

'And what do you suggest we do? We don't have any more food and we're running out of men, where do you *suggest* we get fresh troops from? How are we supposed to feed these starving people?'

'I don't know, by letting the French do it?'

Harker was saved from having to punch Eve by Charlie opening her door and looking at them enquiringly. Dammit. Every word Eve had said had got louder, and Harker feared he'd been shouting, too.

He shook his head at Charlie, who frowned, but went back inside her room.

Harker put his face right up against Eve's, backing her against the wall. He was using his size and his strength to intimidate her, which was a rotten thing to do, but he didn't care.

He saw a spark of fear in her eyes and leaned closer.

'You're right,' he said softly. 'We are starving, and we are dying, but we're still not going to give in to the Coalitionists.

I don't know what version of England you think you're from, Eve Carpenter, but over here we are proud of our country and we're not about to let some thieving French bastards take it from us.'

'Pride won't feed people,' Eve said.

'*Neither will the French*.'

She glared at him, very close and very angry, frightened but defiant, and Harker could feel her breath on his face. Her eyes were clear, bright, fixed on his, and there were spots of colour on her cheeks.

He could smell the soap on her skin. She was so close.

'Well,' she said, nearly whispering the word into his mouth, 'if you're so confident in your people's love for their country, then it shouldn't matter what damn songs I sing, should it?'

She was so close and so pretty and so maddening that it took a second or two for that circular piece of logic to work its way through the heat frying Harker's brain, but when it did he closed his eyes and mentally cursed her.

Then he stepped back, and cursed himself when he saw the relief cross her face.

'Goodnight, Eve,' he said, and she swallowed, hesitated, and nodded.

He watched her walk down the corridor, almost to her room, before he called her back.

'Eve?'

She stopped. Turned. Raised that eyebrow at him again.

Harker didn't even know why he said what he said next. 'You do have a beautiful voice,' he said, and she licked her lips and stared at him for a second.

Then she said, 'Goodnight, Major,' and went into her room, shutting the door with a definite click.

Chapter Thirteen

Neither Tallulah nor Martindale said a word to Eve on the subject, but she knew they'd both heard every word she'd shouted at Harker. In the morning, avoiding their gazes, she dressed and followed them down to the big kitchen, ready to face Harker again – but he wasn't there.

'Left early,' Daz said. 'Went with the LT to reconnoitre around Leeds.'

'Oh,' said Eve, oddly disappointed.

Banks gave her a sly look. 'Looking forward to seeing him, were you?'

Eve opened her mouth to deliver a scathing reply, but nothing came, so she went for a diversionary tactic and asked something that had been bugging her. 'So, all right. I was wondering. You have a co-ed army of serving soldiers, right? What happens if a soldier gets pregnant? Does the army do maternity leave?'

'Not exactly,' Daz said, glancing at the rest of them.

'The army takes ... precautions,' Martindale said.

'Or more to the point, hands out precautions,' Banks said, grinning again.

'Seriously?'

'Yes. Or a lot of women would be taking the easy way out,' Daz said. 'Not everyone wants to be conscripted. And Wheeler takes a dim view of anyone who does it "accidentally".'

'I thought the Catholic Church disapproved of contraception,' she said.

Martindale snorted. 'Do you really think the Catholic Church cares about us?'

After breakfast, Eve asked one of the maids to show her the piano, which Lady Winterton had offered for the squad's use, possibly out of embarrassment over her husband's faux pas last night.

She could hardly remember the last time she'd played a piano before she came here. School recitals, stolen half-hours in recording studios, the electric piano in her mother's dining room, sitting lost and forgotten. Almost certainly sold now, probably trashed.

Funny, but she missed the keyboard more than her mother. Well, it was only fair: Eve was almost sure her mother would be missing Eve's fame more than Eve herself.

Her fingers slowed as she tried to summon up her old resentment, but it didn't come. That whole world, a world of televisions and electricity and temping jobs, of people sniggering at her and her name being used as a cautionary tale, it all seemed very distant, and as hard to see as the foggy Wolds outside.

Maybe that was a dream and this is real, she thought, beginning to play again. *For three years I don't think I felt anything, I didn't laugh or cry at anything, I felt no pain and no happiness and no comfort.* Strange how this sepia-coloured world, full of blood and hunger, seemed more real to Eve than what she'd left behind. Like Dorothy in Oz, only the other way around.

She stared at the low, rolling hills shrouded in mist. Those endless, boggy fens. She'd been so glad to leave the lowlands behind for the Wolds, even if they did seem to resemble mountains in contrast, suddenly steep, the peaks out of sight.

Why did I swap Mitcham for this?

Would I swap back again?

Eve's fingers went still, because she'd just realised she didn't know the answer to that question.

Harker swiped at a scraggy bush, annoyed as hell, wishing he'd brought his sword. A sword was really useful for things like this.

Charlie was keeping her distance, because he'd snapped at her one time too many on the drive from Hatfield Chase in Sir Dennis's nippy little Austin. He hadn't snapped on purpose. Charlie hadn't done anything wrong.

But he couldn't possibly tell her that after arguing with Eve last night he'd been tormented by such hot dreams of his little captive that he'd hardly slept.

He was close to Charlie, but not that close.

'Sir,' Charlie said, and pointed through the trees to where Kirkstall Abbey was visible. But instead of the tall, peaceful house of God that ought to be standing there, Harker saw only a garrison, scarred and ugly with soldiers, the enemy crawling all over it like cockroaches.

He moved closer, and realised that the huge camp didn't contain just soldiers. It was full of refugees, and it went on for miles. Miles of threadbare tents, small fires, crying children and hungry people. Miles of barbed wire and guards with guns.

Miles of people who had nowhere else to go, and wouldn't be allowed to go there even if they had.

He frowned. 'I thought they'd have set up inside the city,' he said.

'They've probably got a barracks there,' Charlie said. 'Who do you think keeps the refugees out of the city?'

They'd tried to enter at several of the city's gates earlier in the morning, but were repeatedly told that they'd need papers issued by the garrison at Kirkstall.

'Out of the city, and inside the camp,' Harker said. He didn't expect many of the people sent to Kirkstall came back to the city gates with papers in their hands.

'Well, at least we know where their HQ is,' Charlie said,

shading her eyes.

'Yeah.' Harker shaded his eyes, and glared at the Abbey. 'Hey, Charlie, if you had a valuable piece of equipment, where would you hide it?'

'Me, sir? In a hole underground where the enemy couldn't find it.'

He dealt her a look.

'Or HQ,' she conceded.

'So we break into the Abbey,' he said. 'Should be fun.'

Charlie raised her eyebrows, but said nothing.

Harker sighed and swiped at a thorny bush. 'Look, I'm sorry I snapped at you this morning. Didn't sleep well.'

'That's all right, sir. It was a long journey, and ...' she hesitated. Charlie rarely hesitated.

'And?' Harker prodded.

'And I know how Eve provokes you. You shouldn't let her get to you, sir.'

Harker closed his eyes, because all night he'd been tormented by dreams of letting Eve get to him. Letting her sweatily, repeatedly get to him.

She's either mad, or she's a spy. Mad or a spy. Mad. Spy.

The mission was important. The squad was important. His hormones weren't.

'I know,' he said shortly, and gestured back to the thicket where the car was concealed. On the way, he asked as idly as possible, 'Charlie, do you know what she was talking about with that Dracula business?'

'It's a book, sir. About a monster. There's someone in it called Harker.'

'He's not the monster, is he?'

Charlie gave him a sideways look. 'No, sir. Dracula is. Harker saves his wife from the monster.'

'How very chivalrous of him,' Harker said. Then a thought occurred. 'What's the wife called?'

'Mina,' said Charlie, and Harker attacked another thorn bush.

Brothers in Arms hadn't really been scored for piano, but it was easier to imitate an almost vocal guitar solo with black and white keys than with a Spanish guitar. At least, it was for Eve, who'd never been particularly good at the fiddly bits.

She played the song out a few times, working out the kinks, the bits she could play and the bits it was safer not to attempt, glad there was no one listening when she got it wrong. Maybe the squad might like it. And Harker couldn't possibly object, seeing as it was all about brotherhood during times of war.

Well. He probably would object. He seemed to object to her very existence, some of the time.

'Bastard,' she muttered, and let her hands drop from the keys. What was she doing, trying to find songs that might please him? It was an impossible task, and she didn't want to accomplish it anyway.

She bashed the keys a few times, annoyed, then shook her head and let her fingers take over, playing things they knew by heart. Chopin. Beethoven. Things she'd learned working her way up the grades at those after-school lessons with old Mrs Mason, whose house had always smelled of roast dinner. Even now, the scent of roasting chicken brought those melodies into her head. Or even just the thought of it, since no matter how hard she sniffed she couldn't smell what was cooking downstairs.

'That,' said a voice from the doorway, making her jump, 'is very beautiful.'

Eve glanced over her shoulder at the speaker, who was lounging there as if he owned the place. Well, he probably nearly did. Very shiny shoes and what Eve could only describe as a lounge suit, and a face that was clearly used to sneering. It wasn't hard to imagine him addressing women by their cleavages and everyone else by sighting down his nose.

She turned back to the piano and resumed playing. 'Beethoven,' she said. '*Moonlight Sonata*.'

'I didn't mean the music,' drawled the man, and Eve rolled her eyes at the piano.

When she didn't respond, he said, much closer this time, 'And you are ...?'

'I am,' Eve said, still playing, still not looking at him.

'I meant, what's your name,' he said, apparently not getting the joke, weak as it was.

'Eve,' she said.

'*Rarely*,' he said, almost yawning the word. 'I'm Adam.'

I bet all the money I lost that you're not, thought Eve, who had heard that line more times than she could count.

'Gosh,' she said flatly.

'Actually,' he came to lean against the side of the piano, so she'd have to look at him smiling what he probably thought was a charming grin, but actually made him look rather like a lopsided weasel, 'I'm Frederick.'

When that got no response, he added, 'Frederick Winterton. Sir Dennis is my father.'

'Hello, Frederick Winterton,' Eve muttered, reaching the end of the piece and starting again so she wouldn't have to pause while she thought of something else.

He held out his hand to her, murmuring, '*Enchanté*.'

Eve ignored it and continued to play.

'I expect you're with that frightful army squad my father has staying,' Frederick went on.

'What gave it away?' asked Eve, not even glancing at her khakis.

'Your uniform,' he said, flashing that damned horrible

grin again.

'Tell me,' Eve said, her fingers stilling, finally looking up at him, 'do you know what rhetorical means?'

He smiled lazily and reached out to twirl a lock of Eve's hair, which actually rather needed washing. 'I know it's a very long word for a girl as pretty as you,' he said, and Eve felt bile rising in her throat.

Outside, a car door slammed, and Frederick glanced towards the window. It was a stupid thing to do, since the drawing room didn't look out over the drive, but he looked anyway, and Eve smiled to herself. That car was, in all probability, the one Harker and Charlie had taken. Sir Dennis's car. It probably looked like something out of *Gosford Park* – it sure sounded like it – but it had to be faster than their wagon.

She turned back to the piano, and started banging out some of the tunes she'd learned in the production of *Oh! What A Lovely War* her amateur operatic group had done when she was about fourteen.

I knew this stupid memory for songs would come in handy some day, she thought, starting to sing loudly about not wanting to be a soldier. That ought to get Harker going. He must be useful for something.

'You sing like a nightingale,' said Frederick, raising his voice over her caterwauling.

Eve broke off for a second to smile and say, 'That's what my boyfriend says.'

His smile faltered, but not for long. 'Boyfriend? Well,' he placed his hand on the back of her neck, which caused Eve to hit several wrong notes, 'we don't need to worry about him.'

Come on, Harker, where are you? Eve thought, hammering at the keys and yelling out *Do You Hear the People Sing?* from *Les Mis*, which had got him going before.

'Now,' Frederick was saying in what he probably thought was a silky tone of voice, 'why don't you stop playing for just a moment, and–'

'Eve?'

'Oh, thank God,' Eve muttered, leaping up from the stool and telling Frederick triumphantly, '*This* is my boyfriend,' only to turn and see Daz standing there, looking somewhat trapped.

'Uh,' he said, and Eve gave him a determined smile, marched over and threw her arms around him. He wasn't as big and broad and scary as Harker, but he was no slouch and the stars on his shoulder denoted a captain. Above all else, he was *here*, which was good enough for her.

'Help me,' she muttered in his ear, and Daz gave her a confused look. Her colour rising, she pretended to nuzzle his ear while hissing furiously, 'This is the odious son of the house and he wouldn't leave me alone so I told him I had a boyfriend and now you're going to have to be him. Okay?'

'Ah,' said Daz, relaxing a little. 'Oh. Okay. Yes. Right.'

He turned to glare at Frederick, who looked mildly nauseated by Eve's nuzzling, but didn't seem to be remotely embarrassed that he'd been coming on to someone else's girlfriend.

'Captain,' he drawled. 'Lovely filly you've got there.'

'I'll thank you not to refer to her like that.'

'Will you, indeed?' Frederick let his gaze rake over Eve, who glared at him and wrapped her arms around Daz. 'Bit of skirt from the ranks, is she?'

'*Skirt?*' Eve said.

'Officers don't marry girls like you,' Frederick informed her, apparently deciding that if he couldn't have her, he didn't want her.

'Er, marry?' said Eve, glancing at Daz to see if the customary male panic at hearing the M word had set in.

But since he knew it wasn't for real, he didn't seem to be too perturbed.

'I'll have you know, we're very much in love,' Daz said, and Eve felt like sticking her tongue out. *So there*. But before she could, Daz had whirled her in his arms and kissed her.

It wasn't a great kiss. In fact, it wasn't even a good kiss. It was a little closed-mouth peck, but it was done with such ceremony and flourish that Eve doubted anyone noticed the total lack of passion.

Then Harker said from the doorway behind Daz, 'When you two lovebirds have quite finished,' and her blood went cold.

Chapter Fourteen

Okay, Eve thought, *this is how I'm going to die. Not drowning in the Thames, not shot as a spy, not even of disease or old age. I'm going to get run through by Major Harker's sword.*

Which was insane, because it was absolutely none of his business who she did and didn't kiss, despite the raging heat that had kept Eve awake ever since he'd argued with her in the corridor last night. But surely, she had no reason at all to be worried–

–except for his voice. It was as if his words had been frozen solid, blasted by liquid rage, cold fury freezing each syllable into a deadly weapon. It was the same voice she'd heard speaking to the oleaginous Captain Sholt back at the Tower. A voice filled with utter hatred.

Daz straightened, dropping his arms from Eve, which made her stumble, and as she righted herself she caught a glimpse of Harker in the doorway. His face looked like marble, his eyes black with rage, and every still, terrifying line of his body told her he could kill her in a second if he wanted to.

And right now, he looked as if he wanted to.

She opened her mouth to say something, anything! Then spied Charlie flanking Harker, her hand moving to her hip and the pistol resting there. Eve swallowed and remembered about the rage, and then she realised that Harker was in civvies, and therefore hopefully wasn't actually armed.

Oh good, that means he'll just kill me with his bare hands.

But Harker was looking past Eve and Daz, whose cheeks were bright pink, to the young man leaning against the piano and sneering faintly at them all.

'I know you,' Harker said, and Frederick raked him with an extremely disparaging glance which took in the workman's clothes, muddy boots, unkempt hair and unshaven jaw.

His lip actually curled.

'I don't believe you do,' he said, his tone so bored he was almost yawning.

'No,' Harker said, and his tone was so sharp he'd have no need of a sword if he wanted to hurt someone.

Eve did not find this a comfort.

'You insulted my wife,' Harker went on, and Eve saw Charlie's knuckles go white.

'Did I?' Frederick yawned. He straightened, and made to leave the drawing room by its other door.

'Oh yes,' Harker said. 'Frederick Winterton, who never addresses a lady while looking her in the face.'

'I doubt *your* wife is a lady,' Frederick said without turning, and Daz winced. So did Eve.

Charlie cocked her gun.

The sound made Frederick stop, and he turned with an expression of such extreme distaste it took Eve's breath away. The man didn't actually seem to be afraid, which was incredibly stupid, since Charlie had her gun out and Harker was looking like Death having a bad day.

'God,' Frederick said, rolling his eyes. 'Father said you were a common little oik, but now you've got your lackey threatening me with a gun. Major Harker, isn't it? How terribly vulgar.'

'Oh aye,' Harker said, his voice as soft and low as the growl of a cat before it pounces. 'That's me. Vulgar through and through. A common little oik like me'd think nothing of murdering a man like you for insulting my wife. It's the sort of thing us vulgar men do.'

Frederick snorted elegantly. 'You're not even armed,' he

said dismissively.

'*I don't need to be.*'

That got his attention. Eve saw the first hint of fear in the man's expression.

'If I were you,' Charlie said, 'I'd apologise right now.'

'For what?' Frederick said, still smirking, although less convincingly. 'I don't even know his wife.'

'Oh, but you do, Frederick,' Harker said. 'Her parents are very good friends of your family.'

Frederick looked disbelieving.

'Saskia Watling-Coburg,' Charlie supplied, her gaze darting to Harker, who still hadn't moved. It occurred to Eve that he probably didn't need to. If she were in Frederick's place, she'd probably die of sheer dread.

But Frederick just said, 'Oh God, yes. She married some dreadful thug from the ranks, didn't she? Shame. Pretty filly.' His gaze raked Harker again. 'Even she couldn't make a gentleman of you.'

Harker said nothing, but his fingers flexed minutely. Frederick saw the movement, and sneered, 'Always said you were no better than you should be.'

'Oh no,' Harker said, his voice by now very soft. 'I'm exactly as good as I should be.'

Frederick scoffed, but not very convincingly. He seemed quite disconcerted to find Harker still agreeing with him.

'But what with me being such a thug, I don't need to be very good at all, do I?'

He let that sink in. Frederick gradually stopped smirking.

'And I have *not* been having a very good day,' Harker added, and Frederick suddenly remembered he had to be elsewhere.

As the door clicked behind him, Eve let out a breath she hadn't realised she'd been holding. Daz gave her a weak grin. Charlie tucked her gun back in its holster as if nothing had happened.

Eve braced herself, then turned to Harker and waited for the explosion. But it never came.

He didn't even look at Eve as he left the room.

The only other person who'd ever made Harker feel such white-hot fury had been Sholt. Even Saskia had never pushed him this far. The world was blurring, spinning slightly, going red at the edges.

He wanted to kill someone. Preferably Frederick, but Daz would do.

He was kissing Eve. I'm *not allowed to kiss her, but* he *can.*

Bastard.

And now she was whispering to Daz as they scurried after him. Whispering. It was one step from giggling together, like lovers. Were they lovers? Had Eve gone to him last night? When had it started? That day the barricades had broken and she'd spent all that time with Daz? Had they really been tending to the wounded or were they shagging frantically in the wagon? Were they–

'Um, sir?' said Daz, and Harker heard a growl coming from his own throat. 'That – back then – that wasn't what it looked like.'

The red mist flared. Harker halted a second to let it fade before he walked into the door at the top of the servants' stairs. Charlie came to a complete stop behind him, Eve and Daz clattering to a halt, probably walking into each other, probably enjoying it–

'I don't care what it looked like,' Harker said, his voice wooden, opened the door and started down the stairs.

'It's just, um, Frederick was hassling Eve, so I sort of stepped in, and we were – look, it's not–'

'I don't care,' Harker said, more emphatically this time.

Maybe he could make himself believe it. 'Charlie, why don't I care?'

'Uh,' Charlie said. 'Because ... um ...'

'Because I care about the squad and the mission and I'm not letting anything interfere with that,' Harker snapped.

'Oh,' Daz said. 'Right. Er ... good?'

'*Yeah*,' Harker said viciously, and shoved open the kitchen door. Tallulah and Martindale were sitting at the table, Banks was flirting with one of the kitchen maids, and the large room was full of noise and movement, which all stopped when Harker walked in with his face like a storm cloud. He threw himself in a chair and glowered at his empty plate. He was hungry, but too angry too eat, and besides, if he got a sharp implement in his hand things might go poorly for the next person to annoy him.

Right on cue, Eve sat down opposite him.

He glowered at her. She ignored him.

'So how come Sir Dennis is so damn rich?' she asked Tallulah. 'I mean, he has this huge house, and a car, and electricity, and everyone else in this country is living in some sort of medieval poverty.'

'Don't be ridiculous,' Harker snapped. Eve made a face at him, and he thought longingly about the pistol he'd hidden in his waistband. He really needed a cigarette, but the cook had snapped at him for lighting up this morning, and even in a blind rage, Harker knew better than to get on the wrong side of someone who fed him.

'I think it's coal,' Tallulah offered. 'He owns lots of land, of course, but it's the coal mines that make him the most money. That's how he can afford electricity.'

'Wow, next you'll be telling me he has a phone,' Eve said, her voice rich with sarcasm.

Actually, that was something he needed to find out. Wheeler had told him Sir Dennis did have a telephone, but she wasn't sure if it was connected. Maybe Daz could fix it.

That is, if he could spare time from his busy Eve-shagging schedule.

Bloody, sodding, damn Daz. All right, so she probably wasn't sleeping with him, that was a little far-fetched, but why had she kissed him? Why? What had Daz done to deserve it?

How come he could have her when Harker couldn't?

'Oi,' said Eve, kicking him under the table, and he stared at her, because he couldn't quite remember the last time anyone had been familiar, or stupid, enough to do that.

'Did you find out anything useful?' she asked him. 'Do you need ID papers or anything?'

He glared at her, actually met her eyes for the first time that day and saw the sparky defiance there. She was doing this on purpose, again. She was needling him. Her eyes were all hard and bright, her chin sticking out. She looked reckless. She looked beautiful.

'I didn't find anything,' he said eventually, 'which you need to know about.'

Eve made a choking sound, her eyes blazing. 'Oh for heaven's sake,' she snapped. 'Look, just because you're in a foul mood, don't take it out on the rest of us, okay? If you're still mad at me because I yelled at you last night, then take it up with me, don't make the rest of the squad feel like hell for it. And if it's about Frederick, oh my *God*, Harker, get over that. Seriously. So he letched at your *ex*-wife, so what? He does it to everyone. He was doing it to me. He's a slimy, arrogant twat, but there's no reason to get so stressed about it.'

'Shut up,' Harker said, in that same low, dangerous tone he'd been using on Frederick, the same tone that had made much stronger men back down, but it had no effect on her.

Dammit, did she really think he was angry because of

something that had happened years ago? Because of a slimy little bastard like Frederick? *No, you idiot woman,* he wanted to shout, *I'm angry with* you*!*

'No, I will not. Just because–'

'Don't push me, Eve,' Harker said, shoving back his chair and standing in one abrupt movement. He needed to get out of here, before he hurt someone. But Eve leapt to her feet too.

'Why not?' she said. 'Why bloody not? Someone has to. Everyone else here is subordinate to you, they have to follow your orders, for right or wrong, and not argue with you. But I'm not one of your men, and I don't have to follow your orders, and I'm sure as hell not sitting around letting you brood and sulk–'

'I am not sulking!' Harker shouted.

'You bloody well are, and it's not good enough! And you can glare all you like at me, I'm not going to run away like Frederick because you know what? I'm not scared of you.'

'You bloody ought to be,' Harker snarled.

'Oh yeah? Why? Because you look like a vagrant and you've got a good line in glowering? *Oooh.* I'm *scared.* What're you going to do to me? I'm a damn prisoner. You've locked me away and lied to me and coerced me and made me walk for a week through boggy fens and you never tell me what the hell is going on, or thank me, and at the end of this, even if I help you out and get you your stupid computer and make it work and win you the war, then what are you going to do? Put me back in that prison-that's-not-a-prison, while you take all the glory and probably get a promotion or something else shiny and wonderful you can pretend you don't care about.'

She was breathing hard now, her cheeks pink, and there was nothing else in the room but the two of them, and he wanted to *shake* her, because she was being so stupid and so blind and she was driving him bloody *crazy*–

'So, yeah, when you say "don't push me", why the hell not? What are you going to do to me?'

The pistol was suddenly in Harker's hand. He stared at it, finally understanding what drove men to hit women.

'Oh, right,' Eve said, a new edge in her voice. 'You're going to shoot me. Fine.' She kicked her chair out of the way, stomped around and faced him, grabbed his wrist and aimed the gun at her own head. 'Go on, then. Bloody shoot me.'

For a long second, an endless long second, the rest of the world went blurry and all he could see was Eve, in sharp relief, so close and so angry.

I've got to stop fighting with her, my head's going to explode, he thought.

And then, *I wonder if she fights like that in bed?*

And then, *She'd let me shoot her, she actually would.*

'You are crazy,' he muttered.

'Yes,' she said. 'I am.' Her eyes locked on his. 'Or I'm dreaming this, or it's a parallel universe. In which case I ought to be trying to get home but you know what? There's not even anything for me there. I've got nothing.'

She was right up against him now, toe to toe, touching him only at his wrist but nearly pressed against him everywhere else. Nearly.

'I don't care,' she said, honesty making her voice soft. 'I don't.'

In her eyes he saw the reckless light of desperation, and remembered that the most dangerous people in the world were the ones with nothing to lose.

She doesn't have anything. You're treating her like a prisoner.

Damn, she's pretty.

'I'm not going to shoot you,' he said, relaxing his hold on

the gun. 'Let go of my wrist.'

A second passed but it lasted for eternity, and then the pressure of her fingers lessened. Harker kept his eyes on hers, and she eventually dropped her hand.

He exhaled.

'Sir,' said someone, Charlie he thought, and suddenly the room was full of people again.

Eve twisted from him, bright eyes turning away, and stumbled towards the door.

'Eve,' he said, and she flinched.

'I violently dislike you,' she said, and then she was gone, slamming through the door and leaving a sort of shocked silence behind.

Right. Excellent.

'Still worried?' he said to Charlie, but she didn't seem to find that very funny. If anything, she looked more concerned than ever. He lit up a cigarette, daring the cook to say a word. Wisely, she didn't.

Chapter Fifteen

I violently dislike you.

Wind whipped rain against him, hard and stinging, freezing his face and his fingers. Harker could have sheltered inside the car while he waited for Banks, but he needed the cold to numb some of the hot anger inside him.

And guilt. And shame.

Mad. Or a spy.

She could get in the way of everything, everything he and the army were fighting for, and yet instead of worrying about the mission he was worrying about Eve. Even now, Banks was inside the city, purloining papers for the squad, and Harker stood in the cold rain and wind, thinking about Eve. How hurt she looked. How lost.

A parallel universe. She was crazy! She ought to be in an asylum. Either that, or back with the Coalitionists, where she belonged. Because all that could have been a masterful performance to convince him she was harmless, so he wouldn't suspect her of being a traitor ...

Harker wiped his hand across his eyes. He couldn't even convince himself he even half-believed that any more. Not Eve. Mad, perhaps, infuriating definitely, but not a traitor.

A familiar shape ambled along the road towards him, and Harker shook himself, getting back inside the car.

'Got them?' he asked Banks, who grinned as he climbed inside the car's shelter.

'Candy from a baby,' he said, displaying a sheaf of papers. 'Shouldn't be hard to alter. Oi, sir, you want to be a Mister Shipley? Teacher at a school in a village. Farnley, it says.'

Harker nodded. Farnley. They'd driven past a turning

to it, and he set off back that way. No harm in doing his research.

Farnley was a depressing place, a sorry collection of cottages servicing the local colliery. The buildings were black with soot, and so were the people. The only building of any size was the school, which he guessed probably served a lot of the surrounding villages.

He parked the car outside the village and walked in. Depressed-looking kids huddled in the gloomy school playground. It was mid-afternoon, and by Harker's guess the kids were probably waiting for their parents to pick them up.

He frowned. One of the kids had a shock of bright red hair, and something about her was familiar–

'Hell of a place,' said Banks, shivering in his thin coat.

'Yeah,' said Harker, watching the little girl. She was a skinny thing, maybe eleven or twelve. Maybe a little older. Hard to tell. But she had oddly dark eyes, and Harker had only ever known one other person with that strange combination.

'I want to thank you, Sarge–'

And she had a very slight limp. It couldn't be anyone else.

The girl was playing a skipping game with her friends, who patiently made allowances for her lack of co-ordination. She wore a pinafore and thick tights, but Harker was almost sure that had it been summer, he'd have been able to see the faded scars on her legs.

He nearly called out to her, but before he could even remember her name, the little girl scampered away from her friends towards a group of women approaching the school gates.

One of them was Mary. She had a scarf tied over her pale hair, but she could have shaved herself bald and Harker would still recognise her.

She smiled when she saw her daughter, leaned down and hugged her tight. But he saw her flinch when one of the other kids brushed her accidentally.

'Sir?' said Banks quietly. Harker had completely forgotten him. 'Who is she?'

He watched Mary talking to her red-haired daughter, smiling, animation erasing some of the tiredness in her face. It was good to see her smile. He hadn't seen it in … hell, twelve years.

Not since Sholt.

'Mary White,' he said, and Mary glanced towards his voice.

And went still.

'Sarge,' she whispered, and he nodded, and she rushed over, dragging her daughter behind her. 'Is it you? Sergeant Harker!'

Harker put his finger to his lips, and she nodded. 'Perhaps we can have a chat, Mary?'

She nodded again, glancing briefly at Banks, who gave her a smile full of curiosity.

'You stop here,' Harker told him, 'keep an eye on things. Mister Banks.'

Banks's eyes narrowed at the Mister, but he nodded and stayed where he was. Harker looked back at Mary, gripping her daughter's hand tight, and said, 'Maybe a walk, Mary? In full sight, where everyone can see us?'

'Of course,' she said. 'Around the square?'

They set off, Mary still holding her daughter's hand. 'I'm so sorry,' Harker said to the little girl, 'I just can't remember your name.'

'Emily,' Mary said. 'Emmy, most of the time.'

'Emmy. Of course. She's so like her father.'

Mary gave a tight nod. Harker waited to see if anything else was forthcoming, then said, 'I didn't know you'd come north. Last I heard you were down in the west.'

She gave a brief smile. 'Oh, we've been here a few years. When Sal and Smiggy – do you remember Smiggy, Private Miggles? And his wife Sal, she was always very kind to me. He was born here, you see.'

'Is that why you came up here? Because Smiggy and Sal came?'

'Yes. All the others had left or ... or been transferred–' most likely killed, thought Harker, who'd kept track of some of his men – 'and Sal always said they were going to come back north when Smiggy's time was up, and it was quiet and ... well, I didn't have anywhere else. And there was work in Leeds, Smiggy's family said. I do work for a tailor there.'

Harker closed his eyes guiltily. 'I'm sorry, Mary, I should have kept in touch–' he began, but she shook her head fiercely.

'No, Sergeant Harker. Don't you ever be sorry. You did more than you ever needed to, for me and for Emmy. Smiggy told me how you sent money for us back when – when Emmy was a baby. And I never thanked you for it.'

'You don't have to,' said Harker, who still felt bad that he'd stopped sending the money when Mary had become too hard to track down.

'You fought for us, Sergeant, and I'll never forget it,' Mary said.

Harker didn't say anything. Yes, he'd fought for them, but not hard enough. If he'd fought hard enough, James might still be alive and Sholt, with any justice, would have faced a firing squad.

'Oh!' said Mary, apropos nothing. 'I'm so sorry.'

'For what, Mary?'

'I've been calling you Sergeant, only Smiggy told me how you'd been promoted, got your commission, sir.'

'You don't have to call me sir,' Harker said gently. 'James

never did.'

'No. He called you Sarge.' She smiled distantly. 'I remember that, he said Sarge was a great man.'

No, Harker thought, *a great man would never have let it all happen in the first place.*

He hesitated, then figured if he could trust anybody, it'd be Mary. After all, she trusted him, which in itself was a miracle. 'Mary, you might be able to help me with something ...'

By the time he went back to Private Banks, who was sharing a cigarette with a couple of miners, he'd got what he wanted. Banks, somewhat reluctantly, gave up his cigarette, and walked with Harker back to the car.

'Sir?' he said, after a minute or two.

'The wife of one of my men,' Harker said, because he knew what Banks was going to ask.

'Ah. I didn't recognise her,' Banks fished.

'No. He served under me when I was still a sergeant in the 17th. You wouldn't've known him.'

'Wouldn't've?' Banks said. 'Is he ... not serving any more?'

'No,' Harker said, and when he blinked, just for that split second he saw James White's flayed and broken body. 'No, he isn't.'

Eve had intended to spend the day lurking in the chilly and unused sunroom at the back of the house, judging correctly that no one would be using it at this time of year, but even in that she was thwarted.

Charlie sniffed her out, and like the good guard dog she was, warned Eve off her beloved Major.

'He's a senior officer, promoted from the ranks in an army where promotion is purchased,' she said calmly. 'If he were to get involved with a spy he would lose his commission.'

It took a short while for this to sink in to Eve's brain.

Firstly, that Charlie thought she was a spy, which she knew was one of the squad's theories about her. But then she realised why she was being warned. Charlie didn't want Harker to get involved with a spy – with her.

She opened her mouth, but she wasn't sure what to protest about first.

'I know there's no proof against you,' Charlie said. 'But there's not much to prove your innocence, either. I'm sorry, Eve. My first duty is to the army. My second is to my friends. Harker falls into both categories. He is the closest thing I have to family, and I won't see him hurt. Not professionally and not personally.'

Eve gaped.

'I'm asking you, please, for the sake of everyone's sanity, to just stop winding him up. We'd all appreciate it. And stop–' she broke off, as if she couldn't find the appropriate words.

'I am not interested in Major Harker,' Eve said flatly.

Charlie gave her a brief smile. 'Good.' She stood up. 'I'll see you at dinner.'

With that she was gone, and Eve stared at the space she'd vacated. Quite apart from the fact that she'd just been warned off by Harker's personal Rottweiler – did they really think she was attracted to him? *We'd all appreciate it. Everyone's sanity.* Did they all think–?

'He's not even that good-looking,' she said out loud. His lips were too thin and his nose was too big, and he was always scowling or mocking, and would it seriously kill him to shave, or wash his hair? All right, so he was tall and he was undoubtedly in great shape, but so what? He was also rude, unpleasant, angry and sarcastic. He was bitter, he was brooding, and what was that thing he had about pretending not to be the major? 'I think I can bring him to mind', yes, hilarious.

Angry now, she reached for her guitar. She'd prefer the piano – better for pounding notes – but that would involve going out into the house, where she might meet Harker, and she really didn't want to do that.

What the hell was wrong with these people? All right, so there was that one time when she'd tried to kiss him, but he'd promised not to tell anyone about that, and for some reason Eve didn't believe he was the type to break his promises. He might be arrogant, rude, bitter, angry, brutal and the most annoying man she'd ever had the misfortune to have her life saved by, but she didn't think he was a liar.

Although he did seem to enjoy bending the truth enormously.

The guitar was altogether too soothing for Eve, who was far too angry to even want to calm down. She picked it up and stalked through the house, preparing herself to meet Harker and do battle with him – *no, bad idea Eve, what did you just promise Charlie?* – but she didn't see any of the squad.

Eventually stomping into the drawing room, she found the piano seat open and sheets of music loose inside.

Beethoven. Chopin. Schubert.

Eve stared, then pulled out the top sheaf. Ludwig von Beethoven: *Sonata No. 14 in C# Minor op.27 no.2 3rd movement*. The end of the *Moonlight Sonata*. The fast, fiddly, tricky but incredibly wonderful third movement.

Eve stared for a long time at the notes dancing over the page. *I remember that arpeggio, and that fortissimo mark, I could never get my electric keyboard to sound fortissimo.* She bashed the keys, and it sounded the same as it had in Mrs Mason's front room. The piano needed tuning and Eve's fingers were too sluggish for the fast, intricate notes, exactly as they had been fifteen years ago.

The music was the same.

They don't know Brothers in Arms *and they've never heard of the Beatles, but they have Beethoven.*

Eve pinched the bridge of her nose. All right, so none of these composers were English – a quick ruffle through the remaining music told her that the majority was French – but they did exist. She had heard of them.

It ought to have been comforting, but Eve felt less sure than ever.

Mist rolled in over the Wolds, swirling around the house at Hatfield Chase like a thick cloak. Like, Harker thought, remembering a distant cocktail party with Saskia, a lady in a fur coat.

Well, now he was getting poetical. It was surely time for a drink.

He drove the car around the back of the house to its garage in the stables, ignoring Banks's chatter and heading through the dark courtyard to the golden square of light oozing from the kitchen window. *Hot food,* he thought longingly, *no more damn stew or stale bread.*

But as they passed one of the wings, music spilled, flowed and trilled from a window just above their heads.

''Cos I ain't sure–' Banks went on, and Harker said, 'Shut up.'

'Shutting up, sir.'

They both stood still, listening to the intricate piano notes. The music tripped and flowed like fast water, lyrical and complex, sometimes light and sometimes heavy, but one of the most incredible things Harker had ever heard.

'That's amazing,' Banks breathed.

Harker just nodded.

'If she can play the piano like that, I bet she's great in – uh,' Banks broke off as Harker blinked and glanced at him.

'Who?'

'Eve. Who else is it gonna be, sir?'

'Right,' Harker said distantly. He'd never heard anything like it before. His feet took him onwards, through the kitchen and up the stairs, occasionally losing the sound, then catching it again as he opened the stair door, turned a corner of the hall, came closer to the glorious sounds, stood outside the drawing room and listened–

He closed his eyes, let the music twist and twirl around him, those golden notes coming from Eve's fingers, and tried not to imagine what else those fingers were capable of.

'... probably come to tell us to turn it down,' Eve's voice sounded, and Harker tried to pull himself together. The door opened, and Eve stood there, and the music continued, and they frowned at each other for a long minute.

'You're not playing,' he said eventually, his voice coming out a little hoarse.

She shook her head, and opened the door wider to reveal Tallulah at the piano, her fingers flying.

'I couldn't,' Eve said. 'There's no way I can play like that.'

'You play very well!' Tallulah protested, without even pausing in her playing. Her hands moved so fast Harker couldn't even see them.

'I think the best I could be allowed is "quite well",' Eve said. She looked at Harker, still frowning a little, and added to Tallulah, 'Back in a sec.'

She came out into the hall, closing the door behind her, muting the music.

'She's amazing, huh?'

Harker nodded, wondering why he felt so disappointed. 'Yeah. I ... I didn't know she was that good.'

'I mean, that's almost concert standard. And she dances too, did you know that? Ballet.'

'I've a vague recollection.'

'Yes, of course you would,' Eve said. She bit her lip.

'Look, I ... I'm sorry about what happened at lunch. I'm crazy; it's the only explanation I can think of.'

Harker felt his lips twitch in a smile. 'If you think you're crazy, doesn't that mean you're not?'

'Who knows? Look, Harker. I'm trying to deal here with a lot of stuff I don't really understand. This world, and everything in it. Do you know, that piano music is the first thing here I've actually recognised? Half of the time, I think I really must be mad. I'm on edge. A lot. But I shouldn't have yelled at you, and I'm sorry.'

It took guts to apologise. Harker nodded. 'It's okay.'

'Well, at least, I shouldn't have yelled at you in front of the squad,' she qualified, and he smiled again. Tallulah's playing had changed, to something slower, more melancholic, and he could feel his heartbeat slowing from its frantic race.

'Look, Charlie came to have a chat with me this afternoon,' Eve said, and from her pained expression he knew it hadn't been a cheerful, friendly natter.

Not that he could quite imagine Charlie *nattering* with anyone, but that was by the by.

'She ... well, she seems to think there's something going on between you and me. Like, I'm just fighting with you because I fancy you. Which is ridiculous, right? I mean – look, no offence and all, but you're so totally not my type.'

'Right,' Harker said automatically. 'Yes.'

'And she – well, look, she was just concerned that, I don't know, I'd be really bad for you or something. Which is crazy, because I'm just, I'm not – I'm not interested, okay?'

'You violently dislike me,' Harker said, and she winced.

'Um. Yeah. Well, not violently. Well, not all the time. Just sometimes. When you wind me up. But look, Charlie seems to think ... apparently they all think there's something going on. Which is ludicrous.'

'Ludicrous,' Harker agreed. Her cheeks were flushed, he

noticed. 'And anyway,' he snapped himself out of it, 'I'm not either. I'm not. I don't. I mean, I have a job to do here–'

'Right,' Eve said, looking relieved. 'Yes, you do. And I'm ... well, I could be a spy or anything–'

'Are you? A spy?'

'Like I'd tell you,' she said, and Harker's lips twitched again. Eve gave a half-smile too.

'Right,' she said again, taking a breath and smoothing down her shirt. 'So I just thought ... look, you just wind me up, okay? And I swear you do it on purpose.'

'I don't,' Harker protested. 'Why would I?'

'I dunno,' she said, fiddling with the hem of her shirt. 'S'fun sometimes.'

He ducked his head, trying to meet her eyes. 'Does that mean you do it on purpose, too?'

'No.' She looked up, and her gaze hit his. It forced a smile. 'Well, sometimes.' Her eyes narrowed. 'What do you mean, do I do it, too?'

Harker felt himself start to grin, and Eve broke eye contact, smiling.

'Truce?' Harker said. 'I'll stop pushing you if you stop pushing me?'

Eve put her head on one side. She was still smiling, although it had faded a little. 'No,' she said.

'No?'

'Someone needs to push you, Harker,' she said, slowly, as if she was still working it out. 'When was the last time anyone challenged you?'

Saskia, he thought, but figured that was something he ought to keep to himself.

'I mean ... look at you. I think you're bored. You're always challenging other people.' When he opened his mouth to protest, she went on, 'Look at Sir Dennis.'

'Sir Dennis is a pompous twat,' Harker said.

'True. But you pulled the same trick on him that you did on me. "I think I can bring him to mind"?'

Oh yeah ... an old favourite. Harker didn't realise he was smiling until Eve said, 'See? You love it.' Eve looked at her hands for a moment, then said, 'Why should life be dull? I spent three years just existing, and I might as well have been dead. At least here there's something to do.'

'Are you telling me I'm your "something to do"?' Harker asked incredulously, and for just a second something flared in Eve's eyes that he'd very much like to have seen more of.

'–' she said, and Harker laughed. After a second, she laughed too, her cheeks decidedly pinker.

'Just don't challenge me in front of my men,' he said. 'I do need to have some authority over them.'

'Okay,' she said. 'And I'm sorry I went ballistic earlier.'

'I'm sorry I told you what not to sing.'

'I'm sorry I accused you of sulking in front of your men.'

'That's okay.'

'No, this is where you apologise for sulking.'

'I was not–' Harker began, then saw the glint in her eye and broke off. 'All right. Very funny.' She shrugged. He sighed. 'Listen, I'm – we're – going to need your help. Tonight, after dinner, I need you to describe as fully as you can what this computer will look like.'

Eve held up a finger, disappeared inside the drawing room, where Tallulah had fallen silent and probably heard every word they'd said, and came back with a notebook.

'Here,' she said, showing him some pictures and notes. 'It's a bit basic, I'm not much of an artist, but that should show you what you're looking for.'

The sketches were labelled. Harker stared at them for a moment, then looked up at her.

'Thank you,' he said, and meant it. 'That's ... exactly what we needed.'

She blushed. 'I ... well, I felt kinda bad about–'

Harker shook his head, and smiled properly. 'Don't.' He lifted her chin with one finger. 'I'll see you at dinner?'

She nodded, and disappeared back inside the drawing room. Harker stood looking at his finger for a long moment, before he turned away and went to find Charlie.

Lady Winterton continued to attempt to make amends with Harker, mostly by inviting him, Charlie and Daz to dine with the family. Harker declined, not impolitely, citing inappropriate dress.

'Oh, but that doesn't matter,' Lady Winterton assured him. 'We're not snobs.'

Eve compressed her lips.

'We're also working very long and unsociable hours,' he said, ignoring her. 'I doubt we'll be able to reliably promise that we'll be there.'

Lady Winterton professed her sorrow at this, but Eve was pretty sure she looked relieved. She grinned at Harker as the lady left the kitchen.

'Oi,' he said. 'Not a word.'

She made lip-zipping gestures. He grinned back at her.

The squad spent three days 'reconnoitring the site'. Eve was never allowed to know where 'the site' was, and if Harker ever seemed in danger of speaking it out loud in her presence, Charlie's expression usually quelled him.

'We've had a stroke of luck,' he told them over dinner the first night. 'An old friend of mine lives nearby and works in Leeds. She thinks she should be able to get us the layout of the – of the site. She was married to one of my men when I was a sergeant in the 17th. Her name is Mary White.'

Charlie's expression changed. 'Ah,' she said.

Eve looked at the others to see if they knew what that

meant, but they looked as nonplussed as she felt.

'Are you sure we can trust her, sir?' Martindale asked.

'Yes,' Harker said, in a tone that said the matter was closed.

Eve made copies of her diagrams and sketches for each of the squad, and explained as well as she could what each component of the computer ought to look like, where it would be and how it would be connected.

'Make sure you bring all the wires,' she said, watching them put their boots and coats on in preparation for leaving on the third night. They were each dressed in the more modern uniforms of the Coalitionist army, which someone – she suspected Banks – had nicked at some point. 'And for the love of God don't drop anything. Or get it wet. Broken pieces are more than useless. And don't forget that things might look different from how I described them. There are different kinds of computers.'

'World of help, you are,' Banks said, grinning.

Christ, I forgot to tell them about laptops. And what if they're using ancient computers, what if they're still on Enigma machines or something? 'Maybe I should come with you,' she said.

'No, I don't think so,' said Charlie. Eve glared at her back.

'Stay here,' Harker said. 'Sleep.'

Eve blinked: was he being kind to her?

'Then when we bring it back you can wake up and make it work in time for morning.'

'I'm back to violently disliking you,' she said, and he actually winked at her before he strode out.

'Take heart,' said Daz, when they were all gone. 'At least you won't be getting shot at.'

'No, but now I'll be sitting here worrying that they all

will be.'

He grinned and followed her up to the drawing room, which had become her own haunt. The family rarely used it now that it was so often full of soldiers, and she hadn't seen hide nor hair of Frederick since Harker had chased him off.

'Now, Eve. I might almost think you cared about the squad.'

'Well, some of them at any rate,' said Eve, thinking about Charlie, who could get shot for all she cared.

'Might one of those be the Major?'

Eve flopped on to the piano stool. 'Don't you start.'

'What? Just because you've been ignoring him the last couple of days doesn't mean we can't all still see it.'

'Then I think you need an eye test, Captain, because there's nothing to see,' said Eve, and launched into the chorus of *Don't Stand So Close To Me* before he could say any more.

'I still can't believe they did this to a church,' Tallulah muttered, looking up at the high walls and flying buttresses. The past three days had been spent infiltrating the Abbey staff, with the help of Mary White and several of her acquaintances, none of whom were fond of the Coalitionists' rule. Tallulah and Martindale, joining the laundry staff, had easily stolen five uniforms.

The nave of the tall and beautiful church had been made into barracks for the rebel forces stationed there. Inside, all the pews had been smashed into firewood, and rows of ugly metal bunks had taken their place. The place stank, and rang to the rafters with the sort of language that Harker believed should never be uttered in a church.

'Well, believe it, Lu,' he muttered back. 'They're bastards, and I don't care if I'm swearing on holy ground, God agrees with me. Come on.'

Their target was the guesthouse, which was where

the more senior officers of the rebel army spent most of their time. It, unlike the rest of the Abbey, had its own generator, and even now a faint glow came from some of the windows. A telephone wire had also been strung across to the guesthouse roof, and Banks had, under the guise of fixing a couple of broken tiles, ascertained which part of the building it serviced.

Harker concentrated on their destination, mentally counting the yards of empty ground to cover. The number of armed soldiers who might realise they were all strangers. The chances of being shot to hell.

Then he gritted his teeth, and nodded to the squad to follow him.

He gave a smart salute to the guard on the door of the guesthouse, then as the other man saluted in return, Harker drew the knife he'd palmed and stabbed the guard in the stomach. As the guard folded, Harker caught him, stopped his mouth, and drew his knife across the man's throat.

Contrary to what Eve might have thought, he didn't enjoy killing people. But it was part of his job. It was necessary.

And at least it was done quickly.

Their target was a room on the ground floor, guarded day and night. The squad had ascertained that the Coalitionists only used men on active duty, but that plenty of women worked in auxiliary roles. Thus he had Martindale lead them down the vaulted stone chamber towards the guards, Tallulah beside her.

'Who're you?' said one of the guards.

Martindale gave the man a quick once-over. 'The Colonel sent us. We've a component for the computer.'

'Show me.'

She gestured Tallulah forward. Pretty, sweet Tallulah, with her big eyes and long lashes. She unslung her pack and made a show of rummaging, letting her cap fall off so her shiny dark hair swung free, blushing prettily when she couldn't find what she was looking for.

When she had the full attention of both guards, Charlie and Harker stepped smartly forward and dispatched them in the same manner as their comrade outside. When Martindale pushed the door open, Banks was ready to shoot anybody inside.

He fired one shot, the sound muffled by the big silencer on his pistol, then nodded.

Harker and Charlie dragged the guards inside, then Harker looked at the bluish glow coming from the screen of the computer, and grinned.

'Jackpot,' he whispered. 'Be quick, that one made a noise. Lu?'

She obediently held her pack open, and Harker shoved aside the man Banks had shot to grab at the board he'd slumped over. He thought it might be called the keyboard, but he wasn't sure.

He yanked at the piece of plastic, but it only came a few inches off the desk before being pulled back by a wire.

Harker swore. So did Martindale, her ear to the door.

'Footsteps,' she said.

Harker yanked at the keyboard, which came free, while Banks freed the box under the desk of its wires.

'No, she said we need the wires!' Tallulah hissed.

'All of them? There are millions!'

'I don't know! That's what she said!'

Martindale gestured for them to shut up. Harker grabbed the screen, which went abruptly blank.

'Shit,' he said. 'Is it supposed to do that?'

Tallulah gave him a frantic look, and he wedged it in anyway, trailing wires. 'Is that everything?'

She pointed to the little thing Eve had called a mouse, and he grabbed it as Martindale said, 'Sir!' urgently. She pointed to the door.

'... are they?' said someone on the other side of it.

Harker winced.

'Sir, are you all right in there?' called the voice.

Harker glanced at the dead men on the floor, shrugged, and called back, 'Fine. Leave me.' He gestured frantically for Martindale to lock the door, then pointed everyone else to the window.

Banks hurried over and opened it, checking first then dropping out on to the grass. Charlie followed, and Tallulah passed over the two packs with the computer pieces in them.

'Are you sure, sir? Dunscroft and Walton were supposed to be on guard–'

'I sent them away. I need to concentrate,' Harker said. He glanced around the room again, checking for anything else. There were more computers, more pieces of electrical equipment he didn't recognise. Did Eve need them? Hell and damnation, how was he supposed to know?

'Well, all right, sir, but–'

'Now go away!' Harker said, following Tallulah outside. Martindale came after him and landed awkwardly, gasping as her ankle gave way. Charlie hauled her unceremoniously to her feet as Harker reached up and shut the window, wincing as the sash fell with a thud.

'*Run*,' he said, and they did.

Chapter Sixteen

Eve was woken by Tallulah giggling, somewhere on the other side of the door. It took her a minute or two to figure out which door, since she couldn't remember where she'd fallen asleep, but then she realised she was on the chaise in the drawing room. A loose sheet of music was stuck to her cheek.

'Oh my goodness,' Tallulah gasped. 'I thought for sure that was it when the guard asked what was wrong with you!'

'That was *brilliant*,' said Banks, as the door opened and Harker looked in. Eve hurriedly snatched the sheet of music from her cheek as Daz woke with a start in the chair opposite. Harker rolled his eyes and jerked his head for them to follow him.

Eve raised her eyebrows at Daz. He shrugged, got to his feet, and held the door for her.

'Never fails,' Martindale said. 'Whatever they say, it's still a man's world, and you can always get them by faking some gruesome female complaint.'

'Yeah, but did you have to be *so* gruesome?' Banks said.

Eve yawned and tried to see what they'd got in their packs. Laptop? Desktop? Massive pre-war adding machine broken into parts?

'I thought you said it was brilliant?'

'Well, it was, but it was gross, too.'

She followed the squad through the lobby and up the stairs to Harker's suite. He'd taken to briefing the men in his own private sitting room, usually leaving Eve out. She'd pretended not to mind. Anyway, the room stank of cigarette smoke. Even now, he was lighting up.

Harker shut the door of his suite behind them all, took Tallulah's pack from her and drew out a computer keyboard.

Eve's heart did a backflip. 'Oh, brave new world,' she said, staring. 'You have no idea how happy I am to see that!'

'Is it an important part?' Tallulah asked.

'Well, yes, sort of. But,' she closed her eyes, and re-opened them. The keyboard was still there. 'But I was starting to think I'd imagined such a thing. Do you have anything else?'

Harker gripped the cigarette with his teeth and took a flat screen out of Tallulah's bag.

'Swanky!' Eve exclaimed. 'And here's me worrying I'll be working on ancient machines. Did you get me a CPU?'

'You mean this?' said Banks, carefully extracting a tower system from his own pack.

'Oh, I love you,' Eve said. 'Were you careful with it? Didn't drop it or get it wet or anything?'

'Nope.'

She ran over and touched the smooth metal and plastic. It seemed real enough.

'And a whole bunch of wires,' Harker added, withdrawing some from Tallulah's pack. Banks showed her some more, and even Charlie had a few. Eve grabbed a bundle of them; most weren't connected to anything. Tangled in the mess was what looked like a power cable, although the plug at the end of it was a European two-pronged affair. Her heart sank, and she looked around the walls.

'Where's a plug point?' she said, and Daz pointed.

As she went to examine it, he said, 'I spoke to Lady Winterton about a phone line – you said you'd need one for an Internet? She said they had one, but it would need connecting up.'

Eve glanced up from the plug socket, which seemed to be compatible with the plug. 'Can you do that?'

'I can try.'

She looked around, spotted a writing desk by the window and pointed to it. 'Bring that over,' she said, 'and I'll plug it in.'

She was dog-tired, but she figured she'd been through less than the rest of the squad, and she could at least see if it worked before she started negotiating some sleep. Harker announced that they should celebrate, and Banks produced a bottle of mead he'd apparently liberated from the kitchen. He poured a mug for everyone, including Eve, who politely ignored hers.

'There are a lot of things to connect up,' she warned them as she put the CPU on the desk. 'I can't do it all instantly. Especially since these wires are in such a tangle.'

'Oh, I'm sorry, next time I'll stop to carefully wind them all up separately,' Harker said, and was ignored.

'How long will it take?' Daz asked.

'I dunno.' Eve looked at the mess. 'Last time I moved a computer halfway across a room it took me the best part of three hours.'

'*How*?' said Harker.

'Well, it had to be disconnected from the printer and scanner and modem, and there were wires to speakers, and table legs and lights and things getting in the way,' she said. She peered at the keyboard, spattered with something red and sticky. 'Er, do I want to know what that is?'

'Probably not,' said Banks.

'I did say keep it clean and dry,' Eve said despairingly.

'Banks, next time you kill some bugger, use a blunt instrument,' Harker said.

Eve's head snapped up in horror. 'Did you *kill* someone for this?'

Charlie rolled her eyes. 'No, we asked politely. What do you think?'

Eve looked at the computer, disconnected and disjointed,

and realised that no matter how bored or depressed she'd been every time she waited for Windows to boot up, she'd never been in danger of getting shot.

'Right,' she said. She glanced at the clock over the fireplace. 'I'll ... if I make a start on this now ...'

'Could have it all done and dusted by morning and we can go home,' Banks said.

Eve yawned. 'Right,' she said again. 'Okay.' She picked up the power cable and started trying to untangle it. That cable looked like a USB, and that one might have been Ethernet, but she wasn't sure. And that one–

'Sarah,' Daz said, and Martindale looked round. 'You're limping.'

'Just fell badly, sir.'

He gestured for her to sit down, and knelt by her, feeling at her ankle while she protested there was nothing wrong with it.

'We should have a light day tomorrow anyway,' Harker said, 'you can rest it then.'

Sure, Eve thought, *she can rest her ankle, when I busted mine I spent the next day hopping up steps and getting locked in prison*. She tugged the end of the power cable free, lost her grip and dropped the whole knot on to the floor.

'It's all right, nobody help,' she said, when nobody did.

'It's not swollen,' Daz said, pressing on Martindale's ankle. 'Just twisted, I think. Take it easy tomorrow.'

'Reckon we all ought to get some rest, sir,' Charlie said, smothering a yawn.

Eve sat down on the floor and started to pick through the knot of wires again. She gave another yawn.

'Right, bed everyone,' Harker said. 'Sleep in tomorrow. Good work tonight.'

They all trooped out. Charlie cast Eve a distrustful look. Eve ignored her, and unwrapped a USB cable from the prongs of the plug.

'Cold down here,' she said, to no one in particular. The squad had all gone.

'You could drink your mead,' said Harker, making her jump – and drop the cables again.

'I'd rather not.'

He stubbed out his cigarette, picked up Eve's mug and swigged from it. 'Is that really going to take hours?'

'Probably.' Especially since she was tired, and not thinking straight, and her fingers were clumsy, and she *was* cold.

'Eve.' He hunkered down and peered at her. 'Go to bed.'

She looked at the wires, which were so blurry they could have been snake-dancing for all she could tell.

'Thought you wanted me to make a start on this tonight.'

'Since when have you ever done anything I've said?'

She smiled at that, and Harker took the wires from her, put them on the desk, and held out his hand. She hesitated for a moment – but it was only his hand, she could touch his hand without bursting into flame – and took it.

His grip was strong, of course, and his hands warm, of course, and as he tugged her to her feet she lost her balance and fell against him, just for a second. Just long enough to register how very big and hard he was, before she jerked away, mortified.

'Night then,' Harker said, and Eve swallowed and looked away and mumbled, 'Night,' and half-ran from the room.

'Did you sleep all right?' Tallulah asked Eve the next morning as she lay there trying to summon the will to get out of bed. The trundle bed wasn't the most comfortable thing in the world, but it was warm, and Hatfield Chase wasn't centrally heated.

'Fine,' said Eve, who'd been disturbed by dreams of falling against Harker's hard body in various states of undress.

'You were talking in your sleep,' Tallulah said.

Oh God. 'Really?' Eve said weakly.

'Well, sort of. You were making noises, maybe not actual words.'

'Bad dream,' Eve managed, which seemed to pacify Tallulah, even if Martindale didn't seem to be entirely convinced. She didn't say anything, but after the look she gave Eve, she didn't need to.

At breakfast, everyone was giving Eve expectant looks, except for Harker, who seemed to be ignoring her.

'Well?' Banks said eventually. 'Are you gonna fix the computer today?'

'Look,' Eve said. 'I'm not an expert on this. I know how to use a computer, I don't know how they actually work.' At their blank looks, she tried to explain. 'Like when you use a ... a car. Do you know how they work?'

'Yes,' said Tallulah.

'Or a gun,' Eve tried.

'Yes,' said Harker.

'But I mean ... if something went wrong, could you fix it?'

'Yes,' said Tallulah.

'Yes,' said Harker.

'Or put one together from component parts?'

'Yes,' said Martindale. 'Worked in munitions before I joined up.'

'Didn't you join up at eighteen?' Eve asked.

'Yes.'

When Eve frowned, Harker said, 'Not everyone has the luxury of spending their teenage years – what were you doing, Eve? Singing?'

'Yeah, and it was damn hard work,' Eve snapped. 'Fine, look. I'll go and fix your damn computer.' She threw her toast back on her plate. 'I'm not hungry anyway.'

Her stomach betrayed her by growling as she stood up.

Banks stifled a smile. Harker's lips thinned.

'Oh, get lost,' she snarled, and stomped upstairs to Harker's sitting room, where the computer sat in pieces, looking oddly sad.

She'd barely sat down before the door opened and Harker came in, bearing her plate of toast. Eve said nothing, so he set it down on the floor next to her.

'I said I wasn't hungry.'

'And you lied.'

'I can't eat it now, I'll get the computer all … toasty.'

He nearly smiled at that. 'Well, then. Don't want it to go to waste.' He picked up a piece.

'Bastard!' Eve yelped, because she really was hungry.

Harker grinned and handed it back to her. 'You'll just have to wash your hands.'

She made a face, but ate the toast, which had been spread with honey and was delicious, while Harker sat opposite her on the floor, his back to an overstuffed chair and his legs stretched out.

'Can you really fix this?' he said. 'Or is it all too broken?'

'I don't know,' Eve said. 'Is there any reason why it should be broken?' He shrugged. 'Was it working when you got it?' *When you shot someone for it?*

Harker looked nonplussed at that, so she sighed and elaborated, 'Was it on? Were there lights here?' she pointed to the front of the CPU. 'Was there anything on the monitor? Colours, pictures?'

'The monitor is the screen thing? Yeah. I didn't see what they were, though.'

'Doesn't matter.' Eve finished her toast and clambered to her feet, wiggling her sticky fingers at Harker, who pointed to the bedroom. 'No, I want to wash them.'

'Bathroom through there.' When her eyes went wide, he grinned. 'Yeah, perks of an officer.'

'Charlie and Daz don't have their own bathrooms.'

'Nope.' Harker stretched. 'They ain't in charge.'

Shaking her head, she went through the bedroom to the small but beautifully appointed, rather Victorian-looking bathroom.

The one she'd been using, along with the rest of the squad, was awash with towels, bars of soap, razors and the rather fancy shampoo and conditioner Tallulah had produced from her pack. Unlike the others, Eve had no toiletries of her own and was using what had been provided by the housekeeper, so she'd been able to leave nothing personal in there.

But Harker, it appeared, had also left virtually nothing personal in his bathroom. There were a couple of towels, presumably hung up by the maid, since she couldn't really see him as the tidy type, and some soap and a toothbrush, along with a pot of the weird-tasting paste they all used to clean their teeth, and that was about it.

He probably didn't own a razor. Or a comb. Eve would bet good money he'd never even heard of conditioner. But now she thought of it, he was rarely actually dirty. Just untidy. He didn't smell.

Actually, he did, he smelled of soap and cigarettes and hot skin and other indefinable things that made her pulse speed up just a little.

But since she wasn't attracted to him, that didn't matter.

Eve finished washing her hands, and went back into the sitting room, where Daz was kneeling by the computer components, peering at them in fascination. Harker was standing, looking at his watch.

'How long does it take you to wash your hands?' he said incredulously.

Eve stuck her tongue out at him. 'How long does it take you to become computer literate?' she said. 'Because until you are, I'm the one in charge of this, all right, and I'm having *clean* hands touching it.' She glanced at Daz, who rolled his eyes.

'I'm a doctor,' he said. 'I know about clean hands.'

'It's a machine,' Harker said. 'It's not going to go gangrenous.' He looked at it doubtfully. 'Is it?'

'No, but you really don't want to get sticky fingers inside it. I'm still not even convinced that keyboard is going to work.'

'Well, then you'll have to fix it.'

Eve closed her eyes. 'Harker, you can't just fix a keyboard that's had blood spilled all over it. If we're lucky, there'll have been a layer of rubber protecting the components inside. But if there isn't, or if some of the ... liquid got inside, it will have fried the electronics and you're going to need someone with about a hundred times my skills to fix it.'

'Can't you learn? Daz has books–'

'Written in hieroglyphs,' Eve said, because Daz had showed her some of the books and they'd reminded her that the Americas hadn't been colonised by anybody from Europe. 'Do you speak American?'

'Algonquian,' Daz murmured.

'I know a few words,' Harker said.

'Any of them repeatable?'

Harker narrowed his eyes at her, then said, 'Daz. We need a phone line. Can you see what you can do about it? And send Charlie up, will you?'

Daz looked between them, then without smiling in any way at all, nodded and left the room.

Eve gave Harker a look and settled back down on the floor to finish untangling the wires. She figured she'd plug in the CPU first to see if it actually worked, then start on the peripherals.

'Are you going to sit and watch me all day?' she said, without looking up.

'Yep.'

'Marvellous.'

'Would it really stop the ... the ...'

She looked up. He was waving his hand at the desk.

'The keyboard?'

'Yeah. Would getting it wet really break it?'

'Yes. Trust me. I once spilt coffee on one and could only type words on the left side of the keyboard. Unfortunately, I was working for someone called Ogilvie, so his name ended up as 've'.'

Harker was looking nonplussed again. Eve sighed, and debated explaining a QWERTY keyboard to him.

'Never mind,' she said.

She untangled the power cable at last and plugged one end into the CPU. Holding her breath, she plugged the other end into the wall socket, and pressed the power switch.

Nothing happened.

'Well, damn.'

'What?'

'Well, that was supposed to come on.' She sighed.

'The, uh, monitor thing is blank.' Harker came over and peered at it. 'Are these wires supposed to be connected?'

'Yes, eventually, but I need to get this working first. Remember what I said in those notes about this being the brain of the computer? And the rest of it is just how you see what's on it, or input new stuff?'

'Yes, but without anything to display the information on, how do you know it's not working?'

'Well, these lights aren't on for one thing. And it's not making a noise.'

'Should it?'

'Yes. It should.'

She set Harker to locating another plug point, and carried the CPU into the bedroom where he'd unplugged the lamp by the bed. Still nothing.

'Are you sure no one dropped this? Or got it wet?' she said, frowning at the CPU as it lay on Harker's pillow.

'I'm sure,' he said. 'And it was working when we got it.'

She resisted the urge to sigh again. He'd probably just yanked the plug out, which could have caused the damage. It didn't seem likely he'd have waited for it to power down.

'Well,' she said, 'I suppose I could have a look inside it.' She turned it over and inspected the back plate. 'I'm going to need a screwdriver. A small Phillips head.'

Another blank look.

'You *do* know what a screwdriver is?' Eve said heavily.

'Yes, I know what a screwdriver is,' Harker said. 'But I don't know what a small Phillips head is.'

'Well, small means little, like the size of my patience,' Eve said. 'A Phillips head is the crosswise kind, look,' she pointed to the screwheads, and Harker leaned in close.

It rather suddenly occurred to Eve that they were leaning over his bed together, and she drew back sharply.

'Okay,' Harker said, still looking closely at the back of the computer. 'Come on, then.'

'What do you need me for?'

He hesitated, just for a split second, but in that second his eyes darted to the computer, and Eve's mouth dropped open.

'Oh my God,' she said. 'That's why you're here, isn't it? You think I'm going to sabotage it, don't you?'

'I never said–'

'You didn't have to. Or am I going to use it to send messages to my Coalitionist friends?'

'Do you have Coalitionist friends?' Harker said.

'*No*. But then, maybe I should. They'd have to be nicer to me than you are,' Eve said, and snatched up the CPU to stomp back into the sitting room.

'Come on, Eve, don't start on this again,' Harker said,

following her.

'Well, how would you like it if everyone thought you were a spy, huh? If all you did was have a minor accident and get blown off course because no one actually told you how to use the damn thing, and when you woke up you were accused of spying?'

But it seemed odd, talking about the glider and the TV show and the accident. Almost as if she was relating something that had happened to someone else. On TV maybe, or in a book. Not something that had happened in this world.

Harker pinched the bridge of his nose. 'Look at it from my point of view, would you? I've got someone flying over the river – over the Tower, no less – when the only things that ought to be flying through the sky are birds. When you wake up you can't tell me where you're from–'

'I *can*,' Eve said.

'Oh, aye. Mitcham. Remember Mitcham?'

'Yes,' Eve said wretchedly, 'but not the Mitcham you showed me.' She sat down in the armchair and put her head in her hands. Took a deep breath or two.

Maybe she really was crazy. Maybe she'd hit her head. Maybe she was in a coma and dreaming all this. Maybe she was dead.

'Oh God,' she groaned, 'is this hell?'

'No. Hell wouldn't have toast and honey.'

She looked up. Harker was crouched in front of her, concern in his eyes. There was a small scar just under his left eye, on the cheekbone. A tiny dent.

'Look, Eve, I'm trying here,' Harker said softly. 'I've got a job to do.'

'I know,' she said.

'And for all I know you could be innocent. But then, for all I know you might not be. And I just can't risk something so important on a maybe.'

Eve reached out without really thinking and touched that little scar. 'What made that?'

Harker's eyes closed for just a second. He swallowed. 'Don't remember,' he said, his voice slightly husky. 'Did it as a child.' His hand moved up to cover hers, and this time it was Eve whose breath caught in her throat. 'Eve–'

Someone scratched at the door. Eve froze, and so did Harker, then he rose and turned away. 'Yeah?'

It was Tallulah. 'Sir, Captain Haran says he's got the phone line working.'

Harker glanced back at Eve, then at the computer. 'That any good to you?'

'Maybe, once I get the thing working.' She blinked, shook her head. Something had just happened and she wasn't entirely sure what. 'Uh, I forgot to ask if this has a modem. You might need–' She saw his face. 'Never mind.'

Harker gave the computer a dark look. 'Lu,' he said, 'stay here. I'm going to find a screwdriver.'

With that he was gone, and Eve was left with Tallulah giving her a very knowing look.

'Whatever you're thinking,' Eve said, closing her eyes, 'don't.'

Chapter Seventeen

'Ah!' said Eve suddenly, waking Harker from his half-doze.

'What?'

But she wasn't speaking to him. Daz was also sitting on the floor, holding the light for her to peer into the back of the computer. Harker had looked in, and been reminded of a drawing he'd seen once of Manhattan, all these toweringly high buildings full up of tiny apartments, people living on top of each other all higgledy-piggledy.

'See this?' Eve pointed to something he couldn't see. 'It shouldn't be loose.'

She dealt Harker a look that said it was his fault.

'Once again, no one dropped it–'

'Where should it go?' Daz said.

'Well, that's the fun thing. See these tiny sockets?'

'Um ...'

'Any one of those.'

'But there are dozens. Hundreds.'

'Yep,' Eve said with mock cheerfulness. She glared at Harker again. He ignored her, having just heard the car pull up outside. Charlie. He left Eve with Daz – probably safer that way – and made his way downstairs, colliding with Sir Dennis in the lobby.

'Is that my car?' he asked, peering out through the fantail.

'Yep. Lovely machine,' Harker said, striding towards the door.

'You've had it out every day!'

'Nice little runner.'

'I really must protest, Major–'

Harker spun around so fast Sir Dennis lost his footing.

'Are you impeding the war effort, Sir Dennis?'

Sir Dennis's moustache quivered with indignation. 'Of course not, sir!'

'Good. Then you won't mind us making full use of your car, will you?'

He didn't wait for an answer, but went outside into the cold, where Banks was driving the car back around to the garage. Charlie crunched over the gravel towards him.

'Still there, sir,' she said. 'At least for the time being, then they're moving them to Madingly's house tonight.'

The former MP who'd led the secession. 'Guarded?'

'Extremely well.'

'Excellent.' Harker turned to go back inside the house. If Daz and Eve couldn't get that damned machine working, they'd have to break into what was probably the best-defended house in Leeds just to get some spare parts.

'Any progress on the machine, sir?'

'Some. Well, no. She's fannying about with wires and screwdrivers – seriously, Charlie, I've seen entrails less complicated than that. It's all tiny, tiny little pieces of – I don't even know what they are. She calls 'em circuit board.'

'Is someone watching her, sir?'

'Yes, Charlie. At all times, Charlie. Just as ordered, Charlie.'

She gave him a reproachful look. 'I'm only trying–'

'Yeah, I know.' The trouble was, so was Eve.

At lunch, he asked Eve if she'd got the keyboard working. She gave him a harassed look.

'No. I told you, I won't know if that works until I've got the CPU working. There's no point having a fully functioning hand if your brain is missing, is there?'

'I dunno, it's always worked for me,' Banks said.

She left lunch early, trailed by Banks, since Harker figured he'd probably be best at diffusing her. Daz followed them shortly after, and Harker turned to Charlie and said, 'Okay. If she can't get these pieces working, we go into town and break into Madingly's place.'

'Dangerous, sir.'

Harker rolled his eyes. 'Charlie, we're the bloody army. Dangerous is what we *do*.'

Happily, while they were still making plans, a triumphant shout came from upstairs. At least, Harker assumed it was an occasion for happiness. In the back of his mind he still couldn't banish hideous thoughts of Eve and Daz shagging like mad, every opportunity they got.

No, Banks is there too, he reminded himself, and then his treacherous imagination added Banks into the scenario, and he ran up the stairs so fast he nearly tripped and broke his neck.

But when he pushed the door open, everyone was still clothed and clustered around the computer. The CPU box was glowing, at least a small section of it at the front was, and a low humming sound came from it.

Eve looked up, beaming. 'It's working!' she said, grabbing a cable that was linked to the flat black screen, and pushing it into a socket at the back of the computer.

The screen made a noise that sounded like *glonk*, and then a little light flashed down in one corner.

Eve stared at it. Harker stared at Eve. *Damn, she's beautiful.*

'That's it!' she shrieked, turning those big blue-green eyes on Daz and squeezing his arm. 'It's working.' She let out a big sigh. 'Oh, thank goodness for that, I thought it was completely knackered.'

She watched the screen as various things flashed up on it, all of them complete nonsense to Harker, until it settled on a black screen with a couple of lines of text in the corner. The last character blinked on and off.

Eve nodded and brushed some dried blood from the keyboard before tapping a few buttons. She watched the screen, where precisely nothing happened. 'Oh dear.'

Harker's heart sank. 'What do you mean, oh dear?'

'Well, I'm not getting anything out of this.' She hit a few keys. 'See? Nothing on screen.' She peered at the single line of text, which was a couple of nonsensical characters, and added, 'And I have a feeling it's in French anyway.'

Harker rolled his head back. The muscles in his neck crunched.

'I did tell you–' Eve began.

'Yeah, yeah. Can't you fix it?'

Eve peered doubtfully at the keyboard. 'I told you–'

'Yes, I *know*. Can you fix it, Eve?'

She chewed her lip. 'Well, I can try, but I can't promise anything. If the blood's got inside–'

'Yeah,' Harker said wearily. He looked at his watch, then at Charlie. She gave him a look that said he must be joking.

He gave her one that said he wasn't. 'Half-an-hour, men, get ready to leave. We're going raiding again.'

Tallulah groaned. Banks grinned. Charlie glowered.

'Martindale,' Harker said, 'how's the ankle?'

'Fine, sir.'

'Daz?'

'Up to her, sir.'

Harker waved her off, and turned to Eve. 'I'll get you a new keyboard,' he said. 'Without blood on it this time.'

A flicker of a smile touched her lips. 'Don't suppose you could stretch to an iPod?'

Harker blinked at her.

Eve almost laughed. 'No, I didn't think so. Okay, well. Good luck.'

He nodded, and left the room, Charlie trailing after him.

'Sir, do we really need to do this?'

'Yes.'

'But what if she's just pretending it doesn't work? Sir, if she's got it working, she could be sending messages to the Coalitionists about where we are–'

'Yes, Charlie, or maybe it's just not bloody working! She did say don't get it wet–'

'Which makes for a very convenient excuse when we did, don't you think?'

'And how did she know Banks was going to shoot someone right in front of it?'

'I don't *know*, sir, I'm just trying to make sure you don't–'

He spun around so fast she walked into him. 'I don't what?'

Her brown eyes narrowed. 'Forget your mission. Sir.'

Charlie, his oldest and closest friend, was challenging him. Except she wasn't his oldest and closest friend, dammit, she was his Lieutenant. She was a soldier, and so was he, and he had a job to do. He took a deep breath and let it out.

'I never forget my mission, Lieutenant.'

'No, sir.'

He started walking again.

'Uniform, sir,' she said, and he growled at her and reversed course.

'There,' Tallulah pointed to a glint of light. 'That's it.'

'Sure?' Harker whispered back.

'Yes, that's the monitor thing.'

Harker nodded, brought up his binoculars and peered at the truck as the back was closed up, and a soldier banged on the back of it. It set off, slowly, another truck in front of it and another behind. Men on horses flanked it.

Harker swore and crawled from his hiding place to Charlie's. 'Four cavalry, two trucks flanking,' he said, 'probably all full of armed men.'

'Want to wait until they get there?' she asked.

'Centre of town? Nightmare. We do it on the road. Banks? You got plenty of ammo?'

'Yessir.' Banks hefted his sniper rifle.

'Good. You're with Lieutenant Riggs, south side of the road. Go!'

They ran off into the night. With Tallulah and Martindale following, Harker darted through the trees to the north of the compound, chasing fast after the convoy. Good job the computer equipment was sensitive, or they'd surely have been moving too fast.

The trucks blazed with light as they rattled along the road. *Stupid,* Harker thought, *that's like an invitation. They might as well have stuck a foghorn on top.*

'Lu,' he said, as they reached the edge of the road. 'You up to this?'

She nodded and handed him her coat. The only one of them not in Coalitionist uniform, she was wearing something filched from the head housemaid, who'd surely be furious to find it missing. Not that there was much of it to miss. Tight, red, and showing lots of thigh, it was about a hundred times more vampish than Harker was comfortable seeing on someone he really regarded as something like a little sister.

If Saskia knew about this, he thought, *she'd bloody kill me.*

The thought cheered him. Annoying Saskia usually did.

'Off you go, then,' he said, and Tallulah ran towards the road, yanking down her bodice as she did. Harker heard cloth tear and caught a glimpse of pale breast, before Tallulah disappeared into the darkness.

'So that's why you sent Banks with the Lieutenant,' Martindale said dryly.

Harker glanced at her briefly before turning his attention

back to the convoy, half-visible through the thick tree trunks. 'Don't reckon he'd be able to concentrate.'

'He'd probably challenge anyone who saw her breast to a duel.'

Harker, who still didn't really like the idea of Tallulah even having breasts, let alone showing them to anyone, fidgeted awkwardly. Then Tallulah's cry of, 'Help! Please!' sounded over the rumble of the truck engines, and he forgot all about her breasts and started hoping she'd get picked up.

More voices sounded, but he couldn't tell what they were saying. Creeping closer, he saw one of the cavalrymen halted by the side of the road, leering down at Tallulah, who was doing a very good impression of a helpless woman in distress.

Well. A good impression of what people thought a woman in distress ought to act like. Anyone who'd seen Mary White's glassy eyes would disagree with Tallulah's performance.

'I can't leave my post, miss,' the cavalryman was saying to Tallulah, 'but you're welcome to ride with me.'

Tallulah didn't hesitate. 'Are you armed, sir? I'm so frightened they'll come after me!'

'Yes, of course I'm armed.' He laughed, showing her his sword and pistol. 'Come on, then.' He held out his hand, and pulled her up on to his lap. Tallulah wriggled, which he seemed to enjoy – *pervert* – and they set off.

'She can take care of herself, sir,' Martindale whispered, and Harker realised he was grinding his teeth.

'Come on,' he said, and they ran alongside the road, hidden by the trees and their dark clothes, as Tallulah turned big blue eyes on the cavalryman and spoke in a high, breathless voice.

'I'm so frightened, sir! Would you mind – no, it's too silly.'

'No, tell me.'

'Well, sir, I'd just feel so much safer if you had your sword in hand,' she said, and her bosom heaved. Harker shook his head in disbelief. Ballet nothing, this kid could act.

The cavalryman gave what he probably thought was a dashing grin – *he even had a moustache, the twat* – and obliged by drawing his sword and twirling it showily. Tallulah gave him a shy smile.

'And your pistol, sir, how accurate is it?' she asked, as they drew level with the convoy again. The other horseman on the same side looked back and shook his head at his comrade.

'Oh, it's quite accurate. I can shoot a man at a hundred paces.'

Harker shared a glance with Martindale who, like him, could do that blindfolded.

'May I see it?'

The cavalryman, who clearly thought he was well in, drew his pistol, which Harker considered an extremely stupid thing to do. Tallulah clearly agreed, for she pressed it against his chest and pulled the trigger. The sound was lost in the rumble of the noisy truck next to her.

Harker liked fools, so long as they were fighting for the other side. Clearly, Tallulah's cavalryman and the one riding in front of her were both complete idiots, because they were dead within five minutes of her mounting the horse. Harker ran up, gave Tallulah her coat as she kicked the dead man away, and took his place on the other horse.

Everything went well, surprisingly well, in fact, as Banks shot out a tyre on the rearguard truck, and one of the riders on the other side hung back to see what the problem was.

Banks shot the remaining rider, which was when everything started to go wrong. Instead of falling quietly, he cried out, panicked his horse, and the beast reared, then began to gallop as its rider slumped to one side and dragged on the stirrups.

'What the hell?' said a voice from within the middle truck, and Harker swore and rode up to the cab.

'Keep going,' he said, 'it's nothing.'

The driver glanced up at him, and the light must have caught Harker's face, because the Coalitionist soldier reached for a small device on the dashboard, picked it up and said, 'Truck one, we have a probl–'

Harker shot him.

The truck veered and wobbled, making his horse shy away, and the other soldier inside the cab started shooting.

Damn and bloody hell. Charlie and Banks came skidding towards the truck, and Harker pointed them on towards the vehicle at the front, which had stopped. Oh hell, that thing was a *radio*, he'd been talking to the other men, they were in communication!

The radio crackled, and a voice said, 'Truck two, what's your status?'

The soldier inside the truck grabbed for it, then slumped forward as Tallulah's bullet killed him. She swung inside the cab with admirable sang-froid – *just like Saskia* – and shoved the two dead men out of her way to take the wheel.

Handing the radio to Harker, she hissed, 'Tell them we're fine, they need a man's voice!'

He stared at the radio, then hit the button as the Coalitionist had done and said, 'We're fine. Just a problem with one of the horses.'

'Truck three is still back there. Reckon we should stop?'

'Uh, no. Keep going. You know our orders.'

That was a guess. But Harker knew how this sort of thing went.

'Yeah, you're right,' said the voice doubtfully. 'Okay th–'

Another bullet cut that voice short. Charlie and Banks had reached the front truck. Breathing a sigh of relief that things were back on track, Harker dismounted, slapping the horse away, and jumped into the back of the truck as it was moving. Martindale ran alongside and leapt in after him.

'Excellent,' she said, and Harker grinned at her. He looked around the back of the truck, which contained a couple of trunks and a dead guard. He kicked the dead guy aside, unstrapped the trunks from their moorings, and started going through them.

'Just wait for Charlie and Banks to take the front car,' he said, 'and we're home and dry. Might as well drive this home.'

The truck bumped over something in the road, bouncing the boxes to the back of the truck. 'Front truck's moving again, sir,' Tallulah said, picking up speed to follow it.

'What about the Austin?' Martindale asked.

'I'm sure he can survive without it. We'll come back tomorrow. Lu,' he poked his head over the front seat, '*nice* work.'

She shrugged nonchalantly, but she was smiling. 'I told you Saskia taught me to fight.'

'Yeah, but she's an officer. Who taught her to fight that dirty?'

'You did, sir.'

She met his eye through the rear-view mirror and grinned.

'Well, nice to know I'm good for something,' Harker muttered. He ripped open one box and found another CPU. Might be useful. A second held what Eve called the peripherals: a keyboard, mouse and a box of small devices he didn't recognise. They looked like they might plug into one of the many sockets on the back of the computer. He picked up a couple, turned them over in his hand, and tucked them thoughtfully into a pocket.

A sudden burst of machine-gun fire made his head whip around. Harker, keyboard in hand, shoved it inside his jacket in case he needed to make a run for it.

'Lu, is the first truck still moving? Charlie's got it?'

'They threw out a couple of men, sir. That's what we ran over.'

The truck shook with the force of more bullets, jolting Harker against the back of the seats.

The last truck, the men hadn't stayed with it, they'd come after them on foot–

'Lu, get down!' Harker yelled. He glanced at Martindale, who already had her shotgun out, then grabbed the dead guard to see if he had any weapons worth using. A submachine-gun. Very nice; nicer than anything the army had.

Harker requisitioned it.

'They've stopped, sir, Lieutenant Riggs has–'

The rest of Tallulah's words were drowned in another hail of fire, this time denting the back of the truck. A second later something heavy hit the back door, and it flew open.

Harker ducked. Bullets sprayed the inside of the truck, peppering the walls, the boxes, *everything* with shot. Martindale, her gun raised, jerked in the air.

'Drive!' Harker yelled, hoping like blazes that Tallulah hadn't been hit. But the truck surged forward, and he raised the submachine-gun to blast the buggers who'd shot in. The gun barked and blazed, and in the sudden burst of light he saw Martindale's slumped body slide towards the back of the truck as it leapt forward.

He grabbed her wrist, but couldn't stop the computer trunks from sliding out.

'Drive, Lu, faster,' he yelled, blindly spraying bullets out the back of the truck. Martindale was still, heavy, blood darkening the front of her stolen uniform. A pulse thudded in her wrist.

'But Riggs and B–'

'Can take care of themselves, but Martindale is dying, Lu, so overtake and drive!'

The stolen gun ran out of bullets. Harker grabbed for his own, but his arm didn't seem to be working properly. Something was restricting his movement – that damned keyboard!

Well, it had probably saved his life.

Unfortunately, Martindale didn't seem to have been so lucky.

Chapter Eighteen

Daz was dozing in the armchair as Eve carefully clicked the last key back into place.

'Come on,' she muttered, 'work. I am not taking you apart to fix you. Last time I did that the whole thing gave up on me. And I–'

Something clattered outside, a poor engine ragged to the limit, gravel spraying and brakes squealing, and she scrambled to her feet. Daz started awake as she ran past, to the window, just in time to see a car – no, a truck – rattle around to the back of the house.

Oh God, it's the Coalitionists, they've found us!

'What?' said Daz, as she turned back.

'That's not Sir Dennis's car,' Eve said, her voice very nearly steady. She looked around. 'Are you armed? No, of course you're not.' There was a hefty-looking vase by the window, and she grabbed it. 'Where do you think Harker keeps his guns?'

'On his person at all times,' Daz said. 'Look, it's probably nothing–'

'Knives, there'll be knives in the kitchen,' Eve said, and swept past him, heart pounding but for some reason not terribly afraid. Adrenaline, she figured, it had always kept stage-fright at bay. She'd go and get a knife – damn, it was so dark, away from the light in Harker's suite the landing was inky–

Footsteps thudded on the stairs. Eve tensed.

Then the shadows shifted and it was Harker, dark and stormy, the dim light glinting off the sweat on his brow. He loomed big and angry in the darkness, and Eve was horrendously glad he was on her side.

He stared at her for a second. Then he looked past her and said, 'Daz. Get your kit. Martindale. In the scullery. It's bad.'

Daz nodded and ran past them to his room.

'How bad?' Eve said, and Harker didn't answer for a second. The tension in his face was enough to clue her in.

'Very,' he said, and moved into life, shouldering past her into his room.

'But – shouldn't I – I mean, is anyone with Martindale?'

'Tallulah. She's some medic training and a cool head.' The corner of his mouth quirked. 'Besides which, she wouldn't leave her. Come on. I need you.'

She trotted after him into the sudden light of his suite. 'That car – it wasn't Sir Dennis's – was that you?'

'Who else would it have been?' He put down a bottle of something on the table, then went to the kettle by the fire, peered inside and hung it on its hook, poking at the fire to brighten it.

'Well, never mind.'

'Eve, what are you doing with that vase?'

She looked down, slightly surprised to see it in her hands. 'Um. I – uh, it doesn't matter.' Hastily she replaced it on its little table.

Harker grunted, shrugged his jacket off one shoulder. Now she could see his face clearly, and it was gleaming not just with sweat but smears of blood, Martindale's blood. His jacket was dark with it too, and torn, and–

'What's that?'

He extracted something from the ripped camouflage. 'Brought you a new keyboard,' he said, handing her some shards of plastic and metal, which Eve took in despair.

'Didn't I tell you not to drop it? This is worse than useless, it's–'

She broke off suddenly. Harker had dropped his jacket on the floor, and most of the keyboard had gone with it, pieces of torn and twisted metal and plastic keys that scattered on the ground. But only most of the keyboard fell.

The rest seemed to be stuck in his chest.

Blood saturated his shirt, which in places was ripped wide open enough for her to see the torn flesh beneath. But what horrified her, really horrified her, were the bits of metal and circuit board actually sticking out of his skin. Pieces were embedded.

Eve stared in horror. 'Oh my *God*,' she whispered.

'I wouldn't call it useless,' Harker said. 'In fact, it makes decent armour. I could suggest this to General Wheeler for standard issue.'

His breathing was a little ragged, Eve realised. She'd put it down to exertion before: carrying Martindale inside, running up the stairs.

'Oh God,' she said, unable to think of anything else to say.

'Eve,' Harker said warningly. 'I need you to help me get this crap out of my chest and stitch it up.'

'But – you should see Daz–'

'Daz is busy.' His face was grim. 'Got far more important things to worry about than this. Charlie and Banks won't be back until they've got the enemy off our scent. There is no one else, do you understand?' He strode over to the bowl she'd been using to wash the keyboard letters, and thrust it at her. 'Go and clean this out, and wash your hands.'

Eve remained frozen, staring at the ripped and weeping skin surrounding a sharp fragment of circuitry.

'Eve!' Harker put his face close to hers, so close she could see the tiny beads of sweat – *not from heat, not from exertion; he's in pain* – and blood. 'I need you to help me.'

Her eyes were rooted on a tiny bit of wire.

'If you're going to get all girlie on me, I'll do it my bloody self.'

Girlie! She opened her mouth in outrage, but there was a gleam of humour in his eyes.

She nodded, shaking herself back into life, and took the bowl, hurrying into his private bathroom and scouring it with soap. Her fingers shook, but she glared at herself in the mirror, told her pale reflection to pull its damn self together, and strode back into the bedroom.

All the lamps were on, electric and oil, the flames from the latter flickering a soft, warm light over the room. Harker's pack was open by the bed, and extracted from it was a basic medical kit, laid out on the nightstand, bandages and needles and a set of tweezers. She wondered how often he'd had to doctor himself, or the others, that he needed to carry a med kit in his pack.

She set the empty bowl down by the bed, laid towels next to it, and was just about to call Harker when he came in, stripped to the waist, and Eve was glad she wasn't carrying anything because she'd certainly have dropped it.

It wasn't just the blood trickling down his stomach from the dozen tiny wounds, or the bits of plastic sticking out of his chest and shoulder, that made her gut clench. It was the other wounds, old wounds, scars both healed and healing, that covered his entire torso. A long, jagged mark running down the side of his flat stomach; the short cuts of sword thrusts; the neat little punctuation marks where bullets had hit; a speckle of tiny pockmarks on his arm that she thought might have come from shotgun pellets. And everywhere, little lines and curved scars where someone had cut him open, either in malice or to dig something out of that tight, hard flesh, until there were barely two inches clear of scars anywhere on his body.

Harker moved past her and set the kettle on the nightstand,

apparently unaware of her horror. On his back were several jagged, asymmetrical marks that looked as if someone had smashed a chair over him.

'How are you still alive?' Eve breathed, and he looked down at himself.

'It's not that bad,' he said, turning. 'None of 'em have gone deep.' He frowned, and poked at a rather hideous pink gash on his shoulder. 'Although I ain't sure if there might be a bullet in there.'

'I don't mean that.' Her hand reached out, and her fingers traced the long jagged scar on his stomach. 'You look like ...'

But she didn't know what he looked like. Couldn't possibly think of a comparison. She'd never seen a scar half as horrible as a single one of these. An ex-boyfriend had borne a tiny scar on his knee from a teenage bike accident, and he'd been terribly proud of it, even though it was barely noticeable.

But these weren't scars to be proud of. These were reminders, every one of them, that someone had really and truly wanted to kill Harker.

She looked up and met his eyes, but they were hard, blank, cold steel. His face was shuttered. *Don't push him on this one.*

'Right,' she said vaguely. 'I – right.'

Harker sat down on the bed, poured steaming water from the kettle into the bowl and dabbed a towel into it, which he then used to wipe away some of the blood from his chest.

Eve glanced around for some sort of disinfectant or even an anaesthetic, but her eye fell on a bottle of gin, and for some reason she knew it was going to serve both purposes.

Harker grabbed the bottle and poured a healthy quantity down his throat. Then he took a breath and sloshed some over the ugly wounds on his chest. His breath hissed between his teeth, his fingers clenched in the sheet, and even Eve winced. She half-expected his skin to sizzle.

'Hell,' he muttered, 'you think you'll never forget how much it hurts.' He slugged some more of the gin, then held the bottle out to her.

'You want me to do this drunk?'

'You want to do it sober?'

He had a point. Eve drank some, shuddering as it burned down her throat.

'Good girl.' He lay back on one of the towels, which was already smeared with blood. 'In your own time.'

He might have looked calm, Eve thought, were it not for the tightness around his eyes and mouth. She glanced at the medical kit, laid out neat and clean, then back at the bloody mess of Harker's chest and shoulder.

'Are you really sure you want me to do this?'

His gaze was steady. 'You've assisted in amputations,' he said.

'Yes, *assisted*. What if I get this wrong? What if I miss a bit, and it gets stuck inside you?'

'Eve, I've probably half-a-pound of shrapnel inside me somewhere. I'll live. I always have before.'

'Yes, that's probably what Nelson said,' Eve muttered, but she took a deep breath and bent over him to pick out the largest piece. He tensed, and she reached back for a roll of bandages to tuck into his hand. Harker glanced at it, then gave her that half-smile, and closed his fist around it.

Eve grabbed the piece of metal and yanked. It came free quite easily, although judging by Harker's expression it had hurt like hell.

'You don't have any sort of anaesthetic, do you?' she asked, dropping the piece of shrapnel in the water glass on the nightstand. It went *glink*.

'Why, yes, bottles of it. But I prefer not to use it.' He

glared at her. 'What do you think? That's why I brought the gin up.'

'Oh. What about Daz – has he a supply?'

'No. Don't disturb Daz.' Harker closed his eyes. 'He needs to concentrate.'

Eve peered at the wounds for the next biggest piece, located it, and wiggled it gently. 'Is Martindale really that bad?'

'Yes.'

'What happened?'

He sucked in a breath as she pulled the piece free. 'Bad luck.'

'Bad luck in the form of someone with a gun?' *Glink*.

'Several someones. We were attacking a convoy. It's always a risk. Three trucks and two were full of soldiers.'

'You brought one truck back. What about the other two?'

'We disabled one. Charlie and Banks had the other.' He closed his eyes. 'I hope they're all right.'

'You left them there?' That didn't sound like Major-gotta-save-all-my-men-Harker.

'It was either that or stay and get shot to hell. Besides, I didn't know how much time Martindale had.'

Eve went for the next piece. 'Where was she hurt?'

'Hard to tell. Here ... somewhere.' He ran his hand over his own chest and stomach. 'Maybe all of it.'

Eve made a face, partly for Martindale, and partly for Harker, because the third piece seemed to be lurking iceberg-style, with much more of it stuck under the skin than above it. 'This one's going to hurt.'

'And the others were so much fun.'

She counted to three and pulled, but it didn't move. Again, she tugged, abandoning the tweezers and using her fingers, but it was slippery with blood and wedged in at an angle.

'Um, it's stuck ...'

Harker jerked his head at the table. 'Scalpel,' he said. 'Can you sew?'

Eve cast him an incredulous look, but she reached for the scalpel and cut a careful, short line from the edge of the tear out along where the piece of circuit board was embedded. Harker sucked in a sharp breath, then another, his knuckles white as he gripped the bandage roll. He grunted when she pulled the piece out, but out it came, and she dropped it in the glass with the others, glancing back at him.

His whole body was sheened with sweat, his jaw tight, his teeth clenched.

'Isn't there anything I can do to make it hurt less?' she said wretchedly.

'Yes. Hurry up.'

Eve bent to look for the next piece, and as she was testing its give, she said, 'So. Where did you grow up?'

'What?'

'I'm trying to distract you. Where did you grow up?'

'Leicester.'

'Oh yes, you said. Is it a big place?' In Eve's world, it was a city with a university, but then in Eve's world, people didn't go around with scalpels in their personal luggage and drink gin as anaesthetic.

Well, not often, anyway.

'Not really. Lot of home industry, spinning and weaving and that.' He flinched as she pulled another piece out. *Glink*.

'Is that what your family do?'

'Did,' Harker said, and from his tone she knew they hadn't just retired.

'I'm sorry.'

'Don't be.'

'Were you close to them?'

Harker shrugged, and from his expression, immediately regretted it. 'I suppose. My dad died when I were twelve, and my sister too, so I didn't get much chance to be close to them.'

'They both died at the same time?'

'About two months apart. Cholera,' he explained. 'Took hundreds.'

'I'm so sorry.' *Glink*.

'Aye, me, too. My sister was only sixteen. Apprenticed to an embroiderer, used to make beautiful stockings.' He tensed as she dug in for a small piece of shrapnel. 'Going to marry a local boy, training to be a clerk. Wonder what happened to him?'

'Probably joined up,' Eve said.

'Nah, can't see that. Far too smart. Got a career ahead of him.'

Eve was surprised. 'Harker – you said you'd been in the army sixteen years.'

'Yep.'

'So ... isn't this a career for you? I mean, if you were conscripted then it'd only be five years, Tallulah said.' *Glink*.

'Aye, but I enlisted. Army's a decent career choice for a lad with no education. Stick it for twenty-five years, you get a full pension. Retire as a sergeant, that's a very decent pension. Could buy a little house, raise a family. Couldn't do that if I followed in my father's footsteps.'

'But, look, you're smart. I mean, couldn't you have trained as ... I dunno, a clerk, or–'

Harker actually laughed at that. 'Eve, you're asking like I had a choice. My father died. I was twelve, got a mother to support, I was a strong lad, she sent me out to work.' He hesitated, then added, 'I was trying to earn the money for the grammar school, but I could never save it. There's always something else to pay for.'

Eve nodded. 'I hear you on that one. What about your mother? Did she want you to go to the school?'

'Oh, aye. Proud of me when I passed the entrance exam. It were just bad timing.' He held his breath as she went after another small piece, embedded deeply, then said, 'She was the one suggested I try the army. Of course, there weren't a war on then.'

His accent was getting stronger, Eve thought as she fished out the small piece of circuitry. Talking about home, thinking about his childhood. His voice was rough. She wondered if he'd spoken like that back when he met Saskia. Wondered if the young officer had fallen for his low voice and soft dialect, rough words to go with his rough appearance. Wondered if Saskia had been attracted to the intelligence that hid behind his street accent.

She glanced up, her face very close to his skin, so close she could feel the heat rising from it. Harker was watching her, one arm behind his head, and he might have appeared relaxed if she couldn't feel the tension in every line of his body.

She cleared her throat. 'So. Nine more years and you can retire. And a major's pension, that's got to be more impressive than a sergeant's.'

'Aye, a lot more.'

'What will you do? Settle down and raise that family?' *Find a nice girl, a damn lucky girl, and live with her, and love her, and–*

'Dunno. Maybe.' *Glink*. 'Think I'd get bored doing nothing. I might ...'

'What?' Eve determinedly inspected a particularly gruesome cut that seemed to have several very small pieces of metal in it.

'Well, before my father died, when I thought I might go to the grammar, I thought I might become a teacher.'

Eve glanced up, and saw a kind of defiance on Harker's face. She smiled, more at his expression than anything.

'Sure,' she said, 'why not?'

He looked wary. 'You think I should?'

'Harker, you're clearly not stupid,' Eve said, bending to the cut again. 'And you're good with people. Well, most people. Well, most people who aren't me. You're good at leading, and giving instructions. And reading people. I mean, I have no idea how you figured out about the guitar ...' She cleared her throat. 'And if there's ever a playground fight I'd put money on you.'

She heard and felt his soft chuckle, but didn't look up.

'Thank you,' he said.

'You're welcome. Now hold still.'

He did, and after a minute or so said, 'You know, that's what my mother said. Not about the leading but the rest of it. She reckoned I'd be good at teaching.'

'What happened to her?'

'Tuberculosis.'

'How old were you?' *Glink. Glink.*

'Twenty-one. I'd just made sergeant. Reckon she told the whole town.' He smiled, and Eve thought how nice it must be to have a mother like that.

'Unfair, isn't it,' she said, 'how the good ones die and the crap ones just hang around forever.'

Harker raised his eyebrows, and Eve sighed, digging in for another tiny piece of shrapnel.

'I mean, your mother, right, wanted to send you to grammar school, picked out your best qualities, understood you, suggested things you'd be good at, and she died when you were still pretty young. Whereas my mother never paid the blindest bit of attention to me until I started landing decent roles in plays and musicals and then she could brag about it to her friends–'

'Maybe she was proud of you,' Harker said.

'Hah. If she was proud of me, wouldn't she have come to

my recitals? Or encouraged me with my piano exams? Or come to watch the plays when all I was doing was standing at the back being Third Villager with no lines to say? You know, the only times she ever exhibited any pride in me was when she could show off to her friends. Or when I made her lots of money. She was made up when I landed the Grrl Power thing. All that lovely money to spend on whatever she liked, and lots of magazines she could show to people, and people taking her picture–'

Harker caught his breath with a sharp sound, and she realised she'd been poking him with the tweezers, right in that deep cut with all the tiny pieces in it.

'Sorry. Sorry.'

He nodded, exhaling. 'You're not close to your mother, then?'

Eve sat back, tweezers in hand. Harker regarded them warily.

'My mother,' she said, 'spent most of the money I earned on holidays and parties and clothes that she ruined. The only thing she bought that retained any value was a beach house in Miami, but she put it in her own name. So when the taxman came knocking, it wasn't among my assets to be sold off. In fact, nothing was in my name. I think, now, she was in cahoots with the accountant. She found him. He was the one who told me not to bother putting things in my name. It was better for tax purposes in my mother's name. Apart from a couple of thousand kicking about, she'd spent everything. And when I was presented with a tax bill to rival the national debt of Ethiopia, she did precisely nothing. So, no. I'm not close to my mother. And if I ever am close to her, I intend to use the opportunity to punch her, hard.'

Harker whistled.

'Yeah,' Eve said, and bent to the cut again.

'Dare I ask about your father, or will I need more gin?'

She passed him the bottle wordlessly, watched him drink.

'My father was a nice guy. And he died of a heart attack when I was fifteen. There's no bloody justice, is there?'

'Did you expect there to be?'

'No.' Eve sighed, extracted another piece of shrapnel. It *glinked* in the glass, which was getting pretty full now. 'You know, they should stop letting kids read those fairytales where everything is nice and good and bad things only happen to bad people. Because then when something bad happens to you, you just can't figure out why. You spend your whole life working hard and loving your family and being nice to small fluffy animals, and then your parents get divorced, your father dies, your mother spends all your money, your accountant takes what's left, the taxman shoves you in a tiny flat with mildew on the walls, you spend three years getting sneered at by people who know you used to be famous and love gloating over you, and then you fall through a damn hole in the world and get thrown in jail for being a spy.'

Harker's fist was white. Damn, she'd been poking him again. 'Sorry.'

He let out a ragged breath. 'Hole in the world?'

Eve shrugged. 'I dunno. Maybe this is a parallel universe. It's as good a hypothesis as any. Better than being mad or in a coma. Your England made all the wrong choices and mine got things right. Well, mostly right. Clearly we need to clear up a few issues surrounding the tax system.'

'You reckon it works in any universe?'

'Probably not.'

She found a small smile, and somehow so did he.

Taxes seemed a very distant problem right now.

Eve sat back and regarded the dozen tiny cuts and weals in Harker's chest and shoulder. A couple of them she'd cleaned out entirely, but there were plenty with lots of tiny pieces of metal and plastic in them.

Then there was the circular puncture in his shoulder, which she hadn't seen before for all the blood and shredded flesh and bits of keyboard in the way. Harker had thought there might still be a bullet in there. Certainly there'd been no exit wound on his back.

She sighed, attempted to make herself more comfortable on the edge of the bed, and bent closer again.

'Tell me about this England of yours,' Harker said after a little while.

'This blessed plot, this earth, this realm, this England,' Eve murmured.

'What?'

'Shakespeare.'

'Who?'

She sighed. 'Do you not even have Shakespeare? Tell me what, exactly, do you have in this country to be proud of?'

Harker closed his eyes. 'Please don't start that again.'

'All right. But only because you're bleeding.' *Glink*. 'Shakespeare was a playwright. Almost certainly the greatest who ever lived. And he was English.'

'Was he?'

'Yes. About four hundred years ago, he wrote some of the most amazing, beautiful, and enduring plays the world has ever seen. You know those theatres on the south bank? The Rose and the Curtain and the Globe?'

'Aye, what about them?'

'Well, Shakespeare worked in them. Especially the Globe. I think he owned it. You know, people come from all over the world to see Shakespeare's Globe. It's not even the real thing, it's a reconstruction. And his plays are translated into Japanese and Hungarian and everything in between. *Everyone's* heard of Shakespeare.'

'I haven't.'

'Well, maybe that's because you're a philistine,' Eve said, extracting another piece of shrapnel. 'Or maybe it's because in this stupid bloody world, no one seems to know what they've got. He probably wrote all those plays and they just got forgotten.'

'Probably,' Harker said, settling with his arm behind his head again. 'I mean, it's not like we have Bram Stoker or anything.'

Eve went still. She lifted her head.

Harker was watching her, his eyes half-shut.

'I asked Charlie,' he said. 'That book about the monster. Drank people's blood. There was a hero called Harker.' He gave her a crooked grin. 'Of course, he was Irish.'

That shook Eve back into life. 'I'm pretty sure he wasn't.'

'He was. Bram Stoker was Irish. Charlie said.'

'And Charlie is always right,' Eve said sourly.

'You want to argue with her?'

Yes. I actually rather do. 'What exactly is going on with you two?'

He tilted his head and looked like he might be smiling. 'What do you mean?'

'I mean you're practically joined at the hip. I don't think she does anything without your permission. I've seen sheepdogs less loyal.'

'This is the army, Eve. Loyalty is a good thing.' He frowned. 'In fact, loyalty's always a good thing, isn't it?'

'Yes, but she's insane about it.' *And she doesn't like me.*

'No, she's not. Look,' he sighed, 'I go through this with everyone. Charlie is my second. Has been since she was my sergeant. She's the best second I've ever had. We work well together. We understand each other. She's very loyal to me because she likes and respects me, and I like and respect her. I don't know why everyone finds it so hard to comprehend.'

'Most people who are as close as you two are sleeping

together,' Eve said, and it came out a lot more petty than she'd wanted.

'Jealous, Miss Carpenter?'

'Are you kidding? Do I look like the sort of person who'd do a good sheepdog impression?'

Harker just grinned at her.

Eve scowled and decided to change the subject. 'You said Bram Stocker was Irish,' she said. 'What about George Bernard Shaw and Oscar Wilde?'

'What about them?'

'Have you heard of them?'

'Not really.' Harker yawned, and Eve thought about pushing it but figured that if Harker had never heard of Shakespeare, she was wasting her time with Wilde.

'I dunno,' she said. 'Sometimes I think all this is just nonsense, but then there's Beethoven, and ... well, look, what about the First World War? Archduke Ferdinand's assassination?'

'What about him?' asked Harker, who was beginning to sound sleepy. How that was possible when she was digging around in an open wound on his chest, she had no idea. She supposed it was part of being a manly man. Shrapnel wounds? Splash of gin and a kip, that'll cure it.

Gritting her teeth, she went after a particularly deep shard of plastic, intriguingly wedged in sideways. That seemed to wake him up.

'If I'm digging bits of circuitry out of you, the least you can do is stay awake,' she said.

'Not an issue,' Harker said.

'You were dozing off there!'

'I tend to do that during history lessons.' He took a deep breath, which did interesting things to the movement of muscles in his chest. 'What was that about Archduke whatsis being assassinated?'

'Franz Ferdinand. It sparked off the First World War. The biggest war the world had ever seen. The War To End All Wars.'

'No, that was in 1939, after Hitler–'

'That was the Second World War.'

'Then clearly yours wasn't the War To End All Wars,' Harker mocked.

'No. That's what they call "irony",' Eve said. 'Do you still have that here?'

'I'm familiar with the concept.'

'Well, at least you've got that to be proud of. Are you familiar with the concept of the British Empire?' Eve asked.

Harker laughed.

'Don't do that, I almost got my tweezers stuck in you,' she scolded.

'Then don't make jokes.'

'The British Empire is not a joke. The British Empire, my granny told me, used to cover a third of the world. When she was a little girl, geography lessons consisted of colouring in the bits belonging to us with a pink crayon, and she'd use up a whole crayon and need another one before she was done.'

Harker frowned. Then he flinched, as Eve went after a piece of plastic that had splintered.

'All right,' he said, 'but how did you get this empire?'

Eve opened her mouth, then shut it again, and used the excuse of digging out the splinter of plastic to think about it. Well, how had such a small, damp island managed to conquer a third of the world?

'I think,' she said eventually, carefully grasping the shard, 'it had a lot to do with not believing we couldn't.'

Harker seemed to think about that. 'I'm sorry, you've lost me.'

'It's like bumblebees,' Eve said, and he gave her a look that questioned his own sanity in allowing someone as bonkers as her to perform minor surgery on him. 'No, I mean – a bumblebee is the least aerodynamic thing there is. Look at it, all round and fluffy, it shouldn't be able to fly. But it can, because no one's ever told it it can't.'

Harker was still staring at her. 'Okay,' he said. 'I'm in severe pain and dosed up on spirits. What's your excuse?'

'I'm insane,' Eve said, and yanked out the plastic splinter triumphantly.

Chapter Nineteen

The flicker of the oil lamps clued Eve in to the fact that she'd been kneeling on the edge of the bed pulling bits of keyboard out of Harker's chest for several hours. That and the blurring of her vision.

Harker lay back against the pillow, his skin gleaming with sweat, his mouth tight. Eve, who'd spent the last few hours arguing and contradicting him, was secretly filled with admiration that he'd withstood it all with very little reaction.

Well, he'd complained. He'd actually complained a lot. But it occurred to Eve that this was really because he liked to annoy her. He wasn't whining in pain.

'Okay,' she said eventually, dropping the last piece of plastic into the glass. 'Only one left now, and it's the big one.'

'You had to leave that 'til last?' Harker murmured. His eyes were closed, and over the last half-hour or so his responses had become decidedly less animated.

'Hey, you want me to do this my way, or not at all? It's the bullet – damn good job it hit your shoulder, huh?'

'Oh yeah,' Harker said. 'I'm really grateful it hit me.'

'I mean,' she tapped his other shoulder admonishingly, 'you should be grateful it didn't hit six inches to the left.'

'No, that was reserved for the shattered keyboard.' He yawned and shifted, wincing as the movement stretched the muscle in his shoulder. 'I'm sorry, you know.'

'What, for keeping me up half the night doctoring you? You're the one who'll be sorry come morning,' Eve said lightly.

'No. For messing up the keyboard. You said it was important.'

His words were starting to slur now. Eve couldn't blame him, she was exhausted and she wasn't the one with bits of metal stuck in her.

'It's okay,' she said, leaning close and peering into the bullet wound. 'I might still be able to get this one working. And if not then, I dunno, maybe Daz can think of something else. Improvise.'

Harker nodded sleepily.

'Okay,' she said, 'I'm going in. And this looks pretty deep, I'm guessing it's wiggled in further as you've moved around, so it's going to take some digging. Okay?'

He grunted.

'Harker–' she broke off. Well, he was going to wake up as soon as she started digging deep in his shoulder.

She took a deep breath, reminded herself that she was a competent, intelligent person on a mission of mercy, and stole a glance at Harker's face, angled slightly towards her as he rested. His hair was starkly black against the white of the pillow, his eyes shadowed by dark circles and his jaw by more than its usual level of stubble.

What would you look like clean-shaven? she wondered. *Would you be handsome, or are you too harsh, too strong for that? Are you too bitter, too hard and worn?*

She touched his face with the back of her hand, his jaw rough against her skin, and said gently, 'Harker? I'm going after the bullet now. It's going to hurt.'

'More?' he mumbled.

'There's that possibility.'

He took a breath and opened his eyes, his warm, gunmetal eyes, and met her gaze. His hand came up, touched her face just as she'd touched his. He nodded.

Eve dug into the wound.

It was deep, maybe two inches, and she thought she saw bone as she moved aside, as carefully as she could, layers of torn skin and muscle. She heard Harker's harsh intake of breath, felt his whole body tense, and determinedly kept her eyes on the wound.

There it was! A dark ball of metal, hidden behind something pink and squidgy she had no wish to identify. *It could be important. A nerve or artery or – no. Worry about that and you'll lose your own nerve.* She angled her tweezers, but couldn't quite grasp it.

'I'm going to have to try and nudge it a bit,' she said. 'It's stuck.'

'Leave the bugger,' Harker said through gritted teeth.

'I will not! I've spent all night digging out tiny fragments of plastic, I'm not going to leave a whacking great ball of metal in there.' She peered closer. What she needed to do was nudge it a bit to the right, and then hopefully, she could grasp it with the tweezers. If only they weren't so slippery with all that damned blood ...

'Your dedication is ... impressive,' he panted.

'Yes, it damn well is. Now, you know what I'm going to do?'

'Cause me more pain?'

'Uh, yes. But, I'm going to remember what it was that made Britain great. What made the Empire so huge that the sun never set on it. And you know what that was?'

'Lunacy?' Harker muttered.

'Of a very specific kind. We succeeded,' she slipped the tweezers into the wound, 'because it never occurred to us that we could fail.'

It was a terrible line, but Eve squared her jaw, chased the bullet out into the open, and yanked it out without allowing herself to consider how much it would hurt Harker.

Judging by the blood trickling from his lip when she finally looked up at his face, that hurt had been considerable.

She dropped the bullet into the glass. It went *glunk*.

'All done,' she said, and when he opened his eyes she smiled at him. He gave her a rather weak smile in return.

'All done bar the stitches,' he said, and Eve's shoulders slumped. 'Oi, don't you make that face. It's me going to have the needle stuck in me.'

She shoved her hair out of her eyes with the back of her arm and nodded. She'd already sterilised the needle and thread but forgotten about them. Well, how much stitching could there be to do? There weren't all that many long or deep cuts.

When she'd sewn the last one, she poured a little more gin over the lot, especially the bullet wound, and handed the bottle to Harker. 'Finish it.'

He lifted his arm and looked at the half-inch left in the bottle. 'Sure you don't want a sip?'

'Like you wouldn't believe,' she said, 'but I think you need it more.'

He gave her a crooked smile that did strange things to her insides. Eve put it down to exhaustion and the complete surrealness of spending the evening doctoring first a keyboard, then a hard, lean man who complained more about her explanation of history than the fact that she was sticking sharp pieces of metal into his tortured flesh.

'Okay,' she said, yawning. 'Dressing?'

'Mm,' said Harker, eyes closed again. 'Prefer undressing.'

Eve ignored a low stab of heat and said, 'I meant bandages.'

He grunted again. 'Clean the gin off first.'

'Sir, yes, sir.'

'And don't call me sir.'

'I'll call you what I damn well like,' Eve said, 'I've still got this scalpel, you know.'

He smiled at that, but he didn't open his eyes.

'And while I'm cleaning the gin off,' she said, wetting the last towel, 'you might try washing your face.'

At that, Harker's expression turned to such little-boy sulkiness that she laughed.

It helped if she thought of him as a little boy, not as a rather large, hard-muscled, brave and stoic man. Because thinking of him as a large, hard-muscled, brave and stoic man made more strange things happen to her insides, and she wasn't quite ready to deal with them yet.

Eve made him sit up to wrap the bandage around his chest and shoulder, which brought her into disturbingly close proximity with his hard, naked torso. *Dammit,* she thought, *he's doing this on purpose. He's being all lean and sexy on bloody* purpose.

She let him fall back to the bed with a slight thump, which Harker didn't even seem to register. His head fell to one side, his hair feathering against his cheekbones, his breathing deep and even.

'I can't believe you're asleep,' she said, and jumped when he murmured, ''m not. Stop staring at me.'

Eve stuck her tongue out.

'Saw that,' he mumbled, snuggling against the pillow.

'Liar,' Eve mouthed, because his eyes were closed, and started gathering up all the kit she'd used. She threw the bloody towels in the bathtub, washed the implements and left them in the bowl to dry, then splashed water on her face and scrubbed at her hands until most of the blood had come off.

'What, will this hand never be clean?' she muttered, looking at the pink stain around her nails. 'How can he have heard of Stoker but not Shakespeare?'

When she went back into the bedroom, the last oil lamp was guttering, so she turned it off, then did the same for the dim overhead electric lights. The fire in the sitting room had reduced itself to ashes a long time ago, so she left it.

Her shoulders ached, her limbs were heavy with fatigue, and as she stood in the doorway to Harker's bedroom, cold crept over her. She thought of her chilly little trundle bed in the room she shared with Martindale, who was probably still being operated on, and Tallulah, who was assisting with the operation. The thought occurred to her that she maybe ought to go down and see if they needed any help.

'No,' she said out loud. 'I can't bear it.'

Besides, she was so tired she'd be useless anyway.

She shivered in the cold, dark room. Funny how she hadn't noticed the heat fading away while she was working. But then, Harker had been generating enough heat of his own.

She frowned. *Hope he's not getting a fever.*

Maybe I ought to stay and keep an eye on him.

As her eyes adjusted to the dim moonlight, she watched him sleeping. At least, probably sleeping. He was bare to the waist, and without decent light she couldn't see most of the scars marring his body. All she could see was his flat stomach, his broad chest, the curve of his hipbones before they disappeared below his waistband.

There was no fat on him, none at all, and none of the showy muscle she'd become used to with the over-pumped backing dancers who'd gyrated on stage with Grrl Power. Harker didn't have the sort of carefully designed physique generated by hours of weight training in the gym. She doubted he'd ever even seen a gym. What he had was a lean, hard body, with the narrow waist and broad shoulders of a man who'd been used to hard physical work before he'd even finished growing.

She regarded him for a long time, her head on one side. *Would you be handsome?* No, he never would. But he was already quite beautiful. Gently, she pulled the quilt over him. 'Harker,' she said softly. 'Are you asleep?'

He didn't stir.

'Harker?' she said, louder this time. 'Charlie's outside with a gun pressed to her head. She's going to kill herself because I've spent so much time in here with you, all alone.'

Nothing.

'That's after she's killed us both.'

Still nothing.

Sleep softened the harsh lines of his face. The moonlight made the bandage on his chest gleam stark and white, rising and falling with each breath.

'Harker,' Eve said softly, and watched him a while longer before whispering, 'I think you're amazing.'

Then, without entirely working out a valid reason other than *I really, really want to,* she toed off her boots, unbuttoned her shirt, and crawled into the bed next to him.

In twisted dreams Harker watched, over and over, Martindale's body jerking in the air. And over and over it became, as injured friends inevitably did, James White, the tattered ribbons of flesh on his back leaping with each thrash of the whip, even after his body had gone still, sagging in its bonds.

Mary White lay curled on the floor, her hands tied and her mouth gagged, beaten and bloody and flinching with each cry of her baby. Harker couldn't forget the sound of that baby. In the lonely hours of the night it haunted him, screaming and screaming with pain and fear.

He woke with a start into a silent room, pale daylight creeping past the open curtains. The day was grey and misty, impossible to tell how early or late it was.

His right shoulder throbbed. His left was weighed down by something.

The right shoulder made sense. He remembered the failed raid, the keyboard that had probably saved his life, and Eve's subsequent care. Well, if you could call it 'care', when she'd bitched and argued and poked him with the tweezers until he'd very nearly burst into tears.

What confused him was the weight on his left shoulder and the warmth pressing against his body. It felt almost like a woman curled up next to him, but that made no sense.

He cracked open one eye.

He quickly shut it again.

Okay, he was still dreaming. There was no way in hell Eve was curled up next to him; and not just next to him but half on him, too, her arm stretched across his waist and her leg propped over his. Her other hand curled in his hair, and that was curiously more intimate than the rest of it.

The quilt had slid down so he could see that she was wearing an undershirt and trousers, which answered one question – thank goodness he hadn't done anything he'd forgotten about – but raised another. Namely, what the hell was she doing there?

He opened his eyes, and she was still there.

Well, damn.

She was soft and warm and fitted against him very nicely, her head tucked into the hollow of his unhurt shoulder, resting against the bandage she'd wrapped around his upper chest. In the gap between her trousers and t-shirt was an inch or so of exposed skin, wonderfully silky, which Harker was surprised to realise he could feel because he had his arms around her.

Apparently some men didn't like women who clung to them. Harker had never minded, so long as the reason she was clinging was that they'd just had really hot sweaty sex and she needed to hold on to something to stop the room from spinning.

Unfortunately, he'd done no such thing with Eve, but for some reason he didn't mind her cuddling up to him.

Besides, the day was still young.

She shifted and sighed in her sleep, all that softness pressing against him, and for a few minutes Harker allowed himself to indulge in the fantasy that she'd curled up there because they had spent the night having hot sweaty sex. All that fire and anger, those fast fingers and faster mouth, all that warmth and softness – damn, she could drive a man insane.

She could certainly drive a man to hold on to her to stop his world from spinning.

Eve made a soft noise in the back of her throat and shifted again, her arm stretching over his stomach, her fingers idly caressing him. This was entirely too much for Harker, who swiftly changed from fantasising about Eve to hoping she wouldn't move her leg any more and see just how much she was affecting him.

Then she went still, as if she'd just realised what she was doing, where she was and who she was stroking – who did she think he was? – and she very, very slowly raised her head.

Harker waited.

Her blue-green eyes were sleepy, her hair tousled, and there was an imprint on her cheek of the bandage she'd been resting on. Her lips were parted and dry and she licked them, her eyes meeting his.

Her fingers curled in his hair. Her heart thudded against his ribs. And Harker forgot all about the stitches in his shoulder and the potentiality of Eve being a spy, and leaned forward to kiss the most desirable woman he'd ever seen.

But he never got there, because someone banged on the suite door and it swung open, and the idiot who'd designed the house had made it so that the person standing in the hallway could see through the bedroom doorway, to the bed.

Where Harker lay with Eve cradled in his arms, his lips inches from hers.

'Sir, we can't find Eve and–'

Banks trailed off, his fist still raised to knock, his eyes growing wider. In a split second he took in Harker's bare chest and Eve's arm stretched across it, and he started to grin nervously.

'–but, uh, there she is. Um, never mind,' he said quickly, and backed out, yanking the door shut, and Harker was left with a petrified motionless replica of the soft warm woman he'd been about to kiss.

'–' she said, and swallowed, and managed, 'I should go,' in a frozen whisper.

He started to tell her no, but she was already pulling away from him, and in a tiny split second her gaze darted down to his bare chest, then skittered away, and his stomach turned to lead.

The way she'd looked at him last night.

He released her instantly, appalled, and Eve scrambled away, off the bed, grabbing at her shirt and tripping over her boots.

Horror on her face, revulsion in her eyes.

She shoved her arms into her shirt and stumbled away from the bed.

'How are you still alive?' Because he looked like he ought to be dead, punctured and ripped open and smashed with glass and knives and shrapnel and shot.

'I–' Eve began, pausing in the doorway, then her nerve deserted her and she ran, out of the bedroom and the sitting room and Harker's reach, leaving the suite silent and cold.

Harker sat motionless in the empty, suddenly huge bed, staring after her for a second, then he swung to his feet and strode into the bathroom.

His reflection glowered back at him, six foot-odd of glowering scars and bruises. No wonder she'd run.

He kicked off his clothes, washed and dressed and glared at the computer, the source of all this damn trouble, before slamming out of his room and stomping downstairs for breakfast.

So what if she really found him that hideous? Did he want a woman who looked at him like that? No, he didn't. She knew who and what he was: a soldier, a serving soldier; did she think he was going to be pristine? What kind of numpty survived sixteen years in the infantry without gaining a few scars? Granted, he had a few more than most people, certainly than most officers, but then most officers treated shaving cuts as war wounds.

Harker was *proud* of those scars, dammit – or if not proud then at least not ashamed. They were part of him, his life, his career – he was a *survivor*, and –

The kitchen was very quiet. Tallulah looked up at him from the table, her face drip-white.

'What?' he said, his anger evaporating, and then the answer hit him like a sandbag. 'Martindale.'

She nodded, swallowed, and said in a half-whisper, 'Banks has gone with one of the maids to fetch the priest. It won't be long now.' Her breath hitched. 'Sir, we tried–'

He stared at her for a second, then shoved past the cook and into the scullery, where Charlie stood and Daz sat and Martindale lay, all of them unmoving. But Daz and Charlie looked up when he came in.

'She told me,' Harker said. He looked down at Martindale, who was still and waxen, looking dead already.

'We were up all night,' Daz said, 'I tried, sir, I tried–'

'I know,' Harker said, his voice hollow.

Daz took a ragged breath and let it out. He nodded. 'I'll stay with her,' he said. 'Until the priest comes, until ...'

Harker exchanged a look with Charlie. She gave a slight nod, and said, 'I'll stay too.'

Harker left, passing the cook again on his way out and daring her to make any comment about needing her scullery back. To her credit, she didn't say a word.

Eve was sitting with Tallulah at the table, her arm over the younger girl's shoulders. Tallulah was praying.

So, Harker, good morning. Snubbed by the only girl you've been interested in since Saskia, and one of your men is dying. And it's not even nine o'clock.

Again.

Chapter Twenty

Sir Dennis, to Harker's mild surprise, offered the family plot for Martindale's body. Frederick complained, and his father slapped him, which made Harker grudgingly respect the old man.

Martindale lingered, while the local priest and Daz sat with her. Harker ordered Charlie to get some sleep, Banks and Tallulah to fetch Sir Dennis's car, and Eve to fix the computer keyboard.

She sat on the floor of his suite, not looking at him, using his tweezers to pick out bits of dirt from the keyboard's innards, and by midday she'd fixed it. But she didn't cheer, didn't smile, just asked him for a few words in French and typed them in.

'There,' she said, as the French flag came up on the screen. 'All yours.'

He dealt her a heavy look. 'You're the one who knows how to use it.'

'Sure,' Eve said. 'But what do you want it to do?'

'Well, use it to connect to that Internet thing you talked about.'

Eve gave a sigh, and he knew what she said next wasn't going to be good news.

'You need a modem to connect to the Internet. I told you that. And you need an ISP, and who knows what you people use for that around here–'

And Harker lost his patience.

'You know, I just knew you were going to come up with something else we needed for this,' he snapped. 'If it's not one thing, it's another. Martindale is dying because of some part you said you needed and now it turns out you didn't–'

'Hey, I didn't know this was going to work,' Eve said.

'And now you tell me you need this piece–'

'I told you it would need a modem, but look, it might–'

'If any more of my men die because of this stupid computer, you can bloody well go with them,' Harker roared, and Eve drew back just a fraction of an inch, her face going tight.

'It might have an internal modem,' she said quietly. 'I'll check.' She turned back to the keyboard, paused and said, 'A French dictionary would be useful.'

'Ask me. I can–'

'You don't have to stay. Daz would be more helpful.'

His fists clenched. 'Daz is busy.'

'Or Tallulah.'

'Basket-case,' Harker said, because his youngest soldier wasn't taking Martindale's condition well.

Eve took a deep breath and let it out, still not looking at him.

'Look, if you really can't bear to be in the same room as me–'

'I can, if you'd just stop yelling at me,' Eve said. 'This is not my fault. I'm doing the best I can. And if you have to go in after a modem, then I'll come with you and you can put me at risk instead of one of your precious men. I know what the damn thing might look like, anyway.'

'You–' Harker began, but right then someone tapped on the open door and he turned to snarl at them. But it was Daz, his face drawn, and he said quietly, 'I called it. Five minutes ago. The gardeners are helping Tallulah and Banks dig the grave.'

Harker wiped his hands over his face and nodded. *And then there were six*. Well, five, because Eve wasn't precisely a member of the squad.

'Will the priest stay and read a service for her?'

Daz nodded. 'And Tallulah asked if you,' he directed his attention to Eve, 'would sing, a hymn or something.'

Eve looked surprised, but she nodded, and Daz left. Harker remained staring at the door for a while, then he glanced at Eve and said, 'Do you know many hymns?'

'Probably not any you're familiar with. I sang *Abide With Me* when my dad died. Will that be acceptable?'

He hesitated. He'd never heard of it.

Eve sighed, scrubbed her hands over her face, and he saw the rawness in her eyes.

'Sure,' he said, 'it's fine. Come on.'

And then life went on again.

When they got back to the house, Harker allowed Eve to pick a fight with him over the computer, just to keep from thinking about how many times he'd spoken the same words over the graves of different men.

Eventually there came a point when there just wasn't anything different to say.

He even allowed Eve to bully Daz into checking over his shoulder, just for another kind of distraction. From the bed, he could see Charlie arguing with Eve over the thing she called a mouse.

'If you have that, then what did you need the keyboard for?' Charlie said.

'Inputting words,' Eve said without looking up.

'You're not doing that now.'

Eve sighed. 'Lieutenant, why do you carry a gun and a sword?'

Charlie looked taken aback. 'I'm an officer,' she said. 'We're allowed swords.'

'Yes, but do you need it if you have a gun, too?'

'Yes,' Charlie said impatiently.

'Well, I haven't seen you use it.'

'Would you like to?' Charlie said with a hint of threat in her voice. Harker almost smiled.

'Not especially. My point is you carry both because you need them for different things.'

Charlie made a noise of annoyance, but didn't say any more.

'This all looks fine,' Daz said to Harker. 'Good work, Eve.'

'Thanks,' she said, again not looking up.

'Do you need a hand with the computer?'

'No, it's all right. I think you should get some rest.'

'Excuse me, who is the doctor around here?' Daz complained.

'You are, and do you really think it's a good idea to stay awake any longer?' Charlie said.

Daz grumbled, but left the room, and they heard his door closing.

Harker pulled his shirt back on and went back out into the sitting room. Eve was frowning at something on the screen. He didn't understand what any of it meant – lots of little pictures and tiny, tiny text – but Eve was nodding and mumbling to herself.

'I just wish it wasn't all in bloody French,' she grumbled.

'We need Tallulah. I can't speak French,' said Charlie.

'And there's no funky music,' Eve muttered. 'But don't wake Tallulah.'

Charlie opened her mouth, but Harker waved her into silence. For once, he and Eve were in agreement.

He fetched the bloodstained jacket he'd been wearing the night before. 'There was a box of these,' he said, taking out the small metal and plastic sticks he'd picked up. 'Are they any good?'

She took them from him, rather carefully not touching him, which didn't do much to help Harker's general mood, and examined them.

'They look like USB sticks,' she said. 'You use them for storing files.'

'Files?' said Harker, thinking of the huge filing cabinets lining the walls of the offices at the Tower. 'But they're tiny.'

'Electronic files,' she said impatiently, and stuck one into a slot at the front of the computer. While Harker was trying to work out what an electronic file might be – a file about electronics? – she clicked a few things and a new square popped up on the screen.

'Oh my God,' Eve said.

'What?' The square was filled with more of the little pictures.

'This is ... well, it's in English, see, it's been written locally and not in France somewhere ... Look, Manchester Barracks One, Two and Three, Kirkstall One – hah, Two has gone out, that's because it's here – it's a list of computers, the computers they have networked. Look, Leeds Grammar One. Does Leeds have a grammar school?'

'Yes,' said Harker.

'There's a computer there. And ... look, there are two in Lincoln, and ...'

'Peterborough,' read Charlie. 'Oxford.'

'Southend's not connected,' Eve said. 'I guess that means they're having trouble there.'

'Good,' said Harker.

'Oh hell,' said Charlie, and pointed.

They all read it.

'That could be any Tower,' Eve said.

'Can you find out more?'

She frowned, clicked something and a square came up on screen. Harker could read about half of the words, which were in French, but one thing lashed out at him. *Destination*: Tower of London.

'That's not possible,' he said.

'Destination?' Charlie said. 'It's going there?'

'No. That means location,' Harker said. 'It's already there.'

When the shock had cleared, a new horror occurred to Harker. The telephone here was connected, which meant he'd be able to call Wheeler and tell her about the computer at the Tower.

But what was he going to say? 'I think there's a computer right under your nose, but I can't tell you any more because I don't understand what the spy is saying.'

Yeah. Wait for more information, Harker.

'Find out more,' he said to Eve, who clicked a few more times but kept shaking her head.

'I can't. Look, I need to connect up, and unless there's an internal modem I can't do that.' She clicked a few more times, asked him to translate a word or two, but Harker's knowledge of French was extremely basic.

'Do you see the word "modem" anywhere?' Eve said. 'Or... I don't know what it'd be called if the French invented it. I need something like ... access point, or device – basically anything that is a device for connecting to a network. See anything like that, shout–'

'Device?' Harker said, and her eyes lifted hopefully to his. 'There: *pas de device trouvé*.'

'*Pas*,' Eve said. 'That means none, right?' He nodded, and her gaze fell. She flopped back in her chair. 'Well, there's your answer. No internal modem. If there is one, then it doesn't work, so we'll need a new one anyway.'

'Like you needed a new keyboard?' Charlie said.

'Hey, I didn't think this one could be–'

'Because of you *not thinking*, Lance-Corporal Martindale is dead,' Charlie said, and Eve flinched.

'All right,' Harker said. 'Stop it, you two.'

They scowled at each other like kids in a playground, and Harker had a sudden urge to laugh. Instead he said, 'Eve. Do you really need this modem thing?' She nodded. 'You said there was a computer at the grammar school. Do you honestly think it will have one of these modem things that you can use?' She nodded again, and Harker, not quite believing himself, said, 'Okay then. You can come with me to get it.'

Charlie rounded on him, disbelief bright on her face. 'Sir, you're not seriously suggesting–'

'No, I am not seriously suggesting,' Harker said. 'I am ordering.'

'You can't order me,' Eve said. 'I'm not one of your men.'

'No, but I have a very big gun and very little patience, and I've been having a really, really bad day, and you told me you'd do it, so just ... do it, would you?'

Eve looked like she was going to say something, but she flexed her jaw, shrugged her shoulders, and stayed silent.

'Sir,' Charlie said, her jaw tight, 'you can't just walk into the grammar school and walk out again with a computer.'

But Harker was already rummaging in the pocket of the civilian jacket he'd worn while reconnoitring the city. He produced his forged papers and waved them at Charlie, unable to help a grin.

'Of course I can,' he said, and pointed to the section of the papers where his fictional profession was written. 'I'm a teacher.'

As she followed Harker to the drawing room, Eve could hear Banks gossiping from the other side of the door.

'... curled up in bed together. I swear! Charlie'd kill him if she knew.'

Eve's face went very hot, and her gaze immediately

skittered away from Harker.

'She must be blind if she can't see what's going on between them–'

Tallulah broke off as the door opened and Harker strode in, giving them a suspicious look.

'My my,' he said sourly as Tallulah spun around on the piano stool, her cheeks bright pink, 'the romantic assignations that take place in this room. There must be something in the air.'

Eve followed him, rolling her eyes.

'Play us something cheerful, Lu,' Harker said, throwing himself at an exquisite imported sofa. 'Me and Eve are going out to get shot at as soon as it gets dark.'

'Oh, cheers, thank you so much for making me feel better,' Eve said, hurling herself at the chair opposite him. She felt slightly sick, and not just at Harker's plan to walk her into enemy territory.

She wanted him, everyone knew she wanted him, including the man himself, and all he wanted from her was a computer technician.

'I don't really know anything cheerful,' Tallulah ventured. 'All the pieces I know are classical.'

'Eve, then. Make yourself useful.'

'You're a real piece of work, you know that?' Eve said, but she stood up to fetch her guitar.

Harker wiped his hands over his face in an expression of exasperation. Eve stuck her tongue out at him. Tallulah pointed at Harker and pulled a face.

Harker said, from behind his hands, 'Stop whatever you're doing.'

'What are you, psychic?' Eve snapped, her nerves shredded.

'Yes,' Harker said, watching her pick up the guitar and stalk back across the room.

Tallulah giggled. Eve scowled, sat down opposite Harker again and gave him a smile that wasn't at all friendly. Then she started to play Sheryl Crow's *All I Wanna Do*, and when she got to the line about William's name, Harker glowered, Tallulah giggled, and Eve knew he'd played the Gosh-I-don't-know-who-Major-Harker-is-my-name-is-just-Will trick on her, too. Presumably when his ex-wife had first taken him home to meet the family.

'Yes, very clever,' he scowled. 'Now, if you've done insulting me?'

'Who said that song was about you?' Eve said innocently, feeling she'd redressed the balance somewhat. 'It was about LA, and bars, and lowlifes.' She played a few more chords, smiled again, then started *You're So Vain*.

Harker looked pissed off, but even he had to smile when she sang the chorus.

'All right,' Eve said when she'd finished. 'I'll stop now.'

'Not a moment too soon,' Harker murmured, and she decided to stop torturing him.

She thought for a moment, then glanced at Tallulah and started *18 Til I Die*. By the time Daz came in, complaining about the noise, Banks and Tallulah were singing along with the chorus, and by the look on Harker's face, he wasn't entirely hating the whole thing.

After a minute, Daz joined in.

Eve caught Harker's eye, and he smiled at her. An actual genuine smile. She smiled back, caught unawares, and then Daz interrupted, and the moment was lost.

'What was that song you played the other day?' Daz asked. '*I Never Really Loved You Anyway*?'

Eve tore her attention from Harker and dutifully started playing. She liked the song, but it never failed to remind her of Kevin Hayes, a boybander she'd walked out with a time or two during her Grrl Power days. He'd been pretty enough, but about as clever and interesting as an old carpet sample.

And when the taxman had come calling, Kevin had suddenly found lots of elsewheres he needed to be.

When she'd finished the song, she shook her head and said, 'Wish you hadn't picked that one, Daz. Reminds me of someone I'd rather forget.'

Harker's face didn't move in any way, but somehow his expression did.

'Ex-boyfriend?' asked Tallulah, a touch slyly.

'Whom you never really loved,' Daz guessed, grinning.

She shrugged. 'Well, no. I liked him ... well, most of the time I liked him. It was just ... convenient, you know? And we did look good together.'

Harker rolled his eyes. 'A very important factor.'

'Yeah, well, I was famous, remember? Had to think about my press coverage.' She strummed a few chords, but broke off to say, 'Why do we do those things? I mean, when I was about fourteen I went out with the ugliest boy just because he was the only one who asked me out.'

'Saskia says it's low self-esteem,' Tallulah opined, and they all looked at her. 'She says it's because you think you're not good enough, so you settle for something worse than you deserve, because you don't know what you do deserve.'

'Smart girl, your sister,' Eve said.

Harker slid down in his seat, glaring half-heartedly at her.

'It's true, though. So many really smart, pretty, funny girls go out with total losers because they just don't think they're good enough for anything better.' She hit a few more chords for emphasis. 'What's the difference between men and women, Lu?'

There was an embarrassed silence. Tallulah went pink again.

'It's that when we look in a mirror, we think we look

terrible. A man looks in the mirror and thinks he's God's gift.'

'Oh, come on,' Harker protested, and Eve gave him a once-over.

'Well, okay,' she conceded, strumming a couple more chords. 'Maybe not you.'

Harker looked surprised: was she being nice to him? But then Eve said, 'I reckon it's been some time since you were on nodding acquaintance with a mirror.' And she launched into her next song.

Banks stuffed his fist in his mouth. Daz looked away. Tallulah tried as hard as she could not to laugh.

But Harker looked at Eve without a shred of merriment in his face, and Eve wondered if she'd gone too far this time.

Harker looked at himself for a long time in the mirror, which wasn't something he usually did. He knew what he looked like, and he'd never seen any point in liking or disliking his appearance, since there wasn't much he could do to change it.

Okay, his hair could probably do with a cut, since he couldn't actually remember the last time Charlie had nagged him into it.

Or the last time he'd shaved. Well, what was the point? It just grew back. Every time there had been some high-toned and fancy do, Saskia had asked, begged, argued and then finally locked him in a room with a barber and refused to let him out until he was clean-shaven.

Harker, who had a pathological aversion to other people waving sharp things near his face, had always thanked the barber and done it himself. But since he no longer went to fancy shindigs with Saskia, he'd stopped bothering. Besides, it seemed to annoy the other officers, and Harker liked annoying them.

He was wearing his uniform. He couldn't see much point wearing anything else, and besides, he *liked* his uniform. And he at least conformed to regulations with it. Well, sort of. Probably regulations stated he was supposed to look a damn sight neater and tidier, but if he was going to arse around making sure his clothes were always perfectly pressed, he'd never get anything done.

He pulled off his shirt, slowly, and then his undershirt after it. Eve's bandage was still wrapped around his chest and shoulder, pristine and stark against the ruin of skin covering the rest of him.

How had it got to be like this? How had he gone from not really minding a few scars here and there to being so disfigured he repulsed pretty girls? Saskia hadn't minded. At least, she'd despaired a little each time he got hurt, but he'd figured that was concern for his well-being. Not how he looked.

His civilian clothes were set out on the bed, fresh from the laundry. His uniform was a crumpled heap on the floor next to his pack.

Harker regarded himself for one more long minute, then took a dull blade from his pack, and started sharpening it.

Eve was teaching Tallulah how to play *Brothers in Arms* on the piano when the harsh ring of a telephone bell startled her.

Weird, she thought, *three weeks ago I'd barely have noticed it. Now it's the most incongruous thing in the world.*

Benson the butler entered the drawing room, viewed the squad with slight distaste and said, 'A General Wheeler for Major Harker.'

Charlie told him Harker was upstairs, and the distaste on Benson's face grew as he realised he'd have to put himself out to find the Major.

The telephone was in the hall, and the whole squad, including Eve, shamelessly eavesdropped on Harker's conversation. A lot of it consisted of 'Yes, sir,' and 'Fine, sir,' but then he said, 'Actually, sir, we do have some information on where the other computers are.'

Charlie glanced at Eve, who raised her eyebrows.

'Well, I think we need to confirm it first, sir. Eve thinks we might be able to connect to the others, but we need a special device for that ... No, sir, I mean we can connect to it remotely. Keep it here and see what they've got on their computers there.'

He hadn't mentioned the computer at the Tower. Eve wondered why.

'Hull? Well, yes, I suppose so. I – when? Right, sir. I'll bear that in mind.'

They listened a bit more.

'Ah, that might be a problem, sir. Eve says we need a phone line to connect to the other computers. That's how the information is sent ... Something to do with sound waves or something, I'm not sure. Daz – Captain Haran might be able to explain it, sir.'

They all looked at Daz, who shook his head rapidly, eyes wide.

'Oh, fine, sir. Very co-operative ... No, sir, I think this is all we'll need ... Yes, sir, as soon as we have it all working. We can go in for the final piece tonight and be in Hull by tomorrow. Yes, sir.'

There was a click as the telephone was replaced – evidently General Wheeler wasn't big on goodbyes – and the squad hurried to look as if they hadn't been listening at the door. Eve scrambled after Tallulah to the piano, and had just hit a totally random collection of notes, explaining, 'See, you play it like this,' when the door opened and Harker came in.

'I should bloody hope not, that's horrible,' he said, and

she turned to snipe at him only to find her mouth totally useless.

He was wearing an open-necked shirt and dark trousers, and while it was weird to see him without his uniform it was even weirder to see him without his stubble. Because Harker was clean-shaven, every inch of his face smooth and perfect. Without the week-old beard that usually graced his jaw, he looked sharper, younger, and as handsome as she'd doubted he could be.

Eve had just realised she was gaping at him when Daz said, 'Oh, my saints.'

Everyone else looked up.

'Saints be praised,' Charlie said.

'Yes, all right,' said Harker, who could clearly scowl just as well without facial hair as he could with it. 'I own a razor, get over it.'

'I thought you was someone else,' Banks said.

'Last time I saw you look like that, you were getting married,' Tallulah said, and Eve lost a few seconds while she pictured Harker in morning dress.

'Well, I ain't getting married today,' Harker said. 'I'm going nicking a computer piece.'

'You look very respectable for a thief,' Charlie said.

'Well, I'm breaking into the grammar school,' Harker said. 'And my papers say I'm a teacher.'

'You need to be clean-shaven to be a teacher?' asked Daz.

'Hah, not my teacher, he was a weird beardy old guy,' Banks said.

'Look, can we stop this?' Harker said. 'Eve. Why ain't you ready yet?'

Eve licked her lips, swallowed, and found her voice. 'I, uh. Well, after Tallulah ripped that dress, none of the maids were particularly inclined to lend me anything.'

Harker made an impatient sound. 'Look, this is the

bloody army, go and *requisition* something. Do you even have a cover story?'

'Do I need one?' Eve said. 'You're the teacher, I thought you were going to be the one getting us in there.'

'Yes, you need one. And don't make it complicated.' He waved his hand at the piano. 'Tell 'em you're a singer, in case they ask you to prove it, you can–'

His face changed.

'No,' Eve said pre-emptively.

'Oh yes.' Harker's newly beautiful face lit up. 'Lu, go and get that dress.'

'But it's torn–'

'And you know how to sew, I've seen them tapestries you did. Go on.'

Tallulah scampered away, and Harker turned to Eve with a look in his eye she wasn't sure she liked. Even if it did make him look devilishly attractive.

'You're a singer,' he said.

'No, I'm not,' she said nervously.

'In that red dress of Tallulah's.'

'Actually, technically I think it was the head housemaid's–'

'Banks, have you put her occupation on those papers yet? Singer, then. Entertainer. Whatever. You're a nightclub floozy in your red dress–'

'Hey,' Eve said, affronted. So much for devilishly attractive, he was just devilish.

'And what is a nightclub floozy doing with a respectable, clean-shaven teacher?' Daz asked. Eve was pretty sure he was making fun, but she was also pretty sure she knew where this was going.

'What do you think she's doing?' Harker said. He grabbed Eve's hand and whirled her into his arms, which was most avowedly not an unpleasant place to be. 'Reckon you can put aside your violent dislike of me for an evening?'

Eve couldn't quite manage to speak, so she nodded, because right then it was hard to imagine ever disliking this man, with his smooth, hot skin and beautiful throat, his warm eyes dancing at her.

'I'm very glad to hear it,' he murmured, and let her go so abruptly she crashed into the piano. 'Now, go and get that frock off Tallulah.'

Eve stumbled away, quite eager to get away from Charlie's ferocious glare and Harker's raging pheromones.

It's not just because he's had a shave and washed his hair, she thought. *He was damn good-looking before that. It's just that now ... now he looks ...*

God, I wish I'd kissed him this morning.

In a slight daze, she found Tallulah ripping lace from the hem of the dress and tacking it over the rip in the bodice of the dress, which was red and shiny and the sort of thing Eve didn't usually touch with a bargepole.

'It might be short on you,' Tallulah was saying as her fingers flew. 'The head housemaid isn't particularly tall. It was very short on me.'

Tallulah practically had to sew Eve into the dress, which was low-cut and fiendishly tight and left no allowance at all for underwear.

Until she had fallen through the hole in the world, Eve had regarded herself about average in height and weight, but now she'd landed in a twilight zone of men and women who apparently lacked the health and nutrition to grow to what Eve considered normal proportions. Tallulah, tall and willowy, was a notable exception.

As was Harker, tall and broad and strong and–

'You look fantastic,' Tallulah said, regarding Eve as she stood in front of the mirror, seams bursting.

Either the head housemaid was exquisitely petite, or she was a slut who liked overly tight dresses, because the frock, which had looked like couture on Tallulah, looked cheap and tight on Eve. It suctioned in her waist and shoved her breasts up under her chin, far too high for comfort. There was a high split, which enabled her to walk, but also displayed rather a lot of thigh. After a battle and an explanation of who Britney Spears was, Eve had been allowed to keep her knickers on, but no bra.

'I look like a – well, a tart,' she said, depressed.

'You look fantastic,' Tallulah repeated firmly.

She requisitioned some stockings that had been darned a couple of times and were secured with a red lace garter, which showed through the skirt's split, and also rustled up shoes that were Eve's approximate size, and pinched like hell.

'There,' Eve said, having crayoned on lipstick and exaggerated her eyes with kohl. 'Do I look like a nightclub floozy yet? Or do I just look like a drag queen?'

'A what?' Tallulah asked uncertainly.

'Never mind.'

'You look very glamorous.'

'I look like I'll split this damn dress if I try to sit down,' Eve sighed. 'All right, let's go.'

If she'd been hoping that Harker might return the favour and stare in astonishment when she made her entrance to the drawing room, she was disappointed. He barely glanced at her, grumbling, 'You took bloody long enough. Right, we need a getaway driver. Banks, I'm volunteering you.'

Banks, who gratifyingly *had* stared at Eve, stumbled off to the back of the house.

'Well?' Eve asked Charlie and Daz. 'How do I look?'

'Cheap,' Charlie said.

'Excellent. Just the effect I was going for.'

'You look incredible,' Daz said admiringly.

'No, she looks very credible,' Harker scowled. 'Come on,

Miss Credible. Got your papers?'

'Yes, but I don't know where the hell I'm going to put them.'

'Does she get a weapon?' Tallulah asked as Eve followed Harker out.

'Nowhere to put that, either,' Harker said.

Outside the kitchen, one of the footmen was sharing a cigarette with a couple of stable boys. They all whistled when they saw Eve, who grinned and curtseyed.

'Stop that,' Harker snapped. 'Get in the bloody car.'

Eve rolled her eyes at him. 'Somebody woke up on the wrong side of the bed this morning,' she said without thinking, and Harker caught her arm as she climbed into the car.

'Yes,' he said, his eyes hot, 'and it wasn't me.'

Chapter Twenty-One

As the car moved away, Harker was desperately craving strong liquor.

This is the woman, he reminded himself as she pressed up against him in the back of the dark car, *who has the potential to ruin your whole mission. Who could even now be taking a message to the enemy. She couldn't just ruin the whole mission, she could ruin your career. Maybe even the whole army. The whole war.*

And you've encouraged – no, ordered *her – to put on a tight red dress and impersonate your girlfriend. When you fancy her rotten and can't have her. Well, that was a nice move, Major Fathead.*

'So,' she said, all round and lush next to him, as he determinedly didn't look at her. 'Is there a plan?'

'Yes,' said Harker, who'd been too sandbagged by the sight of her to think of one.

'Are you gonna share it with me?'

'No.'

'Excellent.'

Her tone said she wasn't happy with him. Yes, he should have complimented her, but if he'd looked directly at her for a second longer, he'd have gone blind. Or dragged her off to his room and ripped that dress off her–

'Not being funny or anything,' Banks said from the driving seat, 'but you don't smell right.'

There was a short silence. 'Pardon?' Eve said.

'I mean ... look, cheap women should smell cheap. Like, cheap perfume or something.'

'He's right,' Harker said. 'Or at least alcohol.'

'Know a lot of cheap women, do you?' Eve asked, and he ignored her.

'Banks, I need you to drop us at the Kirkgate, and then go and wait for us at that weak spot in the defences, remember it?' Banks nodded. 'All going well, we shouldn't need to use it, but I'd rather have a contingency plan.'

'So, you have a contingency plan, but not an actual plan?' Eve sniped.

'Yes, I have an actual plan. Stop bothering me.'

The car bounced on. Harker could smell the scent of Eve's skin, and that expensive shampoo Tallulah used. Only, on Eve it smelled different. Hotter and richer.

Eve muttered something to herself, and Harker said, 'Pardon?'

'I said, thank God I'm only pretending to be your girlfriend. If anybody ever fills the role for real, remind me to send her a condolence card.'

Harker tried to count to ten, failed completely and rounded on her after five.

'Look, what have I done to you?'

'Oh, you want a list?'

Banks sucked his breath between his teeth, and Harker suddenly remembered he was sitting there up front. Listening to every word. Probably taking notes so he could recount it to the others later.

'No,' he snapped. 'I don't. Just do me a favour and shut up, would you?'

Eve did. In fact, she stayed pointedly silent for the rest of the journey, curling away from him and staring out of the window.

Hell and bloody damn. If he survived the night it'd be a miracle.

Banks pulled up half a mile from the Kirkgate, which was busy with people rushing to beat the curfew. Harker came round to open the door and Eve gave him a murderous look but said nothing, stalking off towards the road to join the crowds, her heel getting stuck in the mud within thirty seconds.

Banks watched her go. 'Good luck, sir,' he said.

'I hope you're referring to the mission there, Private,' Harker said severely.

'What else would I be referring to?' Banks said with an innocence that didn't suit him.

'Go,' Harker said. 'Wait for us. Could be a while.'

Banks's mouth stayed still, but his eyes gleamed with a grin.

'Yessir,' he said, and got back in the car.

Harker trudged after Eve, who had her arms wrapped around herself as she walked. Belatedly, Harker realised she'd be freezing in that skimpy dress, and was trying to calculate the chances of her accepting his jacket when he drew level with her and saw the way her crossed arms pushed her breasts up even further. Half-an-inch more and they'd be spilling out of the dress.

'Here,' he said, hurriedly taking off his respectable teacher-man jacket, which he'd nicked from the head coachman. 'You must be freezing.'

'I'm fine,' Eve said.

'You're lying. I can see goose-bumps all over you.'

She shrugged.

'Besides which, you're about to fall out of that dress.'

She looked down, adjusted her arms, and said, 'Thought you wanted me looking cheap.'

'Yes, but you're going to get arrested looking like that.'

Grudgingly, she took the jacket and wrapped it around herself.

'And please try to look as if you actually like me.'

She gave a brittle smile. It was the least convincing thing

Harker had seen since Saskia had pretended she liked drinking Old Whiskers, when she was trying to impress him by drinking a working-class brew.

As they neared the gate, he put his arm around her shoulders, perversely enjoying the way she stiffened up. But as soon as they got within sight of the gate guards, she changed completely, leaning soft and warm against him and smiling as she tilted her face up to his and murmured, 'Where are our papers?'

'In my jacket.' Which she was still wearing.

'Hadn't you better get them, then?'

Damn. Harker reached inside the jacket, which involved a lot of brushing against tight satin and lush curves, and bloody Eve only made it worse by lolling in his arms and nuzzling his neck. He'd kept a cool head during sieges and pitched battles and even during divorce proceedings, but with Eve Carpenter's splendid assets pressed up against him, he couldn't put two thoughts together.

Oh dear heaven, she's going to kill me, Harker thought, trying desperately to remember which of the inside pockets he'd put the papers in before he gave in and ravished her up against the city wall.

Finally he found them, thrust them at the gate guard, and leaned in close to Eve to whisper, 'What are you doing?'

She pressed her body full against his. 'Being a floozy. Is it working?'

O, hell, yes! 'The guards are impressed.'

'Well, good.'

The guards seemed far more interested in Eve's stockings and glimpsed cleavage than in checking their papers. They were waved through with no questions asked, although one of the guards did give Harker an enormous wink.

'What was that for?'

'Probably fancied you,' Eve said. She was still pressed

tightly against his side as they walked. 'Your papers say you're married, don't they? And yet here you are with me.'

Yes, here I am. With you.

She took his hand, reaching across his body for his left hand, and tsked. 'No wedding ring,' she said.

'Never wore one,' he said without thinking. 'Oh – you mean – no, well, I must have taken it off, eh, while I'm out picking up floozies.'

'Never wore one?' Eve said, her eyebrows raised.

'Ain't really practical, is it? Gets in the way, don't want to worry about losing it, sliding off if it gets too bloody.'

'Well, you're an old romantic,' Eve said, and before he could even think of a response, she asked, 'So, where's this grammar school?'

'By the river,' he said. 'But we're not going there first.'

'We're not?'

'No. First, we're going to get drunk.'

He took her to a tavern – a real noisy, dirty, smelly tavern, with rushes on the floor and men with beards spilling foul-smelling beer from leather tankards. Eve started to wonder how many bacteria were living in the place, but quickly tried to distract herself before she went mad and refused to touch anything.

You're a floozy, she reminded herself. *The tavern is your natural habitat. Act like it.*

She slid Harker's jacket from her shoulders and handed it back to him, adjusting her cleavage and smiling at all the men who noticed.

''Ello, luv,' leered one. 'What's your name, then?'

'What do you want it to be?' Eve said with a flutter of her eyelashes, and Harker grabbed her arm and yanked her away as the man and his friends roared at her.

'Ow,' she said pointedly, and he relaxed his grip a little.

'Are you trying to cause a bloody riot?'

'No, I'm trying to act like a floozy.' Eve leaned over the bar and smiled at the grizzled landlord. 'What are we drinking?'

Harker glanced at the big barrels lined up behind the bar and said, 'Old Whiskers.'

The landlord looked surprised, but drew two pints directly from the barrel by means of a tiny tap. The beer was thick and dark and poured into two leather tankards that made Eve's stomach curl.

Harker handed over some coins and pushed one of the mugs at Eve.

'Must I?' she muttered.

Harker took a long drink of his beer. *Must have an iron stomach,* she thought, *to survive drinking from something that unhygienic.*

Then she thought about just how hard his entire body was, and gulped some of the beer to cool herself down.

Then she spat it out.

A couple of drinkers nearby sniggered at her. Eve narrowed her eyes at Harker, who was grinning. 'You did that on purpose,' she said.

'It's an acquired taste.'

'It's disgusting.' Eve looked at the treacle-like brew in her mug, then down at her tight satin dress, and thought, *what the hell.* She stumbled and tipped the beer all down her dress.

'Oh *no,*' she said theatrically. 'And now I'm going to smell of beer all night long.'

Harker laughed at that, and ordered her some cider instead. It came in a wooden mug, which she supposed was marginally more hygienic than leather, and was actually quite pleasant. He lit up a cigarette, and she took it from him, puffed a few times but didn't inhale.

She wanted to smell like cigarettes. The fact that she was

smoking the same cigarette Harker had put between his own lips was completely by the by.

'So,' she said, 'where does your wife think you are?'

He shrugged. 'Oh, working late. Doing all that ... teacher paperwork.'

'That sounds very boring.'

'It is.'

She adjusted her cleavage again. 'I can see why you came looking for me.'

He smiled at that, a slow smile that did fizzy things to her insides, and she gulped more of the cider. When someone pushed past her to the bar, Harker curled his arm around her waist and pulled her close against his body, and Eve lost her breath. His whole body was so lean and hard, as if he'd been made from rock, steady and invincible.

Eve found herself leaning into him, her arms around his neck, trying not to breathe in the hot-man scent she'd nearly overdosed on outside the gate. Trying not to betray that she was actually developing a giant-sized crush on Harker, who after all didn't even like her very much.

She tried to draw back a little, give herself some breathing space, and then she caught his injured shoulder and he flinched, ever so slightly.

'Sorry,' Eve mouthed, wincing, looking up and meeting those hot gunmetal eyes.

He nodded silently, holding her gaze.

The background of the tavern seemed muted, distant, like a TV burbling in the background, and all Eve was aware of was the tall, broad-shouldered and very handsome man holding her close against his hard, perfect body.

This isn't fair, she thought wildly. *He's not even nice to me. God, I must be going mad if I'm this attracted to someone I don't even like.*

Searching desperately for something to distract herself,

she said, 'So, this plan! Do I get to hear it?'

Harker cleared his throat, and she watched the muscles in his beautiful neck move. 'Plan,' he said. 'Yes. Right. We ... uh, go to the school.'

'And? Do we have a reason for going there?'

He hesitated, then in a voice that suggested he was expecting to get shot down said, 'Uh, you get turned on by books?'

Eve laughed. She couldn't help it. 'Books,' she said. 'Right. Fine. I'm an intellectual floozy.'

He smiled again, that slow and gentle smile, and brushed a strand of hair away from her eyes, which was wickedly unfair of him. How was she supposed to resist him when he kept doing things like that?

Forcing herself to breathe deeply, she closed her eyes.

'Are you all right?' Harker asked.

'I'm fine.' *Just having palpitations.*

'It's warm in here. Do you want to get some air?'

Eve nodded, because maybe outside she could get some distance from him, get her brain working again, remind herself he was just pretending with her, and she was pretending with him, and that as soon as they'd stolen this modem he wasn't going to be cuddling her any more.

Dammit.

Taking her hand, he led her out of the crowded tavern, sat her down on a bench outside, and crouched down in front of her. 'Better?'

She took a deep breath, which he watched with interest, and that forced a laugh from her.

'I know they're right there,' she said, looking down at her heaving bosoms, 'but you don't have to stare at them so much.'

It was hard to tell in the dim light outside the tavern, but she thought his clean-shaven cheeks got a bit pink.

'Why, Major Harker,' she said, 'are you blushing?'

'Of course not. I don't blush.' He stood up abruptly. 'You're obviously feeling better. Come on, then.'

He didn't extend his hand to her this time, but started walking away, and Eve frowned and stayed where she was. After a few paces, he stopped and turned back, scowling at her.

'Well? Are you stopping there?'

'I am if you don't stop this hot-and-cold rubbish,' Eve said. 'Either be nice to me or don't, but stop turning on a dime because you're confusing the hell out of me.'

He came back, looked down at her for one long, inscrutable moment, then said, 'Turning on a dime?'

'Never mind,' Eve said. 'Are you going to be civil to me?'

Harker gave a sigh, as if it was all too much trouble for him, and said, 'Yes. Fine. Miss Carpenter, would you do me the honour of accompanying me?'

He gave her back his jacket and held out his hand. Eve looked at it for a moment, at that missing little finger and the scars edging his palm, then took it and stood up.

'Lead on, Macduff,' she said.

'Macduff?'

'Never mind.'

They walked along the riverbank, slowly, Eve's hand tucked into the crook of Harker's arm. It felt nice, companionable, as if they were friends or maybe on a first date. Eve wasn't exactly sure what a first date was meant to feel like, though, since she'd never technically been on one. When she was a teenager, 'going out' with someone meant being seen with them at lunchtime and sitting next to them in double maths once or twice. At fourteen, the price of a cinema ticket and bus fare had been beyond most of the boys she knew, and anyway, most of her evenings had been spent in rehearsals for musicals with boys who played for the other team. Once she hit fame in Grrl Power there'd simply been no possibility of going for dinner or a movie. She and Kevin had just appeared together at various parties and premieres, and then sort of drifted into couplehood.

Evidently it had rained recently in Leeds, because the cobbles were damp and slippery, hard to walk on in heels. It gave her an excuse to hang on to Harker, with his rock-hard biceps and strong forearms. Eve had always had a thing for a nicely defined forearm, the mark of a man who used his hands a lot. Holding on to Harker was like clinging to an iron bar. He felt solid, indestructible, and more than once he kept her from falling when she stumbled on an uneven cobblestone.

To distract herself, she watched the lights dancing in the river, unexpectedly pretty in this slightly seedy part of town. She didn't realise she was humming until Harker said, 'What's that song?'

'Oh,' Eve said. 'Uh – it's called *On My Own*. There's just a verse about lights on the river, and I was thinking of it. Sorry.'

'How does it go?'

Without really thinking, she sang the first three lines of the verse, and then got to the line about being with him forever and forever, and broke off abruptly.

There's no 'him and me', he thinks I'm a spy, and crazy to boot. Stop being sentimental, girl.

' "And"?' Harker said.

'Um ... I can't remember that line,' Eve fumbled. 'Sorry. It's from the same musical – the same play as the song you wouldn't let me sing on the way up here, do you remember? *Do You Hear The People Sing*?'

'Is it? Sounds different.'

'Well, that one was a call to rebellion, and this one is about a girl who's in love with someone who doesn't want her.'

'I thought it was about trees and rivers,' Harker said, but when she looked up at him, he was smiling. Eve smiled back, and something sparked between them that made her a little dizzy. She stumbled, losing her footing, and as he pulled her closer to his body to keep her upright, she forced her gaze out at the river, away from him.

Beautiful as it was, *On My Own* was also sad. The only time Eponine got to be held in the arms of the man she loved was when she was dying, and Eve didn't think she wanted to go that far.

Eponine died, and Marius survived, victorious, to marry his chosen bride and live happily ever after. Without her, his world went on turning.

'Harker?'

'Mmm?'

She tried out various ways of saying it before eventually going for the simplest.

'What's going to happen to me? I mean, after we get this modem and you have your working computer, and presumably take it back down to London ... you won't need me any more.'

Harker looked away, out at the river.

'Will I just be going back to St James's for the rest of my life?'

He let out a sigh and stopped walking. 'I wish you'd come up with a bloody reason for flying over the Thames,' he muttered, and turned to face her. 'Eve, I don't want you to be a spy. I want you to have a bona fide explanation and be pardoned and go free.'

Eve caught her breath at the intensity in his voice.

'And I will do what I can to see you free, but without anything to prove you're innocent ...'

He was gripping her arms, looking so fierce she was

terribly glad he was on her side.

'And helping you? Won't that earn me some Browni – some points?'

'Aye, a few. But the army likes proof,' Harker said, more than a trace of bitterness in his voice. He dropped his hands. 'Come on,' he said, offering her his arm again, and Eve took it. Her heart was thumping.

'Harker?' she said after a few more steps.

'Yeah?'

'Um. About this morning. I ... um.'

'It's all right.'

'No, it's not. I shouldn't have stayed, I was just ... I was really tired, okay, and not thinking straight, and I was freezing and the bed was warm and ... and I didn't really want to go back to my own room, without Tallulah or Martindale–'

Harker reached over and touched the hand she had curled into his elbow. 'Yeah,' he said.

'And ... well, now Banks probably thinks ... and who knows what he's told everyone else–'

'Ignore 'em,' he said.

'Well, I do, but that's not the point.' *The point is, I woke up and nearly kissed you, because you were lying there looking so warm and vital and sexy, and if Banks hadn't come in I'd have taken advantage of the fact that you were nearly naked to pin you down and ravish you.*

Harker was frowning at something in the distance.

'I just didn't want you to – to think that I'd– What are you staring at?'

'There's someone hiding in the shadows there,' Harker murmured. 'Wait here.'

'Wait here?' Eve hissed, as Harker tried to disentangle her arm from his. She clung on. 'Are you serious? We're walking by the river, I'm dressed like a bloody hooker, and you want me to wait here?'

'Yes,' he said patiently. 'That's why I said "wait here".'

But there's someone hiding *in the* shadows, Eve thought, watching him walk away, her iron bar. *They don't do that for honest reasons!*

But he just walked up to the darkened gap between buildings and reached straight in, pulling out a huddled, skinny woman, whimpering and looking as if she might faint with fear.

Okay, he can be scary, but honestly woman, grow a spine, thought Eve. Then the light fell on the woman's face and Harker dropped her instantly, raising his palms and looking horrified.

'*Mary*? What the – what are you doing here? I thought you were a thief or something.'

Mary was holding herself very tightly, arms wrapped around herself, tears trickling down her face. She looked utterly petrified.

'Eve, come over here,' Harker said, and she frowned but did so. 'Mary, this is my friend Eve. She's nice. She won't hurt you.'

Eve tried to look friendly. Her initial assessment of the sobbing woman as a bit of a wuss changed when she got a look at her colourless face and the soul-deep terror in her eyes. Mary's whole body was rigid, her hands shaking slightly, her posture huddled and submissive.

'You're Mary White,' she said, and Mary's eyes snapped to her. 'Harker told me–' She glanced at him, and there was warning in his eyes. He hadn't actually told her anything other than Mary's name, but Eve knew him well enough by now to recognise the tightness around his mouth when he said it.

'He told me he'd met up with the wife of one of his men,' she said carefully.

Mary gave a stiff little nod, and Harker said gently, 'Mary, I'm so sorry. I didn't mean to frighten you.'

She nodded again and whispered, 'It's all right.'

'No, it's not.' He looked frustrated. 'What are you even doing, walking around here by yourself? In the dark?'

'I missed the curfew,' Mary whispered. 'I had some things to finish for the tailor, and I worked so late I missed the curfew. It's all right though, my friend Prudence lives in the city. Her husband works nights, so there'll be someone up.'

'And Emmy?'

'She stays with Sal and Smiggy when I'm working late,' Mary said. Her eyes darted between them both. Eve smiled and tried to look non-threatening.

'Well, look. We'll walk you there. You shouldn't be out alone,' Harker said.

'I'm fine, really–'

'Are you? What if the next person who catches you lurking in shadows isn't James's old sergeant?' Mary flinched, and Eve glared at Harker, because that had been unnecessarily harsh.

'We'll walk with you,' Eve said. 'We're in no hurry.'

Mary gave another jerky little nod, and they set off, flanking her, taking narrow alleys and dark lanes, saying little. When they reached the low, leaning cottage where Mary's friend lived, she turned and thanked them.

'No problem,' Harker said. 'I'm sorry I frightened you.'

Her shoulders were still stiff. 'It's all right. I was just ... startled. I was hiding because I heard voices and I didn't want to attract any attention,' she added, with a slight smile.

'Next time you're working late, get someone to come and meet you at the shop, okay?' Harker said, and Mary nodded as she knocked at the door.

It was answered by a man holding a tetchy-looking baby. He didn't seem surprised to see Mary, but he blinked at

Harker and Eve.

'Friends of my husband's,' Mary said, and he nodded and thanked them for walking her home.

As they turned away, Harker glanced at Eve and said, 'Don't ask.'

'I think I can guess.'

'I bet,' he said grimly, 'you can't.'

They walked to the end of the little lane, unlit by gas or oil lamps, and Harker pointed down another street that ended at the city wall.

'See that low roof against the wall?' he said. 'You can climb up there and be over the wall. If we get separated, go there, it's where Banks is waiting.'

Eve nodded, and they turned back towards the river. The night air was cold and damp, and she shivered in Harker's jacket. When he put his arm around her it seemed entirely natural, and she leaned into his warmth and strength.

'When I was in Grrl Power,' she said, 'we did a skit for Comic Relief. And as part of the whole thing we met some women who were running a women's shelter in London. They didn't film us with any of the victims because they all wanted to keep their identities private, but we talked to a few of them.'

Harker frowned. 'Okay, I only understood about half of that. Comic Relief?'

'It's a charity thing,' Eve said. 'It doesn't matter. My point is, I've seen women act like Mary before. They were victims of domestic abuse, most of them. One had been kidnapped and raped.' She hesitated. 'What did her husband do to her?'

At that Harker looked surprised. 'He didn't do anything. He tried to defend her, and it ended up getting him killed.'

Eve considered that. 'Why was he defending her?'

'Because he loved her.'

'No, I mean–'

Harker sighed. 'This was back when I was still a sergeant, in the 17th. James White was one of my men and his wife was allowed to stay with the regiment. They had a baby, less than a year old. He was devoted to them both. And then ...'

'And then?'

'Then a vicious conniving lying cheating bastard of a man called Sholt bribed and blackmailed his way to a commission, got assigned to my company, and took a liking to Mary White.'

Eve winced.

'Yeah,' Harker said. 'And he planned it out, the slimy bastard. Didn't take any chances. Waited until James was out on manoeuvres with me and the rest of the men and ambushed her in her tent.'

'So there was no one there to hear her?' Eve said.

'No. Or the baby, who cried and cried, and eventually he shoved her on the floor, knocked over a candle and burned her leg. She still limps now.'

'And Mary?'

Harker's face was grim and dark, his eyes ferocious with anger and disgust. The fury he'd shown Frederick Winterton was a mere shade of this.

She never, ever wanted him to look at her like that.

'You don't want to know what he did to Mary.'

'I think I can guess.'

'Can you though, Eve? Has anyone ever bound and gagged you and cut you with a knife in places–' He broke off, his fingers curling into a fist. 'And the worst of it was that James knew who'd done it and went after Sholt, and threatened him and hit him in front of other officers, for which he was sentenced to a flogging.' He delivered the story in a curiously flat tone, as if he was reading it from a book, but anger simmered under every one of his words.

'A flogging? How barbar–' She broke off, shook her head.

'But – surely he was provoked? Didn't they take that into account?'

'They did not. The army,' Harker said flatly, 'likes proof. Besides, Sholt bought his commission with bribery and blackmail, remember? He had several officers in his pocket. He said James beat her. He said she dropped the baby. And they listened. They bloody listened to him. Not one bugger listened to a word James said or gave a damn about the only person defending him.'

'You?' Eve said.

'Me. I'd only been a sergeant less than a year. Didn't know Saskia then, either. Stood up for James's character but it was just pissing into the wind. They'd already decided to have him killed.'

'I thought you said he was flogged?'

'Twelve hundred lashes'll kill most people.'

Eve shuddered.

'Yeah,' Harker said. 'They made Mary watch, too, the sadistic bastards, while Sholt's standing there smirking the whole time, watching a man flogged to death. We tried to take care of her, me and the men, and their wives – not too many women in the army then, but we had plenty of good lads. They looked after her.'

'You looked after her,' Eve said. 'You look after everybody.' She paused, and added sadly, 'She wasn't even one of your men.'

'She was James's wife,' Harker said, as if it was obvious. 'That makes her one of mine.'

Eve looked up at him, at his hard, strong face, determination evident in every line, and wished that she was one of his, too.

But Harker said nothing, and she knew his thoughts were both miles and years away, and didn't include her.

Chapter Twenty-Two

Meeting Mary had unsettled him, but for once in his life Harker didn't dwell on it. He wanted to – he even tried to; anything to distract himself from Eve's attentions as they approached the grammar school in The Calls.

But she leaned into him and looked up at him with those big eyes, and pressed all that softness against him, and smiled so provocatively that even the guard at the school gate couldn't concentrate on anything but her.

'Are you sure you're not an actress?' he asked as they crossed the small lawn, and Eve looked up at him with an unfathomable look in her eyes.

'No,' she said, 'I'm really not.'

Harker didn't stop to try and work that out, mostly because he'd just spotted a second guard prowling around the inside of the school. Eve saw him too, and said, 'Quick, come here.'

She drew his face down to hers, but just when he was sure she was going to kiss him, she darted to one side and kissed his cheek.

'There,' she said, 'lipstick all over you. Better.'

Harker, his heart racing, took a second or two to focus on her, before he nodded and said, 'Yep. Right. Good one,' incredibly fast, and dragged her inside.

It was dark inside the school, but he could hear the hum of electricity and see a dim light coming from a set of tiled stairs.

'Lot of security for a school,' Eve murmured as she followed him, hand in hand.

'A school with a computer,' Harker said, and she laughed

silently. 'What?'

'Nothing, it's just to me ... it'd be a pretty poor school that didn't have any computers.'

'Well, your world ain't my world,' Harker said, wondering as he did whether he actually believed that. Was she from a different world? Or was she just crazy? No, she was too lucid to be crazy.

He refused to believe she was a spy. Not after everything she'd said and done.

Nonetheless, he was taking her right into enemy territory. And if she turned tail and handed him over to the Coalitionists, he'd never hear the end of it from Charlie.

Come on, Eve, he begged her silently as they climbed the staircase and turned towards the half-open door from where the pale blue light was coming. *Prove me right. Help me steal this piece, make the computer work and come home safe and sound. If you do that, Charlie will have to accept you're on our side.*

'Why is there a light on?' Eve mouthed as they approached the door, as silently as possible. Harker gave a facial shrug. Probably there was someone in there.

'Well,' Eve whispered, sliding her arm around his neck and speaking into his ear, 'sneaking around won't help. We have a right to be here, remember?' Then, much louder, she said, 'Go on, then, show me these books.'

'I don't know where they bloody are,' Harker hissed, but there didn't seem to have been any reaction from the other side of the door.

'What's in there? There's a light on,' Eve said. Her words were rougher than he was used to, slightly slurred and shouty. She was clinging to him and stumbling as if she was drunk. Well, she certainly smelled of beer, her own trick in the pub had seen to that.

He grinned a little. Old Whiskers, that had been mean.

Nobody liked the stuff. He didn't even like the stuff. He'd only been drinking it because ... well, because he'd wanted to impress her.

Which was rather pathetic of him.

'Why don't you come and see?' he said out loud, reaching for the door handle and swinging it inwards. His free hand slipped into his pocket, where a cosh would help him knock out anyone inside the room, but there was no one there.

The light was rather dim, coming from the screen of the computer set up on the desk. The rest of the room was filled with books, clearly the school's library, and they stretched off into the darkness, shelves and shelves of them.

'Oh, wow,' Eve said, still in her floozy voice. 'Look at all these books, Will!'

'Yep,' he said, 'look at 'em.'

'Close the door,' Eve said, and he did, and she immediately dropped the act and went straight to the computer, moving the mouse and tapping at the keyboard.

'Might need you to translate,' she murmured. 'All the commands are in French ...'

Ducking her head, she peered at something sitting on top of the CPU box. It trailed wires, one of which went to the back of the computer and the other to a telephone.

'Bingo,' she said. 'That's our modem.' She unplugged it and handed it to Harker, who turned her to face him and tucked it into the pocket of the jacket she was still wearing. She stood still, not reacting at all when his hands brushed her body, then turned away quickly, saying, 'Let me just check the network settings, okay?'

Harker, who still didn't really understand what network settings were, nodded and watched her get on with it. She was frowning slightly, leaning over the desk so that his jacket rode up and her curvy backside was exposed in all its tight red satin glory.

'Harker?' she said after a minute or two.

He was still staring at her. 'Mmm?'

'Stop staring at my arse.'

For the second time that night, he felt colour creep into his cheeks.

'Do something useful,' Eve said, nodding at a strongbox next to the computer. 'See what's in there.'

'How?'

'I dunno, can't you break the lock or something?'

Harker, who did in fact own a lockpick and knew how to use it, scowled. 'Yes, but I'm disappointed you expected me to,' he said.

As she clicked on things and asked for translations, he worked on getting the box undone. Whatever was inside rattled rather alarmingly, and he set it down on the desk to work on it as quietly as possible. But then Eve sucked in a sharp breath and he turned to look at her too fast, catching the strongbox and knocking it on to the floor, where it clattered, rolled and clattered some more, incredibly loud in the silent building.

Harker froze, so did Eve, her expression turning to horror as a distant voice said, 'What the hell was that?'

Harker grabbed for the box, only to have the lid fall open and the contents spill everywhere. Swearing, he scooped up dozens of the little sticks like the one Eve had taken information from earlier in the day, shoving them into his trouser pockets as footsteps sounded on the stairs. Eve snatched up the box and set it back on the desk with the lid shut, if not locked.

'Oi, who's in there?' said a voice outside the door as Harker straightened, and Eve suddenly grabbed him, pulled his head down to hers and, as the door opened, she wrapped her arms around his neck and touched her lips to his.

But her lips were slightly parted, soft and warm and

irresistible, and Harker found himself leaning into her, pressing her back against the desk and actually kissing her.

The guard said something but Harker didn't even hear. Eve's mouth on his was a miracle, her eyes widening with surprise. He liked that she didn't close her eyes, because then instead of the thick make-up on her lids he could see, even in the computer's cool light, how her eyes warmed up, how her pupils dilated, and most of all how she looked right at him and knew it was him she was kissing.

There was a distant sound that he later realised was the guard saying something else and shutting the door, but he didn't really pay much attention. Eve's body was pressed against his, round and lush in that satin, and he slid one hand down to the curve of her waist, feeling the heat of her skin through the cheap fabric.

You shouldn't be wearing this, he thought, *it's not you.* He wasn't sure what was her at that moment, but he had a sneaking suspicion that it was somewhere between very little and nothing at all.

Eve had her arms around him, one hand warm on the back of his neck. Her fingers curled in his hair, her ankle twined around his and she leaned back against the desk, letting him settle between her thighs, which was where he really, really wanted to be.

He'd never felt anything like this before. It was just *kissing*, for heaven's sake, but it was magical, intense, and kind of surreal because he didn't think this sort of thing happened to real people. But here he was, kissing desperately, unable to stop, unaware of anything or anyone else in the world apart from Eve and her hot mouth and her hot body and how very, very much he wanted her.

She bit his lower lip, her eyes dancing at him, then licked away the sting, and Harker groaned and slid his hand down to press her hips against his more fully. He wanted her desperately, and she didn't seem to mind. In fact, she seemed quite enthusiastic about the idea.

His hand moved to her breast and he felt the lace give, the hastily sewn rip re-open as she arched her back, pushing herself into his hands, and *heaven help him* she was naked under there.

You're going to kill me, he thought, and then a terrific bang behind him suddenly made them both freeze. *Must be the world ending to rip me away from that*, Harker thought muzzily, and swung his head around to see what it was.

A man wearing a dark suit and a ferocious glare stood in the doorway. He was flanked by soldiers with large guns.

'What,' said the man, 'do you think you are doing here?'

Making out with a woman I want so incredibly badly I'm considering killing you just so I can get back to it, Harker thought, but he said, 'I work here.'

'No,' said the man, 'you do not.'

And a cold feeling stole through Harker, killing most of his ardour, and from the way Eve tensed in his arms he guessed she felt it, too.

'Uh, who are you?' Harker asked.

'I am the headmaster, young man.'

'Ah,' said Harker, glancing back at Eve. 'Bollocks.'

Where were they? First floor. Great. Was there a roof outside the window? Well, was there? Could they jump off that? No telling what they might hit, and besides, they'd almost certainly be shot at. And apart from the cosh, he wasn't armed.

With great reluctance he released Eve and turned around, using his body to shield hers. 'She just wanted to see the books,' he said, trying to sound contrite and wondering if he even knew how to.

The headmaster looked disgusted, but one of the soldiers sniggered.

'Come on then, out, before I have you arrested for trespassing on private property,' said the headmaster, and Harker nodded, relieved.

'Yes, sir. Sorry, sir.'

'And don't get smart, boy.'

What is it about schools that make you feel like a kid again? Harker thought as he took Eve's hand – enjoying the tingle he got from just touching her – and walked after the headmaster out of the library.

The soldiers followed behind them, and they'd got halfway down the stairs when one of the men said, 'Hang on a minute.'

Harker gripped Eve's hand tighter and kept going.

'That ... what do they call it? That computer, it looks different.'

They were almost to the bottom now.

'Different how?' said the other, who was closer behind Harker and Eve.

'I dunno. 'Ere, did you two do something to it?'

'What, us?' said Harker, as they hit the ground floor. 'Wouldn't know how to.'

'Did you touch it?' asked the headmaster suspiciously.

'No,' said Harker.

'At least, not on purpose,' Eve said with what he thought was a perfectly charming grin, but which seemed to annoy the headmaster.

'Check if something's missing,' said the headmaster. 'There have been some thefts of computing equipment, haven't there?'

One of the soldiers nodded, and withdrew from his pocket a radio.

Oh hell, thought Harker, and willed it not to show on his face.

'Right, turn out your pockets, please,' said the headmaster, and Harker glanced at the two soldiers. One was at the top of the stairs, speaking into his radio, requesting back-up. The other was peering through the open door at the computer. Harker squeezed Eve's hand, and she looked up at him. He flicked his gaze to the door and she gave an infinitesimal nod.

'Now, please,' said the headmaster, and they ran.

Behind them the headmaster shouted, and there was a sudden burst of gunfire. They were firing automatics, and Harker could only hope they didn't have many bullets. After all, they were only guarding one computer, housed in a school ...

A computer that was a prime target for attacks by the army.

Hell and bloody damn!

His fingers wrapped tightly around Eve's, Harker raced her down the steps and across the lawn, to the background of more shouting and some thankfully inaccurate gunfire. The guard on the gate turned and saw them running and Harker waved his hands frantically.

'Misunderstanding,' he yelled. 'Don't shoot!'

The guy was clearly more gullible than Harker had first realised, because he held back, right up until Harker reached him, brained him with the help of his cosh and stole his gun, all without breaking stride.

'Very impressive,' Eve panted, and he grinned at her before yanking her out through the gate and on to the street, where a few people had stopped to peer up at the school. Ignoring them, he darted down the first alley he saw, took as many fast turns as he could, and paused in a gap between buildings, holding Eve against him and enjoying the way her chest heaved against his.

'Do you think we lost them?' she whispered, her breath coming hard.

Harker listened. He nodded. Eve exhaled, smiled and reached up to kiss him.

Feet pounded on the cobbles a few feet away.

Alarm flared in her eyes.

'Maybe not,' Harker muttered, and tugged her deeper down the alley, so narrow it was hardly an alley at all, emerging at the other end dirty and damp and only a few streets away, he reckoned, from their escape over the wall.

'This way,' he said, and tugged Eve after him. She stumbled, her face twisting in pain as those treacherous heels caught in the cobblestones.

'I can't,' she panted when he tried to pull her upright. 'Just ... gimme a second.'

'We don't have a second. They'll kill us if they catch us.'

On cue, an automatic weapon spattered bullets somewhere very close by, and Eve glanced back the way they'd come.

'Look,' she said, 'take the modem and the USB sticks. If they catch me I have nothing on me. They can search me,' she added, ripping off his jacket and handing it to him. 'I can tell them it was all your idea and that you've run off towards the river.'

'I ain't leaving you,' Harker said, because that was a ridiculous plan.

'Sarge, I see them!' yelled someone, and he saw the panic rise on her face.

'Harker, I just can't run in these heels and it'll take me forever to get these straps undone. I'm going to turn my ankle and then I'll be completely useless and you'll have to leave me anyway. Go after Banks, dump the stuff there and come back for me. Or send him. I'll be fine,' she insisted, her face pale and entreating in the moonlight. Her red lipstick was smeared – *I did that*, he thought with a touch of pride – and her eyes were wide.

'Eve–' he began, and a shout from the alley made his head

whip round.

Eve grabbed him and pressed her lips against his. 'Go,' she said. 'I'll totally make it worth your while when we get back.'

Heat flashed through him and he couldn't help a smile. 'I'll come back for you,' he promised, before he turned and ran, hoping like hell he was doing the right thing.

But that was the way of it, wasn't it? There was never any time to make a proper choice, you had to follow your gut and deal with the consequences.

He reached the city wall, hauled himself up on to the low roof and over the wall. More machine-gun fire echoed as he dropped to the ground and ran the couple of hundred yards to where the car was hiding in a small copse, as arranged.

Banks had his rifle out, but relaxed when he recognised Harker. 'No Eve, sir?'

'No. She stayed behind to put them off the scent,' Harker said, chucking his jacket on to the back seat. 'I said I'd go back for her.'

'Sir, would it be better if I did?' said Banks. 'They won't recognise me.'

He hesitated. On the one hand, he'd promised Eve. On the other, Banks was right, and he stood a better chance of going unnoticed.

'Okay,' he said. 'But be careful.'

'Yessir,' Banks said, no questions asked, which was just the way Harker liked it. He gave brief directions, then flopped into the car, his heart racing.

She'll be fine, he told himself. *Remember how she's always getting the better of you? Well, those guys are stupider than you, and more susceptible to a pretty girl in a torn dress.*

Not much more susceptible, though.

He grinned, running his hands over his face and remembering how she'd felt pressed against him, her mouth soft and hot on his, her hands clutching at him. *I'll totally make it worth your while.* Oh, God, yes. She would, too, he knew she would. All that passion and fire and creativity, she'd be incredible. He wanted her and she wanted him, and she'd gone into the enemy's territory and returned – well, nearly returned – with him, and now Charlie would have to shut up and leave him in peace with the girl he wanted more than anything he'd ever wanted in his whole life.

The gunfire came closer and Eve walked fast, her head down, sticking to the shadows. Maybe they wouldn't see her, and then–

'Halt!'

Did they have to say that? Now she couldn't keep a straight face.

Composing herself, she turned, ready with a smile, and faced six men with very large guns.

'Oh, you frightened me,' she said, trying to smile disarmingly. 'I was just on my way home. Working late. I'm a singer,' she babbled.

'Papers,' said one of the soldiers. In the dark, she couldn't see any insignia, but she guessed he was a sergeant.

Cold dread stole through her as she realised the flaw in the plan: her papers were in Harker's jacket.

'Um, I must have left them–'

'Take her,' said the Sergeant.

'No, you don't understand, I live just around the corner,' Eve said desperately, as two soldiers clamped down on her arms and started marching, dragging her with them. Maybe if she could get to Mary's friends, maybe they'd take her in, maybe–

'Where?' asked the Sergeant, and Eve tried to remember, panic fogging her brain. She pointed, but the Sergeant wanted an address, and Eve didn't even know the name of the road they were on.

'Um,' she panicked, 'um, um ...'

'Nice try,' said the Sergeant.

Banks hadn't come back. Eve hadn't come back. Harker, his elation fading somewhat, waited another five minutes then got out of the car, and climbed over the wall again.

The lane where he'd left Eve was empty. Harker forced himself to calm down, told himself she'd just have gone somewhere else to hide, or taken a different route, and started searching, keeping to the shadows as much as possible.

He heard voices. A woman, a man, heavy footsteps, several soldiers. Oh no, what if they'd found her? But she had nothing on her–

–nothing at all, not even papers–

–*idiot!* Harker started to run.

One of the soldiers was leering at her breast, half-exposed by the torn dress. Wildly, Eve started to wonder how far she'd go to save herself. Or Harker. Fear thudded through her with every thump of her heart. Mary White. Sholt. Harker.

Harker.

'Look,' she said to the Sergeant, 'maybe we can make a deal?'

They were right ahead, around the next corner. The Coalitionist patrols didn't bother to hide themselves. They had the whole town terrified of them.

Harker slid along in the shadow of a house with a heavy overhang, and very, very slowly peered around the edge.

'What kind of deal?' the Sergeant said, and Eve smiled at him. His eyes narrowed, then he smiled back. He gestured to the men to release her.

There are six of them, I can't take them down, maybe one at a time but not six, Eve thought wildly, her smile fixed in place as she moved to press herself against the Sergeant. He was tall, broad-shouldered, hard-muscled, and her body was like ice, frozen with fear and disgust.

'I can be very co-operative,' Eve said.

Like the moments when he'd faced mortality, Harker's world seemed to slow down, to crystallise, and the city faded into blurriness as the image of Eve pressed up against the Coalitionist soldier roared into life right before his eyes.

She smiled at him, stroked his neck, let him manhandle her. He touched her breast and she closed her eyes, and nausea rose sharply in Harker's throat.

You bloody fool, you said yourself she was quite an actress.

She didn't think the Sergeant believed her bluff, but she was gambling without any cards at all now. *Are you going to do this?* asked a terrified voice inside her. *He's not going to let you go, he's going to rape you!*

Sacrifice my body, save my life, Eve told it blindly, offering another smile to the Sergeant.

'Maybe at your barracks, we can go somewhere more private?' she said. *Where I can kill you and escape. Maybe I can escape.*

Oh God, I'm not brave enough for this.

'Who needs to wait until we get back?' said the Sergeant, grinning horribly. 'They'll take you straight off my hands when we get back. No ... we can be more private here, my lovely.'

Harker found himself running back through the streets, almost blind, seeing nothing, hearing the echo of Eve's words with every step his stupid feet took.

'We can go somewhere more private ... more private ... co-operative ... private ...'

She was supposed to be mine.

Of course she'd sparked something in him. She'd made them all like her, but who had she paid most attention to? Who had she provoked and teased and flirted with? The guy in charge, that's who. Gain his confidence, and nothing anyone else says can touch you.

Charlie was right, he thought as he hauled himself over the wall and out of the city. *She was bloody right.*

So much panic arose in Eve that things went black for a moment, then she found herself in an alley with the Sergeant pushing her against a wall, pawing at her dress, fumbling with his own clothing–

– using both his hands, his gun slung over his shoulder –

Eve's knee shot up, right into his groin, acting almost without thinking about it, and as he yelped and doubled over she shoved at him and ran.

She got almost to the end of the alley before the crack and whine of a gunshot rang out, and things went black again.

He'd been there ten minutes when Banks came panting up, looking worried. 'Sir, I can't find her, do you know where–'

'Get in,' Harker said, starting the engine.

'But, sir, what about Eve?'

Harker blinked, and when he did he saw Eve walking away with the enemy Sergeant.

'She ain't coming,' he said.

Chapter Twenty-Three

Eve came to when someone threw cold water on her face. She was lying on a stone floor, her leg throbbing and her head doing a decent job of keeping up. She'd ... what the hell had she done to end up like this?

Harker, the school – *that kiss*, she smiled – and then the soldiers ... Her smile faded. The Sergeant. She'd so nearly escaped. But someone ... one of his men must have seen her running because her leg was throbbing and bleeding and she thought, she wasn't sure but she *thought* she'd been shot.

Shot. With a goddamned bullet. *Shot*.

I want to go home now.

About a metre in front of her was a carved stone pillar, the sort of thing you might find in a church, but leaning against it was a man in a Coalitionist uniform. It had braid and things on it, so she guessed he was an officer.

She attempted to sit up. It didn't go well.

'State your name,' said the officer.

'No.' It came out as a croak.

'State your name.'

'Why? Are you going to set me free if I give you the right one?' She wasn't chained or handcuffed, but she didn't really need to be. Her leg hurt incredibly. Eve had never broken a bone or been seriously injured before, and she was discovering that the pain was incredible. She was having trouble concentrating because of it.

I've probably lost a lot of blood, too. Bet they don't care.

Clearly they didn't, because as Eve was thinking that, the officer gave a nod and a large boot aimed itself at Eve's ribs. Gasping with new pain, she turned her head and saw the sort of large, bald man traditionally hired by villains to beat people up and enjoy it.

This man could have come from Central Casting. He gave Eve a toothless grin.

'My name,' she wheezed, 'is Louisa Butcher.'

There was a tapping sound. Someone behind her was using a computer.

'Who was the man you were with?'

Eve licked her lips. 'My boyfriend. And I tell you something, he's a liar and a bloody cheat, because he told me he wanted–' She grunted as the boot hit again.

'His name,' said the officer calmly. He looked totally normal, neither handsome nor ugly, but well-built and clean-shaven.

Think of Harker clean-shaven and smiling instead. There's a thought to keep a girl warm on cold nights.

'Kevin Hayes,' she said. 'He's a teacher. And he's married.'

More tapping. The officer glanced at whoever was behind her, then back at Eve, his expression remaining blank. Charlie could do the same thing. Harker, too. Daz had called it Officer Blank. He was still practising it, apparently.

'No, he's not,' the officer said. 'We have no Kevin Hayes on record as a teacher.'

'Well, did you spell it right?' Eve said, wondering why she was even bothering. 'It's H-A-Y-E-S, and did you check him as maybe a lecturer, or tutor, or something else?'

'Don't play games with me, young lady,' said the officer. He straightened up and moved over to a fireplace. There was a poker hanging next to it.

Eve had a sudden terrible premonition.

'I'm not playing games,' she said. 'Look, I want to get out of here. If I tell you what you want to know, will you let me go?'

'Perhaps,' said the officer, and – yes, he picked up the

poker and stirred the fire with it. Eve was mesmerised by the way the tip heated up and brightened in colour.

'Well, what do you want?'

'Who are you working for?'

'I–' she began to say she didn't understand, when an idea came into her head. Dulled by pain and fear, her brain wasn't functioning at full capacity, but she figured this one had legs. More legs than her attempt at seduction, anyway.

'The army,' she said.

The officer took a deep, satisfied breath. 'Your rank?'

'I don't have one. I'm not a soldier. They just co-opted me as a civilian.'

'What was your mission?'

'I – they didn't tell me. Not totally. I was a civilian,' she repeated quickly, because he had the poker in his gloved hands now and he was bringing it closer, closer–

Take good care of your hands, and they'll take care of you, said a long-forgotten session musician in her head, as the poker swung and Eve's right hand darted out to stop it, because it was glowing and he was going to smash it into her face, and if Harker could survive without his little finger then she could live through this–

But it hurt, dear God, it hurt, and she could hear the sizzle of her own flesh as her eyes met the officer's.

That's taken Officer Blank off your face, she thought, watching the surprise flash over his features. *That's right, I'm not afraid of you.*

Well, I am, but I don't want you to know that.

'Captain Sholt,' she said. Sweat poured down her face, stung her eyes and made her blink, losing that brave eye contact. 'Of the 75th Infantry. He was in charge. You want him.'

The officer stared at her for one more long moment. Eve thought she might pass out. She could smell something disgusting, and a distant little part of her said, *That's burning flesh, you're cooking your own fingers.*

Then he pulled the poker back with a ripping sound she really didn't want to investigate, and his gaze flickered to the man at the computer.

'Captain Sholt,' he said. Waves of pain threatened to drown Eve. Above her, she saw the officer talking but above the blood pounding in her ears she couldn't hear a thing.

Then the officer leaned closer and said to her, 'What's his first name?'

Eve stared up at him, speechless, and a cruel smile twisted the officer's face.

'No, I didn't think so,' he said softly, and to the big thug he added, 'Put her in the cells.'

'No,' Eve said, as she was grabbed by the huge man's meaty hands. 'No, you said – you'd let me go, and–'

'I said perhaps,' said the officer, smiling thinly. 'Take her away.'

No, Eve thought, picked up and slung over the thug's shoulder. Her right hand hung limp and she stared in horror at the useless, charred flesh of her fingers.

Harker didn't sleep. He threw his civilian clothes on the floor, lay down on his cold bed and stared at the ceiling. The cuts on his shoulder throbbed, and he tore off the bandage Eve had wrapped around him to shy it at the wall, where it failed to make any sort of impact at all.

Unlike Eve. He'd seen mines leave smaller craters.

I'll totally make it worth your while.

And he'd believed her. He'd believed her when she had clung to him after the skirmish at the Fen Causeway. He'd believed her when she had fought with him about those songs – how did she know them, anyway? And those songs about France, what an idiot he was!

He'd believed her when she had kissed him.

That was the problem. He'd wanted to believe her, and been willing, desperate in fact, to believe her. He'd made excuses and allowances, and he'd pretty much talked himself into trusting that, despite a total lack of evidence, she was innocent. All because she was the first woman who'd sparked anything in him since Saskia.

You were an idiot, Harker, he told himself savagely, rolling on to his back again and staring at the ceiling, his eyes burning. *You were a bloody idiot, and I don't know what the hell you were using for brains but it wasn't what you keep in your head.*

He fought for his country. For the army, and for England. He'd done it all his life. He'd never been distracted before. He'd forgotten what was important.

He should have listened to Charlie. He'd known her twelve years, and Eve less than three weeks. Stupid Harker, stupid, stupid Harker.

This morning I woke up with her soft and warm in my arms. This evening I kissed her, and the world went away.

Tonight I hope she rots in hell.

The cell was dark, and it was cold. Things scuttled. Eve thought she might have been underground. But then, she thought she saw leprechauns at one point, so she wasn't entirely certain she was thinking straight.

Her leg hurt so intensely it sucked away huge chunks of consciousness. Waves of pain throbbed through her, and when she had a second to concentrate on her ribs, they didn't feel so good either.

But her hand ... that didn't hurt much at all. It was red and black and white, like the old joke about the newspaper, and she couldn't move it much, but it didn't hurt a lot.

Harker will come for me, she thought. *He said he would*

and he keeps his word. He'll come and get me, and he'll look all dishevelled and heroic, and he'll carry me back to the Chase where we'll have hot sweaty sex and everything will be fine.

Weak as a newborn, she curled on the floor, cradling her ruined hand, watching the leprechauns and singing softly to them.

'Are y'sure you won't be staying?' asked Sir Dennis as Harker chain-smoked his way through the day and watched Banks and Tallulah pack the wagon. Tallulah kept casting him sullen looks. He didn't know what her problem was. She wasn't the one who'd been hoodwinked.

'No. We have to get to Hull. Thank you for your hospitality,' Harker said, the words coming without him really thinking about them, just as they had yesterday at Martindale's funeral.

If it wasn't for Eve, would she still be alive?

No. Don't start that.

'I called the Tower, sir,' Charlie said, coming out into the cold stable yard. 'The Humber Bridge is being blown up at midnight; we have until then.' She hesitated.

'Yes, Lieutenant?' *Mention Eve and I will hurt you.*

'Sir, about the location we saw on the computer yesterday ...? I didn't say anything to Wheeler's aides, but–'

'Good. She's going to have to get some top people on that machine, make sure it's not all been made up for our benefit.'

Charlie's eyes narrowed. 'You think it was a fake?'

'I think the army's right, Charlie,' Harker said, watching Tallulah load Eve's guitar on to the wagon. 'Never do anything without proof.'

He went back inside the warmth of the house in search of some alcohol with maybe a hot drink in it. He could take up drinking. That might be something to do.

Saskia always said you were too cocky. She said one day, doing things your way would backfire on you.

He stomped up to the drawing room, ignored the piano, and started raiding the drinks cabinet Sir Dennis thought was well-hidden.

'Major Harker?' said someone, and he looked round to see one of the footmen standing there. 'A young lady for you, sir. She came to the back door.'

His heart leapt. Stupid heart. 'Did you recognise her?'

'No, sir. She said her name was Mary White.'

That got his attention. Straightening up, he followed the man down to the kitchen, where Mary was indeed standing, holding Emmy back against her, both of them wide-eyed at the size of the kitchen and the scale of the activity.

'Mary,' he said, and she looked up at him. *If it wasn't for Frederick I'd get Sir Dennis to hire you here.* 'What are you doing here?'

Mary looked around nervously, and Harker, realising she wanted to talk somewhere quieter, led her through into the laundry room. It was still visible from the kitchen, which seemed to make her feel better.

'Major Harker,' she began. 'I wanted to ask if ...' She took a deep breath. Emmy clutched her hand reassuringly. 'If you needed any help rescuing your young lady.'

The temporary distraction of Mary's presence faded, and the sick pain he'd been feeling all day came back to nestle in his stomach like rancid meat.

'She's not my young lady,' he said. 'And she doesn't need rescuing.'

Mary opened her mouth, then shut it again. 'But ... Frank said he saw her being taken to the Abbey.'

'Did he,' Harker said flatly. 'Who's Frank?'

'Last night, you met him? Prudence's husband. He's on nights at the foundry, and he was walking to work when he saw them with her.'

'Recognised her, did he?' Harker said sourly, thinking of that damned red dress and the effect it had had on him.

'Yes ... and she was unconscious, and she was bleeding,' said Mary.

Serves her bloody right. But a nasty tightening in his gut made him ask, 'Unconscious?'

Mary nodded. 'That's what he said. They were carrying her.'

Harker shut his eyes, and once more the memory of Eve nuzzling the Coalitionist flashed in front of him.

It used to be James White who haunted him, but since last night, it had been Eve.

Harker made himself open his eyes and said, 'It could have been anyone.'

'No, sir, he recognised her dress.' Mary looked even more tense than usual. 'It was torn.'

Because she'd let Harker manhandle her.

But why was she unconscious? And bleeding?

Charlie tapped at the open door. 'Sir? Wagon's packed. We're ready when you are.'

She was unconscious and bleeding. Harker glanced from Mary to Charlie, then back again.

She was acting. I know she was acting.

'Sir,' Charlie said, and wibbled on about the wagon and supplies and provisioning.

Who was she acting with?

Mary's eyes were huge, full of fear. Of course she was afraid; she knew just what a soldier could do to a woman.

And Harker knew what a woman could do to a soldier. She could make his fears and doubts persuade him that he was seeing lies instead of the truth.

Or the truth, instead of lies.

'Sir?' Charlie said to Harker, who had his eyes resting

on a pile of laundry, but was focused on a dark alley and a woman in a red dress.

'You said she was hurt,' he said distantly.

'He couldn't see where exactly, but there was blood on her clothes. He could see it even against the red of the dress.'

'They were going to the Abbey,' he said.

'They take everyone there. People who disagree with them, or fight … and they don't come back, sir.'

'Sir, you said she went with them,' Charlie said.

'I know what I said,' Harker muttered.

You were wrong.

'Maybe she didn't go willingly,' Charlie said cautiously.

'*No one* would go willingly,' said Emmy, speaking for the first time.

What would Harker do if he was faced with six enemy soldiers? He'd fight. But Eve? Eve wasn't a soldier, she didn't know how to fight. She knew how to smile and flirt and pretend.

She was trying to save herself. Maybe she was trying to save you. And now look what you've–

'Sir,' Charlie said, touching his arm, and he snarled at her, and Mary flinched back against an ironing board so hard it clattered. Emmy turned to her mother immediately, soothing her, and Harker watched them, breathing hard.

Mary's risked an awful lot to come here and tell you this, to offer her help. It could get her hurt, killed, or back in the hands of men who beat and rape.

He remembered with horribly vivid accuracy the blood and the bruises and the silent, white-faced sobbing when he and James had found her.

And Eve's hurt, there was blood soaking through her clothes–

'We'll go in after her, sir,' Charlie said, her voice calm and quiet. There was a look in her eyes he hadn't seen before.

She was wary of him. 'Tonight, if you want.'

The sooner the better.

He nodded, strode out to tell the others, and cannoned into Banks, who said, 'Sir, butler's looking for you. Telephone; it's General Wheeler.'

Annoyed at this diversion, Harker took the back stairs two at a time and snatched up the phone. 'Sir?'

'Ah, Harker. I'm glad I caught you before you left. The telephone at the Hull base isn't working. I thought with your clever captain you could get it fixed.'

'Yes, sir,' Harker said distractedly. Then reality smacked him in the face. 'Uh, sir, when did you say the Humber Bridge was being blown up?'

'Tonight. We simply can't leave it up, it's an open invitation for the Coalitionists to spread further north.'

'Tonight,' Harker repeated. Behind him, Charlie winced.

'Yes, Harker. Did you have something else planned?' There was a note of slight humour in her voice. 'Riggs said you were leaving this afternoon. You've got everything you need, haven't you?'

'Yes, although we don't know if it all works,' Harker hedged. 'The new piece we got last night, sir, it might not–'

'Well, if it's damaged I'm sure we can repair it. Your Miss Carpenter should be able to help, you said yourself how co-operative she's been.'

'Yes, sir. That's the thing, sir. She's actually been – well, sir, she's been captured by the enemy, and–'

'Captured?' Wheeler said sharply.

'Yes, sir. While we were fetching that piece last night. That's why we don't–'

'By the Coalitionist rebels in Leeds?' Wheeler drew in her breath. 'It's a shame, Harker, because she might have been useful.'

'Yes, sir, very useful, which is why we're going in tonight

to rescue her.'

There was a pause. Then Wheeler said, her voice firm, 'Major Harker. Lieutenant Riggs informs me that you are down to four men plus one medical officer untrained in combat. Leeds is one of the biggest Coalitionist strongholds and I cannot possibly imagine that it is poorly defended. You may have managed to sneak in and out on your raids but a person captured while stealing a computer component is, I am sure, going to be held at the highest level of security.'

'Yes, sir,' Harker said, already mentally calculating how much firepower he had and how much more he'd need.

'We have lost men to the Coalitionists before,' Wheeler said. 'Only five were returned alive, and I doubt they will ever live full lives again.'

'Yes, sir, which is why we have to go in now,' Harker said.

'Major. She is probably already dead. And if not, then she almost certainly will wish she was. You do not want to know,' Wheeler added quietly, 'what state our female officers were returned in.'

'Exactly, sir, that's why–'

'Harker, I need you to go to Hull.'

He closed his eyes. 'Can't the bridge be delayed until tomorrow?'

'No, Major. My orders are for you and your remaining men to go to Hull. Do not go back to Leeds. There is nothing for you there.'

'But, sir–'

'Those are my *orders*, Harker.'

Orders. It was like a magic word. He couldn't ignore it.

... soldiers don't need to think. They need to obey. They need to have it hammered into them that when they're told to march, they march. When they're told to run, they run. And when they're told to abandon the woman they're mad about to go and fix a telephone line–

'Major?' Wheeler's voice echoed down the line.

'Yes, sir,' he said.

'Telephone me from Hull when the line is fixed,' she said, and ended the call.

Harker replaced the receiver slowly, turning to see Charlie and the squad watching him silently.

He got out a cigarette and lit it, moving automatically until he'd sucked in a lungful of nicotine.

It's a bridge. It's a telephone line.

It's Eve.

They knew what their orders were. They'd known since Wheeler had told Harker about the bridge the day before.

And they knew about Eve. They'd known how he felt about her before he did.

'I take care of my men,' he said.

'She's not one of your men, sir,' Charlie said quietly.

'I know that,' Harker said. He dragged hard on the cigarette, burning half of it down in one go. 'And I don't care.' He nodded to them all and turned to go. 'See you in Hull, then.'

'No, you won't,' Charlie sighed, and he turned back to see them all standing behind her.

'We're with you,' Tallulah said.

'Got to follow the Major,' Banks added.

'Can't leave an injured woman unaided,' Daz said.

Harker met Charlie's eyes, and a world of communication passed between them.

She sighed. 'She's one of us.'

'Damn right she is.' Harker ground the cigarette under his heel, pride swelling in him. 'Right, men, fall in. Let's go and do something stupid.'

Charlie stared at the Abbey, a dark shape against the glow of hundreds of fires from the refugee camp, and then she stared at Harker.

'When you said something stupid,' she said, 'I didn't think you meant this stupid.'

'Thank you, Charlie, for that valuable input.' Harker kept his eyes on the Abbey and the gate guards.

'We don't even know where she is.'

'Well, I do.' When Charlie raised her eyebrows, Harker said, 'While you lot were fannying about stealing uniforms, I learned the layout of the place. Cells are underneath the kitchen. Used to be the cellars. Have their own entrance.'

'So we just make a run for that, all guns blazing?'

'Got a better idea?' Harker said.

'I suppose the old sneaking in as washerwomen trick isn't worth considering?'

'No, it is not. Besides, we've sneaked in before, and we've raided one of their convoys, and last night I got recognised by half-a-dozen guards at the grammar school. We ain't going to be able to sneak anywhere.'

Charlie looked up at the Abbey again, and sighed.

'All right,' she said. 'Something stupid it is.'

Breaking into the compound hadn't been as hard as the Coalitionists might have hoped it would be. The soldiers patrolling the refugee camp had let them through after a quick glance at their forged papers, and never checked for weapons. Now the squad spread out around the more heavily guarded Abbey, and waited for Harker's signal.

He sent Tallulah round to the far side of the compound to lob a few grenades over the fence before she ran back to ready their getaway. Banks's sniper rifle took out three guards on the attack side before the rest noticed what was happening, by which time Harker had opened fire with the submachine-gun he'd requisitioned from the raid on the convoy.

They were under the shadow of the Abbey in minutes.

Harker's heart was racing, and not just from the rush of the fight. Eve was in there, just the other side of this wall, and she had to be okay. He prayed it with every beat of his heart.

The sloped cellar door was just visible in the darkness. Harker grabbed a grenade from his belt, yanked out the pin with his teeth, and threw it over the kitchen roof and into the cloisters for another distraction. As it went off, he blasted the cellar doors with his stolen gun.

A grin fought its way out. He'd forgotten how much bloody fun this could be.

The doors flew open but, judging by the yells coming from the other side of the building, most of the coalitionists were too preoccupied to notice.

He ran in, shot the first guard and Banks got the second. They were faced with a low corridor, cheaply subdivided into cells with many, many narrow doors.

'Shoot the locks off,' he said, 'all of 'em,' and Charlie and Banks nodded.

When Harker caught a glimpse inside the first cell, his smile faded. Inside huddled a family, filthy and emaciated, with what he was pretty sure was a dead child.

'Go,' he said, and didn't wait to see if they obeyed.

He blasted door after door, panic rising as it occurred to him that they might have kept her somewhere else, but then Banks yelled, 'Sir!' and he ran that way.

She has to be okay, she has to be okay, he repeated to himself, and then he heard the faint, rather wobbly but unmistakable sound of the melody Eve had sung last night by the river, and relief made him smile just a little.

She was singing about being found, and he shoved through her door to find Banks crouching over her. He looked up, and his expression killed Harker's smile.

The light from the corridor illuminated a small figure curled on the ground, shivering, cradling one hand against her exposed chest. Her dress was ripped at her breast, and also at the split on her thigh, ripped high enough for him to see the red, swollen wound there. It was crusted, and oozing, and stank of infection.

Eve's head lolled on the floor and she was mumbling the verse she'd sung to him about lights on the river, and this time she remembered the last line, because it was about being with him forever and forever.

Banks's eyes met his, and he looked frightened. And no wonder. Eve was lying on a filthy stone floor, an infected wound in her leg, shivering and sweating with fever.

This is not my definition of okay, Harker thought furiously as he took off his overcoat and knelt down beside her.

'Eve?' he said, and she ignored him. 'Eve, it's me, Harker.'

Her gaze fell briefly on him before sliding away. Her pupils were unfocused. 'Great,' she mumbled. 'Now I'm hallucinating.'

'You're not hallucinating.' He laid his coat over her and she huddled into it.

'Then explain the leprechauns.' Eve giggled.

Harker exchanged a look with Banks, and picked Eve up, which stopped her giggling and made her yelp in pain.

'Sorry, sorry,' he said, standing up and cradling her against his body, indescribably glad to have her back.

He followed Banks, who led with his gun, and met up with Charlie, who was kicking down the last of the cell doors. A stream of people was running, limping and in some cases crawling out of the cellar. Not one of them looked to be in particularly good shape.

Eve moaned in his arms, her face twisted in pain, and Harker shoved through the crowd to the cellar doors. Why hadn't he brought Daz? Why leave him and Mary back at the Chase? Stupid, stupid Harker. Eve needed help *now*.

She's survived twenty-four hours, she can manage another

thirty minutes, said a small sensible voice, but the part of Harker that had seen that swollen wound on her leg ignored it.

Charlie led them, somehow finding the soldiers among the civilians and taking them out. People milled all over the compound and some soldiers were firing at them. Other soldiers ran around, half-dressed, unarmed, trying to restrain prisoners who clearly were in no mood to be locked up again.

Harker and his men ran towards the hole Tallulah had made in the fence, which was now being guarded by men with machine-guns. Banks, impressively, took them out without losing stride, and they ducked through into the chaos of the refugee camp, which was crawling with frightened people.

Frightened people, Harker knew, were the fastest route to complete anarchy, and no one managed to stop them as they raced out and back towards Tallulah and the car.

She had the engine started as soon as she saw them, and set off before Banks had even closed the passenger door.

'Is she all right?' she asked. Her eyes were on the road, but her voice was tense.

'Not exactly,' Harker muttered. He held Eve against him, trying to shield her from the knocks and jolts of the car as it bounced over badly made roads. They'd never taken it this fast before, because it was damned uncomfortable, although Tallulah had reached similar speeds in the truck trying to get Martindale home the other night.

Don't think about how that ended, just don't, he told himself, and touched Eve's face to bring her attention back to him.

'Nearly there,' he said, 'and Daz'll fix you up. You'll be fine.'

Her head lolled against his chest.

'Is she awake?' Tallulah asked.

'She's in and out,' Harker said. He reached inside the overcoat for her hand, and she flinched away from him. 'It's all right,' he said softly, 'I won't hurt you.'

And so help me, if that Sergeant raped you I'll burn that whole Abbey to the ground.

''m already hurt,' Eve mumbled.

'Yes, but we'll get you fixed. You'll be fine.' *You'll have to be. I need you to be.* He moved the edge of the coat aside and went for her hand again, but she had her left hand cupped protectively over her right and wouldn't move.

Shit, and she's a musician, if they've hurt her hands–

'Is your hand all right?' he said, and she frowned. 'Let me see. I won't hurt you, I promise.'

She made a face, but allowed him to move her left hand away. In the dim light of the car, he couldn't see much, and then with a sudden flare of light Charlie had lit a lantern and held it over Eve, who flinched away, squeezing her eyes shut.

The harsh light fell on her right hand, which looked fine until he gently turned it over and heard Charlie's gasp.

Harker stared in increasing horror at the ruined skin of Eve's palm and fingers, white in places and deep red in others. Something had burned her, something deep and awful, and it had mutilated her beautiful hand.

Rage swallowed Harker for a second, and then he heard Eve say, 'You know, that's the second time you've been the last thing I saw before I died,' and his vision cleared just in time to see her eyes close.

For the second time in as many nights, the kitchen was full of chaos. It wasn't quite late enough for the cook and her staff to have finished, which meant the squad were getting in everyone's way. He collided with Frederick in the doorway and shoved past, ignoring the sneering voice as he carefully laid Eve on the table and bellowed for Daz.

'Really, Major, must you–' began the cook, and Harker snarled at her.

'God, what is that smell?' drawled Frederick as he sauntered over. He regarded Eve through his nostrils. 'Ugh, it's disgusting.'

'I'd advise you to step back and shut up,' Charlie said in a low voice before Harker could murder the little insect.

'Where the hell is Daz?' he growled. 'Banks, Lu, go find–'

'He's talking on the telephone,' Frederick yawned. 'General Wheeler called. Apparently you're not supposed to be here.'

Everything in the kitchen slowed and blurred as Harker turned to face Frederick. The loathsome cockroach didn't even have the balls to look afraid.

'How does she know,' Harker said, struggling to breathe through the fear and rage threatening to strangle him, 'that we are?'

Frederick looked bored, but there was a telltale gleam of malice in his eye that said he hadn't forgiven Harker for humiliating him earlier in the week. 'Well, she asked what time you'd left, and I told her it was only an hour or so ago, and she said–'

'Is it bad?' Daz said from the doorway, and Harker turned away from Frederick before he shoved him in the meat grinder.

'Eve or Wheeler?' Harker said.

Daz looked up from examining Eve and winced. 'Someone,' he shot Frederick a poisonous look which bounced right off, 'told her you'd gone into Leeds to bring Eve back.'

Harker didn't even see Charlie step in to stop him killing Frederick. His world had narrowed to pain and revenge, all his blood turned to fire, roaring through his veins–

'Sir, concentrate,' she said.

'I'll bloody *dismember* him–'

'Yes, but first tell Daz about Eve's hand.'

He turned, shaking, back to Eve and managed to gesture to her right hand. Daz wordlessly picked it up. He winced again.

'Will she be okay?' Tallulah asked, her voice hopeful, and his eyes returned to the ooozing, swollen wound on Eve's leg. He'd seen men lose limbs over infected wounds. And he'd definitely seen amputations carried out on extremities burned less severely than Eve's hand.

'She'll be fine,' he said firmly, and Daz glanced up at him as he laid his fingers on her forehead.

'Sir, I can't promise–'

'*Promise*,' Harker said, and the violence in his tone made even Charlie flinch.

Right then Benson appeared, apparently not at all disturbed by the scene he found, and said, 'Excuse me, sir, but General Wheeler begs me to inform you that she is becoming most impatient.'

Since this was directed at Harker, whose attention was rooted on Eve, it got no response.

'She wants to talk to you, sir,' Daz said, and Harker shook his head.

'Not now.'

'Sir, she is the General,' Charlie said, and Harker's conscience stabbed him in the back.

Daz was examining the wound on Eve's leg again, checking her temperature, frowning a lot.

'Daz,' he said hollowly, and the doctor looked up. 'What does she need?'

'Hospitalisation,' Daz said. 'This is more than I can do here. I don't have the drugs or the equipment. The Hull base has a decent hospital. We'll take her there.'

'Ought to keep the General happy,' Charlie said. 'Right.

Put her in the car. The wagon can follow. Banks, go make sure the car has enough fuel. And you,' she pointed to Harker, 'need to talk to Wheeler. Longer you leave it, angrier she'll get.'

Harker stared at her for a moment.

'Sir,' Charlie said in the tone she used to command troops on the battlefield. 'Go and pick up the telephone. *Now.*'

He moved automatically, and was halfway across the room before it occurred to him to disobey. He looked back to see Charlie and Tallulah carefully picking up Eve, and very nearly turned back to take her from them.

'Go,' Charlie said, and Harker did.

He imagined Wheeler would probably be organising a sunny wall and a cigarette for him. He knew she'd yell.

He found he didn't much care.

But when he picked up the phone and her voice was quiet, cold, and calm, he knew he was in trouble.

'Kindly explain why I have been waiting so long.'

'Eve,' he said, and cleared his throat. 'She's injured, sir, but we're ready to leave–'

'Leave?' Wheeler cut in, her voice made of ice. 'Major Harker, tonight you disobeyed a direct order given by the highest authority in this army. Do you have the faintest idea what that means?'

'Yes, sir.' *It means Eve is still alive.*

'It means, Harker–'

'Sir, we're ready to go.' Tallulah's soft voice intruded over Wheeler's.

'I have to go, sir,' he interrupted, which was probably his worst move all night.

'Go?'

Harker flinched.

'Sir, we really have to leave now if we're going to get there before the bridge blows. Everyone's in the car.'

'Do you have another conversation to participate in, Major?' Wheeler asked in a voice made of needles.

Harker looked at Tallulah for an unending moment, and covered the mouthpiece. 'Tell them to go,' he said. 'I'll follow.'

Tallulah frowned, but when Harker raised his eyebrows at her, she nodded and went, and Harker uncovered the mouthpiece again.

'I'm sorry sir,' he said heavily. 'It's a bad line.'

Wheeler paused for a long moment, and he wondered if that was actually true. Then she spoke, and this time the needles were made of ice.

'I would not have entrusted just any of my officers with the task I gave to you, Major. You have consistently shown yourself to be a man of intelligence and resource but, most of all, of huge loyalty and trust. I trusted you with this mission and I trusted you,' she spoke slowly and deliberately, 'to follow my orders. All of them. You are not in a position to pick and choose which orders to obey.'

His torn fingernails dug into his palm. 'No, sir.'

'And now you force me to wonder if I can trust you at all. I am not unreasonable, Harker. I shall confer with my aides and other senior officers and in the morning I will let you know when and where the court will be held. And I expect you to be there to take my call, is that clear?'

In the morning. Eve would be in Hull, the other side of a bridgeless river. In the morning–

'Court?' Harker said.

'Your court-martial.'

He stared at the gaping abyss between his life and his reality.

'I can't convene a general court-martial while you are on the other end of a telephone. It will take some time to gather enough officers of sufficient rank.'

'Yes, sir,' Harker said distantly. He heard the car rattle past the house and down the driveway. Away from here.

Tallulah appeared in the doorway again. She didn't say anything.

'And I warn you, Harker, it will go very hard for you if you are not there in the morning. If you do not answer the telephone when I call tomorrow, I will consider you a deserter, do you understand?'

'Yes, sir,' he said mechanically. 'Oh, and sir? There's a traitor at the Tower. Just thought you should know.'

He hung up the receiver before she could answer.

You could just run away. Take Eve and disappear with her.

The abyss yawned and stretched, and then Tallulah spoke and the entrance hall of Hatfield Chase snapped back into place around him.

'Lieutenant Riggs has gone with Eve, sir,' Tallulah said. 'I said I'd stay. Help you drive the wagon, guard the computer.'

But he'd never run away from anything. He wasn't a coward, never had been. He faced things. Dealt with the consequences of his actions. He'd deal with this.

'When do you want to leave, sir?' Tallulah asked, and Harker finally managed to look at her.

'In the morning,' he said, and walked away before she could ask why.

Chapter Twenty-Four

Eve woke to the smell of antiseptic, an unfamiliar bed, and the terrible fear that it had all been a dream.

Then her leg gave a twinge, her hand throbbed, and she opened her eyes to see a nurse in a silly headdress at the next bed.

'Oh, thank God,' she said, and wondered what she'd have done if it turned out the nightmare wasn't real.

The nurse gave her a disapproving look, and Eve saw the large cross hanging round her neck.

'Oh, come on, it's not blasphemy. I'm thanking Him,' Eve said, privately thinking that getting shot was a perfect excuse for blasphemy.

The nurse turned away, but to Eve's eternal relief, it was to call a doctor and she was ridiculously glad to see it was Daz. He grinned at her. 'Well, you're a sight for sore eyes.'

Eve, who was just beginning to catalogue the many ways in which she ached, grimaced.

'How are you feeling?'

'Even worse than the last time you asked me that,' she said, and they shared a smile.

Daz called the nurse over, and they poked at Eve, sticking a thermometer in her mouth and a blood pressure cuff about her arm. Daz looked happy with the results.

'The fever broke yesterday,' he said, 'but you've been asleep since then. Seems to have done you some good.'

Eve shifted in the bed and winced. She remembered getting shot in the leg, and by the looks of the heavy bandaging on her hand she hadn't imagined her foolhardy poker-grabbing, either.

'Of course, I wouldn't recommend you, you know, *move* yet, but it does look like the infection has finally cleared,' Daz said.

'Infection?'

The nurse adjusted something hanging above Eve's bed, and when she looked up she saw an IV drip, which appeared to be plugged into her arm.

'The wound on your leg. It was pretty nasty. Hence the fever. I think you're out of the woods now, but we'll have to keep an eye on you.' He gave that cartoon grin. 'If you get so much as a bedsore, the Major will kill me.'

'Harker?' Eve said, trying to ignore the rather unappetising idea of bedsores.

'Yes, Harker.' Daz grinned at her. 'How many other majors are madly in love with you?'

'None,' Eve said, and told herself the reason her stomach felt all squirly was the fever and the IV, and nothing else. 'Including him.'

'Sure, that's why he was so adamant you recover properly. Don't you let me down now. He really will hurt me if you're not okay when he gets here.'

'Why, where is he?' *I must look like hell*, Eve thought in a faint panic. *How much time do I have?*

Daz laughed. 'Don't worry. He's not about to come striding in. I'll let you know when he arrives. He had to stay at the house,' he explained, 'to talk to General Wheeler on the telephone.'

Eve tried to remember whereabouts Hatfield Chase had been, and then she tried to remember where Hull was, and eventually she gave Daz a hopeless look, and he laughed and explained it to her. While Daz, Banks and Charlie had brought her in the car, Harker was having to bring the wagon, and take a slower route around the estuary, since the bridge had been destroyed for some security purpose or other.

'Personally, I'm not sure how stopping ordinary people moving about is making anyone more secure, but then I don't pretend to understand how these things work,' Daz said, and Eve had to smile at that.

He told her she'd been kept sedated for several days, but that now the fever had largely gone, she should be feeling better and might even be allowed out of bed soon.

'Stop, that's far too exciting,' Eve said. She chewed her lip. 'How long would you say it takes to drive a wagon around the Humber Estuary?'

'It'd say at least as long as it's taken already, plus maybe a day or two more.'

She nodded distantly. 'And how long would you say until I could, for instance, take a damn shower and wash my hair?'

Daz laughed at that. 'Less than that. Later today, if you're feeling up to it, you can try crutches, and if you're steady enough on those, you can try taking a shower.'

'Okay, good.'

'I'll probably have to send someone in to help you, though.'

Eve made a face at that. 'Less good.'

'Sorry. Can't have you losing your balance or getting shampoo in your wounds.' He hesitated. 'Eve, about your hand ...?'

She looked at it. The fingers were all bandaged individually, except for the very tips, and her palm was also heavily swaddled.

'The tips of your fingers weren't burned, so we've left them uncovered. I need you to tell me how much sensation you have in them, and if at any time they start going numb, or very cold.'

Eve tapped each fingertip with the nails of her other hand.

'They feel okay.'

'And can you move them at all?'

'With all this stuff on them?' Eve attempted to waggle her fingers, and let out a scream. 'That hurts!'

Daz exhaled. 'That's good. That's really good.'

'That it hurts like hell?' Eve said, incredulous.

'Yes. It means the nerves aren't destroyed. And if you can move them at all, it's good news for the muscles. It's hard to see straight away how much damage there is to the nerves, muscles and blood vessels, which is why it's really important for you to tell me if there's any change in what you can feel with the tips, because a restricted blood flow is very bad news for the healing process.'

Eve nodded, her eyes still watering.

'To be brutally honest, the skin on your fingers is very badly damaged. We're still in a process of cutting away the dead flesh, which is another reason we kept you sedated, but until we have it all and can see what, if anything, is growing back, we really can't tell just how well it's going to heal.'

Eve stared at her mummified hand. *I could probably still hold a plectrum*, she thought distantly. *But I think it's adieu to the Beethoven sonatas.*

'I've been speaking on the telephone to a colleague at St Thomas's in London who is a burns expert. We're doing everything we can, Eve, I promise you. But we really do have to wait and see.'

She nodded again. *Take good care of your hands, and your hands will take good care of you.*

'Well, great,' she said.

The body in his dreams wasn't that of James White, or even of Mary. It was Eve, pale and bloody, worse each time he saw her. Sometimes she laughed with the Coalitionist soldiers, kissing them and taunting him, and sometimes it was them pinning her down, ripping her dress and raping her, violating her. And sometimes she just lay there, still and blue, a corpse because of his own idiocy.

He woke with a start, hand on his sword, but it was only Tallulah tapping his shoulder. The wagon had stopped its jolting, and he was stiff from trying to sleep wedged into a corner of it while it moved.

Still, it was probably the most he'd slept all week.

'Sir, we're nearly there. See?'

She pointed to the large compound, bigger than it had been last time Harker had seen it, but back then it hadn't been a base for the Navy, too. Now that they were operating open blockades on all ports, rivers and bays, the Navy had taken up residence in a lot of army bases.

Climbing out of the wagon, he stretched and ran his hand through his hair by way of grooming. Tallulah had lit the lanterns on the front of the wagon against the dark clouds and the heavy fog which was halfway to drizzle.

He was cold, he was tired, he was hungry and he ached pretty much all over. Still curled in the pit of his stomach was the cold little ball of dread that whispered, *You're going to lose your rank, and all over a woman who might be dead anyway*. He'd been trying to ignore it all week, and only partly succeeded.

'Right then,' he said to Tallulah, who'd been unfailingly helpful and chipper for the whole journey, and who he had, on occasion, felt like strangling. 'Let's go.'

They set off, both walking, Tallulah leading the horses. There'd been no opportunity to stop and change them along the way, not when they were so close to Coalitionist territory that all available beasts had been requisitioned by the enemy. So their progress had been slow, horribly, painfully slow, and each time Harker looked at his map and realised how far they hadn't come, the cold little ball of dread grew a little colder, and a little larger.

'She'll be fine, sir,' Tallulah said.

'I know she will.' He'd given up pretending not to be interested in Eve. He'd disobeyed orders over her, it had to be pretty clear to everyone now how he felt.

The guards on duty were clearly expecting them, and told Harker that Charlie had even organised accommodation for him.

'Hope it has a shower,' Tallulah murmured as she led the wagon in.

'Are you being impertinent, Private?' Harker said.

'Actually, sir, I was being quite pertinent,' Tallulah said.

He sniffed. Okay, maybe she was right. Soap didn't exactly grow by the side of the road, and since he'd had to plough through boggy patches to dig the wagon out several times a day, his clothes had never seemed entirely dry, let alone clean.

The fog had fully turned into rain by the time they entered the compound. Harker wondered if that was enough to get him clean, decided not, and headed off to find his quarters.

Charlie, bless her heart, had evidently bullied the duty officer into assigning Harker the cushiest accommodation available, with a double bed and its own, fully plumbed bathroom. He took advantage of it, put on the cleanest clothes he had, and crossed the parade ground to the hospital wing, rehearsing things to say as he went.

Stop being so nervous, he told himself. *You weren't this nervous when you got married.*

Yeah, but when I got married, it wasn't to someone who'd nearly died because of my stupidity.

'Her name is Eve Carpenter,' Harker told the duty nurse, who checked her clipboard and shook her head. 'She should have got here on Thursday night, or maybe early on Friday.'

She checked again. The dread grew in Harker's stomach.

'Gunshot wound to the left thigh. Burned right palm. She had a fever, she would've needed, I dunno, one of those drip things–'

'An IV,' said the nurse absently.

'Yeah, one of those.' Harker leaned forward to see her insignia, panic setting in. 'Corporal. She was here.'

'Yes, sir, but now she's not.'

'No,' Harker said forcefully, leaning over the desk, 'she is here. She has to be.' Because if she wasn't any more then that might mean – it might mean–

'She's fine,' came a voice, cutting through Harker's panic, and he turned to see Daz, once more in a white coat. 'Well, she's recovering. I discharged her this afternoon. We need the beds.'

Relief shot through Harker, making him weak for a second. He closed his eyes, leaning back against the desk. 'Recovering?' he said. She couldn't be too bad if Daz had discharged her.

'Yes, sir. I think Banks took her to the NAAFI.'

Harker nodded. There was probably a piano there. 'Her hand?' he asked.

Daz paused, which told Harker enough. 'We're doing everything we can,' he said eventually.

Harker thought of Eve sitting by the fire and playing the guitar to herself. Music was her comfort and her strength, and if she couldn't play then what did she have?

'Do more,' he said, and went out into the rain.

The NAAFI bar was housed in a more than usually ugly hut on the far side of the parade ground, behind the much more attractive officers' quarters. As he got closer, he could hear noises under the sound of the rain: people talking, laughing and most definitely drinking.

Ducking inside, he shook off the rain and searched for

Eve's blonde head.

There were so many people here, men and women, jostling for space and trying to avoid the raincapes and caps hung up around the walls. He eventually spied Banks near the bar, looking delighted to be able to buy Tallulah a drink, and strode over to them.

'Sir!' Banks looked slightly startled, and rather annoyed. 'Uh, what are you doing here? The officers' mess is–'

'I'm looking for Eve.'

Banks pointed around the corner of the bar, which Harker hadn't seen from the door. There was a snooker table there, and also an old upright piano, pushed against the wall. A smallish blonde in a very large sweater was sitting there, playing notes with her left hand and apparently singing to herself. The sound was largely lost under the noise of the bar.

Nodding vaguely to Banks and Tallulah, Harker moved across the room, and as he did people seemed to notice his uniform was slightly different, that there were pips on his shoulder, and little by little they grew quiet, until he could hear what Eve was singing.

She'd played it once or twice back at the Chase, but he'd never caught the words. She was singing about fields of destruction; she was singing about baptisms of fire ...

She was singing about not being deserted by her 'brothers in arms', and the words hit Harker like a knife in the chest.

For the first time in his life, his nerve failed.

He shoved out of the hot, crowded bar, silence dropping down around him until his footsteps thudded loudly on the cheap boards, and slammed outside into the rain, which was coming down heavier than ever, soaking him in seconds. He needed to damage something, hit something, because Eve had been hurt and she was so precious and it was *all his fault*, but he wasn't armed and he ended up punching the sign announcing the NAAFI bar, which was rough and hard and bloody hurt.

Sucking his bleeding knuckles, he decided to go to the officers' mess to get very drunk, and headed back towards the parade ground and the main entrance to the building.

He'd probably got halfway when Eve shouted, 'Harker!' and he froze.

She hopped out of the bar on one crutch, ducking against the rain, and reached him as he turned, slowly. She was smiling, but it faded when she saw his face, and for a second she stared at him uncertainly.

'You're here,' she said, and Harker just nodded, taking her in. Her face was pale, her wet hair flat to her head, and her right hand was tucked inside its sleeve. She looked small, smaller than he remembered.

'Are you all right?'

He nodded again. He wanted to grab her and hold her against him and tell her all kinds of mushy stuff that appalled even himself.

When he didn't say anything, Eve asked, 'Is Tallulah all right?'

'She's in there.'

'Oh.' Eve glanced back at the comparative cheer of the bar, then at Harker again. She looked unsure. 'Well, I … Where are you going?'

'Officers' mess. Nicer bar.'

She nodded. 'Yeah, probably.' She shivered.

'You should get back inside,' Harker said, gesturing to the pounding rain.

Eve nodded again, and he turned to go, aching for her.

'Wait,' she said, and he spun back. 'I don't believe this.'

'Believe what?'

'This! Last time you saw me I was incoherent with fever, I had a gunshot wound in my leg and a burnt hand and needed hospitalisation, and you can't even ask how I am?'

Her cheeks were pink now, her eyes flashing angrily, and it was taking all of Harker's self-control not to grab her, strip her naked and find out exactly how she was.

'How are you?'

'Cold, wet, and annoyed.'

Harker, angry, frustrated and *aching*, moved suddenly, picked her up in his arms and she struggled, but not particularly effectively. 'Hey! What are you doing?'

'You need to get inside. Shouldn't get those dressings wet.'

'Oh, so you have noticed I'm hurt?'

'*Yes*,' Harker said grimly, striding towards the officers' quarters.

'Right, but I can walk, you know!'

'No, you can't.' Was it his imagination, or was she slightly less soft and round than she used to be? More fragile. Heaven help him, he was going to kill each and every Coalitionist in Leeds.

'Well, I could if you'd let me have my crutch back! You just left it there, someone's going to trip over it.'

'I don't care.' He kicked open the door, ignored the duty officer, and carried Eve up the stairs to his quarters.

'And where are you taking me?'

He hesitated on the stairs. Eve glared at him.

'Do you have a bunk somewhere else?'

'Well, no,' she began, and Harker started walking again, 'but if you take me back to the hospital then–'

'Daz has already reassigned your bed.'

'Well, yes, but–'

He shoved open the door to his room with his shoulder.

'Um, whose room is this?' Eve said, looking around.

'Mine.' He set her down carefully on the bed, but to his annoyance she sprang back to her feet again. At least, that was probably her intention, but the end effect was that she moved carefully on to one foot.

'Oh,' she said, looking uncomfortable, her arms wrapped around herself. Her injured hand was still tucked into her sleeve. 'Well, don't you get the nicest accommodation?'

'It's called "pulling rank",' Harker said, 'and I might as well while I still can.'

'What?'

'Never mind.' He threw his sodden jacket on the floor, which made Eve scowl.

'Don't you *ever* pick up after yourself?'

'Look, don't start,' Harker said. 'I have spent a week trawling through the mud in that damned wagon, it hasn't stopped raining, Tallulah has been trying for the Most Cheerful Soldier award, and I am tired, and hungry, and soaking wet through, so don't bloody *start*, okay?'

He'd moved closer to her, and she'd backed up against the bed so they stood nose to nose. Her hair curled slightly at the ends, tendrils of it clinging to her neck. She smelled of rain on hot skin.

'All right, so it sucks to be you,' she said, nostrils flaring. 'I've spent the week lolling about in bed by choice, have I?'

'No.' He closed his eyes. She was infuriating. 'Look, those dressings could be wet–'

'They're fine.'

'Let me see.'

'No.'

'*Eve*.' He leaned closer, but there was no point trying to intimidate her with his height or his strength. She just glared back up at him.

'Look, the one on my hand is supposed to be wet, it's called a wet-to-dry dressing, it's–'

'Meant to be dry on the outside.'

Snarling under her breath, she drew her right hand out from her sleeve and thrust it in front of his face. 'There.

Happy now?'

Not really. Her hand was practically mummified, each finger wrapped up separately, the palm swaddled with bandages. Waves of anger and guilt crashed over Harker as he took her hand in his, gently, careful not to put any pressure on the injured side. The dressing was, at least, dry.

'Does it hurt?' he asked.

'Little bit. Some times more than others. Daz has me on lots of painkillers.'

Harker turned her hand over and very, very gently kissed the bandaged palm. 'I'm so sorry.'

'Yeah, well, you should be.' She took her hand back belligerently. 'Banks told me how you decided I'd defected to the other side, so thanks for leaving me to rot. They could have raped me or killed me–'

'But they didn't?' *If they raped her I'll kill every one of them, I'll burn them alive, I'll bleed them and–*

'I'm still alive, aren't I?'

'No,' Harker said wretchedly, 'I mean–'

'I know what you mean. And no, they didn't,' Eve said softly, then rallied. 'Which is just as well for you, because if they had, I'd have to beat the crap out of you.'

Relief flooded him, and he nearly smiled, which probably would have been a mistake.

'Beat the – Eve, you're half-a-head shorter than me, and can you even lift a sword?'

'Oh, so now you're picking on me because I'm hurt?'

'No, I am not picking on you, I'm just saying there's no way you could take me in a fight.'

'Oh, I so could take you.'

She was really close and really hot, and Harker thought, *Hell, yes, take me*, but then the light caught a fading bruise on her cheek, and he cursed himself.

'You're soaked through,' he said, stepping back to a safer

distance.

'I'm okay.'

'No, you're not. You've only just recovered from one infection, your body is weak, if you catch a chill now it could be fatal, and that dressing on your leg could be soaked through.' *This is going to kill me*, he thought, even as he added, 'Take your clothes off.'

'No.'

'Eve–'

'I don't have anything else to put on. I had to borrow these as it is.'

'You can wear my clothes.'

'I can't, they're all in wet heaps on the floor.'

'If that dressing is wet, there could be maggots crawling in there, right inside the wound, eating–'

'All *right*,' Eve shouted, and unfastened her belt. She kicked at her boots, nearly losing her balance, and shied them across the room. One of them hit his shin.

'Ow,' he said.

'Bite me.'

Love to, Harker thought, but then she was shoving off her trousers and standing there wearing only an oversized wool sweater and a bandage, scowling at him.

'Sit,' he said, a touch hoarsely, relieved to see as she did that she was at least wearing underwear. There was only so much he could take.

The bandage was wrapped around her left thigh and didn't leave much of it uncovered. Harker knelt by the bed, reminded himself that he'd do this for any one of his men who was injured, laughed internally at his own feeble attempts at justification, and ran his hands over the pale linen.

'See?' Eve said. 'Dry.'

With one hand, he lifted her foot, making her thigh come

off the bed, and ran his other hand under it.

'Any maggots?' she asked, and he looked up at her, wondering if she was being this beautiful on purpose. It was the sort of thing she'd do.

She was so warm, and so soft; yes, she'd lost weight, but her skin was smooth and he could see her breasts moving under her sweater as she breathed, and he wanted her so much he was nearly blind with it.

Abruptly, he dropped her foot and stood up. 'You're fine,' he said. 'You should – you should get some rest, and – dammit, you don't have a room, I'll–'

'I also don't have any dry clothes.'

Her sweater was damp. She should take it off, but Harker honestly didn't think he could handle any more without pinning her down and ravishing her.

'Look, stay here, I'll go and find somewhere else to sleep.'

'No, it's fine.' She reached for the damp trousers and boots she'd just taken off, and he lost his patience.

'Eve, don't be so bloody stupid. You can't put wet clothes back on.'

She glared at him, standing up again and resting on one foot. 'I can and I will. I'm even old enough to dress myself, you know.'

'What, with one hand?'

'Oh, that's below the belt.'

'You can't take care of yourself–'

'I don't *believe* you just said that.'

'No, I meant–'

'You know what?' Eve threw the wet clothes back on the floor. Her boots thudded. 'I just don't get you. What is wrong with you?'

'Me? I'm not the one who thinks I can take care of myself after a gunshot wound and infection that nearly killed me.'

'It didn't nearly kill me.'

'If Daz hadn't got you here–'

'Yes, *Daz*. I didn't see *you* rushing to be by my side. Half the time you don't even seem to like me very much, but I remember you kissing me, Harker, and that was *not* fake. I wish you'd make up your bloody mind, because I never know if it's one thing or the other–'

And Harker kissed her. Just grabbed her and kissed her, as deep and hard and passionate as she'd kissed him in that darkened library at the grammar school a lifetime ago. He kissed her to shut her up, he kissed her because her mouth was driving him crazy, but most of all he kissed her because he couldn't stand not kissing her any longer.

'Don't like you,' he said when he let her go, and they were both breathing hard. 'Don't *like* you? Eve, I'm bloody crazy about you, and if you don't know that then you're more insane than I ever thought.'

Chapter Twenty-Five

Eve touched her lips. They tingled.

Harker was looking down at her, his eyes fierce, his hands gripping her arms.

'Did you just call me insane?'

His eyes lightened a little with incredulity, but there was still tension in his face when he said, 'I also said I was crazy about you.'

'Yes, I was working up to that bit.'

He stared at her, those gunmetal eyes hot and hard on her, but she couldn't find anything else to say, her brain wasn't working properly, so she reached for him and pulled him back and kissed him again.

She hadn't expected fireworks when she'd kissed him in the school. She'd never had fireworks with anyone else. But with Harker, she couldn't seem to stop. When he kissed her, the world went away and she didn't hurt so much, she wasn't so tired and angry or just so lost and confused any more.

He held her in his arms, his body strong and hard and so wonderfully invincible. And his mouth on hers was like a miracle, his lips rough but his mouth soft. He kissed her with such passion and heat she was trembling when she pulled back.

'I'm crazy about you too,' she said. 'But I didn't know if I was just crazy in general, because you don't even seem to like me, and–'

'I do,' Harker said. 'Hell, Eve, I disobeyed orders for you. I endangered the mission for you. And I don't think you're insane.' He brushed his lips against hers. 'You're shivering.'

'Please don't ask me to take this sweater off.'

He drew back a little, doubt creeping into those beautiful eyes, and Eve smiled and said, 'I can't do it with one hand.'

At that Harker smiled, then he laughed, and kissed her again, drawing the sweater up her body as he did, leaning into her and kissing her right up until the last second when he pulled the damp wool over her head. He pulled the sleeve over her injured hand so carefully, with such concentration, that it wasn't until he'd tossed the sweater on the floor and turned back to her that he noticed she'd been naked underneath it.

He blinked, as if in shock, then reached out, ran his hand over her shoulder, making her shiver again. Then his gaze dropped, and he sucked in a breath.

'Oh hell, Eve,' he said, gazing at her with what looked like horror on his face.

'Okay, that's not the reaction I was looking for,' Eve said, then his hand touched her ribs and she recalled the boot-shaped bruise there.

And she remembered, with a sudden flash of insight, how she'd reacted the first time she'd seen him with his shirt off. Had she immediately swooned at what had honestly been a very beautifully defined torso? No, she'd stared in horror and asked him how he was still alive.

She winced, and Harker snatched his hand back. 'Sorry.'

'No – no, it's fine, I was just ... look, take this off, would you?' she said, plucking at his shirt. It was dry, his jacket having taken most of the rain damage.

Harker did, apparently not concentrating, and Eve reached out to touch the long, jagged scar on his stomach. He flinched and turned his face away, his jaw tightening, and she realised he was ashamed.

'Harker,' she said, sliding her hand up to his neck, feeling the rough stubble there. He didn't look at her. 'I never said how beautiful you are with your shirt off.'

That got his attention.

'I just got a big dollop of what it's like to stand there nearly naked and have someone only see the ugliness.'

He touched her shoulder again, his hand moving down gently to cup her breast, and this time there was no horror in his expression.

'There's no ugliness on you,' he said. 'You're perfect, and beautiful–'

'Well, you haven't seen my hand,' Eve said sadly, looking at it.

He took it and kissed the bandaged palm again. Just as it had the last time, it made Eve's insides go hot and liquid. She wrapped her other arm around his neck, kissed him, and said, 'Neither of us are wearing much here. Don't you think we should do something about that?'

The look he gave her was one Eve would remember and use to keep warm on cold nights. He picked her up again, laid her on the bed, and got rid of the rest of her clothes and his. His legs were as scarred and battered as the rest of him, but instead of staring Eve pulled him down to her and revelled in the feel of his lean, hard body pressed against hers. His chest was hard, his thighs were hard, and his–

'Oh no,' she said, sitting up, and Harker gave her a warning look.

'Don't "oh no" me now, woman,' he said.

'Condoms,' she said. 'Banks said they're standard issue, but–'

Harker laughed, kissed her mouth, then rolled away to grab his pack and dump the entire contents on the ground. Rather a lot of small shiny packages slithered out.

'I've got bloody hundreds,' he said.

'I'm glad to hear–' Eve began, then forgot how to speak as Harker cupped her breast and stroked the nipple, his other hand soothing her bruised ribs. He caressed her aching body, and somehow it didn't ache as much any more. He kissed her breast, stroked her hip and very gently skimmed her injured thigh.

'Tell me,' he murmured against her skin, 'if I'm hurting you.'

'No,' Eve gasped, because he'd just taken her nipple into his mouth and she was losing the capacity for thought.

When he slipped his hand between her legs her back arched, and her ribs protested, making her gasp in pain, and Harker said, 'Okay, maybe I'll stop that.'

'Stop it and I'll kill you,' she panted.

He grinned and bent to kiss her again, and Eve held him there, both arms wrapped around his lean, muscular body. She kicked her good leg over his hip, felt the heat of his erection against her stomach, and buried her face in his throat. He had a beautiful throat. Hell, he had a beautiful everything.

When he slid inside her she looked up and saw such heat and intensity in his eyes she lost her breath. Stroking the hair from his eyes, she smiled, and he smiled back, looking kind of tense, which made her giggle.

'Something funny?'

She shook her head. 'No.' *I think I'm in love with you.* 'Why aren't you moving?'

'Because if I do, my head might explode.'

She laughed again at that, and he smiled, dipping his head to kiss her, and then evidently he'd got his head in order because he did start to move, and suddenly it wasn't so funny any more.

Everything he did wound her higher and higher. He kissed her neck and she panted. He brushed his hand across her breast and her back arched, and this time she didn't even notice if it hurt. She wrapped her legs around him, licked the sweat from his skin and clutched his shoulders as he surged into her and she lost her mind.

Some time later, she came back from her trip around the stars and found Harker lying heavy on her, his face tucked into her neck, breathing hard. She stroked his back, and he looked up, kissed the corner of her mouth, and made to move away.

'No,' she said, pulling him back, because he felt so good there. She'd spent a night and a day in that freezing cell in Kirkstall remembering what it felt like to hold this big, hard man in her arms and wishing he was there with her, and now she had him she wasn't about to let him go.

'I'm too heavy for you,' he said.

'No, you're not.'

'I'll be right back,' he promised, and although Eve's body was irritated that he'd left the bed, her brain was gratified that the condom was one thing he didn't just throw on the floor.

He came back to her, lay on his back and pulled her into his arms, holding her carefully.

'Am I hurting you?'

'No, and stop asking. I'll tell you if you're hurting me.' She snuggled against him. 'I'm actually feeling better than I have since I got here. Maybe we should make this part of my treatment.'

He stroked her arm. 'Happy to oblige.'

When she shivered, he pulled the covers over them both, but Eve pushed them back down again, tracing that scar on his stomach and asking, 'What did this?'

'Bayonet.'

It was a long scar, uneven and ugly. 'It could have killed you.'

'I think that was the idea.'

She kissed his jaw, because people had tried to kill him and she finally understood first hand how terrifying that was, and wrapped her arm around him, keeping him safe from harm.

Rain spattered the window, wind rattled the panes, but she was enveloped in warmth, more than a little in love and happier than she could ever remember being.

'Hey,' she murmured against his mouth. 'You're not smoking.'

'No, I'm not. I think I'll develop an addiction to you instead.'

Eve nestled her head against his shoulder. 'Good plan.' Her fingers carefully traced patterns between the cuts and stitches on the other side of his chest.

'You're not a fan of smoking, are you?'

'Bad for the voice.'

'Even if someone else does it?'

'I'm going to assume you've never heard of passive smoking,' Eve said drowsily. Come to think of it, she'd imagined kissing a smoker would be less pleasant. She didn't even mind the smell of cigarettes on him. It was just ... part of his Harkerness.

'Passive ...?'

'Ne'mind.' Her sleepy fingers caught a sore spot on his shoulder, making him flinch. 'Sorry.'

'Don't worry about it. I need to go and get these stitches taken out in the morning anyway.'

''s it hurt?'

'It's fine. Eve, go to sleep.'

''s not even late.'

'No, but your body's been through a lot.' Eve giggled sleepily. 'Sleep, sweetheart. I'll be here when you wake up.'

And he would, Eve thought fuzzily as her eyes drifted shut. He kept his promises.

Reveille woke Harker, which in itself was surprising. He

couldn't remember the last time he'd slept so long. Maybe because it had been a while since he'd slept in such a comfortable bed. Or maybe because Eve was there with him.

She stirred in his arms, which in itself was extremely pleasant, and mumbled, 'I hate that goddamned bugle.'

He smiled. 'We all do.'

'I swear he plays it right outside the hospital building. Did not need that waking me up in the morning.'

'It's a special quality of bugles that they sound like they're right outside everyone's window.'

Eve hmphed and turned over – or at least tried to. Halfway, she realised why she shouldn't be sleeping on her left side, and turned back.

Harker laughed silently. Dropping a kiss on her hair, he moved away and slid out of bed.

'Where you goin'?'

Harker was nonplussed. Reveille sounded, and he got out of bed. It was like asking why a bullet came out of the gun when you squeezed the trigger.

'That's Reveille,' he said.

'Do you have to get up?'

Harker stared at her. She was burrowed under the covers, her eyes closed, visible mostly as a mop of blonde hair.

'Look, don't confuse me,' he said, sorting through his clothes to see what was wearable and taking her point about throwing them on the floor. 'I'll bring you something to eat, okay?'

Eve made a soft sound that said she was already half-asleep again, and Harker got dressed, kissed her hair, and left.

He was wearing damp clothes, the sun was invisible behind a sullen clutch of clouds, and he was starving, but he was smiling. He smiled at the flag, he smiled at the morning parade, and he smiled at the canteen worker slopping out his breakfast.

'So did you sleep with a coat hanger in your mouth,' came a voice behind him as he picked up his tray, 'or are there more cheerful forces at work?'

It was Charlie. Well, it had to end some time.

'The latter, I'm afraid,' he said, unable to work up any real anxiety over her reaction.

'Eve?' she said, following him to a table and setting her tray down opposite him.

Harker nodded, grinned, and started eating. The porridge here was weak gruel compared to the honey-laced ambrosia the cook had created at Hatfield Chase, but after the tasteless slops he and Tallulah had been living on for the past week, it still tasted pretty good.

'And I don't care,' he said, 'you can lay it on me, I don't care.'

'Lay what on you, sir?' Charlie asked, sprinkling salt on her porridge.

'You don't mind?'

'Mind about what?'

'Come on, Charlie, I know you ain't stupid. Me and Eve. We weren't playing chess all night.'

'No, I don't suppose you were.' She didn't look remotely bothered. 'You'll probably get more shit from Daz than me, especially if you've torn any of her stitches.'

'She doesn't have any – not visible ones,' Harker reported, a touch smugly, because he'd checked everywhere.

'Sir, look. I know I had doubts about her, but if she was shot, beaten, burned, and locked up in a cell with a fever, then I really don't think the Coalitionists are her friends, do you?'

Some of Harker's glow diminished slightly as his old anger came to the surface. *I'll kill every one of them.* But he banished it, concentrated on the feel of Eve in his arms, her soft mouth and smooth skin and the way she moved under him, the sounds she made–

Charlie cleared her throat, and he shook himself.

'No,' he said. 'They're most definitely not her friends.'

'And if Eve makes you happy–'

'She does, Charlie,' Harker said quietly, because even if Eve had spent so much time driving him spare, it was true.

'Well, then,' Charlie said, and that seemed to be that.

He was still feeling pretty good when an extremely junior Ensign came in and informed Harker that there was a telephone call for him from General Wheeler.

Whereupon reality came crashing down on him, his good mood evaporated and that old sick feeling settled in his stomach again.

'When Daz got the phone working, she insisted you call the minute you got here,' Charlie said.

'Why the hell was Daz working on the phone and not taking care of Eve?'

'Because there's a full medical staff here, and she was unconscious most of the time anyway. Sir, go and talk to Wheeler.'

He stood up, shoved his chair out of the way, and scowled at the Ensign. 'Well, then?'

The telephone was in the Colonel's office. Harker took a deep breath before picking it up. 'Sir?'

'Major Harker. How kind of you to check in.'

Harker nearly checked the receiver for icicles. 'Sir,' he said.

'How long have you been at Hull?'

'Since last night, sir. It was quite late,' he added, hoping the Colonel hadn't already contradicted this.

'Yes, that doesn't matter. Harker, we've found nothing like you've described at the Tower. We need your computer. How soon can you be in London?'

His mind reeled. 'Uh – well, sir, it'll probably take us a couple of weeks to travel, plus–'

'No, that will be far too long. I'm sure Commodore Bletchley can spare a ship to take you at least some of the way.'

'Yes, sir,' Harker said gloomily.

She doesn't trust you to come back by yourself. Suddenly, Harker realised how blessed he'd been to have Wheeler's favour all this time.

'I am informed that your civilian is recovering.'

'Eve? Yes, she's–'

'Fit for travel?'

Harker pounced on this opportunity. 'No, sir. Not yet. Still needs full medical care here, sir, can't travel.'

'Perhaps she could stay there, while you bring the computer down.'

'Uh,' Harker searched for a new excuse, 'well, no, sir, because she's really the only one who knows how to use it.'

Wheeler made an impatient noise. 'Major Harker, I do hope you are not procrastinating to delay your own court-martial.'

'No, sir,' he said, because he'd been procrastinating to spend more time with Eve.

'It will take place upon your return to the Tower.'

'Yes, sir.'

'I shall expect you to telephone me daily with a report on Miss Carpenter's progress and travel as soon as possible.'

'Yes, sir.'

'Hand me back to Colonel Robinson.'

Harker did so, and was dismissed by the Colonel. Leaving the building, he saw Daz coming out of the hospital and waved him over.

'Do you think Eve's fit to travel?'

Daz pulled a face. 'Travel where?'

'London.'

'Nope.'

'Good. Repeat that answer whenever you're asked.'

'Uh, yes, sir. Oh, and sir? Eve left this outside the NAAFI last night.'

It was the crutch she'd been hopping about on. Harker took it, ignoring the twinkle in Daz's eye.

'I found her a bed in one of the recovery wards,' the doctor said, watching him.

'Did you now? She won't need it.'

Daz grinned. 'Right, sir.'

Leaving Daz, Harker picked up some food and fresh clothes for Eve, and found her still curled in his bed, tousled and sleepy.

'Hi,' she said, looking so desirable he couldn't breathe for a moment. She smiled. 'You did bring me food.'

'I said I would.'

'Yes,' she said happily, as he set down the plate and sat on the edge of the bed, 'you did.'

Harker kissed her; a wonderful, sweet, soft kiss, and immediately felt better.

Chapter Twenty-Six

Despite the sword of Damocles hanging over his head, Harker remembered those cold, rainy days in Hull as some of the happiest of his life.

With nothing else in particular to do, he spent most of every day with Eve. She tried to teach him to play the guitar, without much success, and the piano, with even less. In return he showed her how to assemble and disassemble a rifle, and how to shoot, an exercise met with total futility by a uselessly right-handed Eve.

He took her to the officer's mess, where she befriended a young Subaltern who played the piano, and entertained the whole mess with her songs. She was allowed to dine with him, which was just as well as he had to cut up food for her.

He helped her to dress and to bathe, which generally turned into an excuse for something else, and he went with her each time she went back to the hospital, which amused Daz and irritated the other staff. Harker didn't care. He'd seen the wound on her leg, and the state of her palm, and he wasn't taking any chances with some junior quack seeing her.

When Daz told Eve he had to debride her palm, her face went white and her other hand reached for Harker's. He held her as Daz cut away the thick, hard tissue that was beginning to grow back, and even after she'd been given strong medication, she shook and sobbed in Harker's arms while he devised horrific tortures for the Coalitionists who'd hurt her.

That night, she curled in his arms and told him that she deserved the pain, because she'd grabbed the poker and that was just stupid of her.

'Why did you grab it?'

'He was going to smash it into my face. And the end of it was white-hot, way hotter than the bit I touched.'

'Eve,' he said, stroking the back of her hand, 'that wasn't stupid at all. And we'll get it fixed. You're young and healthy, you still have some use of your fingers, and I've already told Daz if you don't get full use back, I'll demonstrate to him just how painful a hot poker really can be.'

'You're evil,' Eve said, but she smiled as she did.

By day she tinkered with the computer, connecting it to the thing she called the Internet and exclaiming over every little thing.

'So, you use one of these a lot?' Harker said, watching her. He had a French dictionary open on his lap and was surreptitiously using it to look up endearments.

'Used to, at work.' She tapped a couple of keys. 'What's French for Wikipedia?'

Her hair was pinned up, but a few wisps had escaped and caressed the back of her neck. Harker found himself wishing he could do the same, then remembered that he could, because he was allowed to touch her now, anywhere he wanted.

She leaned into him as he stroked the back of her neck. 'Have you told Wheeler about the computer at the Tower?'

'Yes. Couldn't really leave it any longer. But I still don't see how something this big and fragile could be hiding there. There aren't many rooms that aren't in constant use, and she's searched everywhere else.'

'Well, maybe it's a laptop.'

'A what?'

Eve described to him a smaller computer which could be folded down to the size of a large book.

'I mean, is there a library at the Tower? It could be

disguised in there. Or just shoved under someone's bed.'

Harker sighed. Searching everyone's private property was never high on any officer's list of Fun Things To Do. The men hated it, and it was usually fruitless, anyway.

Someone tapped on the door and Harker said, 'Yeah?' without looking up. They were in one of the small rooms near the Colonel's office that were usually occupied by relatively unimportant officers. One of them stood in the doorway, saluted, and said, 'Sir, telephone call for you.'

Harker made a face and got to his feet. 'Wheeler again?'

'No, sir. Colonel Watling-Coburg.'

Eve looked up, her eyebrows raised.

'Did she say what she wanted?' Harker asked.

The junior officer hesitated. 'Well, sir.' He glanced at Eve.

'I can leave the room if you want,' she said wearily.

'No, it's fine,' Harker said. To the Subaltern he said, 'You can speak freely in front of her,' and Eve beamed at him. He smiled back, losing his concentration somewhat.

'Well, sir, she said it was, er, about your court-martial.'

Eve started to laugh, but when Harker didn't share the joke her smile drained away.

'Actually, sir, she said "bloody court-martial", but–'

'Yes, all right,' Harker said, his eyes still on Eve and her expression of confusion. 'I'll be right back,' he told her.

'Court-martial? But–'

He took her hand. 'Eve, I'll explain it to you, but let me go and talk to Saskia first.'

She nodded, still looking uncertain, and he gave her a quick kiss before following the Subaltern out to the Colonel's office, where the telephone was. 'Go and find Lieutenant Riggs,' he said, 'and tell her I want to speak to the whole squad. Tell 'em to meet in the office where Eve is.'

The Colonel, who apparently was unaware that the woman on the phone was Harker's ex-wife, stood by expectantly until Harker asked him for some privacy.

Then he picked up the phone. 'Saskia?'

'Will, what the hell are you playing at? Wheeler's got people coming in from all over, leaving their regiments commanded by bloody majors and captains, for heaven's sake, to try you for disobedience.'

'Yeah, she said she would.'

'You know about it?'

'Of course I know about it. I was there.'

'Harker, are you taking this seriously?'

He leaned back against the desk, wiping his hand over his face. 'Yes, I'm taking it seriously,' he said.

'She could put you in jail, Will, or take away your commission.'

'Yeah, I know.'

'She could put you up in front of a firing squad,' Saskia said.

'Yeah.' Harker stared blindly at the wall, where the abyss was opening up again. 'She could.'

'What the hell were you thinking? What did she tell you to do that was so terrible you had to disobey?'

'It doesn't matter.'

'She could have you shot, Will, and it "doesn't matter"? Don't be ridiculous. I'm not asking you this as Saskia, I'm asking you this as Colonel Watling-Coburg.'

Harker rested his eyes on a crack in the plaster. 'She told me to leave someone behind.'

'Who? Charlie? Is she all right?'

'No. Not Charlie.' He hesitated. Well, it was going to come out at some point. 'Eve. Remember? The alien in the river?'

'You took her with you because she knew something about computers.'

Harker snorted. Yeah, and he'd believed that, too.

'She was captured,' he said. 'She was injured, and they had her, and Wheeler told me to leave her behind because she was probably dead anyway, and she wanted us up here.'

Saskia was silent a moment. 'And you went after her?'

'I did.'

'Did you get her back?'

'I did.'

'And ... was she ...?'

'She's okay,' Harker said. 'Well, she will be.'

'Harker,' Saskia began, then stopped. 'Look, I'm asking you this now as your wife.' She hesitated again, and Harker thought, *You're not my wife, not any more.* 'Did you go after her because you needed her for the mission, or because you always go after your men, or because ...'

'Because,' Harker said quietly. He could argue the other reasons in court, but the bottom line was he'd disobeyed a direct order in order to save the woman he loved.

Saskia sighed. 'Oh, Harker,' she said. 'That really was stupid.'

'Oh, right, so if it'd been you who was captured and tortured and about to die from some septic infection, you'd have preferred it if I just left you there?'

'No, but this isn't about me. And besides, I'm your superior officer. She's a civilian.'

'I didn't mean that you were my CO,' Harker said. 'I meant that you were my wife.'

Saskia was silent a moment longer. 'Are you going to marry her?'

Visions of Eve in white danced before his eyes. A whole life with her, the kind he'd never really allowed himself to imagine with Saskia. A life with children, a cottage somewhere, growing old together, spending the next forty or fifty years being challenged and pushed by Eve.

'Find me a priest who'll marry a divorced man, Sask, and

yes, I will,' he said. 'Even if I face a firing squad the next day.'

'There's a wedding present.' She sighed. 'Well. Look, I'll talk to Wheeler, and I'll see what I can do–'

'Sask, please don't try and talk her out of the court-martial, it won't put her in a good mood.'

'I meant for Eve. As I understand it, she's still considered a threat, and she'll be going back to St James's. I don't think marrying her would get her out, but it would at least give you visitation rights. Even if you are cashiered.'

Cashiered. Stripped of his rank. And with it the rights and privileges of an officer: his own room to sleep in, coffee when it was available, extra money for cigarettes, now they were so damn expensive.

And a widow's pension. That was an officer's right.

'Look, Sask, Eve's not well enough to travel yet. She's still recovering. Too many nights sleeping under canvas while she's still weak could–'

'Yes, Will, I know. I'll tell Wheeler you're not ready to leave yet.' She hesitated, then said, 'You know, you could marry in a civil ceremony. You don't actually need a priest.'

'Are you offering your blessing?'

'I'm offering my help. As your CO and as someone who was once very much in love with you. Don't screw this up, Will. I may not want to be married to you any more but I don't want to see you unhappy, either.'

'Thanks,' he said, touched.

'And I really don't want to be the ex-wife of an officer who faced a firing squad.'

'Again, thanks,' he said, less touched.

'I'll keep you informed,' she said, and ended the call.

Harker put the phone down slowly, his eyes still focused on the abyss, forcing it to close. *Plans, Harker, think this through. What do you want?* To be acquitted at the court-martial, to remove the suspicion hanging over Eve and, well, yes, maybe, to marry her.

The court, he felt, would probably be less impressed if he said he went after Eve for personal reasons. But how would it stand with them if he said he was rescuing his fiancée?

Still, probably, not all that well.

But did that even matter to him right now? *Get your head in order, Harker, you can think about Eve later, once you've got yourself out of being shot.*

The door opened, and it was Charlie, looking slightly concerned to find him staring at the wall.

'Sir? I gathered the men.'

Harker nodded distantly. Then he remembered why he'd wanted to get them together in the first place, and made a face.

He found them in the little office where he'd left Eve, who was attempting to mimic some hand exercises Daz was showing her, without much success. Her fingers waggled a little bit, but she couldn't move much more than the tips.

'This is so annoying,' she said.

'It's still very early,' Daz told her. 'The fact that you can move them at all is very encouraging.'

'Yeah? Well, I don't feel very encouraged.' She looked up at Harker. 'Well? What did Saskia want? Are you being court-martialled for sleeping with someone else?'

Was she jealous? He suddenly remembered her inexplicable anger the night she'd discovered his ex-wife and CO were the same person, and very nearly smiled.

'Well,' he said. He leaned against the door and folded his arms. The squad, not even remotely at attention, looked back at him. 'I am being court-martialled.' Tallulah made a sound of dismay, and Harker talked over it. 'When we get back to London. Wheeler's bringing in some fairly senior officers for it.'

‘What are the charges?’ Charlie asked, although by her expression she’d already guessed.

‘Disobedience.’

‘Like a dog?’ Eve said. ‘This is ridiculous.’

‘It’s the army,’ Charlie said. ‘Disobeying an order is serious.’

‘What order?’ Eve said, and there was a sticky silence. No one looked at her, or at Harker.

He lit up a cigarette, and eventually said, ‘I was ordered to leave you in Leeds and come straight here.’

‘You – who ordered you? General Wheeler?’ Harker nodded. ‘But ... why did she care where I was?’

‘She didn’t. But she cared where I was. It’s not about the specifics of the order, Eve; it’s about me not following it.’

‘But you came here, didn’t you? You got me and came here. Eventually.’

‘Yes, eventually.’

‘So it’s not as if there were dire consequences–’

‘No,’ Harker said, losing his patience a little, ‘it’s not about the consequences, it’s about the fact that I didn’t follow the order. It’s a serious offence, Eve. Men have died for disobeying orders, and this one came directly from the General herself.’

Some of the belligerence drained from Eve’s expression. ‘But you’re not going to die,’ she said, her tone uncertain.

Harker let his gaze drop. He didn’t quite know what to say to that. He’d faced the possibility of death from his first day in the army, but he’d never been offered a time and date for it.

‘There were no direct consequences,’ Charlie said, ‘and it wasn’t a major order, and there were extenuating circumstances–’

‘But the death penalty has been handed out to men who disobeyed orders,’ Harker said.

'Has been,' Eve said. 'What, every time?'

'No–'

'So that's the worst-case scenario?' Her voice was rising now, notes of panic creeping in. 'I mean, what else could they do, imprison you or fine you, or–'

'Take my commission,' Harker said. Tallulah sucked in a breath. He'd forgotten she and the others were even there. 'Or all of the above. It's a serious offence–'

'You keep saying that,' Eve said, her tone angry but her eyes frightened. 'You keep saying it's a serious offence, but no one's died, you didn't steal or rape or betray anyone. How can just not following orders be so serious?'

'Because this is the army,' Harker snarled, straightening away from the door, 'and we follow orders. It's what we do. And you don't seem to understand that–'

'Because it's stupid,' Eve snapped back at him.

'I am not having this argument with you,' Harker said, and Eve stood up, glaring at him.

'Ok, don't, then,' she said, and limped out, slamming the door behind her.

He's going to die because of you. He's going to die because of you.

It ran around her head in a terrible little refrain, louder with each step, pummelling her with fear and guilt and anger, and when a hand touched her shoulder and pulled her around she stumbled, her leg giving way.

Harker caught her, and she pushed away from him.

'Go away,' she said. 'I don't want to talk to you.'

'Well, listen then.'

'No.' She limped down the steps from the office building to the path leading to the parade ground. It was cold, the sun sinking down behind the hulking barracks, and she didn't have a coat.

Harker propped his over her shoulders, and she turned, snarling.

'I don't want you catching a chill,' he said wearily.

'Oh, get lost.'

'No.' He walked beside her, slowing his pace to match hers. 'Eve, we're going to have to go back to London. And when we get there, I'm being court-martialled and you're going back to St James's.'

'Thanks for reminding me.'

'And if I die, there's no one to help you. Even if you do get out, you'll have nothing. If I'm executed–'

'Stop saying that!' How could he talk about it like that? And how could he not realise how much it hurt her to hear it?

'Eve, if I'm executed there'll be no widow's pension, but there's some money, enough to live on, at least for a while.'

'Widow's pension?' she said, giving him a sideways look.

'Aye, officer's privilege. If I die in the line of duty, you get money to live on.'

'Harker, I don't get anything, I'm not married to you.'

Harker said nothing for a moment, and Eve's blood pounded loudly in her ears.

'You could be,' he said. 'Marry me now, and you'll be an official citizen, you'll have more rights, and if I die–'

'If you die?' Eve stopped walking and stared at him, incredulous. 'Harker, I don't want to be a widow. And I'm not going to marry you just in case you die.'

He stared at her, and she watched confusion, pain, and anger chase each other across his face.

'You'd rather spend the rest of your life in a POW camp or living rough because you've no money and no citizenship, than marry me? Even just for a couple of weeks?'

Eve gaped. How could he not get this? Offering to marry someone because you thought you were going to die had to be the most unromantic thing she'd ever heard of. And although she'd never pegged Harker for the hearts-and-flowers type, she still couldn't believe he was getting it this wrong.

'I won't marry anyone for a couple of weeks,' she said, 'and if you can't figure out why, you can find somewhere else to sleep tonight.'

With that she started walking for his quarters.

'It's my sodding room,' he shouted after her, but she gave no appearance of hearing him.

Eve didn't speak to him for the rest of the day. She even went so far as to take her dinner with Tallulah and Banks in their mess, and then he found her collecting her clothes and toiletries from his room to go and sleep in a spare cot in Tallulah's bunkhouse.

When he asked, begged, and ordered her not to go, she ignored him and went anyway, and Harker spent a miserable, angry night alone in a bed that was far too big.

In the morning, Daz told him Eve was probably well enough to travel, and Harker dully arranged with the Commodore for one of his ships to take them to Harwich, from where the road was secure enough to march straight into London. Concerned for Eve even if she wasn't talking to him, he organised a wagon to be waiting for them at Harwich to spare her an eighty-mile walk.

The computer was packed, carefully, in a crate, the squad assembled, and still Eve didn't make eye-contact with him. She spent most of the voyage in conversation with Daz about either her hand, or the computer, and when they docked refused Harker's assistance off the ship.

You've only got a few days left, he reminded himself, *before she goes back to St James's and you get court-martialled. Don't waste what you've got.*

The wagon rattled on as the sun came down and he sent Charlie and Banks on foot to scout for a decent place to spend the night. Packed in the wagon were three tents: one for Charlie and Tallulah, one for Banks and Daz, and one for Harker and Eve. He was determined to get her back in his bed at least once before the Damoclean sword fell on them both.

When they stopped for the night he set the others to making camp, and took Eve's arm to silently walk her away from all the others, into the dark woods, until no one else could hear them.

'In two days we'll be in London,' he said to her, 'and you'll be taken away from me and I'm not going to spend the time in between without you.'

'You're not without me,' Eve said, looking sulky, 'I'm right here.'

'Eve,' he said, gripping her arms and making her look at him. 'I want you to know I'll do whatever I can to get you out of St James's and make you a free woman. Saskia promised to help and Charlie will, too, you know she will.'

Eve looked wary. 'Well, thanks,' she said.

'And I know you won't marry me,' which hurt, it really did, 'but I'll do what I can for you anyway.'

Eve tried to pull away from him, but Harker held on. 'Look, let go of me,' she said, 'I'm not going anywhere, and you're starting to hurt me.'

He moved his hands instantly, which earned a small smile from Eve. Harker smiled back hopefully.

Then she said, 'You really are stupid,' which made his smile falter somewhat. 'Harker, it's not – look, you said you'd marry me for a couple of weeks, because then you were going to die. Don't you realise what that sounded like? You're just doing me a favour, and then you won't have to put up with me any more, because you'll be dead.'

Put like that, she had a point.

'That's not what I meant,' he said, and Eve folded her arms.

'Then what did you mean?'

'I meant …' Harker ran his hands through his hair. 'Are you angry because you thought I only wanted to marry you for a couple of weeks?'

She nodded. 'It's not exactly flattering, is it?'

'Eve, I want to marry you forever. I'm just saying, you have to understand that–'

She put her finger over his lips, and he was so happy to have her touching him again that he smiled.

'Stop telling me you're going to die,' she said. 'You're a soldier. I've seen those scars. I know the risks of the life you have. Doesn't mean I'm happy about it, because I'm actually bloody terrified.' She blinked, and the fading light caught something glistening in her eye.

'Terrified?'

'I don't want you to die,' Eve said, her voice breaking slightly, and then to his surprise threw her arms around him. 'I don't. But please stop talking about it, because this is hard enough as it is.'

He held her, grateful to have her back in his arms again. He kissed her cheek, wet with tears, and then she kissed his mouth, her fingers in his hair, her body soft against his.

'I don't want to go back to London,' she whispered.

'Neither do I.'

'Then let's not.' She looked up at him, tense and earnest in the moonlight. 'We could go, right now, you and me. We could just run away, get on a ship or something and leave the country. Or just hide out, you've even got those fake papers, we could just leave, and be together …'

Her voice trailed off, her eyes searching his, and for a second Harker actually considered it. Eve looked up at him, fragile and beautiful and everything he wanted, and her face changed as she read his. He watched the hope slide away and the despair creep in.

'But of course you never would,' she said sadly, touching his cheek. 'Major Harker never runs away from anything.'

He opened his mouth, but she stopped it with her finger again, and added softly, 'And if you did, I wouldn't love you half as much as I do.' She dipped her head, then looked back up at him and said, 'Can we just ... pretend for a while that we don't have to go to London and you're not in trouble and I'm not going to go back to St James's?'

He kissed her softly. 'Yes,' he said, and for the rest of the trip they did. The rest of the squad played along, and Harker figured Charlie had probably had something to do with that. By day he and Eve sat in the wagon and talked and kissed, and at night she sat circled in his arms by the fire, singing to them all until it was too cold, and Harker took her to his own private tent and made love to her, moving hot and perfect together in the dark.

It seemed to Harker that London had moved several dozen miles east, because they came upon it far too quickly. The fires of the Tower shone out through the late afternoon gloom, and Eve clutched his hand.

'What will we do?' she said, her voice pointedly matter-of-fact. 'Go straight to St James's, or the Tower, or what?'

'The Tower, I think,' Harker said, because there was always the possibility that he could talk Wheeler out of sending Eve back to St James's. It wasn't a strong possibility, but it was there.

When they came to the Byward Gate and the sentries recognised Harker, they exchanged uncomfortable looks, and one of them said, 'Major Harker, sir, we've been told to keep you here.'

'I can't go into the Tower?'

'Uh, no, sir. General Wheeler's on her way.'

Eve looked at Harker, trepidation in her eyes, and that cold ball of dread settled in Harker's stomach again.

He took Eve's hand, and said lightly, 'Always nice to get a personal welcome from your host.' To Charlie, who was driving the wagon, he said, 'Move us out of the way, then, we don't want to make the place look untidy.'

The sound of a few dozen pairs of boots marching came closer. Eve's fingers tightened around his, and when he glanced at her, her jaw was tense, her breathing shallow.

'Hey,' he said gently, and she looked up at him. She seemed to be trying to present him with a brave face, but she was making a terrible job of it.

'Don't say anything,' she whispered. 'You can't say anything that won't sound like goodbye.'

'I love you,' he said, and she gave a trembly smile.

'Like that,' she said, her voice breaking, as Wheeler came around the corner, followed by an outrageously heavily armed squad.

Boy, one little betrayal of trust and she turned into such a vindictive bitch.

'Miss Carpenter,' said the General, 'to me, please.'

Harker moved to get out of the wagon to help her down, and Wheeler barked, 'Not you, Major.'

'She can't get out by herself, sir,' Harker said to Wheeler, loathing her, and she motioned one of her guards forward to help Eve down.

Eve wrapped her arm around Harker's neck, kissed him, and Wheeler said tersely, 'Now, please.'

'I'm not one of your soldiers,' Eve snapped at her, and Harker was impressed at the steel in her voice. She turned back, her eyes met his, and Harker thought he might be in danger of starting to cry.

Eve touched her damaged right hand to his, nodded, and

turned to the soldier waiting to help her down.

'Take her to St James's,' Wheeler said. 'Now.'

'She can't walk–' Harker began, and Wheeler gave him a glacial look that had absolutely no effect on him. Eve was assisted on to a horse and led away, and the look on her face as she turned back and gave him a tiny wave broke his heart.

'I'll see you again,' he shouted after her. 'I *will* see you again!'

'Major,' Wheeler said, as the men escorting Eve turned the corner and she vanished from his sight.

He turned to her with absolute hatred. *You did that on purpose, you cruel, stonehearted bitch.*

'Escort Major Harker to my office,' said Wheeler to the man behind her, and he was horrified – but not surprised – to see that it was Sholt. He stepped forward, smiling oleaginously, and Harker got down from the wagon.

If I'm demoted and this creature becomes my senior I will have to kill someone, he thought, and it plainly showed on his face, because Sholt's smile faded slightly.

'This way, sir,' he said.

'I know the damn way,' Harker said, striding off, making Sholt and his men hurry after him.

'What a pretty girl she is,' said Sholt from behind him, and Harker felt his mouth twist. 'And so very co-operative, I'm told.'

Harker spun around so fast Sholt walked into him, grabbed the hideous little man by his collar, and lifted him clear off the ground.

'If you ever even look at her, you repulsive little maggot, I will cut you open and strangle you with your own slimy entrails. I am still your superior officer, do you understand? And you will go nowhere near Eve Carpenter.'

'My superior officer for how long, sir?' Sholt gurgled, and Harker gave serious thought to killing him there and then.

But Wheeler walked past, gave him a disgusted look, and Harker let Sholt drop to the ground.

They left Sholt at the door to the Martin Tower, as Harker followed the General to her office, and was not offered a seat.

'You are in so much trouble, Major, that I'm not sure I know where to start,' she said, sitting down and putting on her glasses.

It begins with an alien falling into the river, Harker thought, *and ends with her too.*

He stared into the abyss, and jumped into it.

'Your trial will take place as soon as Lieutenant-Colonel Compton arrives from Leicester.'

'Yes, sir.' *Wonder if Eve's made it to St James's yet? Wonder if she'll have the same room? Can I still go and visit her? If Coop's still on the gate, he might–*

'There has been massive fighting there, did you know?'

At St James's? No, wait, what was she talking about? 'Sir?'

'You were born in Leicester, were you not?'

'Yes, sir.' *Stop trying to hurt me more, you vicious cow, you couldn't possibly.*

'Any family there?'

'No, sir. Don't have any family now, sir.'

'No, I don't suppose you do,' Wheeler said, as the door opened and Saskia came in. She gave Harker a look that was part sympathy, part anger, and part exasperation.

'Major,' she said.

'Temporarily,' Harker replied. He was starting to feel slightly giddy.

'Captain Haran's setting up the computer in the main office, where there's more room,' she said, 'but he says he'll need a telephone line.'

While that was being fussed over, with the General

overseeing proceedings, Saskia took Harker aside and said, 'I saw that out by the gate.'

'Did you?' *I hope she's okay, and they have a doctor there who can take care of her hand.*

'It was pretty cruel. She's really, really angry with you, Will.'

'I don't care,' Harker said, and at her look of annoyance he repeated, 'I don't. There's not another thing she can do to hurt me now. She can lock me up, she can take away my rank, she can bust me back down to private, and I don't care. And you know what? She knows that. And that's making her even angrier.'

Saskia stared at him. 'Will, have you gone mad?'

'Possibly.'

'She could have you shot at dawn.'

'Yeah.' He frowned. 'Sask, will you do something for me?'

'Well, right now, that depends.'

'If I am shot, will you take care of Eve?'

Her eyes went wide. 'You do realise you're asking your ex-wife to take care of your girlfriend?'

'Yep.'

Saskia shook her head in disbelief, but she said, 'Yes, Will, I'll do what I can. I said I would.'

'I know. I just wanted to ... make sure,' he said, to Saskia's departing back.

While Daz set up the computer in the main office, the rest of the squad were hanging about looking unsure, and Harker's heart sank even further. Hadn't Wheeler promised promotions all round? Poor Charlie would never get her captaincy now, and–

'Ah, Major Harker!'

It was Wilmington, puffing up the stairs with a large box in his arms. Charlie offered him a salute, which seemed to confuse him terribly, since he had no free hand with which to return it.

'At ease, Captain,' Harker said. 'How's my company?'

'Oh, fine, fine, sir, in tip-top condition!' Wilmington handed the box to Banks, and added, 'You'll hardly know you've left them, sir!'

Ignoring this, Harker nodded at the box. 'What's that?'

'Oh, it's addressed to you, sir. It was sitting on your desk, but I took it to my quarters for safe-keeping. It arrived about a fortnight ago.'

Harker exchanged a look with Charlie. 'Who's it from?'

'I don't know, sir.'

Harker thought about asking who'd delivered it, but from Wilmington's pink shiny face he knew there was no point. Sighing, he took out his knife and sliced the top open.

Inside was a flat plastic box, about the size of a large book, and a piece of paper with what would have looked like nonsense to Harker a week ago. But thanks to Eve, he knew what it was and so, when he showed it to Charlie, did she.

'A file address,' she said, and when she looked up at him, her eyes were full of dread.

And Harker knew why. He knew that handwriting same as she did. Only one cockroach of a man wrote in capitals that were both rigid and slithering at the same time.

Harker snapped into life. 'Right, thank you, Captain, very helpful, why don't you pop in there and see Captain Haran work the magic of the computer? Go on, quick march!'

Looking confused, Wilmington did as he was told, and Harker picked up the little flat box. There was a power flex coiled beneath it.

'What is it?' Charlie said.

'It's a laptop,' Harker said, dread mounting in him. And it'd been sent to him.

Two weeks ago.

Shoving the thing back in its box, he raced down the stairs and to the mess, where there was a plug point and no people. Charlie, thinking more clearly than Harker, posted Banks and Tallulah outside while Harker waited impatiently for the computer to start up.

The machine displayed a greeting. *Welcome, Major Harker.*

Harker carefully typed in the file's location, and was rewarded with an image. A map of London. There were two arrows painted crudely on it, one pointing to the Tower, the other to a spot south of London Bridge. The first was labelled, *You Are Here.*

The second was labelled *Eve.*

Chapter Twenty-Seven

'Now, you've already been very useful,' said the oleaginous voice in Eve's ear. 'If it wasn't for you, Sergeant Harker wouldn't be in trouble in the first place.'

Major Harker, Eve wanted to correct him, but his hand was shoved in her mouth and she couldn't.

So she bit his hand, and he yelped and slapped her, and bashed the side of her head with the butt of his rifle. Eve saw stars, but her vision cleared when Captain Sholt shoved a piece of cloth in her mouth and tied it as a gag.

'Don't want you screaming, do we, even if your voice is so pretty.'

He grabbed her injured hand, and the pain made Eve far too weak to struggle as he tied her hands behind her back, again with a piece of cloth that he'd ripped from the uniform of the dead soldier at their feet.

Sholt had intercepted the party escorting Eve to St James's and demanded custody of 'the prisoner'. The poor sod lying in the mud with a bullet in his head was the one who'd voiced an objection and been invited by Sholt in his oiliest voice to accompany them.

'Come on then, pretty voice,' he said now, his breath making Eve's stomach curl. 'Don't you want to see your handsome Sergeant again?'

Eve gave him a death glare, but he just chuckled and continued to herd her through the thick mud edging the riverbank.

'Very clever of you, pretty voice, to give them my name,' said Sholt. 'I set this up straight away when they emailed me, because I'm clever, too. I've been ever so helpful to

General Wheeler since Sergeant Harker left, been telling her about all the times he's held me back, ever so unfairly. Been just waiting for you to come back, I have. Couldn't resist it when they sent me your picture. Sergeant Harker's little bit of fluff.'

Eve, stumbling and frightened, swore at him through her gag.

'Oh yes, pretty voice, you're going to be very useful indeed. Because if your Sergeant doesn't come after you, then he's going to be in lots of trouble for possessing a computer in the Tower. One with lots of lovely emails from the Coalitionists on it.'

Eve stared at him, her eyes wide. Sholt chuckled again.

'But don't worry, pretty voice, because he'll come after you. Doesn't like to leave his men behind, you know,' Sholt told her with mock solemnity. 'You'll see him again. Briefly.'

'Sir, please,' said Charlie as Harker strode across the dark courtyard. 'You're in enough trouble as it is.'

'So a little bit more won't matter,' Harker said. His heart was pounding. At the back of his mind he knew Sholt had tried to frame him, but all he could think about was that the hideous cockroach had Eve.

He kept coming back, over and over again, to the image of Eve lying pale and bloody in that cell in Kirkstall, and mixing it with the deeply etched memory of Mary White, until a red mist descended and he didn't even hear Charlie any more.

Should have killed him years ago. Bullet in the brainpan, heat of battle, no one'd know.

He's got Eve.

London Bridge was choked with heavy traffic, people and carts and animals forming a totally solid barrier. Harker fired his gun up through the narrow gap between buildings and yelled, 'Move out of the bloody way!'

People turned, saw his face, and obeyed.

'You don't have to follow me,' he said as Banks took point and Tallulah marched up beside him.

'I know,' Tallulah said.

'You could get in trouble.'

'I *know*,' she said.

'Your sister'll bloody kill me,' Harker muttered.

'It's not really up to her, is it, sir?'

'Think she'll see it that way?'

'No one told me to come, sir,' Tallulah said, in a voice that said it was final.

Fear gripped him as they searched the wasteland for any structure that Sholt could be hiding in. Charlie kept going on about it being a trap, but Harker didn't care. He was fairly sure she was right, but he still didn't care.

Got to find Eve, got to find her. Maybe that running away idea of hers has merit.

'Sir,' shouted Banks, and pointed with his gun to a trap door, hidden in the cellar of a burned-out building.

Harker ran over. Scratched into the brick besides the trapdoor was an arrow and one word: Eve.

He grabbed the handle and flung it open. A dark tunnel was revealed. Harker took two steps, hesitated, and said, 'None of you have to come, you know.'

'That's what you said last time,' said Tallulah.

Last time. *Last time!*

'I am never letting her out of my sight again,' Harker said, starting down the slippery steps into the tunnel.

It was dark, damp, and freezing cold. In places, it wasn't much more than mud shored up with planks. Underfoot, the ground squelched. The darkness was so heavy and thick Harker wondered occasionally if he was going blind, but he knew striking a light would be like announcing their presence in loud tones.

They walked as silently as possible, weapons drawn, for about fifteen minutes, moving steadily downwards, and then the wall Harker was feeling his way along dropped away and the quality of the air changed.

Something rumbled. The ground shook. And it seemed ... warmer.

'If you come near me, I'll bloody well kill you,' said a voice, and Harker could have wept with delight, because it was Eve.

'If you kill me, I'll be really pissed off,' he said, 'especially since I've come to rescue you.'

'Harker?'

He lit a lamp, and there she was, lying on the ground about thirty feet away, her hands bound behind her back and her clothes streaked with dirt. Behind her was a drop of a few feet, inlaid with dark metal pipes and rails. Harker ran towards her, but she was shaking her head rapidly.

'Stop!' And he did, automatically, wondering if there was a bomb or something he might trigger. 'It's a trap–'

'I know it's a sodding trap,' he said, and started forward again, cautiously. But Eve shook her head urgently.

'Harker, Sholt's still here, he's hiding, you have to go, he wants to kill you!'

'Remember the last time you said that? I ain't going any–'

– and a shot rang out. Eve's eyes widened in horror, and Harker whipped his head around to see Tallulah fall, looking kind of surprised, dark blood blossoming on her jacket.

'*No*,' Banks said, and ran to her, but something exploded nearby and he was knocked off his feet.

Harker fired in the direction the bullet had come from, five shots in quick succession aimed behind Eve, and he heard someone fall and clatter against the metal pipes in the ditch behind her.

'Is that where Sholt was hiding?' Harker said, craning to see.

'Oh God,' said Eve, and Harker began, 'Maybe–' and she shook her head, pointing back to his side of the tunnel. 'Charlie!'

Harker went cold.

Charlie lay on the far side of the tunnel, in the mud, almost out of the reach of the lamp's light. But there was enough light, and Harker's horrified eyes took a second to get the message to his brain that one of her legs was lying a couple of yards away.

'Hell, Charlie,' he mumbled, and ran towards her.

He glanced back, and Eve was struggling to her knees, wincing. The area of the tunnel behind her looked so different, the ground flat and hard, the curved walls covered in tiles, and he thought he saw a symbol under all the grime. A circle with a line across the centre of it.

'There are bombs, charges or something, he was laying them. Will, he's with the Coalitionists,' she said, and Harker nodded, because he already knew that. 'He's had this planned for weeks. The tunnel's going to come down. But listen, Harker, I know where I am.'

Charlie's eyes flickered as he reached her. She focused blearily on him, then on the tunnel behind Eve. Something rumbled again, and an acrid smell hung in the air.

'Is this hell?' she mumbled.

'No,' Eve said. She pointed to the grimy circle. 'It's the London Underground. Harker, this is my world.'

He stared back at her, kneeling there on the hard surface, trying and failing to get to her feet. *My world*.

It smelled different, and there was some kind of heat and breeze in the air, and that strange rumble …

Then hands appeared on the edge of the ditch behind Eve, and he shouted, 'Behind you!' as Sholt appeared, bloody and grimy but most definitely not dead, grinning that horrible grin of his. Harker raised his gun, but Eve was in the way, he couldn't get a clear shot. 'Eve, get down!'

In the distance, a horn sounded. The rumbling grew louder. Bombs, Eve had said. Charges. The tunnel was falling down around them.

Then something – something big, and hideously loud, and incredibly fast, and lit up, glowing, something like a gigantic snake, shot past behind Eve, slamming into Sholt and ripping him apart as it screeched on the metal rails. Eve, still on the ground, stared in horror.

'It's the Northern Line,' she croaked, watching the thing fly past. 'It's the bloody Northern Line!'

Another explosion shook the tunnel. Wet mud splattered Harker and Charlie.

'We need to get out,' he said, 'before the whole thing collapses. Banks, are you okay?'

Banks didn't answer. He was kneeling by Tallulah, who was still and pale.

'She's not breathing,' he said.

Harker's eyes met Charlie's. 'Is there a pulse?'

A few awful seconds passed, then Banks shook his head and started to cry.

Harker got to his feet. 'Eve,' he said, starting towards her, but as he approached the hole between his world and Eve's, something went *boom* right near his ear.

When he opened his eyes, Eve and the platform were gone, and the tunnel was collapsing around them.

The train had stopped just ahead. Its light spilled out over the disused platform, illuminating with a dim glow the dirty rails that were now splattered with blood and bits of torn flesh.

The train had stopped because it had hit Sholt, she realised dimly, but she didn't care about that, because something had exploded and she couldn't see into Harker's tunnel any more. The hole in the curved Tube wall had filled in with dirt, bits of wood, stone and concrete.

Heart pounding, unable to get to her feet, Eve crawled over, her leg throbbing and her eyes burning, and scrabbled at what had once been a platform entrance, and was now solid with mud.

'No,' she said, digging with her good hand, and then her bad one, too. '*No.*'

'Is someone there?' came a voice, and she shouted, 'Yes, and you've got to help me!'

Footsteps sounded, electric torchlight blinded her, and then there was a man in a hi-vis jacket beside her.

'Jesus,' he said, 'I'll get you an ambulance.'

'I'm fine,' Eve said. 'But we have to get through here. The tunnel collapsed and there are people there.' Harker was there. He was right there.

'There's no tunnel,' he said, and she stared at him as if he was mad, then looked back at the cascade of earth. She clawed at it, grabbed chunks of earth and rock and threw them away, gasping for breath and blinking away burning tears, because he was there, they were all there, just out of reach, right *there*–

The man in the hi-vis spoke into his radio, then put his hand on Eve's shoulder and pulled her back. She stumbled, fought him, then fell to her knees and stared at the wall of earth.

I will see you again.

'There's nuffink back there,' said the man in the hi-vis. 'No tunnel. This platform ain't been used for years.' He peered at the blocked archway. 'Reckon there was a landslide or summink.'

Looking back at the train and the rails, he sucked his

breath through his teeth. 'Was there someone wiv you, love?'

'Is he dead?' she asked numbly.

'Fink so. Sorry.'

'I'm not.'

He frowned at her, and she said distantly, 'He was not a nice man.'

'Oi,' said the man, peering at her. 'Ain't you Eve Carpenter? You went missing, dincha?'

There was no tunnel. No portal into another world.

No injured Charlie, no dead Tallulah. No Harker.

'What the hell are you doing down here?' said the man, and Eve whispered, 'I don't know.'

Chapter Twenty-Eight

'Thirty-three days,' said the journalist. 'Thirty-four, by the time they got you to a hospital. You must have been somewhere.'

'I've said it before,' Eve said calmly, looking down at the plectrum she'd spent a month trying to grasp. She strummed a few chords. There was a tune there, but no words.

There's nothing you can say that won't sound like goodbye.

'You "went away"?'

'Yep.' Eve looked at the other woman, challenging her to ask about rehab or slyly question her sanity. She'd heard it all anyway.

The journalist lost her nerve and looked down at her notepad. They generally did these days. Eve had discovered inner calm: it came with having nothing to lose.

'Now, your comeback single, *Missing You*, has been doing really well, and you're working on an album, is that right?'

'That's right.'

'Does it have a title yet?'

Outside, a taxi beeped its horn. A light buzzed overhead. Somewhere, someone was playing a radio.

'Yep. It's called *Rumours of My Death*.'

'Clever,' said the journalist, and Eve thought, *Not really*.

'Will it be similar to *Missing You*?'

'Some of it.' Eve glanced at the bandages covering her newest skin grafts. 'I've got some great collaborations lined up with some producers I really admire ...'

The words came automatically, the way they had for Harker when–

Don't think about Harker. He said he'd see her again, and he always kept his word, but since Transport for London had eventually excavated the landslide and found nothing but more mud, the chances of Harker walking through her door seemed somewhere between slim and anorexic.

'And with *Missing You*, you hinted that it was written about someone in particular. Would you like to elaborate?'

The Tower was different now. She'd visited the other day. And London Bridge was an ugly concrete thing, low and squat and easy to miss. Her old flat still stood in Mitcham, although some other poor sod had been moved in almost as soon as Eve went missing.

Everywhere she went she looked for Harker, but found no traces of him or his world. Nowhere in London held a memory of him; but everywhere, she remembered.

Eve looked at the woman calmly. 'No.'

Again, the journalist tried to outstare her, and failed. Flustered, she looked at her notes again. 'Right, er ... yes, well, what about living in a hostel when you were released from hospital?'

'I didn't have anywhere else to go. And no money.' Eve shrugged. 'I've lived in worse.'

'It was rumoured that you were going to sue the TV company who let you fly the paraglider without sufficient tuition. Why did you decide not to?'

'They'd probably have to fire people in order to pay the settlement, and they'd most likely be people who really needed the money. And I sure as hell didn't want to force anyone else to be as poor as I was.'

The journalist looked around Eve's comfortable, bland hotel suite and tried a smile. 'But now money's not a problem?'

'No,' said Eve, who had found herself at the centre of a bidding war for her album. 'It's not.'

'And your tax problems?'

'It's amazing how fast they go away when you can afford a lawyer who mentions nervous breakdowns,' Eve said. Maybe that had been playing dirty, but she'd offered a cash payment and they'd backed off pretty sharpish.

Now Eve had a lawyer on retainer, and three accountants each desperate to find fault with each other.

'Now, when you left Grrl Power, you cited artistic differences,' said the journalist.

'I hated the songs,' Eve said.

'Did you try writing your own material then?'

'Yes, but,' Eve shrugged, 'I guess I had nothing to write about.'

'So what made you try it this time?'

The songs had poured out of her since she had returned. Good songs. Songs about love and loss and anger and grief and life. *I didn't need songs. I needed something to sing about.*

Eve stared out of the window at Park Lane, which was jammed with traffic. She'd walked to St James's the other day, but found nothing to keep her there.

'Well, as the man said, when you've got nothing, you've got nothing to lose.'

'Right,' said the journalist, making a note. 'Which man?'

In another cell, someone was sobbing, which Harker considered to be pretty pathetic. He was, as far as he knew, the only man there condemned to die, and he wasn't crying about it.

He'd thought about it, but he hadn't really seen the point.

He'd been asked if he wanted a special last meal, but since he'd never eaten well in his life, he didn't see why he should start now. A priest had been sent to give comfort, but the only comfort Harker wanted had disappeared through a hole in the world.

In the morning they'd come and stick a bag over his head, lead him out into a private courtyard, and use him for target practice. Harker tried to be depressed about it, and found he couldn't work up the enthusiasm.

The only thing he was annoyed about was that he'd run out of cigarettes, but then a packet landed by his feet and he looked up to see Saskia standing on the other side of the bars, her hand still raised.

'Brought you something,' she said.

He picked them up. 'You always said these'd kill me.'

'Well, it looks like I was wrong.' She seemed to have something on her mind, frowning down at him. But then no one was smiling much these days.

Harker lit up a cigarette and sucked deeply. Better. Much better.

'Harker ... why did you go down to those tunnels?'

'You know why.'

'I want to hear you say it, to me.'

This was unnecessarily cruel. 'I wanted to save Eve.'

She nodded. 'And did you?'

He frowned. 'What do you mean? Do you see her around anywhere?'

'No, but ... Harker, you said she'd gone back where she came from. But you never said where that was.'

'Another world,' he said, wondering, like Eve, if he'd gone mad.

'And the ... doorway was in those tunnels?'

'Yeah.' Until Sholt's French bombs had destroyed it. Though why he'd wanted to destroy what he and his fellow Coalitionists had gone to so much trouble to dig out, Harker didn't pretend to understand. Perhaps, in the end, Sholt's hatred of Harker had sent him slightly mad.

'Wheeler's having them brought down tomorrow,' Saskia

said. 'Bombing what's left until it collapses. Can't have Coalitionists running around under London.'

'Nope.' First cigarette already exhausted, he lit a second. Saskia watched him a little while, then said, 'I saw Charlie the other day.'

'Yeah? How's she doing?'

'Not too badly. She's on the waiting list for a prosthetic.'

'It'll drive her mad sitting in a wheelchair,' Harker said.

'It is. She's constantly bickering with your Captain Haran – Daz, is it?'

'He's there, is he?'

'Apparently by request.'

Well well. Stranger things had happened, Harker supposed. Like the only woman he wanted disappearing through a hole in the world.

'The two of them are advising a special team on how to use the computer. We've already intercepted a couple of enemy messages. One of them was about an attack on Nottingham. That computer saved lives, Harker. It might even lead to a turning point in the war.'

'Glad to hear it.'

Her skin looked tight and pale. He knew she was thinking the same as him, that the one life that mattered was the one he hadn't saved.

'She can't forgive you, Harker. Wheeler. It hurt her all the more because she'd always championed you.'

'Making an example of me, isn't she?'

Saskia nodded.

'I ain't going to ask for your forgiveness, Sask. I don't deserve it.'

Her knuckles were pale. 'You didn't make her go with you. Charlie and Banks were very clear on that. They followed voluntarily.'

'But still. I shouldn't ...'

'Shouldn't what? Have gone after the woman you loved?'

Her face was tight with pain. Harker wondered if he'd have done the same for Saskia as he had for Eve. Wondered if he'd ever really loved Saskia all that much.

'Tallulah was a soldier,' she said, and there was the very tiniest tremor in her voice. 'She knew the risks. And I ... oh, Harker, I wish–'

Her voice broke, which for Saskia was like a fit of hysteria. Harker waited until she'd composed herself.

'I couldn't influence anyone's decision on your sentence,' she said. 'I don't want you to die.'

'Makes two of us.'

'But I ...' She looked down, then back up again. Her eyes were wet. 'I never hated you, you know.'

'You ought to. I would, if I were you.'

'Well, I suppose I'm a better person than you,' Saskia fired back, and Harker gave her half a smile.

Saskia stared off down the corridor for a long moment, then back at him.

'If there was a way for you to be with Eve, would you do it?'

He was sitting there waiting to be shot in the morning for what he'd done for Eve. What did she think?

'She,' he said, 'is the only thing in the world that I want. But she ain't even in my world any more.'

'Very poetic,' Saskia said.

'Yeah, I thought so. I'd say put it on my headstone, but I don't get one now, do I?'

'No. You're going to be shot in the tunnels where Tallulah died,' Saskia said, her face displaying what Daz had called Officer Blank, but which Harker suspected Saskia had perfected long before she joined the army. 'Wheeler gave me the choice.'

'S'pose that's poetic, too,' Harker said.

'They're going to be collapsed immediately after.' She watched him carefully. 'I supervised the positioning of the charges myself.'

'Did you?' Harker said, without much interest, and then what she'd said penetrated his brain, and he looked up. She gave an infinitesimal nod in the direction of the cigarette packet.

There was a tiny folded piece of paper in it.

What was she planning? Some final degradation, an act of revenge? He looked up at her, her face cold and aloof. He'd taken from her the last thing she had left, the person she loved most in all the world.

'Have you decided whether or not to wear the hood?' Saskia asked.

'Not yet,' he said cautiously.

'I'd advise that you do.' She met his eyes, and Harker told himself it could all still go horribly wrong. He didn't even know what she was planning.

Footsteps sounded in the corridor, and Saskia straightened. 'I'll see you tomorrow, Major.'

'Thanks, Colonel. You've been a great comfort.'

She gave a wry smile, and turned to go. Then she stopped, turned back, and said, 'Good luck in your next life, Will.'

'Thank you,' Harker said, and watched her go. Then he read her note, before burning it, lying back, and wondering if she was going to be able to pull it off.

Wind whipped at Eve's hair as she stood on the bridge, staring out at the dirty Thames. Past the bulk of HMS Belfast she could make out the new, boring, London Bridge, squatting over the river like a concrete toad. *I wouldn't need rescuing from there*, she thought. There were no narrow arches and wooden piers to thrash the tide into a frenzy. The only thing about London Bridge that could possibly kill someone was the sight of it.

There wasn't much separating her from the water. Just a waist-high barrier and a drop that wasn't nearly high enough to kill her. Eve glanced up at the high walkways above the road. Falling from there might kill someone.

'Don't do it!'

Eve closed her eyes for a second, then opened them again to see Jen, her newly acquired assistant, smiling at her own joke. But behind the smile was faint concern. *She really thinks I would.*

'I'm not going to jump,' Eve said, turning her back to the water. 'Well, not unless the album flops.'

Jen smiled. 'Come on away from there before a pappersnapper gets you and runs an *Eve Contemplating Suicide* headline.'

Eve allowed herself to be tugged away, her mind a hundred-and-fifty feet up. *How high was I when the sky changed?* she wondered. *Where did I fall through the hole in the world?*

How could I get back up there?

Morning came, with what he had overheard Eve, standing over Martindale's grave, call a glooming peace. '"The sun for sorrow will not show his head",' she'd added, mostly to herself.

Today I die, Harker thought, *either way, it all ends today.* And he wasn't afraid. They were beating some damn drum as he walked out to the wagon, and he was mildly disappointed that it wasn't a tumbrel. Officers weren't often executed, so a reasonably large crowd had turned out to watch.

No one saluted him. Without headgear, weapons, or even his jacket, he wasn't in uniform and couldn't salute back.

A path had been cleared along the centre of London Bridge. Harker sat in the wagon, smoking his last few cigarettes and ducking the rotten vegetables occasionally thrown his way. General Wheeler was waiting at the entrance to the tunnels, and she marched ahead of him into the torchlit darkness.

'Very dramatic,' he said, following, and was ignored.

In places, the tunnel walls had collapsed in and been re-dug. As part of his trial Wheeler had insisted on coming to see the exact spot where Tallulah had died and Sholt and Eve had gone missing.

At least that bastard was dead. Some good had come out of that horrible night.

He recognised a few faces in the guards standing around the slightly larger cavern where he'd last seen Eve. Only of course he hadn't last seen her there – she'd been through a portal, on the platform of what Harker had eventually worked out was something to do with a train. Eve had talked about trains, and Daz had animatedly passed on information gleaned from his American books. Some metal monster moving faster than light. Harker hadn't believed them, but now he'd seen proof. Real proof of Eve's world. Now there was a wall of earth there instead, impossible to shift, according to engineers, without destroying the whole tunnel.

There was Coop, standing half-hidden in the shadows, and as Harker nodded at him he was suddenly yanked into the darkness, a hand over his mouth, and someone else was shoved out in his place, a man whose head was covered by a hood.

A prisoner from Newgate, according to Saskia's note, one condemned to die anyway. Harker watched, still and silent, as he was led out to the approximate spot where Tallulah had died, and as the firing squad trooped out and took position, someone shoved a private's jacket and helmet at Harker and jammed a gun into his hands.

He pulled the helmet low, lurked back in the shadows,

and watched as Saskia herself gave the order to fire.

Through it all Wheeler stood stiff and straight, but she flinched ever so slightly when the prisoner fell.

She gave a nod and said to Saskia, 'I am sorry, you know.'

Saskia looked down at the dead man – Harker hoped like hell he'd at least deserved it – and said, 'Not as sorry as I am, sir.'

Then she ordered all the men out, and Coop murmured under the noise of marching feet, 'You stay here, sir. Reckon we're even now, eh?'

If it wasn't for you, Mister Harker, I wouldn't have nobody to marry.

'Thank you,' Harker mouthed, falling back into the shadows and waiting for the cavern to clear. Saskia remained, along with a couple of men who lit the fuses as she directed. Then they went, and she followed, lingering in the cavern entrance to set down her lantern and say, 'Goodbye, Will,' without looking at him.

Something good should come of all this, she'd written at the bottom of her note. She really was a better person than him.

Then she was gone, and Harker hit the ground as the first charge went off. When he opened his eyes, he was looking at a hard, flat platform and a circular tunnel with tiled walls. He rolled through the gap, just as another charge went off, and another, cascading earth down through the hole and sealing it again.

The ground was hard beneath him. The air was warm, with a slight breeze and that strange metallic smell. His last match illuminated a maintenance hatch in the tiles above.

For the first time in a month, Harker smiled.

It was harder with one hand mostly useless. Everything was. Constantly afraid she'd fall before she found the hole in the sky, and even more afraid someone would see her and try to bring her down, Eve stood on the roof of the Tower Bridge walkway, and looked out across the river to London Bridge.

High up here. Very high. The wind was fierce. Dropping to her knees to steady herself, Eve unfastened her bag with frozen fingers and took out the first of many pebbles.

She threw one up high, into the air, and watched it fall to the river below. Then she threw another, a little higher. *How high was I? And how far over to the side?*

Below her, the traffic moved on, unconcerned. Eve threw more stones, her teeth chattering. How many more did she have? Enough?

Maybe the portal wasn't there any more. Maybe it moved, and she'd never find it again. After all, if it'd been there a hundred-odd years ago, surely some of the men building the bridge would have found it?

Desperation mounting in her, Eve didn't pay attention to the shouts or the sirens until the loudspeaker got her attention. First a policeman, then a negotiator who gave his name as Tristram. Eve ignored them both.

Her phone rang. Her personal, up-to-the-minute, shiny pink, un-military phone.

'Eve, when I said don't jump, I was joking, I mean, I didn't want to put ideas into your head,' Jen babbled.

'I'm not going to jump,' Eve said. *At least, not until I've found the right place to jump through. And figured out how to get that high.*

I probably should have thought this through more.

'But … what are you doing up there?'

'I'm just looking for something.'

'But that's what the walkways are for, that's why–'

'Not that kind of something,' Eve said, distracted. 'Look, Jen, tell them to go away. I'm not going to jump. They don't need to worry.'

'They're sending someone up to bring you down.'

'No!' Eve yelped, because she still hadn't found the doorway. 'Not *yet*.'

'Eve–'

'Jen, I'm busy,' Eve said, and ended the call. She threw another pebble. It fell down to the river. Her phone rang again, and she switched it off.

Below her, a fire engine rumbled into place. Great, now they were going to bring her down and probably stick her in an asylum somewhere.

I'm not crazy. I know where I was. I just want to get back there.

Something whirred, the hydraulic lift, she supposed, a cherry-picker or something, or did they have those extending ladders? Maybe if she talked to them nicely, they'd extend it out over the water, and she could see if the hole was there.

Although people would follow her. Nosey people. Journalists and scientists. The Untied Kingdom would be swamped with people from this world, like something out of a Hollywood blockbuster. Like *Stargate* or something. They'd try to clean it up and probably fail horribly. Armies of big men with guns, politicians who never listened, packs of tabloid hacks who wanted to see Queen Diana. It would be a huge mess.

But if she found Harker, it would be worth it.

The cherry-picker whirred closer, and Eve's shoulders slumped. No, it wouldn't. She couldn't let anyone else find that world. What good would interfering do? Banks, and Charlie, and Tallulah's grieving family; they'd turn into fairground attractions. Come and see what Britain would have been like without the Empire! Look how sorry we'd all have been! Marvel at a country with no television!

You've never had it so good!

Eve could almost hear Harker's voice saying her name. If

she brought that upon the country he loved so fiercely, he'd never forgive her.

She threw one last pebble, and turned.

And nearly fell off the roof.

'Eve,' said Harker. He was black with dirt, eyes blazing, clothes tattered. Harker, standing next to a fireman in the bucket of the cherry-picker. 'For Christ's sake, don't jump.'

Eve's head whipped around. She hadn't found the hole, how had he got here? How had he found her?

Snapping her gaze back to him, she opened and closed her mouth half-a-dozen times before she managed to get her brain wired back in. Eventually, without taking her eyes off Harker, she said to the fireman, 'Excuse me, do you see a tall man with black hair and extremely dirty clothes standing next to you?'

Looking a little nervous, the fireman nodded. 'He said he knew you. Said he could bring you down.'

Harker's eyes bored into Eve's. 'I crawled out of a hole in the ground,' he said, his voice as soft as it could be under the howling wind. 'I heard people talking to – to –' he mimed holding something to his ear.

'A phone?' Eve said faintly. 'A mobile phone?'

'I don't know. They were talking about Crazy Eve Carpenter. Someone said you were going to jump. As if it was entertainment. So I came.'

'You said you would,' Eve whispered.

'Eve, for the love of God, please don't jump.'

Eve's hand flew to her mouth. She suddenly felt like laughing. 'You bloody idiot,' she said, and gestured to the fireman to bring the bucket closer. To Harker she said, 'This is where I fell from. Into the river. Into your world.'

Sudden understanding dawned in his eyes.

'The only place I was jumping was towards you,' Eve said, reaching for him, taking his cold, dirty hand and gripping it as tight as she could. Then she giggled, light-headed with relief. 'That's a terrible line. Remind me to use it in a song.'

Harker smiled more genuinely, and opened the gate for her. *He said he'd come, I knew he'd come*, Eve thought.

'You took your damn time,' she said, and fell into his arms.

About the Author

Kate Johnson is a prolific writer of romantic and paranormal fiction. Born in 1982, Kate is Choc Lit's youngest author and lives near Stansted. She is a self-confessed fan of Terry Pratchett, whose fantasy fiction has inspired her to write her own books. Kate worked in an airport and a laboratory before escaping to write fiction full time. She is a member of the Romantic Novelists' Association and has previously published short stories in the UK and romantic mysteries in the US. She's a previous winner of the WisRWA's Silver Quill and Passionate Ink's Passionate Plume award.

The Untied Kingdom is her UK debut novel.

For more information visit: www.katejohnson.co.uk

More Choc Lit

Why not try something else from the Choc Lit selection?

Starting Over
Sue Moorcroft

New home, new friends new love. Can starting over be that simple?
When Tess Riddell crashes her Freelander into Miles Rattenbury's breakdown truck, they find they are nearly neighbours – yet worlds apart. Tess discovers the joys of village life and forms an unlikely friendship with Miles, despite the sudden attentions of her ex-fiancé. Then just as her relationship with Miles develops into something deeper, an old flame comes looking for him …

ISBN: 978-1-906931-223

Turning the Tide
Christine Stovell

All's fair in love and war? Depends on who's making the rules.
Harry Watling has spent the past five years keeping her father's boat yard afloat, despite its dying clientele. Now all she wants to do is enjoy the peace and quiet of her sleepy backwater. So when property developer Matthew Corrigan wants to turn the boat yard into an upmarket housing complex for his exotic new restaurant, it's like declaring war.

ISBN: 978-1-906931-25-4

Trade Winds
Christina Courteney

Marriage of convenience or a love for life?
It's 1732 in Gothenburg, Sweden, and strong-willed Jess van Sandt knows only too well that it's a man's world. She believes she's being swindled out of her inheritance by her stepfather – and she's determined to stop it.
Short-listed for the Romantic Novelists' Association's Pure Passion Award for Best Historical Fiction 2011
ISBN: 978-1-906931-23-0

The Silver Locket
Margaret James

If life is cheap, how much is love worth?
It's 1914 and young Rose Courtenay has a decision to make. Please her parents by marrying the man of their choice – or play her part in the war effort?
ISBN: 978-1-906931-28-5

Please don't stop the music
Jane Lovering

How much can you hide?
Jemima Hutton is determined to build a successful new life and keep her past a dark secret. Trouble is, her jewellery business looks set to fail – until enigmatic Ben Davies offers to stock her handmade belt buckles in his guitar shop and things start looking up, on all fronts.
ISBN: 978-1-906931-27-8

The Scarlet Kimono
Christina Courteney

Abducted by a Samurai warlord in 17th-century Japan – what happens when fear turns to love?
England, 1611, and young Hannah Marston envies her brother's adventurous life. But when she stows away on a merchant ship, her powers of endurance are stretched to their limit. Then they reach Japan and all her suffering seems worthwhile – until she is abducted by Taro Kumashiro's ninja.

ISBN: 978-1-906931-29-2

Want to Know a Secret?
Sue Moorcroft

Money, love and family. Which matters most?
When Diane Jenner's husband is hurt in a helicopter crash, she discovers a secret that changes her life. And it's all about money, the kind of money the Jenners have never had.

ISBN: 978-1-906931-26-1

All That Mullarkey
Sue Moorcroft

Revenge and love: it's a thin line …
The writing's on the wall for Cleo and Gav. The bedroom wall, to be precise. And it says 'This marriage is over.'

ISBN: 978-1-906931-247

Introducing the Choc Lit Club

Join us at the Choc Lit Club where we're creating a delicious selection of women's fiction.
Where heroes are like chocolate – irresistible!

Join our authors in Author's Corner, read author interviews and see our featured books.

We'd also love to hear how you enjoyed *The Untied Kingdom*. Just visit www.choc-lit.com and give your feedback. Describe Major Harker in terms of chocolate and you could win a Choc Lit novel in our Flavour of the Month competition!

Follow us on twitter: www.twitter.com/ChocLituk